SECRETS IN THE SAND

The Lost Pharaoh Chronicles Book II

LAUREN LEE MEREWETHER

Edited by
SPENCER HAMILTON

LLMBOOKS
PUBLISHING

LLMBOOKS
PUBLISHING

Copyright © 2019 Lauren Lee Merewether

For permissions and to visit the author's website, see

www.laurenleemerewether.com

eBook ISBN: 978-1-961759-15-2
Paperback ISBN: 978-1-961759-16-9
Paperback ISBN-13: 978-1087298511

THE LOST PHARAOH CHRONICLES TIMELINE

1375 B.C.

1371 B.C. - 1365 B.C.
Wife of Ay
(Prequel Book II)

1368 B.C.
The Valley Iris
(Prequel Book I)

1362 B.C. - 1360 B.C.
Paaten's War
(Prequel Book III)

1365 B.C.

1360 B.C. - 1354 B.C.
The Fifth Prophet
(Prequel Book IV)

1355 B.C.
Egypt's Second Born (Prequel Book V)
or King's Jubilee (Prequel Short Story)

1353 B.C.
The Mitanni Princess
(Prequel Novella)

1355 B.C.

1365 B.C. / 1352 B.C. - 1335 B.C.
Salvation in the Sun (Book I)

1352 B.C. - 1343 B.C.
Exiled
(Complement Book I)

1345 B.C.

1335 B.C. - 1332 B.C.
Secrets in the Sand (Book II)

1332 B.C. - 1324 B.C.
Scarab in the Storm (Book III)

1335 B.C.

1331 B.C. - 1320 B.C.
King's Daughter
(Complement Book II)

1321 B.C. - 1318 B.C.
Nefertiti's Legacy
(Complement Book III)

1324 B.C. - 1292 B.C.
Silence in the Stone (Book IV)

1325 B.C.

CONTENTS

PROLOGUE
THE TIME OF REMEMBERING

THE SUNRISE CAUGHT THE GLINT OF PHARAOH HOREMHEB'S stare into the empty room. His royal guards stood at attention behind his throne. The image of their great god, Amun-Re, towered above the five vacant seats in front of him. He lowered his elbow to rest on his knee, cradled his head in his hand, and peered through his fingers.

There is so much left to tell, he thought.

His mind filled with images from the previous, tumultuous night. The screams and tears of his precious wife, Queen Mut, and the beating she gave his chest, begging him not to condemn her family to erasure, raced through his recent memory.

The morning's grain-rich breakfast rolled in his belly as he sat on the throne. As he had commanded the day before, the five prophets of Amun gathered in their seats at the morning's first light. They looked well-rested, eagerly awaiting any mistake he might make.

I was there, he told himself. *I remember. They will remember as well. I am Pharaoh. There are none greater.*

Mut entered from the shadowed doorway behind him and

took her place behind his throne. Her eyes and cheeks sat puffed and inflamed. Silence lingered in the hall as Horemheb straightened his back and brought his hand to his side, revealing his eyes. The early-morning sun kissed the feet of the Amun-Re, the rest of his stone body still cast in shadow.

Horemheb knew that if he began to recount the rest of the story, it would be time for him to sign the edict to erase the pharaohs before him; and so, at the command of his heart, his mouth stayed closed. He looked at the face of Amun.

So much blood spilled for you. So much sacrifice to keep you as the premier god of Egypt.

He took a deep breath and closed his eyes to gather his thoughts. He clenched his jaw, wishing Pharaoh Akhenaten had never assumed the throne. Had his brother, the Crown Prince Thutmose, lived, history would not have to be erased. They could have declared the Aten as the premier god, restored power stolen from the Amun priesthood to the position of Pharaoh, and returned Egypt back to Amun all within a few years and have been done with it. He closed his eyes as he reflected.

No, Pharaoh Akhenaten had to spend seventeen years tearing apart Egypt, disassembling its economy and faith, lost in his obsessions with the sun, the Aten disc. He brought his murder upon himself, and now condemns his entire family to eternal erasure. . . . He forces me to purge our records. Curse him! By my hand, the people will forget them . . . her, Nefertiti.

He squeezed his eyes, and his brow furrowed. He took a deep breath amid a tight chest and continued to think.

But it is necessary. The people cannot remember what he did, what Pawah did, what I did. For the sake of the future of Egypt and Amun's divinely appointed Pharaohs, I do this—so there is no weakness in the people's judgment.

He opened his eyes, noticing the ache in his jaw from gritting his teeth.

I must finish telling what happened to honor their memories before I sentence them to erasure. Amun, be with me.

The prophets began to fidget in their seats, uncomfortable with Pharaoh's silence, until the sun uncovered the knees of Amun. Finally, First Prophet of Amun, Wennefer, stood and spoke.

"Great King of Egypt, we have all gathered to hear that which is to be erased. Will Pharaoh continue from yesterday the recounting of Pharaoh Akhenaten and his Queen Nefertiti?"

Nefertiti, he thought, taking another deep breath, *the one who sacrificed everything for Egypt and Amun.* He swallowed the growing lump in his throat, his heart breaking for her and what she had gone through—bringing Pharaoh poisoned wine on the threat of rebellion.

Duty and love for his country made Horemheb speak against the will of self.

"Pharaoh shall now speak."

He took one final calming breath.

"Sit down, First Prophet, and all shall hear Pharaoh's words as we begin with the People's Restoration of Egypt and their threat of rebellion if Pharaoh Akhenaten was not removed from the throne."

THE TIME OF WAITING

AKETATEN, 1335 B.C.

THE THUD OF NEFERTITI'S HEART NUMBED HER CHEST AS A bitter taste settled on her tongue. Leaning back into the door of Pharaoh's bedchambers, the thud dropped like a weight to her stomach.

Should I go back? Should I take the poisoned wine back?

Her breath hitched as her arms lay limp at her sides. The agony of the answer to her question attacked what was left of her dignity and seared its red stain upon her cheeks.

No . . . what is done is done, she thought, and lifted her head from the door and straightened her back, raising her chin to the sky.

"Amun"—her thick whisper clogged her throat—"forgive me."

I leave the wine for you, Amun, and for Egypt, she prayed in silence. *I leave it for the safety of my family and myself.* Her hands balled into fists as she thought of Pawah and Beketaten's threat of rebellion, of her children's lives. *I leave the wine for him to drink, if the gods will him gone. When the time comes, I wish him a painless journey west.*

A cry caught in her throat as unshed tears became a

stream down her cheeks. She wiped them away as she stared into the hallway, her face lit only by the hall's torches.

"Goodbye, my love," she whispered and walked down the hallway to face whatever may become of her, knowing she would have to deal with Pawah and Beketaten in the morning.

"Is it done?" Chief Royal Guard Jabari whispered, stepping from the shadows.

Nefertiti stopped in her gait and shuffled back a step as her red-rimmed, widening eyes found his. It took a moment for her to recognize him, and then her shoulders released their tension. *You too, my chief of guards?* she thought. *My father, my commander, my chief royal guard—all a part of this plan to kill my husband.* She pressed her lips into a grimace. *And now, I suppose, so am I.*

Her gaze dropped to the stone floor. "The morning sun shall uncover what is to be." Her words danced to him and painted his expression with confusion.

Not wanting to say more, Nefertiti continued down the long corridor toward her bedchambers.

"When the gods want him gone, he will drink of the poisoned wine," she whispered to herself as she let her fingers slide across the wall's cold stone. *I have said my goodbye.*

JABARI WATCHED HER GO BEFORE HURRYING TO THE council room to tell Beketaten, Pawah, and all those who awaited the outcome.

Beketaten pounded a fist into the table after she heard Jabari's incomplete report. "So? Did he drink?"

"At the morning's first light, we shall see," Jabari said again.

Beketaten shot up. "Coward!"

Pawah took his wife's hand, calming her as he guided her back in her seat. Turning to Jabari, he asked, "Did she at least leave the wine in his chambers?"

Jabari nodded. "She emerged with nothing in hand."

"Then it will only be a matter of time," Master of Pharaoh's Horses, Ay, said from the corner. "My daughter did well."

"We are short of *time*," Beketaten said through her teeth.

"Yes, but let the Coregent keep her dignity," Commander Horemheb said. "She is not a murderer. She knows Pharaoh must be dealt with in order for Egypt to survive, but . . ."

"But *what*?" Beketaten gripped the edge of the table. "We all do what we must do," she said as she leaned toward him. "And if she must give the Pharaoh poisoned wine to save herself, her children, and Egypt . . . what coward would not do it?"

"My daughter is no coward," Ay said, uncrossing his arms and putting his weight firmly planted on both feet.

In the back of the room, Jabari and his subordinates, Khabek, Ineni, and Hori, shuffled their feet, their eyes darting back and forth between the leaders of the People's Restoration of Egypt, Pawah and Beketaten, and the second- and third-highest ranking commanders of the Egyptian military, Ay and Horemheb. They shared glances, wondering where the other would place his loyalty.

"Of course our Coregent Neferneferuaten-Nefertiti is no coward," Pawah said, sensing the tension in the room.

Beketaten's glare snapped to her husband.

"As you said, my wife, one way or another, we must be rid of him. If he drinks the cup laid for him tonight or tomorrow or a month from now, he will still become one with Re. The Coregent did what she said she would do—she brought him the poisoned wine." Pawah looked at Horemheb to confirm his report of escorting Nefertiti to Akhenaten's bedchambers and witnessing the hemlock poured into the wine goblet Nefertiti took to the king.

"Egypt will not suffer more if he is alive one day or seven days," Horemheb said, nodding. "It would matter," he added, "if he were alive for *years* more."

"Yes," Pawah said, resting back in his chair. "And then more *drastic* measures would have to be taken."

"Should a rebellion come, you will spare my daughter and her children in your attack," Ay said. It was less a question than a commandment.

"It is hard to control an armed, angry riot," Pawah said, swirling his finger over an imaginary point on the table. "Sometimes, they just get . . . bloodthirsty." He pushed his finger into the table as his eyes lifted to meet Ay's, making his point.

Ay took a step and leaned forward on the table, both hands supporting his hearty frame. "You will control those who fight for you."

"Of course." Pawah slid his hand from the table as the shuffling of feet in the corner of the room slowed and stopped. "Just as I assume you would as well."

"My men follow my order," Ay said.

Pawah smirked, shaking his head. "Of course, Master of Pharaoh's Horses."

Ay stood up straight and peered down at this enemy he had to call an ally. *When this is all over, I will make you pay for forcing my hand and persuading my firstborn to murder her husband.* He gritted his teeth at the thought and put his hand on the top of the dagger's handle that hung from his belt. *You can threaten your rebellion—you can imply my men will betray me . . . and now, having no other option, I have gone along with your plan to return Egypt to its former glory. But, in the end, I may even kill you for what you have made me do to my Nefertiti, my precious lotus blossom.*

Pawah sneered, adding, "We will follow your wishes . . . for now."

"Why were you defending Nefertiti?"

Beketaten cut her husband off in his saunter down an outer palace hall after they had left the council room. Her shrill hush and her firmly planted feet made Pawah pause and look her up and down.

"Because I only strike when I know I can win," Pawah whispered in her ear as he gripped her shoulder. As he waited for her response, he carefully planned his rebuttal to her every objection. When she only glared back, he added, "There were men in that room whose loyalty was not with me, and I did not want to put us in danger, my golden flower." He traced the outline of her face with the back of his hand and then patted her chin. His chest tingled at his quick wit, and with a smug smile, he sidestepped her and continued down the path.

She grabbed his shoulder and pulled him back, placing herself in front of him again. "You always defend that woman." Her eyes narrowed at him. "Even when she exiled us to Nubia, you defended her."

"I did no such thing!" Pawah grabbed her and pushed her against the wall. Pressing his body against hers, he whispered in her ear, "Nefertiti is only a tool to return Egypt to Amun. My dear wife, when will you trust me completely?"

Beketaten tried to push him away, but his strength surpassed hers. "It is hard to *trust* you when you wouldn't even stand up to my father the first time he tried to exile us. It is hard to *trust* you when you call out other women's names in your sleep."

Pawah smirked. "Those names are from a lifetime ago. Besides . . . you are a better lover when you are jealous."

Beketaten wanted to slap him across the face, but still, he held her arms down. "Even Nefertiti? You called her name once or twice."

Pawah jutted out his chin and peered down at her. "I must have been thinking about the plan and the movement we lead."

"You *lie*," Beketaten hissed. "I thought you loved me. I thought you would make a life for us. But no . . . you have only used me to get what you want. You made me look the fool in front of those men."

Pawah let out a *tsk-tsk* and bit her earlobe with his lips. "No. You looked a fool by yourself. I only stopped you from further embarrassment."

Beketaten huffed.

Pawah kissed her neck a few times, sliding his lips from one spot to the next. "Remember, my love, you begged me to marry you so you would not have to marry your brother. There is a cost to going against your father's command. This is how we planned to get out of Nubia and back into Egypt. If I have to defend Our Majesty, Coregent Neferneferuaten, then so be it. If I have to *marry* her, then so be it. You knew perfectly well the cost."

"You told me you loved me"—Beketaten lowered her chin to block his lips from going farther—"and would do anything for me because you cherished me. *I* should be on the throne. Nefertiti banished me. She stripped everything from me. She slept in her palace while I slept on a bed of straw in Nubia. *I* am Pharaoh's *daughter*. She is no one—and should *be* no one. Yet you call out her name? You *defend* her? You *love* her! You *lied* to me." The burn of envy simmered in her chest as the coals in her stomach added strength to the flame.

"My sweet Nile Reed," Pawah crooned, and he pushed her

wig's hair from her cheek. "I never lie to you." He hovered his lips over hers. "I do love you. I do cherish you, my beautiful daughter of the King."

"I don't believe you," Beketaten said, turning her face away.

He pulled her chin with his fingers so that she faced him again.

"Don't you?" His lips brushed past hers.

"No," she whispered, and closed her eyes, breathing him in.

He kissed her, and not a moment later, she kissed him back, pulling him closer.

2

THE TIME OF LOSS

A FEW DECANS LATER, NEFERTITI HID IN THE SHADE OF THE supporting beams to the outer harbor, peering out over the calm Nile waters that graced the setting horizon. She drew in a shaky breath and pressed her hands to her cheeks, trying to hide the puffiness and blinking rapidly to conceal the redness in her eyes. The plague had taken so much from her four long years ago, and now the People's Restoration of Egypt was taking so much of her own dignity. Trust she only gave to a few; even then, after her father and Horemheb convinced her to become Pharaoh's executioner, she only found solace with a few of her servants, Merytre, and Aitye.

The morning after Nefertiti had brought the poisoned wine to Akhenaten, Merytre collapsed while dressing her. Aitye caught the steward and waited with her as the royal physician-priest came at Nefertiti's call.

"*No breath, no beat of the heart,*" he had declared.

Merytre's passing caused Nefertiti's spirit to break. Her loyal steward for almost seventeen years, Merytre always knew what she needed—a bath, a moment of reprieve, a piece of bread, a wipe of the brow . . . but now she was gone.

Nefertiti's chin quivered as she closed her eyes, wishing she had not taken her servant for granted—especially now when so much was at stake.

A boat docked, and Nefertiti's younger half-sister, Mut, stepped off and then tried to help her aging mother, Tey, who refused both Mut's and the servant's aid.

"Mother!" Nefertiti exclaimed with a quivery smile as she grabbed ahold of her. Safe in the arms of someone she knew she could trust with absolute certainty, Nefertiti's shoulders let their burden down. Her mind went blank as she took in the sweet garden musk that lived in Tey's clothes, and she instantly remembered her carefree days as a child in Waset.

Tey's arms flew out in surprise at the Coregent's informal actions, but soon came to rest around her daughter. Tey loved when Nefertiti called her "Mother"—even though Nefertiti's birth mother, Temehu, had traveled to the Field of Reeds in childbirth.

"My dear Nefertiti."

Mut stood with her hands twisted in front of her stomach and her left foot hiding behind her right. An awkward grin and eyes of admiration defined her face. Nefertiti opened an arm to her as well, and Mut, still a child with her sidelock, bounced into their circle of arms.

"I-I'm sorry you lost Merytre," Mut stammered. Her half-sister, Coregent Nefertiti, elegant and powerful, perfect in every way, rendered her mute most of the time. Her cheeks did not rise as high as Nefertiti's, nor did her eyes open as wide; but even in her youth, a certain beauty beheld her.

The circles under Nefertiti's eyes grew dark again as Mut's innocent sentiment thrust her back into the present day. "As am I," Nefertiti whispered, and pulled them closer. After a moment, she released them. "Come inside. Aitye will bring us wine to drink and bread to eat. It was a long trip for you."

"Thank you, child," Tey said, and they made their way to the nearest courtyard.

Silence followed them.

Once they were seated and Aitye had brought them nourishment, Tey asked as they ate, "Will they entomb Merytre in Akhe-Aten, as well, with Meketaten and . . . ?" She trailed off upon seeing her daughter's contorted mouth.

Nefertiti could not bring herself to remember the year of the plague. It had taken so many from her: three of her six daughters; Kiya, the best of friends; and Queen Tiye, her wise mentor.

Mut returned her bread to the plate and stood up. Walking over to Nefertiti, she put a hand on her shoulder.

"Yes . . ." Nefertiti's shaky voice found strength in the innocence of Mut's eyes. "They will entomb Merytre in Akhe-Aten."

Mut is only a year younger than my daughter would have been. Neferneferure journeyed west so young, Nefertiti thought. *I see her in there somewhere. In the eyes, maybe.*

Her thoughts raced to the last time she saw her daughter alive, holding the wet nurse, gasping for air, coughing up blood, struggling to live . . . her little limp body worn from the plague . . .

She pushed the image from her mind, remembering her failings as a mother: Instead of going to her, she instead went to tend to Egypt in her husband's place. She had brought the plague into Egypt by bringing the military home from diseased lands. Because of her, they were no longer in the land of the living. Because of her, they were in the Field of Reeds.

"Akhe-Aten," she mumbled and pressed her lips together to form a thin line. Her arms tensed, and suddenly the bread on her plate looked unappetizing. Akhe-Aten—where her daughters had made the journey to the afterlife. The thickness in her throat slid to her chest.

Tey rubbed Nefertiti's arms and pressed her lips into a warm smile as she found her daughter's eyes. "Akhe-Aten." Tey nodded. She remembered the long walk from the palace to the necropolis for each of her three grand-daughters.

"Pharaoh Akhenaten will be entombed here," Nefertiti said, her voice stronger, "and, as such, I will be also, along with my children."

It is the truth. I will forever spend eternity in a place dedicated to the Aten—a place that insults the face of Amun.

"Why can't you be entombed with all of the followers of Amun?" Mut asked, seemingly reading her half-sister's thoughts.

The tendons in Nefertiti's neck stood on alert as she pressed a finger to Mut's lips. "You mustn't speak of Amun here." Nefertiti's voice fell to a hurried whisper.

Mut's downward-curled mouth and big, wide eyes searched for truth. "Because Pharaoh is mad?"

Nefertiti almost laughed, partly at the pure sight of her, and partly at the obvious truth even this nine-year-old child could see. A stern grimace replaced a momentary grin. "Pharaoh thinks differently," she said. "Now, Mut, whilst here, you must refrain from speaking directly what comes to mind."

Tey nodded and gave Mut a raised eyebrow and a squint of the eyes. Nefertiti remembered that look from Tey well—a warning to be more cautious of one's words—and had no envy of being young again.

"Nefertiti, your father keeps me in the dark, but I must ask . . . Is all well? He wakes in the night and spends his free time leering out the window, eyes darting." Tey placed her hand upon Nefertiti's knee. "Last time I saw you as well, my daughter, your shoulders seemed heavy . . . and now you hide something in your eyes, something more than just the passing of Merytre."

"It is nothing, Mother," Nefertiti lied.

Curse how she can read me like an open scroll! Father is right to protect her and the children. They have no business knowing what is going on in the palace. With the threat of the People's Restoration of Egypt, she should be out of harm's way in Waset . . . unless an angry mob targets their house. She is the wife of Master of Pharaoh's Horses, after all.

Tey searched her face for a moment, then sat back, removing her hand. "If you say so."

"I do," Nefertiti said, more to herself than to Tey, hating herself for lying to her mother.

Tey nodded and, as she always did, bided her time.

Mut glanced back and forth between them, but, as if remembering Tey's warning from moments earlier, decided not to say anything else.

They ate the rest of their meal in silence, peering up at each other every now and then. Once they sated their hunger, Aitye and another servant came to take their plates and cups.

Tey looked to her daughter, eyeing her golden-banded modius crown; she skimmed her face next, noting the dark circles under her eyes, her hollow cheeks, her pallid skin.

"What, Mother?" Nefertiti asked, annoyed at her mother simply looking her over.

But perhaps it is my guilt of lying to her, and Mother's stare only reminds me of it.

"Nothing. We are *your* guests. What would you have us do? The sun is almost set." Tey tapped her finger on her knee and lifted her chin toward her daughter.

Her response took Nefertiti back a little—she had expected her mother to ask her again about what secrets she held. "We shall . . . adjourn to my chambers."

"Very well," Tey said.

"Mut," Nefertiti said, diverting the conversation to get out from under Tey's stare. "Tell me of your studies. How do they go?"

Mut began to drone on about her tutors as Nefertiti led them to her chambers.

Once the door closed, leaving them alone within the walls of Nefertiti's bedchambers, they settled in the living area and silence once again fell upon the women.

"Any suitors yet, Mut?" Nefertiti asked. "If I'm not mistaken, you only have a few years left before you are of the age to marry."

Mut's cheeks turned red and her once-straight spine bent and caved around her chest. Mut's sheepish grin betrayed her. "No—"

"She likes the servant boy," Tey said with a shake of her head. "He is beneath her, and she cannot marry him. He has nothing to offer for her."

"Don't say that, Mother!" Mut stood and threw her arms across her chest.

Tey's raised eyebrow came forth and Mut sucked in her cheeks and sat down, her arms still pressed into her stomach and her hands clasped as fists.

"She is not as lucky as you, Nefertiti, having a cousin to wed," Tey said, watching Mut as she scrubbed a hand on the side of her face.

"Yes, lucky." Nefertiti thought of the late Crown Prince Thutmose, and even though it seemed like another life, she wished he were alive—then maybe she would have been lucky.

"Well, you could do as Queen Tiye did for you." Tey's eyes grew wide with meaning.

"What?" Nefertiti hunched her shoulders, already anticipating the response.

"Just as Queen Tiye asked you to marry her son, you could

ask Mut to marry Prince Tutankhaten." Her eyes lit at this new potential match.

"Mother, please don't put such thoughts into our heads." Nefertiti curled her lip and threw her hands up. "That boy will never have any of *my* family as his wife. Not if I have anything to say about it!" She stood and walked away to regain her composure. Placing her hands on her hips, she looked to the floor and took a few breaths while her mother spoke.

"What's wrong with him? He is a prince of Egypt, and the one time I have met him, he was kind and polite enough." Tey shrugged with an impatient sneer. "So he may have a bit of a temper. He is only a child—what, two years Mut's junior? There is still plenty of time for him to—"

"No!" A sour taste filled Nefertiti's mouth, and she yelled again for good measure, "No! He is the product of Akhenaten and Henuttaneb. That boy is a constant reminder that my own husband, who promised to love *me* and *only* me, who promised *me* I would bear the next heir, didn't think I was enough. His broken promise to me lingers in that boy's very existence. In his madness, he loved that boy more than he would ever love me!" Nefertiti sucked in her breath, wishing she could pull back her words.

A sly smile crossed Tey's face—and Nefertiti let out an audible sigh; her mother's trickery had worked, and she knew her prodding would come soon enough.

"So you *do* think him mad?"

"Mother!"

Nefertiti clenched her fists. She knew the prodding would come, but not as quickly as it did. Another thought crossed her mind and she looked around, noting the servants peering up from their duties. In her anger she had forgotten they were there. Her eyes darted to and fro as the presence of those in the room fell upon her mind.

"Come. No more talk of this," she whispered, and motioned them to silence until Aitye shut them in alone in her chambers. Finally, a sigh of relief escaped her lungs. "We can't be too careful. There are ears everywhere." She crossed her arms over her chest as she walked to the door to make sure Aitye had shut it behind her.

"I am so glad to hear that! I didn't raise my daughter to renounce Amun." Tey let out the words with a deep sigh as her shoulders rolled forward.

Nefertiti stopped in her walk back to her living area, watching her mother with a vacant stare.

"Egypt believes I have," Nefertiti said, avoiding her mother's eyes.

Instead of rejoining them, she walked to the window overlooking the sun as it sank over the Nile, beyond whose shores the desert looked as barren as her future. She had chosen this room for her living area and her bedroom behind it when they first moved to Aketaten, so she could wake to the rising sun's reflection on the water. Being on the second floor of the palace, the guards only needed to guard her door and the royal road below. It allowed her an unimpeded view of the Nile. Her mother's shuffling made her snap back to the present. She peered out the window and to the ground below, making sure no one lingered there to overhear their conversation.

"My Nefertiti, I am sure they don't believe that," Tey reassured her as she came behind her, placing her hands on her shoulder. "At least not with certainty."

Nefertiti smirked at her step-mother's frankness. But then her heart dipped as she wondered if her own mother, Temehu, would have been that way. She would never know.

"What else bothers you, my child?" Tey asked her.

"Everything," Nefertiti said as she turned and fell forward into Tey's arms. The warmth of Tey's embrace made her feel safe again—a fleeting feeling in this empire, this city, this palace. Even the walls of her own chamber felt as though they had closed in on her in the stillness of the night. Ears always listened. Trust lingered only in some.

"Come, child," Tey soothed as she guided her back to the living area where Mut was seated. "Tell me and perhaps we can figure it out together." She rubbed Nefertiti's back before taking a seat herself.

Nefertiti opened her mouth to speak, but no words could come.

Where to even start?

Her gaze lowered to the floor with a shake of her head. She opened her mouth again, lifting her eyes to Tey, but nothing came.

"Why do you seem as if you have not slept"—Tey motioned to the circles under Nefertiti's eyes—"and yet have not seen the sun lately?"

Nefertiti bit her lip and rubbed her chin. *Because everything is wrong!* her heart screamed. She drew a frown and pulled back, slightly uncertain what Tey and Mut would think of her if she confessed her true thoughts.

"My daughter, tell me." Tey stroked her forearm and leaned in.

"Each day," Nefertiti began, and fidgeted with the beads on her collar. "Each day—" She cleared her throat. She closed her eyes and forced the words out—any that would come. "Each day, I wake up not knowing if death will strike us."

Tey jerked, not expecting those words, but leaned in again and continued to listen in silence. Nefertiti smiled at her; she loved the way her mother made her feel, the way she listened to her, as if what she said mattered.

Mut sat too, leaning forward but staying mute, imitating her mother.

Nefertiti's voice wavered as she spoke, not knowing how

her mother and sister would react. "If Pharaoh passes from this life soon, it will be because of me." Tears ran from her cheeks as she whispered, "I will have killed him." The weight of her confession lifted from her chest as the words spilled into her mother's lap.

Tey's brow furrowed as she tried to comprehend what Nefertiti meant.

Mut's eyes grew wider.

Nefertiti studied Tey's face and knew more explanation was needed. She bit her lip, but pressed herself to continue in a whisper. "There is a movement . . . a movement that wants to kill the royal family and start anew with the followers of Amun," Nefertiti whispered as her shoulders slumped.

Her father had kept this information from his family for a reason, and she knew she violated his will by speaking it. *An eye for an eye.* She thought back to him coaxing her to kill her own husband. *I cannot keep this to myself any longer. I want to be able to sleep again.*

"Not my family," Tey said with a force behind her voice and a shake of her head. "What movement?" Her voice echoed off of the stone walls.

"Mother," Nefertiti hushed. "Be quiet. You don't know who is on the other side of the door listening. This is not a safe place."

"This is the *palace*. This is the safest place there is," Mut retorted, her hands emphasizing every word.

"Yes, I agree." Tey nodded. "You shouldn't feel—"

"Both of you, quiet," Nefertiti hissed. "Loyalties are split. The movement runs deep, even into the palace. They tasked me to take poisoned wine to Pharaoh." Nefertiti gritted her teeth, thinking back to that night, and averted her eyes. She couldn't bear to look her mother in the eyes, knowing what a shameful deed she had done.

Mut gave a nervous chuckle. "You didn't . . . did you? Not

you?" The shrillness in Mut's voice made Nefertiti only imagine the depths she would fall from Mut's pedestal for her.

"I did." Nefertiti straightened her back, but her gaze stayed on the floor below, not wanting to give witness to the disappearance of the respect and admiration from her sister's eyes. She finally lifted her own. "I said the movement runs deep. I had no other choice."

Mut gasped. "You always have a choice!"

Tey shot her the look to quit, and Mut closed her mouth.

But her half-sister was right. "I know," Nefertiti whispered. "I could have refused . . . but they said a mob bent on murder lay in wait. One life or many—it was my choice to make. I chose one life." Flutters in her stomach made her breaths shallow. Her hands closed and opened as she imagined what must be going through their minds.

"Wouldn't the guards protect you?" Tey asked, returning her focus to Nefertiti.

"No." The word came out as quick as a cat's scratch; seeing the wound to her mother's feelings, she softened her tone. "Some would, for they took an oath, but others feel their oath has been violated. They won't stop anyone from removing the single most powerful threat to Egypt—Pharaoh . . . and anyone they believe supports him." Nefertiti chewed on her lip in their silence, then added, "He has let Egypt fall, Mother."

"Does that deserve murder?" Mut asked as Tey stroked Nefertiti's hand. Tey shot a cold stare to her youngest daughter, but not before Nefertiti rushed through her defense.

"He let our alliances fall apart. There is threat of war between the Mitanni, the Libyans, and the Nubians. We had no choice but to try to strike an alliance with the Hittites. The Hittites! Our sworn enemies, who do nothing but try to take our northern Canaan border . . . we had to try to align ourselves with them, because Egypt is desperate!"

Nefertiti's heart beat against her chest wall as she realized her own voice echoed off the walls now. She regained her composure and looked to the door, hoping no one had heard her elevated voice. She dropped her head and held her next words as they trembled on her lips. Doubt from her past raised her voice as memories flooded her soul until, finally, the dam broke.

"If Thutmose had lived . . ."

She took in a loud sweep of air into her lungs. Thutmose. The true Crown Prince . . . the one who loved her and her him . . . the one she would have spent her life with if he hadn't gone to Re at such a young age . . . the one who wouldn't have betrayed her . . . the one who would have been good to Egypt. Tears slide out of the corners of her eyes, and she brushed them away. But that life she would never know.

"We would never be in this position! Thutmose would have been a Pharaoh his father would have been proud of!"

Instead, eventually, she fell in love with Thutmose's brother after his passing, and let Akhenaten beat her down until she brought him poisoned wine. She cupped her mouth with her hands as she rocked back and forth, trying to steady her breath and hold her tears.

"Where is my dignity?" she asked herself.

Tey said nothing, but rather clenched her jaw and rubbed Nefertiti's knee.

"If Thutmose had lived, I wouldn't be a murderer," Nefertiti whispered as she looked at her mother, not trying to hide her tears anymore.

Tey would never condone murder, but still, she pulled Nefertiti up into an embrace. "I will never understand the burden you carry, my daughter," Tey whispered, but then fell silent as she gently rubbed Nefertiti's back.

They locked their gazes upon each other, and that was when Nefertiti saw the disappointment dripping from her mother's eyes. Tey's silence ate at Nefertiti's conscience, but she rested her head on Tey's shoulder anyway, letting the tears fall.

"But Pharaoh lives." Mut cut through the silence trying to heal her half-sister from her grief. "Perhaps the wine spilt."

"Oh, Mut," Nefertiti whispered, and pulled away from Tey. Her chin trembled as she explained, "He lives for now, yes . . . I left the poisoned wine in his bedchambers. He drinks wine as he breathes air. He will find it one day." Nefertiti turned to look to Tey. "Despite what you both think, I had no choice."

Tey opened her mouth to say she understood, but Mut was quicker. "Fine—but then what will happen?" Mut immediately shut her mouth at the sight of her mother's stare.

"Then I will be Pharaoh," Nefertiti said, referring to her status as Coregent, and wiped her tears from her cheeks. She took a deep breath and sat back down again as she lifted her chin.

I am Pharaoh Coregent. I cannot act in this way, even with my family, she chided herself.

"His son is too young and too sickly to take his place—or, in the very least, he will be *my* Coregent." Her jaw clenched as she thought of that dreadful boy, the evidence of her husband's broken promise to their bed. Akhenaten had yet to name a successor, but since she was Coregent, it would fall to her.

"Would they allow a woman to be Pharaoh?" Tey asked, but backtracked her words at the annoyed look she received from Nefertiti. "I mean, you are more than capable, of course . . . but—"

"But what?" Nefertiti crossed her arms and sat up straight.

Tey tilted her head and let out a short huff of air, causing Nefertiti to shrink back a little. Nefertiti pursed her lips and leaned away from her mother as an apology of sorts.

"I just don't see the people accepting a woman Pharaoh." Tey threw her hands up and let them drift back down to her lap.

Nefertiti only stared at her mother. "Women hold equal status to men in this country."

"But we hold different roles. The *King* has been traditionally Amun's divinely appointed *man* since the dawn of our civilization."

Nefertiti crossed her arms tighter across her chest as her mother continued.

"The Egyptians—we . . . we are a proud people. We thrive in our traditions, do we not? Is that not why Egypt has failed in this new religion of Pharaoh Akhenaten's? Do you think your crowning as King would not cause more strife with the people?"

Nefertiti bit her tongue and sat quietly for a moment. Her royalty began with such an auspicious future—to be carved in stone next to her friend and husband, Thutmose—but since he passed, she instead would be remembered next to this heretic Pharaoh, Akhenaten, if she was to be remembered at all. She folded her hands in her lap, not wanting to accept her future.

"Then I suppose I shall have no legacy."

Tey turned and surveyed the room, praying to Amun that this not be the case for her daughter. She crossed her arms as well and dropped her head.

Mut swallowed the dry lump sitting in her throat. "No, they can't do that to you," she protested as her muscles quivered at the unfairness. "You . . . you are Queen Nefertiti,

Coregent Neferneferuaten!" Her eyes lit with admiration once again. "You sat in Pharaoh's place while he rejected his duties! You said so yourself!"

Tey turned to face her daughters, but said nothing, feeling both of their pain sink into the depths of her stomach.

"Mut, Mother speaks the truth," Nefertiti started, "it will—"

"No!" Mut stood up with fists by her side. "You—"

"Silence, Mut!" Nefertiti stood and towered over her small frame.

Mut's mouth contorted; she wanted to say more, but refrained.

"Yes, I did sit in Pharaoh's place," Nefertiti continued as she sat down, having secured Mut's silence. "But that doesn't change anything . . . that doesn't change what I did or what will most likely happen." She bit her lip and slumped her shoulders. With a quick shake of her head, she let out a despairing sigh. Nefertiti looked to her half-sister as the burdens sat heavily on her shoulders. "Mut, I don't deserve your respect. Be better than me."

Mut's lips turned into a frown as she clenched her jaw, and a tear escaped as Nefertiti accepted her fate.

Tey rubbed her neck and closed her eyes, not knowing what to say. Words would not change the future. Words would not take away the shame and anger.

Nefertiti lifted her chin. "The further you distance yourself from me, the safer you will be. Less tears you will cry for my sake."

3

THE TIME OF SUCCESSION

THE SUN ROSE THE NEXT MORNING AS NEFERTITI STOOD awake, Aitye having already dressed her in silence. Her heart ached for Merytre. In the dim candlelight, Nefertiti heard Aitye's sniffles and knew she wasn't the only one who missed her. They would entomb Merytre in the necropolis Akhe-Aten just east of the city Aketaten.

The last walk she took there was a time of great grieving as well, four years ago now. Rubbing her hand against her heart, Nefertiti felt the same pang of sorrow in her chest as when she had to entomb her second oldest, Meketaten, who had been taken by the plague. Her fingers closed around her palm, curling into a tight fist, and her nostrils flared as she envisioned the past. On that same dark day, Akhenaten had named their third daughter, Ankhesenpaaten, his wife, as if Meketaten had never existed.

Never mind the fact that Ankhesenpaaten was only seven at the time, with no business being married at her age, she thought. *Then, shortly after, Kiya died . . .*

Her fist shook now against her corded neck.

Kiya, she thought, *I will never forgive myself for the way I treated you in your last times. I will never forgive myself.*

Angry tears pricked her eyes as she shook her head. Drawing in a deep breath, Nefertiti raised her chin against the past.

Not today. I do not want to remember those days. They are behind me.

This day would be, too, in time; but the more she thought about the life and the next, the more something gnawed at her—or rather, someone.

Akhenaten.

Was he dead? Was he alive? Every morning she asked herself this question, but every day he proved to be alive and a little piece of her soul perished. Would she find relief from her guilt when the morning sun came with news of Pharaoh's passing? Relief. Such a weak word to describe a murderer who has finally completed her task.

A *rap-rap-rap* came at her door, and Nefertiti's stomach swelled as she held her breath. Aitye answered and a messenger came to declare that Pharaoh summoned Queen and Coregent Neferneferuaten-Nefertiti to the throne room. Hushed tones filled the room as Nefertiti strained to hear.

Aitye came back and whispered to Nefertiti, "My Coregent, Pharaoh summons the royal family. He has had a vision."

Nefertiti's eyes rolled as she dropped her head back in frustration. "Why today? Can we not send Merytre to the afterlife in peace?" She brought her head to her hands and again whispered, to no one in particular, "Why today?"

"He doesn't realize," Aitye spoke.

Nefertiti shot her a deadly stare.

Aitye hurriedly added, "He doesn't know what she meant to you because he is lost in himself."

"And he wouldn't care if I told him," Nefertiti said as she

pulled her shoulders up. "Is it wrong, Aitye, to want him gone?"

"When someone causes you a lot of pain"—Aitye glanced down and twirled her fingers—"it is not *un*reasonable to want to remove the cause of your pain." Her gaze rose to Nefertiti and she swallowed before continuing. "I see your tears, my Coregent. I see your tight jaw and swollen eyes. I see the burden of Egypt upon your shoulders." She paused, taking in Nefertiti's silence. "Coregent . . . may I speak freely?"

"You may," Nefertiti said, swaying slightly on her feet. Aitye had been with her for a long time, and Merytre was gone; someone needed to fill her place, and who better than Aitye? She had saved her life when the rebels attacked Malkata more than a decade ago.

With her master's permission, Aitye spoke again, saying, "There are rumors you were going to kill him."

Nefertiti's eyes grew wide. "Rumors?" She bit her tongue. Pawah and Beketaten would spread the truth as rumors. Why did she ever go along with their plan? Because they threatened the lives of her and her children. Her feet stuck to the floor in much the same way as she was stuck in the middle of an unfortunate situation.

"Yes. Rumors," Aitye said, eyes searching her master, whose silence confirmed to her their truth, and the corners of Aitye's mouth fell. "My Coregent . . . don't become someone you hate because another caused you pain."

"Very wise words," Nefertiti said as she patted Aitye's cheek. "But I'm afraid, it's too late for that." A sad grin graced her face. "Put those rumors to rest." Aitye bowed her head as Nefertiti walked past. "When I return from the throne room, we will send Merytre in peace and goodwill, despite whatever mindless thing Pharaoh Akhenaten decides to say this morning."

"Yes, Coregent," Aitye said as she watched the woman

who had lost nearly everything walk out the door. "Stay strong, my Queen," she whispered. "Don't fall from your grace."

THE ROYAL GUARDS OPENED THE THRONE ROOM DOORS AS Nefertiti entered. Her daughter Meritaten and her husband Smenkare stood on her right and her two daughters Ankhesenpaaten and Neferneferuaten Tasherit—or "Nefe," as they called her—stood on her left. Tutankhaten stood next to his nurse, Maia, beside Smenkare. Nefertiti looked to her right and to her left, thinking the royal family had been reduced significantly since the plague.

Akhenaten stood facing his throne; his sun-darkened back faced them. He lifted his face to his open roof as the morning light fell upon his shoulders and bellowed:

"The Aten has spoken to Pharaoh!"

He spun around. His bloodshot eyes searched them for the anticipation he felt he deserved, but found them lacking. "Pharaoh prayed to the Aten all night, and *this* is the response?" He took a step down from his throne. "A vision!" he yelled as he threw a finger into the air, pointing to the sky. "Humble yourselves before the vision the Aten has granted unto Pharaoh!"

Smenkare and Meritaten slumped over as pitiful servants of the sun-disc god, the Aten, and, one by one, the rest bowed their heads.

"Smenkare, my brother." Akhenaten pulled him out in front of the gathered royal family. "For all of your life, your mother—my sister, royal wife of our father, Amenhotep III—Sitamun, kept a secret. A secret that may have changed the course of your life. You are my father's son, the Great King Amenhotep III, just as I am. You were robbed of your right to the throne seventeen years ago when I did not want it. Is this true?"

Smenkare nodded. "Yes, Pharaoh."

Nefertiti's stomach gurgled in dreaded anticipation of what came next. Her arms crossed her stomach to symbolically protect from whatever blow might be dealt to her in the coming moments. Meritaten, along with Smenkare, who were brainwashed into the cult of the Aten, would prove tragic for the future of Egypt if Smenkare was appointed successor. She clenched her jaw, hating how she failed her eldest child in the most important aspect of life—their faith. Amun was the premier god of Egypt, but because of Nefertiti's actions, Meritaten believed the *Aten* was the only god of Egypt.

"Then, brother, in light of my Coregent pleading to allow our precious Egypt to go back to those false gods and goddesses, Amun, Mut, Horus, Anubis, and the like"— Akhenaten glared at Nefertiti, who matched his stare steadily —"I appoint you, my brother and husband to my daughter, the first daughter of Pharaoh, as the next King of Egypt."

Nefertiti's throat closed and her stomach turned to stone. *Why did I not just give you the cursed wine that night?* Her eyes narrowed and her jaw clenched as her breath came out hot through her teeth.

"*I* shall be Coregent?" Smenkare asked, his eyes wide and a smile on his face.

"You shall be crowned at Pharaoh's next sed festival in the coming decans," Akhenaten said, referring to the traditional celebration of a Pharaoh's thirty-year reign; tradition called for one every few years after that, but he had already had several because he simply liked the celebration.

Another sed festival? Nefertiti gritted her teeth. *He has only been on the throne seventeen years. I should have cut his reign short before this happened.* Heat rose to her cheeks; she loathed herself for not making sure he drank the poisoned wine that night. Guilt or no guilt.

"Thank you, brother!" Smenkare bowed to Akhenaten.

Then the room fell silent as they turned to peer at Nefertiti, the current Coregent. She pressed her lips together, dropped her arms to her side and straightened her spine. Her unwavering stare focused on her husband.

I dare you, she thought.

Ankhesenpaaten tried to find her mother's gaze, but it was locked on her father. She looked her up and down, wondering why her mother would plead the return to the false gods. Her lip curled as her soon-to-be-removed sidelock bounced on the side of her head.

"And what of Coregent Neferneferuaten?" Smenkare whispered from behind his hand.

"Ah! The beautiful Coregent Neferneferuaten-Nefertiti, whose cheeks rise as high as Khufu's great pyramid and whose spirit attacks like the great leopard," Akhenaten said as he raised his arms and embraced his wife. "She is Pharaoh's Queen—nonetheless, she cannot see the vision Pharaoh has for Egypt, the future in the Aten."

Nefertiti bit her lip as he pulled back and stared into her cold, dark eyes. An unpredictable man could be her demise. Not knowing what this man would declare next, her heart raced. *Don't let my life be in vain,* she prayed in haste to Amun underneath her confident exterior.

"She shall keep her title as Coregent. To strip it away would be unfitting for such a stunning creature as her." Akhenaten pulled his hands away and turned back to his half-brother. "But you, Smenkare, shall take my place when I go to the Aten, and always remember that the Aten is most gracious—even to those who doubt." He peered over his shoulder at Nefertiti. "Even you, my Queen, the Aten's second mediator. He is disappointed in you, yet he is still gracious."

Nefertiti relaxed her jaw and realized her hands were trembling. Her life spared, she bowed her head and, with a slow exhale to calm her nerves, muttered in grace, "I shall try harder to see Pharaoh's vision."

Akhenaten smiled. "That is all Pharaoh asks, my beautiful one granted to me by the Aten." He then dismissed all except his brother, Smenkare, with whom he needed to share the future plans for Egypt.

NEFERTITI SLAMMED THE DOOR BEHIND HER, PICKED UP A nearby candle, and shot it across the room. Wax splattered on the wall as Aitye rounded the corner with Mut and Tey. Like a bull ready to charge, Nefertiti grunted.

Mut let out a scream and ducked her head in her hands. Tey gasped, her hand stilling the sudden race of her heart, and spun to look at Nefertiti.

"My dear child!" Tey's jaw dropped. "What was that for?"

Aitye went to pick up the candle pieces and peel the wax from the stone. She bit her lip and peered to the tapestry that hid the stash of broken trinkets she had not yet discarded from her Coregent's last tirade.

"Smenkare will be Akhenaten's successor."

The coldness in Nefertiti's voice matched the coldness of her stare.

"Smenkare is Meritaten's husband." Tey walked to her daughter. "Surely you taught Amun's truth to Meritaten?" She grasped Nefertiti's arms to pull her into an embrace, but closed her mouth as Nefertiti's hot glare crept over her.

" 'Surely, you taught the religious zealot's daughter about this so-called false god!' " Nefertiti said, mocking her stepmother. "Surely!" She threw her hands in the air, knocking away Tey's embrace.

Tey pulled her arms to her side and bit her lip. "I thought—"

"No, Mother. I am not a good mother like you. I was not there to teach them about the true gods . . . and when I was, I played the part . . . bringing flowers to the Aten, indulging in Akhenaten's mild obsession. But I was too late in noticing how the Aten had overtaken his mind. By the time I did, Meritaten and Meketaten . . . *all* of my daughters . . . they had all but forgotten about Amun—if they had even ever known him." Nefertiti shook her head. Meketaten, so young to go west, as with her sisters, Setepenre and Neferneferure. They sliced her heart. She failed all of her daughters.

Nefertiti paced for a few moments as she cleared her mind and thought aloud about the present crisis. In a hushed tone so as to not be heard outside her doors, she muttered, "When Akhenaten drinks the wine, Smenkare will take his place, not me. What are they going to do? What am *I* going to do? I would have killed a man for nothing. Nothing! Why didn't I just make sure he drank the wine that night? I am such a *fool*!"

Aitye's gaze dropped, shocked, but Nefertiti no longer cared if she knew the truth of the rumors. Tey just shook her head and clenched her jaw, clearly unsure how to comfort Nefertiti in this moment. But at Mut's contorted brow and diminished admiration in her eyes, dimmed even more with pity, Nefertiti stopped in her tracks.

"Mut . . . I'm sorry, Mut."

Nefertiti came to Mut, crumpling under her lost innocence. She finally found the strength to look Mut in the eyes and stroked her sister's arms. "Be better than me, Mut. Be better." Her cheeks burned. "Egypt can't go on like this."

Nefertiti held Mut's chin up. "I'd rather it be my burden than any of yours."

Nefertiti patted Mut's shoulders at Mut's silence and empty stare. She pressed her lips together and turned to face Aitye.

"Yes, Coregent?" Aitye asked as she stepped forward, acknowledging her master's silent call.

"Send word to my father, Ay, Master of Pharaoh's Horses, that Prince Smenkare will be appointed as successor," Nefertiti said as a tear escaped her eye.

She hated herself for putting them all in a worse situation than she was before. She knew of Smenkare's rejection of Amun, but did anyone else? He was the son of Sitamun, Akhenaten's sister who remained in Waset, at Malkata. They would all assume she taught him well in the ways of Egypt and their gods. If only she had made Akhenaten drink the wine that night, she would not be subjecting Egypt to further oppression.

"As you wish." Aitye bowed her head and went to call a messenger.

Nefertiti wiped her eye as she thought of her friend and servant—Merytre, the one whose soul they were supposed to honor this morning.

Merytre, may your soul rest on your journey to the afterlife. Be glad you do not have to witness this hypocrisy.

❧ 4 ❧

THE TIME OF SCHEMING

AT THE NEWS OF SMENKARE BEING NAMED AS SUCCESSOR, a smile perched on Beketaten's lips as she and Pawah looked at each other.

"Even though Akhenaten says Smenkare will continue his worship to Aten, I know my sister. She would have taught him better than that. He only agrees to Akhenaten's decree as to escape the same fate as Nefertiti. He will bring us back to Amun," Beketaten said, pausing to study her husband's face.

His teeth showed as he grinned and his shoulders rolled back into an upward stance. Narrowing his eyes, he snorted at the news. Glancing at his wife, he muttered through his teeth, "Yes, the son of *Sitamun* should bring Egypt back to *Amun*."

"Then what flusters you?" Beketaten asked, throwing her hands on her hips.

But she already knew the answer. He had made it clear to her during their time in exile. Despite giving up her royalty and blindly following him into a life as an outcast, she knew he wanted another woman. Yet there was something about him. He could always soothe her, even after he would murmur another woman's name in her ear while they lay in bed or while sleeping. But she had nothing left—only him and Amun. He was her husband, and he had never laid a fist on her face. She had no father to take up grievance against him for his philandering. If she left him on her own word for divorce without evidence of his unfaithfulness, she may be entitled to some of his grain; but if not, she would have nothing but her faith. He knew she could do nothing but stay, and it caused her blood to boil when he said those things to her. At the same time, he was the only man she'd known and loved, and she figured he gave his kisses as a truce between them.

"What flusters me is that Akhenaten isn't in his tomb yet," Pawah said. "If the fearless Coregent Neferneferuaten-Nefertiti had just given him the poisoned wine that night, I'd be—" He cut himself off. "*We'd* be rid of him now, and she and the boy would be Egypt's Regents."

"I have already said that, but you made me look a fool in front of Horemheb and Ay!" Beketaten yelled as she pushed her fists down by her sides and leaned forward.

"Your emotions discredit you," Pawah said, waving her away. "Now I must think."

"Think about what?" Beketaten pulled his shoulder, forcing him to look at her.

He caught her wrist and squeezed, like a snake snuffing the life out of its prey. "Do not disrespect me like a child," he warned her. He let go of her wrist when she began to wince. "Now, I must think about how best to transition Smenkare. Why don't you go to your sister Sitamun's house and see if and what she taught him about Amun?"

Beketaten hit him in his chest. "You just want me gone so you can chase the women you call out by name in *our* bed."

"No, I'm asking you to fulfill your role in our plan to

return Egypt to Amun." He grabbed her hand and pushed it away.

"You want to stay here in Aketaten while I go to my sister's in Waset?" Beketaten said. "I don't want you to tell me in a year that it was my idea to go to Waset."

"Why would I tell you that?" Pawah said as he flicked his hand toward her.

"You always do! You tell me one thing on one day and then something else the next and expect me to believe you! I am *done* believing you! You lie about your women. I *know* you do! You lie about everything else too!" Her heart raced and pounded in her ears.

He rocked back on his heels, stunned, then came near to her and grasped her shoulders to settle her down. "My golden grain," he whispered. "You hurt me when you think of me in this light. I have—"

"Why don't you just say it?" Beketaten blinked to keep her tears to herself. "Just *say* it, Pawah!"

"Say what, my love?" Pawah stepped closer to her, taking a wide stance with a straight back and neck, daring her.

"Don't call me your love if you don't mean it!" Beketaten rolled her shoulder to remove his hand. "I know you want other women, and . . . maybe you've *been* with other women too! I gave up everything for you! I even tricked Henuttaneb into having a child with Akhenaten because Nefertiti couldn't bear a son!" Her chest tightened and her throat constricted, remembering her late sister.

"My sweet Nile reed . . ." Pawah smirked. His low tone of voice kept her angry outbursts at bay for a moment. "It was *your* idea for Akhenaten to have a male heir before we attempted to kill him. For me, it would have been fine if Nefertiti became the sole Regent."

Beketaten hit him on the cheek and twisted her mouth. "Of course you would! My sister *journeyed west* having

Akhenaten's son as a part of *our* plan to bring Egypt back to her gods, and all you can say is that you wanted Nefertiti to be the sole Regent?!"

"I had no part in your sister's passing. If anything, her demise is on *you*, my love." Pawah touched her chin with his finger and thumb and watched her eyes glisten with tears as he shook his head. "It was my plan to persuade Nefertiti to grant us pardon from exile when she was ruling in his place while he was worshipping the Aten, and I wanted to kill him then. Remember, Beketaten, *you* thought the position of Pharaoh would fall into turmoil because he had no son. So *you* concocted the plan for Henuttaneb." He squinted and probed her with his eyes. "I did not want to involve your sister, but *you* were the one who went to Aketaten, and *you* were the one who prepared Henuttaneb to seduce Akhenaten. And you also stayed to help her through her pregnancy. You were the one who was there when she journeyed west. I only bring up Nefertiti because I want you to remember it was not my plan to involve Henuttaneb." Pawah cupped her face in his hands and he looked into her eyes. "You—"

"It was *our* plan. *You* said I should go to Aketaten alone. You wanted—"

"No, Beketaten, *you* said those things." Pawah pursed his lips and turned down the corners of his mouth. "Did I go with you to Aketaten?"

"No," Beketaten replied. She paused. Perhaps she did remember incorrectly. Pawah had always been right before— or at least what she could remember. "But that means I alone am responsible for what happened to Henuttaneb." That truth hit her hard in the stomach.

"Yes, but Henuttaneb understood that there is no guarantee a woman will live through childbirth. She knew the risks when she did what you asked." Pawah brought her head close to his chest.

Beketaten stayed her tongue and took short, deep breaths to keep her tears at bay.

"Then, after Tutankhaten was born, the plague hit Egypt." He shook his head and curled his mouth into a frown. "My plan was to have Nefertiti, since she was as powerful as he, be the next Pharaoh."

"Why? So you could marry her and become Pharaoh yourself!" Beketaten said. "So you could forget about me?"

"My precious wife, absolutely not! I would never forget about you," Pawah said as he gathered her in his arms to reassure his love for her. Holding her close and seducing her as he had done in her youth, he slid his arms up and down her back, each time going farther down. "*You* are the only one I see, and *you* are the perfect woman for me. Why would I want any other? Unless you think I am a dishonorable liar, like you have called me many times?"

Beketaten swallowed as she placed her head on his chest and took in his musty scent. All of a sudden, she became aware of her own heartbeat, and her fingers longed to run over his back as he did to her. With each breath she took, she buried herself closer to him.

When she had fully relaxed into him, he cocked his head with a hard smile and rested his chin on the top of her head. He'd done it again.

"Beketaten," he said, pulling her into him even more, "you allow your mind to be ruled by your heart. Please don't twist my words and my actions into your truth. It hurts me so much when you think me a liar . . . when I do nothing but try to look out for your best interest."

"I'm sorry," Beketaten habitually said on the next exhale. She closed her eyes again, hating herself for calling her husband such horrible names. "I know you only look after me. I'm sorry."

Pawah smirked, then transformed it into a smile and

pulled back to look at her face. "I have no hard feelings. And besides, we mustn't live in the past, my dear. Now, we have work to do if we are going to help save Egypt." Pawah released her from his embrace. "Go to your sister Sitamun and see if we can trust Smenkare," he said. "Maybe she can make you feel better as well."

"Yes, I'll go to Waset and visit my sister," Beketaten said, and turned to leave. She spun around one more time. "Thank you, Pawah."

"You are most welcome, my love." He waved to her, but sneered when she turned to leave. Upon hearing her exit, he sighed. "I never thought a daughter of the magnificent King Amenhotep III would have been so needy," he whispered to himself. "Or so malleable. At least that trait is to my advantage."

Then he sat down in his chair and pondered how to adapt his original plan to overtake the throne. It had been adapted so many times before. First, he'd rid Egypt of Thutmose; but then Thutmose's stupid brother still chose Nefertiti instead of Kasmut, the daughter of Amun's prophet. So he'd had to marry Beketaten to gain a footing inside the royal family; but that also was to his detriment when her father exiled them for her disobedience, as she was to marry Akhenaten instead. He'd then tried to take the throne by force when Pharaoh Amenhotep III was entombed; but when that failed, Akhenaten banished them for good. It had been his idea for Beketaten to change her name from Nebetah to Beketaten and send word she worshiped the Aten to be able to gain entry back into Egypt.

He hadn't lied to his wife in totality—after all, she was the one who suggested Akhenaten have a son first, and to keep up appearances with her, he agreed. He would have preferred Nefertiti be on the throne.

She would then have needed a husband to keep her title as Coregent . . . and what better man than me?

"I am a prophet of Amun and, at this time, the only living male royal relative," he said as he smoothed his hand over his bald head. "A very *attractive* prophet of Amun, who could have been Pharaoh by now."

He'd snuffed out Thutmose, and it would not be hard to squash a blanket over Nefertiti's unsuspecting head as she slept, leaving him as sole Regent of Egypt.

"But that cursed boy *Tut* now stands in my way as well." Shaking his head, he reassured himself, "To those who try and are patient, their goals will become reality. Now, to consider Smenkare and Prince Tutankhaten . . ."

He put his feet up on the table in front of his chair, closed his eyes, and began to scheme.

✺ 5 ✺

THE TIME OF MURDER

THE SUN BEGAN TO SET AS NEFERTITI MADE HER WAY BACK from entombing Merytre at Akhe-Aten. Where Amun should have been, the Aten disgraced the walls of her tomb. Merytre knew better in life, but just like the rest of Egypt, she was bound to worship only the Aten.

"Nefertiti," Mut whispered as they walked through one of the palace's many courtyards. "Sister," she said a little louder.

Tey looked between her two daughters.

Nefertiti sighed and hummed in acknowledgment. The world seemed to slow that evening, and a heavy weight still perched on her shoulders. She wondered when she would have to make this walk for her husband. If the rumors were already circulating about her planning to murder him, she debated how she would act: sorrowful? indifferent? weeping? No, not weeping—she refused to be associated with the Aten in any way. And yet, she couldn't give people any reason to believe she had actually done the killing, and so couldn't quite decide between sorrowful or indifferent.

"I have been thinking . . ." Mut bit the corner of her

mouth as she peered up at her sister. "Maybe Pharaoh will take back what he said?"

"What do you mean, 'take back what he said'?" Nefertiti murmured, rethinking through the events of the day.

"Maybe if you go to Pharaoh and tell him you were wrong to ask that Egypt be allowed to worship the way they want, he may reappoint you as his successor." Mut shrugged her shoulder. It was an idea in the very least.

Nefertiti looked over and smiled at her naïveté. "No, Mut. I was never his successor—just Coregent. As Mother said, I am a woman. I guess I was only hoping I would be sole Regent after he journeyed west, but even then, it would still go to his son." Nefertiti's shoulders dropped; but, glancing over at the pursed lips of her sister, she straightened her back and continued. "You know, Mut . . . if you have an idea, you should own it. Be more confident in your decisions."

A sheepish grin crossed Mut's face. "But what if I'm wrong?"

"You *will* be wrong. Expect it sometimes. But what do you have to lose?"

"What do *you* have to lose?" Mut asked

"A lot more than you," Nefertiti responded.

"But with Smenkare as the successor, haven't you already lost most of it?"

She is too smart for her own good, Nefertiti thought.

"Mother, what do *you* think I should do?"

"I think your young sister makes a good point," Tey said as she walked just in step behind them.

They rounded the hallway to go to Nefertiti's bedchambers.

"He may make it worse," Nefertiti whispered as to not be heard by prying ears.

"How?" Tey whispered back.

"I don't know. He has visions that no one can predict.

Sometimes I think he just says what he wants to say and tells everyone the Aten gave him the vision. 'The Aten told me to'—"

Nefertiti stopped speaking with a quick and nervous beat of the heart as a shadow rounded the corner. If any supporter of the Aten heard her, it could be interpreted as treason.

Commander Horemheb suddenly stood in front of her with two lower-ranked military officers, and, knowing where his loyalties lay, Nefertiti felt her heart rate slow down.

He bowed slightly from the waist, as did his guards. His jaw tightened and his brow furrowed in a frantic rush. "Coregent, I must speak with you."

Mut let out an audible breath as her jaw dropped.

Nefertiti glanced to her sister and saw her sun-warmed cheeks and distant gaze upon her commander, then looked back to Horemheb, whose eyes also darted between Mut and herself. Nefertiti bit the inside of her cheeks to keep from smirking. She ran her eyes up and down Commander Horemheb. His tight leather tunic of a military warrior commander did wrap his muscles quite well as the setting sun's rays glistened upon his bronze armor. But her urge to smirk died, knowing that even though he was loyal to Pharaoh, he along with her father had failed her the night they convinced her to take poisoned wine to her husband. A certain coldness set in her eyes.

"Commander, what is this about?" Nefertiti asked, ignoring her sister's instant infatuation with him. She gave him a raised eyebrow to signal she could guess the topic of urgency. A pang of hate stabbed him. She still couldn't bring herself to forgive him or her father for forcing her to play a part in the plot to assassinate her husband while they hid in a back room in the dark, conspiring with Pawah and Beketaten.

"Egypt's new successor," Horemheb said in a low voice, and shot a suspicious look at Tey and Mut.

Nefertiti gestured to each of them. "This is my mother, Tey, and my sister, Mut."

"My pleasure, mother and sister of Pharaoh's greatly beloved," Horemheb said, nodding to Tey, and then turned to look at Mut and stopped.

Nefertiti followed his gaze and elbowed her sister in the arm, causing Mut to shut her gaping mouth. Mut froze, only her eyes darting between Nefertiti and Horemheb. Nefertiti's chest burned as she watched her sister act a fool for none other than a coward.

Horemheb smiled at Mut and bowed his head to the sister of Coregent Neferneferuaten-Nefertiti.

Mut giggled, and Nefertiti threw her gaze upward. *He has a wife, Mut, you ridiculous child!* she wanted to say.

"As is ours." Tey smiled at this man, sizing him up with a polite stare.

"Mother, Mut, I shall meet you in my chambers," Nefertiti said. Her stare fell on one of the officers until he stepped in line to escort the Coregent's family members to their destination.

Tey called back as they left: "My daughter—go to him."

Nefertiti looked to her, expressionless, and took a deep breath as she headed toward the council room with Horemheb slightly behind her, as was his place.

Horemheb leaned forward and whispered to her as they rounded the corner. "Coregent, may I be so bold as to ask: Go to whom?"

Nefertiti looked back to him and nodded toward the other officer. Horemheb dismissed him, ordering him to send word of Egypt's new successor to General Paaten in Nubia.

"He is trustworthy," he mentioned, regarding the officer.

"I am not as lenient with my trust anymore, Commander." Nefertiti's eyes peered up at him and she spoke through clenched teeth. "Those who say they would be slain protecting me might slay me with a wine goblet. That was what happened last time you and I were alone in a hallway, was it not?"

Horemheb straightened his back and stopped walking. He bowed his head toward her and sighed. His gaze stayed on the floor for a moment before he spoke. "Pharaoh Coregent . . . I am sorry this fell to you."

His eyes bore into hers as she stared back at him, not responding. He never broke her stare as she debated what to say in return. Her heart wanted to scream out: *Coward! Murderer! Liar!* But she knew she was all of those as well, and to call Horemheb and her father such names would also mean she could add *Hypocrite!* to her list. Her jaw tightened then loosened, prompting Horemheb to step closer to her. A shaky breath escaped her lungs as he stepped with purpose. She wanted to slap him and spit at his feet, but knew she deserved the same.

"I am sorry we could not do this without you," he whispered, seeing her inner struggle and acceptance of what she had done. With his eyes he said, *If I could take this from you, I would,* but Nefertiti turned her face away.

"Anyone would have done the same without a second thought," she reasoned, and shook her head, trying to believe her own lie. She found his eyes again. They were filled with . . . pity? regret? She couldn't quite tell. She studied his face. Sincerity. "But that doesn't change the fact that *I* brought him the wine."

"No . . . I suppose it does not." Horemheb saw the guilt weigh down her shoulders, and he wished the Pharaoh a quick passing so she could come to terms with her actions before it ate away at her.

He opened his mouth to say more, but Nefertiti motioned toward the council room and returned to the original subject. She didn't want to hear any more from him on the subject.

"My mother and sister think I should go to Pharaoh and admit my wrongdoing so that he will name me successor," Nefertiti whispered as they walked.

After pausing in thought, he said, "If I may speak freely . . . I think you should as well."

Nefertiti's shoulders rolled as she tried to release the tension in her neck. "I don't want to face him before he drinks . . ." She bit her lip and looked up at Horemheb, shaking her head.

A lump formed in his throat. He pushed his lips together and crinkled his eyes. Refusing to further add to her guilt at this time, he mumbled, "I am only one member of your council, Coregent. Ask the remaining members."

"Who is left? Vizier Nakht, who might be as much of an Aten-lover as Pharaoh? General Paaten, who is in Nubia—and my father." At the mention of her father, she gritted her teeth and let out a hot flash of air through her nostrils.

Horemheb opened the door to the council room for her.

Ay, already inside, sat alone. A rage built inside of Nefertiti as she saw him. *I am your little girl. You were supposed to protect me!* she thought as her fingers curled into her palms.

"Master of Pharaoh's Horses," Nefertiti acknowledged him as she entered. She watched his eyes wince in pain at her coldness in referring to him with his title.

"Daughter, please," he begged as he stood up.

"You shall address Pharaoh Coregent as *Pharaoh Coregent*," she said as she took her seat in Pharaoh's place at the head of the council table. The callouses of her heart grew, watching a little of her father wilt inside. He had promised her to return Egypt back to the gods once they had secured the power of the position of Pharaoh over that of the Amun priesthood, but never with murder.

He used me, Nefertiti thought.

"As I am commanded," Ay said with a half-heart.

"Commander Horemheb says you both needed to speak with Pharaoh Coregent?" Nefertiti said, waiting for the discussion to take place.

Horemheb nodded, pushing away the tension in the room. "We both know Smenkare is part of the cult of the Aten, but when the news went to Pawah and Beketaten, they were glad. Do they not know?"

"Let us play the fool and not tell them," Nefertiti said. "Then, when they celebrate in their folly with their followers, we can perhaps regain some loyalty." She lifted her chin as the words flowed, regaining her composure.

"Master of Pharaoh's Horses," Horemheb said as he leaned forward on the table and looked at Ay. "Your wife and daughter suggested Pharaoh Coregent go admit her wrongdoing to Akhenaten and request to be successor. What do you say?"

"My wife and daughter?" Ay asked, befuddled. "Why are they at Aketaten? Why do they know about this?" His voice grew more bold as he looked at Nefertiti.

"They came to visit Pharaoh Coregent and join her in the burial parade for her steward Merytre," Nefertiti said, and sat up straighter. Her frown kept her tears from falling.

Horemheb looked at the table, silent.

Ay bit his tongue, and his eyes told her *I have failed you again, my lotus blossom*; he knew nothing in her life besides the pain her husband had caused her, and it was all his fault for telling her to marry him.

"I see . . ." He hung his head as he drew in a deep breath. He looked at her again and licked his lips, suddenly dry, before he responded. "You may not be fond of my answer, Pharaoh Coregent, but I say . . . go to Akhenaten and attempt to secure the throne from yet another Aten follower."

"I agree," Horemheb said. He shut his mouth before saying anything else.

Silence filled the room as tension grew.

"I know what you are thinking," Nefertiti finally said. "If I had just given Pharaoh the wine that night, we would not have to deal with this."

Horemheb and Ay looked down and pressed their lips together. They had thought it, indeed, but they dared not say anything.

"Well, if you wanted him gone, *you* should have given him the wine instead of turning me into a murderer," Nefertiti said as she stood to leave.

Ay closed his eyes. He had turned his lotus blossom, pure and lovely, into a snake, conniving and cold.

"Pharaoh Coregent, where are you going?" Ay asked as Nefertiti opened the door.

"To see Pharaoh and beg forgiveness," she spat with the venom of an asp.

Horemheb glanced to the floor and bit the insides of his cheeks. After all, he did have a hand in this plot as well. He wished he could have taken the wine to Pharaoh and not involved Nefertiti at all. His heart ached for her as he watched her treat her father the only way a truly hurt person can treat someone closest to them: with walls; with bitterness. He longed to put a comforting hand on Ay's shoulder and reassure him that she would eventually forgive him, but he restrained himself—there were other urgent matters that needed tending.

NEFERTITI APPROACHED PHARAOH'S BEDCHAMBERS AS THE night began to fall into place. She noticed no guard graced his door. Looking up and down the hall, she whistled, but nothing stirred. A slight chill slithered up her spine as she remembered the last time she was here—when she left the poisoned wine in his room.

She knocked on the door once, twice, three times. Nothing.

She took a chance and opened the door. Peering inside, she saw Akhenaten kneeling by his window, looking out to the shadow of the Aten, praying. She tiptoed into the room and closed the door behind her. She fell in line with Akhenaten, knelt beside him, and spread her arms above her head. She heard him mumbling the same song he'd said many times before.

Perhaps he won't notice I came in uninvited, Nefertiti thought as she joined in his song.

> "You are in my heart,
> There is no other who knows you,
> Only your son, Akhenaten,
> Whom you have taught your ways and might."

At its end, a smile curled on Akhenaten's lips. "Ah, my lovely Neferneferuaten-Nefertiti."

"My beloved," Nefertiti said, but her voice held no love. She took a long inhale to soften her heart and focus her mind. If he was going to believe her, she had to be believable.

"At first, I thought you to be the cupbearer who has failed to bring my wine for several days," he said. "He leaves me to look for it in this room."

Nefertiti grew wide-eyed, realizing that the People's Restoration of Egypt were now making their move, correcting her error in leaving the poison that night instead of making sure he drank from it. They were forcing him to find the goblet she left and drink from it.

"My beloved, I came to ask forgiveness from you." Nefertiti half smiled at the gentleness in her voice. *That sounds genuine,* she thought.

"Forgiveness?" Akhenaten asked, turning his head to her. He stood up, looking like an old wise fool, and hovered his eyes upon each wine goblet to see if it were empty as he continued his conversation with her.

"Yes." She pursed her lips. "About the last night I came here, and what I asked of you."

"The Aten has already forgiven you. He is generous with his forgiveness, but you try his patience with your doubt," Akhenaten said, and took a step away from her toward the wine goblets strewn about the room.

Doubt, Nefertiti thought.

She had no doubts—that was the first lie she'd ever told Akhenaten, even before they were wed. He'd had so many doubts of himself, and her father told her to gain his trust because he would need her, so she'd lied to him, telling him she had no doubts in his abilities; she'd encouraged him to indulge in his obsession if it meant his faithfulness to her. It was her false confidence that had brought him to this place, now accusing her of doubt. He had been a good Pharaoh for a while, maybe a few years, but then he became obsessed with pleasing the Aten, whom he believed to be his father and other Pharaohs before. Her heart suddenly fell. Had he this whole time been trying to please his father yet distance himself from him? His father withheld his love from him, his second-born son. O, the twisted irony! Nefertiti shook her head as she saw the young boy desperately trying to prove himself to his father to gain his love and respect, but at the same time hating his father for thinking him a fool and a waste.

"Doubt, doubt, *doubt*," he said as he began to pace. "So much doubt." He shook his finger at her. "You need to not doubt anymore. You need to believe in the Aten! He is our salvation!"

"I have no doubts," Nefertiti said, as if remembering an old line from a long-past memory.

Akhenaten rummaged through the wine goblets, and he stepped closer to the half-empty goblet she had placed there a few decans earlier. "Aha! More wine!" he said, and grabbed the goblet.

"Pharaoh!" she called out.

The cup stopped at his lips before he tipped it to drink and he brought it back down, holding it in front of his chest.

She licked her lips as her exhale shook her.

"Pharaoh . . ."

Her shoulders slumped. *Am I murderer?* she questioned herself. *Only if I let him drink. Only if he drinks. I am not a murderer. Yet.*

"Pharaoh, I have asked forgiveness. Will you appoint me successor? I am but your Queen Nefertiti, your most beloved, your Lady of the Two Lands, your Great of Praises, your Coregent Neferneferuaten-Nefertiti. I have stood by your side since we were married these long years. Do you not remember?"

He blinked once and then again. "But the Aten has spoken. We have appointed my brother Smenkare as successor." He swirled the wine in the goblet as he spoke.

"Can you not ask the Aten to send you another vision now that I have asked forgiveness?"

"You dare insult the Aten?" Akhenaten wrenched his lips back into a scowl of disgust. "No! Smenkare will succeed Pharaoh." He brought the goblet to his lips.

In a fleeting moment, she saw herself lunge for him and knock the wine out of his hand; but just as it had come, she realized she still knelt on the floor, unmoving, watching him down the last remnants of the poisoned wine. He licked his lips and let out a gag. "Gah! This wine is long gone bad! A burning all the way down!"

A burden lifted from her shoulders, but a heavier weight cast down upon her heart.

She had done it. She brought the mad man his last drink, and after time had passed, he drank. It would have made no difference if he had drunk that night or in fifty nights' time—she was still a murderer.

Only now, she had lost the throne.

He tossed the goblet over his shoulder after he finished and, still gagging, he began to rummage through other standing goblets, only to realize they too were empty.

Nefertiti watched him, waiting for the poison to start working.

He hummed his praises to the Aten, searching for more wine until his left leg gave out from underneath him. His cheeks blushed with embarrassment in front of his chief royal wife as he tried to stand again, but his leg was like a new babe's, and he tossed to and fro, unable to stand on his own.

Nefertiti felt tears burn their way down her cheeks as she watched him stumble. She gathered herself up and went to him, offering a hand. He took it just as his remaining leg wobbled and then failed. She caught him, but he was too heavy to drag to his bed, so she lowered his head into her lap as she sat on the floor.

"I have drunk much wine?" he asked her, looking up into her big, almond eyes.

"Yes, Pharaoh," she said as she soothed his contorted brow.

"I have never drunk so much wine as to not feel my legs," he said as he tried to sit up, looking as if to see if they were still attached to him.

"It is getting late. Perhaps the wine and the coming night coax you to sleep?" Nefertiti said, wiping away a tear and biting her lip as she looked away from her victim.

"No, the Aten is disappointed in me for drinking much wine," Akhenaten said, and he covered his face with his hands.

"Amenhotep"—she tried once more to reach the man she married before he changed his name to Akhenaten—"the Aten is not disappointed."

"Amenhotep," he repeated, "is my father," he breathed out. "I am Akhenaten." He pulled his hands back to look at her. "I do not want to be my father."

"You say the Aten is your father and all Pharaohs past," Nefertiti said.

"Then the Aten is disappointed in me and is punishing me," Akhenaten said as he raised his fists to the sky.

"Your father loved you, Amenhotep . . . as did I," Nefertiti crooned as she softened his fists with her hand and brought them to his chest.

"Do you not anymore?" He gazed up at her. "Do you have doubts now?"

Nefertiti closed her eyes and bowed her head, gathering her thoughts. "I love you." She tried to remember the Amenhotep she fell in love with so long ago. "I have no doubts," she repeated from her youth.

For a moment, his mind cleared, and he seemed to see her just as he saw her the eve of their marriage, under the moonlight, as she said those exact words to him then. "The beautiful Nefertiti has no doubts in me . . . then I shall have none myself." He tried to lift his arm to touch her face, but he could only pull his shoulder up from the weight of his arm.

"Help me, my Nefertiti. I cannot feel my arms." His eyes grew wide and a frantic breath accompanied his ever-paling face.

Shushing him and caressing his face, she distracted him in the last moments of his life. "There, there, my love." She attempted to make his head comfortable in her lap. She hoped he wouldn't realize what was happening to him, but just as his tongue began to swell, he looked at her.

"I am poisoned." His eyes held the truth; there was no way to keep him from it anymore.

"Yes," Nefertiti whispered as two tears ran down her cheek, and she kissed his forehead.

"You? Why?" he asked her.

"Because, my love, Egypt was going to revolt against you, and your military's loyalties were not with you. We sacrificed so much to regain power for Pharaoh from the Amun priesthood. If you were to be publicly killed, all would have been in vain."

"This did not have to happen." He tightened his jaw.

"If you had kept your promise to go back to Amun . . . but you stayed with the Aten," Nefertiti said. "You broke all of your promises to me."

"I did . . . didn't I?" Akhenaten said. But instead of anger or hurt, relief overcame his eyes. His chest rose as one walks over a sand dune and fell with a thud. "I do love you, Nefertiti. I never wanted to hurt you."

"It has been a long journey," Nefertiti said as she stroked his forehead, knowing he spoke his own truth.

"It has," he said with a thick tongue.

"I will make sure you have all you need on your journey to join the Aten in the sky," Nefertiti whispered to him as another tear rolled down her cheek.

He mumbled something incoherent as his tongue fell limp. Not able to move his head, he only looked at his wife.

"I'm sorry, my love . . ." She kissed his forehead once again. "I'm so sorry." She kissed his lips. "I'm so, so sorry." She tried to catch her breath, hoping in this last moment it was just too much wine. She wished to take back the poison. She wanted to blink and everything be the way they had planned long ago, but her husband lay dying in her arms and at her own hand.

He blinked as he gazed at her, and a peace filled his eyes, almost as if to say, *It is better this way.*

Nefertiti held his face close to hers as she bit her lip, watching him slip away. She had taken away the father from her children. She did this to the man she once loved, or still loved, in his illness.

His eyes dimmed.

The dizzying world around her spun as she finally caught her breath, tied up in the heaviness of her guilt and the justification behind it.

Then the world stopped to a sudden halt. Nothing but the deafening sound of death pounded in her ears.

It was done.

She closed her eyes, and to her surprise, her heart broke, and she wept like a little child.

❧ 6 ❧

THE TIME OF BURIAL

THE SUN BEAT UPON HER BROW AS THE SANDS ATE UPON HER freshly perfumed skin. She could not be seen shedding tears for the dead man she called Pharaoh and husband if she were ever to gain the people's trust. At least, that was what she finally ended up deciding in her mind.

The funeral procession continued to Akhe-Aten, where Pharaoh Akhenaten would be placed to rest for his journey to the afterlife. This one held no difference from all the other funeral processions of the royal bloodline:

The high priests of the Aten, rather than Amun, with their shaved heads, walked solemnly beside the dead Pharaoh, pulled in his coffin by oxen. The priestesses symbolizing Isis and Nephthys were long replaced by yet more priests of the Aten. The incense the priests held sent smoke swirling about their waists. Crying and wailing women—paid mourners— followed as lower priests mingled among them, playing their sistrums.

Instead of real tears, however, small smiles graced the people's faces; they cried out in a façade of mourning. Rumors of celebrations lining the streets of Waset and Men-nefer at this Pharaoh's passing spread through Egypt's capital city of Aketaten. The nation of Egypt was glad to be rid of their heretic King, who indeed would be missed by very few.

Little do they know, she thought as she looked to the golden thrones that carried the new Pharaoh Smenkare and his Queen—her daughter, Meritaten—at the front of the processions behind the sarcophagus.

Would the people rise up against them when they found out about their new Pharaoh's devotion to the Aten? Would the people feel betrayed even further? She feared for her daughter, but only time would tell how zealous Meritaten was for the Aten. Maybe Nefertiti could still reach her before it really was too late.

In her own golden throne as Coregent, she glanced over to her twelve-year-old daughter, Ankhesenpaaten, who sat next to her; having both been married to Pharaoh Akhenaten, they both now wore the title of great royal wife. She glanced at the other children being carried behind them: her youngest living daughter, Nefe, who was a year younger than Mut; and the evidence of Pharaoh Akhenaten's betrayal of his promises, the seven-year-old prince, Tutankhaten.

He saw her looking at him and smiled at her. The boy's eyes twinkled at his stepmother. In truth, she pitied him—he never knew his mother or his father—but she also hated looking at him. She observed the boy's sickly appearance: his club foot, his exaggerated overbite, his somewhat bent spine, his pale skin; this cherished boy, who had to walk with a cane, and whom her husband hadn't even named as his successor, despite thinking it was worth betraying their bed to produce a son.

His face fell when she didn't smile back, lost in her thoughts as she was. Taking note, she forced a smile, and his reappeared, beaming at the only woman he could call Mother.

WHEN THEY RETURNED TO THE PALACE, THE FUNERARY feast continued. Horemheb was speaking to Tey and Mut when Nefertiti walked up to them, the three of them bowing before her at her approach. Silence overcame them as they stared at the floor. Horemheb knew better than to offer her condolences. He cleared his throat.

"I . . ."

He had no clue what to say, but the three women looked at him. He cleared his throat again. Mut's eyes peered up at him, and he wished the innocent way in which she saw him was not misguided. He licked his lips as the dry air and silence made him thirsty.

"I can bring us something to drink," he offered.

"We would be much obliged, Commander," Tey said, and patted his large bicep. After he left, she looked at Mut, who was watching him walk away. "He is too old for you," she whispered.

"No, he's not, Mother," Mut said, and immediately her eyes grew wide as her cheeks blushed. "He's the same age as Nefertiti," Mut whispered, jabbing a thumb at her sister.

"That is still too old for you," Tey said, shaking her head. "Although he is very well established." Tey bobbed her head back and forth, as if weighing the pros and cons were Mut to marry an older man.

"He already has a wife, Amenia, an out-of-work chantress." For her part, Nefertiti just wanted them to be quiet about Horemheb. She rubbed her temple and closed her eyes for a moment. He had never spoken freely like that to her before all of this happened, and she didn't know how to interpret his words. He seemed as though he understood her, and he'd even apologized, but she couldn't forgive him or her father for forcing her hand.

"He could afford another. He is the commander of Pharaoh's armies," Mut argued, and bobbed her head as though she knew better.

"Trust me, Mut. Believe me, you do not want to be the second wife," Nefertiti said as she peered over to Horemheb. "Or the first wife who can't bear sons."

Nefertiti ran her hand over her hip and stomach. Her late husband had not touched her since she conceived Setepenre almost seven years ago. She forced her thoughts back to Mut, not wanting to entertain any ill memories of her husband—especially at his funerary feast. But she also didn't want her sister to get entangled in an idea of a husband with multiple wives. "It's hard enough being the first wife and having to live with your husband and another woman."

Mut shook her head. "I would still be a second wife"—she looked to the ceiling, imagining life—"if it were with Commander Horemheb," she whispered and smiled dreamily.

Tey let out a sigh and jokingly slapped Mut's cheek right as Horemheb returned. Mut's cheeks gushed from embarrassment at her mother's slap. Tey just smiled and shook her head at him. Horemheb smiled politely back at the three women as he offered them their drinks.

They speak of love and marriage at the funeral of the man I murdered, Nefertiti thought. *The man I murdered . . . my husband. I murdered my husband.*

All of these months, she had wrestled with her actions, justifying them in every way; but at the end of the day, as the sun set behind the mourners dancing in the courtyard, she had killed a man. Her brow tensed as the gravity of what she had done sank into the depths of her soul. There existed nothing but hate. Whatever the reasons, she took a life. She had wondered if she would be relieved when Akhenaten was finally put to rest, but now she knew the answer: relief was far from her mind.

HOREMHEB WATCHED HER THINK AS HE HANDED TEY HER wine goblet and Mut a barley beer in a cup. He held Nefertiti's wine goblet in the hand with his own, but as the wine swirled about, he debated giving it to her, knowing they had used wine to kill Pharaoh. He remembered the servers drawing wine from the barrel and knew the wine was most likely harmless. But perhaps it was in poor taste.

Nefertiti's eyes found his goblet as she peered in. Her gaze drifted to Horemheb, who pulled his hand away.

"I will call the royal cupbearer to taste of the wine first," he said, and made a motion, but Nefertiti placed her hand on his arm.

"I am not thirsty," she said, and walked away with her shoulders down. She didn't know where she was going, but knew she needed to be alone with her self-destructive thoughts.

Horemheb watched her. *At least she looks sad at her husband's passing. She very well may be, but I think she wrestles more with the poisoned wine.*

Tey's gaze darted between him and Nefertiti as she walked away. Mut did the same with a scowl.

He sighed as he watched her slide out of the light and into the shadows. He returned his attention to Tey and Mut, noticing their stares. *Do they know about Nefertiti's involvement in Akhenaten's death?* he asked himself.

"We all care about our Coregent." Tey offered, as her warm smile hid her wisdom regarding what a man feels when he lingers in watching a woman walk away.

"She is sad about Pharaoh Akhenaten," Mut said as she pulled her shoulders straighter. "But she will move on. She is strong. You needn't worry about her." Mut admired her sister, but clearly, she didn't want Nefertiti to be the object of his attention.

"Yes, Mut. She is strong. She bears many burdens," Horemheb said, and again glanced to where Nefertiti disappeared.

Ay came up to their circle. "Ah, Commander, I see you have met my wife and daughter," Ay said, gesturing to them.

"Yes," Horemheb said. "You have a fine family, Master of Pharaoh's Horses."

"They are a fine family indeed. I could not ask for better."

Ay beamed with pride and rubbed Mut's baldness. Mut's neck shrunk in her shoulders as the pink blush passed over her cheeks. Tey slightly shook her head at her husband. Ay quickly removed his hand and gave Tey a look that said *We will talk later*.

"Commander, I must speak with you," Ay said, changing the subject, and cleared his throat.

This prompted Tey to say, "Mut and I were just leaving."

After they were alone, Ay said, "General Paaten sends word from Nubia. Relations are not going well." He looked around for his daughter, as she needed to hear the report as well, even under the circumstances. Time was not on their side.

"Relations are not going well here either," Horemheb said, looking to Pharaoh Smenkare.

"I know," Ay said, still searching for his daughter.

Horemheb tightened his jaw, knowing the man spoke of his relationship with Nefertiti. "She will come around."

Ay found his eyes and responded with a shake of his head. "You don't know Nefertiti as I do. She is strong to the point of stubbornness. She is a lot like her mother in that way."

"She will come around," Horemheb said again. "It will take time, but she will. You are her father."

"Speaking of Nefertiti, do you see her?" Ay asked, brushing off what Horemheb said.

"She was here, but I think the weight of the day sent her away. She walked off into the shadows." Horemheb pointed in the general direction of where she had left.

"Help me look for her," Ay said, more command than request. "I need to know she is safe, and also to let her know of the Nubians."

Horemheb nodded, and the two men went in search of Nefertiti.

ANKHESENPAATEN SAT IN HER THRONE AND WATCHED THEM from afar. Tut sat next to her as he twirled his thumbs and let out a big sigh. She peered over at him and then returned to watching her grandfather and Commander Horemheb leave, most likely to go look for her mother. *Not once did she ever ask how we were coping with our father's journey west,* Ankhesenpaaten thought to herself. She grabbed her elbows and sunk down in her lap.

"What's wrong?" Tut asked, and poked her arm.

"I don't feel right," Ankhesenpaaten said, not looking at him.

"Well, our father has just been entombed," Tut said, and accidentally kicked his cane to the ground. Maia, his nurse, picked it up for him and resumed her dutiful position a respectable distance behind him. "*Nothing* feels right."

"I guess you're right." Ankhesenpaaten tried to find Tey and Mut in the crowd. They had disappeared too easily. She finally spotted Mut with Nefe. "I'm going to talk with Nefe and Mut."

Tut grabbed her arm. "No, don't leave me, Ankhesenpaaten!"

"But I want to talk to my sister." Ankhesenpaaten tried to pull her arm away, but Tut scowled and dug his fingernails into her skin.

"No!" he yelled.

Ankhesenpaaten winced, but instead of angering the young prince further, she grabbed his cane and offered it to him. "Come with me, then."

Tut released his grip on her arm. "Fine." He yanked the cane from her hand and scooted off of his seat.

They made their way over to the other girls. Ankhesenpaaten was the only one among them to wear a woman's wig. It had actually been not that long ago when her mother acknowledged her twelfth birthday and gave her the beautiful beaded wig. She loved it, but now, looking at the other three children with their sidelocks, she felt somewhat out of place.

"My sympathies, royal wife and King's daughter, Ankhesenpaaten," Mut said with a bow of her head.

Ankhesenpaaten lifted her chin. "Thank you, Mut." Her heart seemed sad now that her father was gone, but she wondered if there was something wrong with her that she wasn't as sad as she thought she should be. The passing of her sister Meketaten five years ago still carried more burden than that of her father. She had wept for days when her sister began her travels to the afterlife, and even longer when they entombed her; but for her father, she only shed tears initially, and at his funeral procession, she had felt nothing but flutterings in her stomach.

She saw Ay behind the hall's pillars, surveying the room, looking for her mother. *I doubt I will be as sad as a daughter should be when my mother passes too. I may even have no tears.* A grimace accompanied her thoughts. She didn't want it to be that way, but her mother never actually lived in the royal harem like most queens did—or so her tutors told her—and so she never really knew her. Most of the interactions she'd had with her mother were rushed, or else something more important took precedence over her spending any time with her. She knew the late royal wife Kiya better than she knew her own mother.

"What are you thinking about, Ankhesenpaaten?" Tut asked, and poked her leg with the end of his cane.

"Tut, a prince shouldn't do that," Ankhesenpaaten chided and shook her head.

He shook his head in mimicry. "Well, you didn't answer me the first time I asked you."

"Nothing. I'm thinking about nothing."

The three of them stared at her with suspicion perched on their lips.

"I am your sister, and I know you are lying," Nefe said, and pushed her elbow teasingly.

"I'm thinking of Father and Mother, and what is it with you two touching me?" Ankhesenpaaten said, and swatted her sister's hand away. "The only one here who is giving the respect and solemnity appropriate for this time is Mut." She nodded in Mut's direction. "And *she's* not even royalty."

Mut's chin drooped.

"She's Mother's sister!" Nefe pointed out. "She's royalty enough!"

Ankhesenpaaten sighed and shook her head again. "No, Nefe." She debated whether it was worth explaining to her why Mut was not considered royalty, but ultimately decided she would soon learn those nuances in the Kap.

"Yeah, she's royalty enough!" Tut said, grabbing Mut's arm and shaking it. Mut slowly emerged from her self-imposed cocoon and smiled, feeling supported by Nefe and Tut.

Sighing and shrugging her shoulders, Ankhesenpaaten let it go. *There is a reason why Mut does not stand next to my father's stone image as we do,* she thought.

They all stood there in silence for a moment. Mut's foot hid behind her other as she wrapped her hands behind her back. Ankhesenpaaten remembered she used to do the same, and passed her tutor's words on to Mut.

"Mut, my tutor always told me: Stand straight, hold your head up—you are a daughter of the King, and you must stand like so!" She reached out to Mut's chin and lifted it up. "Even though you aren't a daughter of the King, it would help you in finding a husband."

"Gross," Tut said, sticking out his tongue. "Marriage. You have to *kiss*."

Ankhesenpaaten laughed. "She is nine years old, and the age of marriage is almost upon her . . . like it is for me now." She brushed her new wig proudly as if she'd won it.

"You were married a long time ago," Nefe pointed out, and flipped her sidelock.

But at this mention, a weight set on the conversation as they all remembered that they were at a funerary feast honoring their father, to whom Ankhesenpaaten was married.

Nefe huffed and continued speaking. "Mother gives you that wig and all of the sudden you know so much more than all of us—and I'm only a year younger than Mut, so marriage is almost upon *me* too." It was easier to talk of marriage and tease her sister than to dwell on the fact that they would never see their father again.

Tut pulled his lips back to show his distaste of what happens with marriage. "I'm just glad *I* don't have to think about that for a long time!"

"Oh, Tut," Ankhesenpaaten said, and patted his shoulder. "It will be here before you know it."

7

THE TIME OF WOUNDS

THE SOFT TORCHLIGHT LIT UP HER WHITE-AND-GOLD ROYAL dress like a star in the night as she strolled along the stone pathway situated between the small lakes filled with lotus blossoms. He watched her for a second as she strolled the empty gardens.

Her slender frame would have lured any man in this light, he thought, *except for the mad Akhenaten.*

He shook his head at Akhenaten's dismissal of such a woman. He rubbed his bronze armor, signifying his military rank, as he admitted to himself he had admired her from afar for a long time. He drew in a deep breath; he should go tell Ay where he had found her and let him approach her, but he had never really spoken to her before, and a desire to comfort her, this woman who held so much burden, came over him. An anxious breath escaped as he looked around, making sure she was not in harm's way, then made his decision and approached her.

NEFERTITI BREATHED IN THE FRESH NIGHT AIR AND LOOKED to the stars. Her head dropped as tears fell.

I am a murderer.

The beat of her heart died as her chest grew numb.

I mourn my own innocence and not my husband. I must be heartless as well.

"Coregent, I spoke with your father," Horemheb said, his voice unwavering professionalism.

A sudden cold hit her belly like a blast of wind at the sound of his voice in her solitude. Her shoulders rose and she lifted her head, trying to blink back her tears. She didn't turn around to conceal her tears.

"He looks for you."

Nefertiti hummed in acknowledgment. She smiled slightly at the sound of Horemheb's voice. She wanted to be alone . . . but also did not want to be alone.

"I told him he had a fine family," Horemheb said as he walked up behind Nefertiti. She detected a hint of anxiety in his voice; clearly, he was hoping she wouldn't dismiss him.

She snorted. "A fine family indeed." She clenched her jaw and knelt to a nearby pond, drawing her hand through the water. Her back still faced him. She snuck her other hand to her face to wipe her cheeks. Peering over her shoulder, she saw him study her and scratch his chin as if debating what to say. Her gaze fell back to the water as she swirled her finger around a closing lotus blossom. She wished him to stay, but she wished him to leave—just as the lotus both opened in the day and closed at night.

He cleared his throat and she heard him shuffle his feet.

What is he wanting to say to me?

She slumped. No one would ever be able to understand why she did what she did. Was it truly for Egypt, out of self-preservation, a little revenge? She wanted to speak to someone about it but knew no one else was left. Tey and Mut judged her. Her father and Horemheb put the fatal weapon in her hand. With a slight shake of her head, she let out a breath, realizing she was utterly alone.

But Horemheb walked around to her front.

He is breaking his rank, she thought as she peered up at him with a furrowed brow. *Why? What more can he convince me to do?*

"Speaking of family, I think your sister might be taken with the uniform." He motioned to his leather tunic and bronze breastplate. He held a small smile on his lips.

A moment of silence, and then Nefertiti let out a chuckle, mostly at his awkward smile and the randomness of his remark. Just the release she needed.

Horemheb's small smile spread into a large grin.

"If you tell her I laughed, I will deny it." She beamed and pointed a finger at him, but immediately regained her composure. She had never seen this side of Horemheb before; his smile seemed almost playful. It made her forget her burdens, if only for a while. Maybe that was why he broke his rank. "I told her you are already married to a wonderful chantress."

His smile dropped. "Who is currently out of work. The god for whom she chanted is no longer welcome in Egypt."

"She will be in work soon enough," Nefertiti said, and huffed at the entrapment back into the present. "Well, *if*—" Her gaze fell back to the water as she drew her hand through the sparkling liquid. She shook her head, hating herself even more.

From her peripheral vision, she saw his weight shift and his jaw clench.

At least he is trying to help me—or is he trying to soothe his own conscience for turning me into a murderer?

"You know, I've always wanted children," Horemheb's

voice cut through her thoughts, "especially if they are as sweet as Mut."

"And if your wife only gave you daughters, would you marry another to get a son?" Nefertiti peered up at him. She knew the answer. All men would answer yes.

Horemheb bit his tongue as he bent forward, as though she had hurt his pride.

Good, she thought. *He can feel a small amount of the pain women feel when their husbands break their promises to them.*

"Well, Amenia is infertile. She *cannot* have children . . . and yet I have not married another."

"Oh," Nefertiti said as she dropped her head, wondering if he spoke the whole truth.

A man with no children—even with an infertile wife—could adopt orphans. Why has he never tried to build such a life with Amenia? Why wouldn't he try to marry another? He is a rich man. He can afford two estates. Even more so, why is he here, speaking with me in this manner? I am Coregent. He is the commander. What is he doing?

But despite her racing mind, etiquette won in her speech. "I'm sorry. I didn't know."

Horemheb shook his head. "The Coregent does not apologize. And I'm sorry Pharaoh Akhenaten did that to you . . ."

He trailed off, seeing her brows knit together, and once again he wished he could learn when to not say anything. He had sat at negotiations between warriors, sat at Pharaoh's council for many years; and now, alone with a woman—albeit a powerful woman—he found himself saying the wrong things in trying to help her. He let out a breath and knelt down next to her. She didn't flinch or ask him what he was doing, so he decided to try again, against his better judgment.

You fool! Keep your rank! he yelled at himself, but his heart knew she needed someone to be with her at this time. *Just as a friend,* he finally came to an agreement with himself. He wouldn't let his admiration of her become something else.

"I should probably explain my marriage a little more." He nodded, as if to give himself the courage to continue. "Our marriage was arranged by our fathers, and even though we both could have chosen another spouse, we agreed to the arrangement—it was easier than protesting. Our fathers could be . . ." He chewed his lip as he searched for the right word. ". . . dogmatic."

Nefertiti nodded, letting him continue, thinking, *At least he is trying.* The thought repeated in her mind. *At least he is trying. And I can better see if he is lying or not.*

"She lives in Men-nefer, presiding over my household." He tapped his finger on his arm as quickly as his toe tapped the ground.

He is nervous, Nefertiti thought, and a half-smile crossed her face, appreciating the risk he was taking by speaking to her in this way to get her mind off of Akhenaten.

"We rarely see each other, but I cannot imagine life without her. She takes care of my entire estate without wanting anything in return."

"Do you love her?"

Nefertiti felt the words come out of her mouth as though with a will of their own. *Of course he does. Why would you ask such a thing?*

But he paused.

"I will be truthful with you, Coregent. I do love her in a sense. I took the blame when we failed to produce children because I knew my father would start a grievance against her family and force us into a public divorce, which would be hard on the both of us, more so her. It would tarnish her name and make known her infertility. Most likely, it would abandon her to a life of solitude in her father's house—or as a concubine, because she is very skilled in music and has a beautiful voice."

"A chantress would have a beautiful voice," Nefertiti remarked, wishing her own deeper voice could be higher, more like other women's voices.

"Her singing is very pleasing to hear," Horemheb said, nodding. "But I don't want that life for her. I'm grateful she doesn't divorce me. I'm never there. I'm never home. I would think we would both agree it is just easier to stay married and live apart."

"I see." Nefertiti took a deep breath. "Thank you for your honesty."

He may have put her off, but at least he protects her from a life of solitude or that of a concubine. Did Akhenaten ever protect me?

She shook her head and turned away from Horemheb.

He followed her gaze into the water.

"Do you like the lotus blossom? I hear your father call you that sometimes."

She nodded thoughtfully. "My mother tended a lotus garden. It was her favorite. He calls me 'lotus blossom' as a term of endearment," Nefertiti said as she cupped water in her hand and drizzled it over one of them.

"Oh! Then I'll have to bring Tey a lotus next time I'm in Waset," Horemheb offered, clearly trying to further her mind's distance from Akhenaten.

"My mother has gone to the Field of Reeds. Tey is my stepmother." Nefertiti paused to take a breath, remembering the disappointment in Tey's eyes after confessing what she'd done. "My mother traveled there in childbirth. They thought her infertile too, but I was the miracle baby that took her life from this land." Nefertiti hit the water with the palm of her hand, dashing her reflection. "How can you miss someone you've never known?"

Horemheb shut his mouth, as he had no response.

Nefertiti continued talking. "Tey is a wonderful mother, but I've done a major wrong in this . . ."—a lump formed in her throat as she tried to describe the murder she had committed—"in this crime." She whispered so low that Horemheb leaned closer to hear her. "Tey can't comfort me. I feel like my mother would know what to say."

Horemheb clenched his jaw. "Sometimes it is best not to say anything."

She found his eyes. A warm smile arose upon his thick lips. He reached out his hand to pat hers, but instead, he pushed up to standing. He had almost forgotten she was still Pharaoh Coregent—and he the commander.

"If you need to talk to someone . . ." he began.

"I don't," Nefertiti said as she stood up as well. She realized their personal space dwindled as the earthy musk of his leather tunic filled her nostrils. "I don't need to talk to anyone," she repeated and took a step back to regain her status. "I have nothing to talk about. Not with you, not my father, not Tey."

"I admire you for your strength, Pharaoh Coregent," Horemheb whispered as he looked around as if hoping they were still alone. "The three of us—as with General Paaten, when he returns from Nubia—we all care for you and would do anything for you."

"Yes, that is why you and my father abandoned me to Pawah and Beketaten!"

Horemheb took a deep breath. "Pharaoh Coregent, deep down, you know why we did such a thing. We cared about the safety of you and your family."

"No, if you cared, you would have kept us safe," Nefertiti retorted, and she hit him in the chest. Her hand throbbed as it hit the tiny ridges in his bronze breastplate, but she didn't let it faze her. She knew he spoke the truth. She figured there wasn't another way, but she needed to blame someone to keep from collapsing there on the stone walkway in her grief.

"Your hand, it's bleeding." When she did not respond, he pulled his shoulders back and looked her in the eye. "You're right. *I* should have kept you safe." He licked his lips in the dry evening air, and his jaw twitched before he continued. "I talked your father into the wine as well."

Nefertiti's jaw dropped, but then she closed her mouth as she studied his face and noticed his ticking eyebrow. "You are a horrible liar. My father did so on his own accord."

He dropped his head. "Pharaoh Coregent, I am the Commander of Pharaoh's Armies. I should have kept you safe. Hate me, not your father. You need him, and he needs you."

"I don't need him! My father outranks you in both profession and relation to me. I could accept it coming from you but from him? He is my *father*! He is supposed to protect me." The heat of her anger evaporated her tears away, but more followed. "You wouldn't understand." She shook her head and threw her hands up as she turned to leave.

"Pharaoh Coregent," Horemheb called.

Nefertiti stopped walking but kept her back to him.

"May I see your hand?"

Nefertiti's shoulders slumped. "I'm fine," she whispered, clutching her hands at her chest.

Horemheb walked around to face her; their personal space dwindling again.

She shook her head and blinked back tears. At the sounds of the funerary feast in the distance, a heavy breath filled her lungs. "I have blood on my hands," she whispered and peered up to Horemheb with utter despondence.

"No—*we* have blood on our hands," he whispered back.

Nefertiti closed her eyes, thanking him in her head for taking some of her guilt away. He brushed her upper arm with his fingers—a gentle brush, just enough to send tingles down her back—and she tensed, but then her relief rolled on her breath. She licked her lips in the dryness of the evening as the sparks from the torchlight fell and simmered in the ponds.

He ran his fingers down her forearm to her hand. Examining the wound in the dying torchlight, he whispered, "It looks like only the surface skin is broken." He clasped his other hand over hers and held her gaze. "It shall heal in time."

A flutter of trust and friendship passed over them as they shared a moment of understanding.

The light was almost out, and she wished for this one moment she was not Pharaoh Coregent so she could be wrapped up in his strong arms and let her sobs fall on his shoulder. The past few decans—nay, *years*—were almost too much. But at the test of her strength, she kept her pain inside.

They stood for a few moments with their hands clasped.

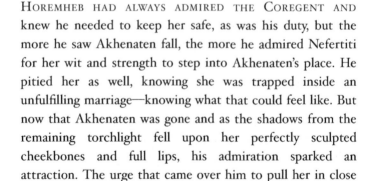

HOREMHEB HAD ALWAYS ADMIRED THE COREGENT AND knew he needed to keep her safe, as was his duty, but the more he saw Akhenaten fall, the more he admired Nefertiti for her wit and strength to step into Akhenaten's place. He pitied her as well, knowing she was trapped inside an unfulfilling marriage—knowing what that could feel like. But now that Akhenaten was gone and as the shadows from the remaining torchlight fell upon her perfectly sculpted cheekbones and full lips, his admiration sparked an attraction. The urge that came over him to pull her in close and possibly even kiss her startled him enough to break their connection.

He drew in a deep breath and gestured for her to come

with him back to the funerary feast. "Your father looks for you," he whispered.

NEFERTITI AND HOREMHEB FOUND AY SEARCHING THE corridors for his daughter. He debated calling her daughter or Pharaoh Coregent, but in the end, to not anger her more, he decided on the latter.

"Pharaoh Coregent," he said with a nod of his head as he walked up to her and Horemheb. "Commander, thank you for finding her for me."

Horemheb nodded.

Ay looked down and saw blood on her hand. "Daughter, are you hurt?" he said and reached for her hand.

She yanked her fist behind her back. Words jumbled in her mouth, not wanting to admit to her father she had lost her temper and hit the commander.

Horemheb eyed Nefertiti, sensing her hesitation to tell Ay what happened. He nodded again to Ay as he spoke. "We were in the lotus garden, and she cut her hand on the stone as she rose from one of the pond's edges. I have already sent a message to a stone mason to fix it." He tried very hard to keep his eyebrow from twitching, and, finally, he just had to look away, even though Ay seemed to accept his answer. "I will leave you to discuss matters with the Coregent."

Nefertiti pulled her lips into her mouth as she looked to the floor to keep her smile hidden from sight.

"No, this involves you too, Commander," Ay said. "General Paaten sends word from Nubia. We should speak somewhere more private."

He let Nefertiti lead them to the council room, but Nefertiti slowed down so that Horemheb was by her side. She sent a gentle jab of her elbow into Horemheb's arm. He smiled at the sight of her grateful beam before she quickened her pace to enter the room so her father would not see her token of appreciation to Horemheb.

Once they were all seated, Nefertiti asked, "Should we send word to Smenkare?"

"That boy doesn't know anything." Ay shook his head, rethinking his words. "We probably should, but . . ."

"But what?" Nefertiti asked. "He is Pharaoh now that Akhenaten is gone."

Ay squared his shoulders and faced his daughter. "He is just another Akhenaten. I don't trust him to defend Egypt. We need to act before the Appearance of the King ceremony, while you still have the title of Coregent."

As much as she hated to admit it, he was right. Besides, it was her fault the crown would not fall to her tomorrow. She pursed her lips.

"What word does General Paaten send?" Nefertiti eventually asked.

"The Nubians have invaded our border. The general is resisting them but at a great cost. They demand one hundred containers of grain to stop the attack," Ay said. "We have never bartered for our borders before, but given the state of the military and the economy, we need to consider it. The Nubians are an honorable people, and they usually keep their word—"

"It is a risky venture," Horemheb interrupted as he pressed his forefingers and thumbs together in front of his chest. "Did General Paaten describe the cost?"

"He did not, but for General Paaten to say 'at a great cost' . . ." Ay shook his head. "It must be great."

"Send the containers," Nefertiti said, her voice firm. "Make sure General Paaten ensures their surrender before they release the containers." She waved away any more discussion regarding her decision and stood up. "Thus,

Coregent says." She squared her shoulders to her father and then walked from the room.

When she was gone, Ay took in a long inhale and let his chest fall with a deep exhale. "Commander, do you have children?" he asked as he pushed his palms into his eyes.

"No, I do not."

Ay let his hands fall to the table, and then stood to leave.

"In times like these, do not be envious."

8

THE TIME OF THE ATEN

AT THE LAST DECREE OF PHARAOH AKHENATEN, HIS HALF-brother, Smenkare, took the throne, and an Appearance of the King celebration was held first in the capital, Aketaten, and then in Men-nefer, in the North.

The new Pharaoh Smenkare and company went to Waset for his third and last celebration, which General Paaten was able to attend, given that the threat of the Nubians' advance on the Egyptian border had subsided thus far.

Rumors and whisperings filled the streets, lining the people's hearts with hopeful thinking, and they began to see an auspicious future ahead of them. Talk of unity and a return to prosperity swept over Egypt's people.

The celebration was held in Malkata—the palace of her father-in-law, Amenhotep III, the father of Akhenaten and Smenkare. Nefertiti sat on her throne to the left of Smenkare and Meritaten as she looked to the crowd that had gathered, and remembered when she was first crowned Chief Royal Wife, on the same steps where her daughter was just crowned. She held her wine goblet in her hand, swirling her finger over the top of it as she watched the festivities. Her throat cried for drink, but fear silenced her thirst. She tipped the wine onto the floor.

"Mother," Ankhesenpaaten said as she moved her foot away from the splatter.

"I'm sorry," Nefertiti said. She saw a passing servant and gave him the goblet, then put her head in her hand.

"Mother, are you feeling well?" Ankhesenpaaten asked as she rubbed Nefertiti's shoulder.

Nefertiti took a deep breath as she swiveled her chin to face her daughter.

"Yes, my sweet one."

Tut leaned over to look at her from his throne next to Ankhesenpaaten. A child in the big throne chair was probably quite the sight, she thought, but even as a child, he repulsed her. Nefertiti's jaw tightened as she held her head up and straightened her shoulders.

"I am fine. Enjoy the celebration."

The nobility had made their way into Waset to support their new King in their assumption he would bring a unified Egypt back to Amun-Re. Pawah and Beketaten were among Smenkare's supporters. Now, Beketaten walked up the steps to Smenkare's throne with her arms held open wide.

"Brother," Beketaten said. She stopped at the second to the top step. Then she and Pawah, who stood off and behind her, bowed from the waist.

Nefertiti cocked a half-grin at their ignorance to which god he gave his loyalty.

Smenkare stood and walked to the top step with a smile gracing his face. "My sister!"

As Smenkare embraced her, Beketaten exclaimed, "How you have grown since I have last seen you!"

"Why did you leave my mother's house so long ago? I have missed you so!" His eyes grew brighter as he recalled the memories of them when he was a boy.

"Our brother, the Pharaoh before, Akhenaten, and his Queen"—Beketaten shot a look at Nefertiti over Pharaoh's shoulder—"exiled us to Nubia for five long years."

"Why would they do such a thing? His own sister?" Smenkare looked to Nefertiti with eyes wide in disbelief.

"We tried to return Egypt to Amun-Re," Beketaten said, her voice loud. "But now, we are back and ready to follow your reign."

"Ah, I see," Smenkare said, and his smile became polite. "Well, I am glad you came to your senses—even changed your name to honor the Aten."

A moment of confusion crossed Beketaten and Pawah's faces.

"It is good to have you back," Smenkare said, and his smile grew with sincerity.

Nefertiti bit her tongue to keep from laughing at the poor fools. They would find out soon enough—O, the new Pharaoh was not for their god!—and then what would they do? Have her murder her own daughter and son-in-law as well?

Why not just murder the whole royal line? she thought bitterly.

"Yes, of course," Beketaten said flatly.

Pawah stepped forward. "My Lord of the Two Lands . . . may you reign forever and ever with your beautiful Queen always by your side."

At the mention of her title, Smenkare gestured for Meritaten to join them on the steps. Meritaten obeyed and glided to her husband. "Thank you, Pawah," Pharaoh said, "Fifth Prophet of the Aten—"

"Amun," Pawah corrected.

Smenkare and Meritaten looked at him with their lips thinned and their brows furrowed. "You were a prophet of Amun . . . now you are a prophet of the Aten?" Smenkare said, raising his chin and peering down at Pawah over the bridge of his nose.

Pawah looked past Smenkare to Nefertiti, who watched their interactions like a lion watches its prey.

Meritaten glanced at her mother and gestured for her to join them. Nefertiti stood and walked over to them. "Mother and Coregent," her daughter said, "when you granted pardon to Princess Nebetah and her husband, Pawah, was it not because she had changed her name to Beketaten and they had decided to worship the one true god, the Aten?"

"It was," Nefertiti said. "That was the word I had received."

She tilted her head as she looked at them. She held their lives in her next words, and Beketaten narrowed her eyes in acknowledgment of this power. The People's Restoration of Egypt could be ended. But in doing so, Nefertiti would make Beketaten and Pawah martyrs—and martyrs are hard to silence. She shook her head and dismissed the idea. If she did not protect them, they could then point the finger at *her* for getting rid of Akhenaten. She hoped Meritaten would believe *her*, not them. But it was too risky to try.

"Yes, of course," Pawah said in one breath, backpedaling. "My previous position was that of the Fifth Prophet of Amun, but after our exile, I became a prophet of the Aten, for whom I have spent much time in worship, my king—as you have correctly stated." Pawah stepped in front of Beketaten, closer to Smenkare, as he continued. "I hope that my presence with you as a child in your mother's house, in sanctuary from your father's order of exile against us, and my previous position with Amun does not spoil your opinion of me."

"Not at all," Smenkare said and placed his hands on Pawah's shoulders. "I cannot harbor a sour opinion of the man I grew to call 'Father'—in the absence of my *real* father, who hid me behind the palace and never claimed me as his own."

Pawah put his hands on Pharaoh's shoulders as well, and a sly smile crossed his lips. "I am so proud . . . my *son*. You are wise beyond your years and will be greatly remembered for what you are to accomplish."

Smenkare nodded, the burden of doubt lifting from his expression. "*You* are the wise one. I only wish I had more time with you as a child."

"We have time now, and I have much to *advise* and teach," Pawah said as he squeezed Smenkare's shoulders.

"How fortunate for you to mention advice! I need a second vizier," Smenkare said. "Duties of both the Upper and the Lower appear to be too much for the aging Vizier Nakht."

Nefertiti bit her tongue as she watched Smenkare play right into Pawah's hands, both figuratively and literally. If Smenkare thought of Pawah as a father, then Meritaten's word would most likely not be enough to go against Pawah's if he told him Nefertiti had killed Akhenaten. Her smug smile disappeared as she realized she no longer held their lives in her hands. Beketaten peered at Nefertiti, and, as if reading her thoughts, the corners of Beketaten's mouth upturned into a devious grin.

"I would assume so. It is much to oversee," Pawah said, and his chest puffed and swelled in victory.

"I'm glad you feel the same way, my new Vizier of the Upper," Smenkare replied. "My mother taught me about the ways of Amun, and she never told me *my* father was *her* father. She kept from me the truth that I was a son of Pharaoh Amenhotep III. She lied to me for all of my life. My father disowned *me*, so *I* shall disown *him*—and put you in his place."

Smenkare clapped his hands loudly, and as the room grew

silent, he declared from his platform, "In honor of my crowning as King of the Upper and the Lower, Pharaoh of Egypt, I give praise to the Aten and shall carry on my brother's work! As I will need much advice to oversee my edicts and to ensure they are carried out, I have named Pawah, Fifth Prophet of the Aten, as Vizier of the Upper, and Nakht will remain as Vizier of the Lower as he served under my brother, Pharaoh Akhenaten."

He waited for some sort of applause from the audience but was only greeted with wide eyes until another prophet of the Aten began to clap slowly, and it was joined by reluctant hands.

Nefertiti stood stiff as a statue, anxious about what Smenkare would say next.

"For my first decree as Pharaoh, send military men to tear down all the temples dedicated to any false god. Only temples to the Aten are to remain."

Pawah, Beketaten, and Nefertiti swallowed the lumps in their throats. Beketaten shot a glance to Nefertiti that said, *If you had only killed Akhenaten that night instead of waiting.*

Nefertiti's nostrils flared—she didn't know if her anger was toward Beketaten or because she too felt the same way.

"Furthermore," Smenkare continued, and all ears turned to his next words, "death will meet any who utter Amun's name."

A simultaneous gasp was heard throughout the hall, but Smenkare continued oblivious.

"Thus Pharaoh says." He waited for the people's jaws to close and their incredulous stares to cease, but when they didn't, he added, "We shall begin with the purge at the first morning light! Enjoy your food and beverage, for tomorrow we finish what Pharaoh Akhenaten began."

Chief Royal Guard Jabari stood off nearby, his nostrils flaring at the decree as the room broke out in murmured whispers. His subordinates Khabek, Ineni, and Hori's knuckles went white as they squeezed their spears and rubbed their thumbs along the smooth wooden handles. They all exchanged glances and knew Smenkare would soon meet the same fate as his brother.

As the scribe wrote Smenkare's declaration, he turned to Meritaten with a big smile on his face. Her eyebrows squeezed together as she pulled her lips into a grimace. He came near to her.

"What pains you, my beautiful Meritaten: the one the Aten loves?"

She took a hard swallow. "My love . . . not even my father was so severe," Meritaten murmured low enough for only his ears.

"My love . . . my Queen . . . Egypt will never truly worship the Aten when there is temptation at every corner to worship a false god. I do this for Egypt, for the greater good of its people," Smenkare reasoned and stroked her arm with the tips of his fingers.

She took another moment to gather her words, then looked at him and said, "Many will be killed."

"Yes, my love, but my brother and I talked a long time about what we should do. Because he journeyed west and was unable to give the decree, I will do it for him. It will be my legacy—the Pharaoh who ultimately brought Egypt out of ignorance."

COMMANDER HOREMHEB AND GENERAL PAATEN stood in the back corner of the great hall, each lost in their own thoughts at the new edict, until Horemheb spoke.

"There will be much bloodshed," he whispered.

"Yes, there will be." Paaten's sturdy legs stood as pillars, but his voice revealed his sadness.

Horemheb wondered if the general thought the same as him and Ay. He didn't know about Akhenaten's murder. The People's Restoration of Egypt had never approached him. "Do you believe the soldiers will carry out the edict?"

"The ones who take their oath seriously will carry out whatever edict Pharaoh utters," General Paaten responded. "As will I."

Horemheb nodded and blew out a hesitant breath. "Even if it means killing innocent people?"

General Paaten's jaw twitched as he wrestled with his morals. "Innocent to me, but not innocent to Pharaoh's law."

"And this deserves execution?" Horemheb asked with a scowl and stiffened his stance.

"I have already killed for the crown many times—even when I did not agree. I have fought wars to expand the empire under Pharaoh Amenhotep III, when a trade agreement would have sufficed. Under Pharaoh Akhenaten, I have ordered the torture of men accused to be part of the rebellion for information about its leaders . . ." He trailed off, then finished, "Pharaoh's law is the law I uphold."

"And now you would order the execution of Egypt's people?"

"We took an oath to protect Pharaoh and to uphold his throne and edicts. To do otherwise lessens Pharaoh in the eyes of the world, no matter who sits on the throne. Power was restored to Pharaoh. If I do anything other than what I swore when I became a military steward of Egypt, I give that power away, and all our efforts are in vain."

Horemheb bit his tongue from saying anything more. He understood and felt the same, but knew Egypt would not last if nothing was done. Balancing both objectives proved to be a difficult task. He watched Pawah and Beketaten from afar as they squirmed under Nefertiti's eye and spoke with Pharaoh Smenkare. He couldn't deny, either: it felt good to watch them wallow in their mistake—at least until they would probably come to them again, demanding the immediate removal of Pharaoh Smenkare under threat of rebellion. He wagered with himself that it would be a day or two after they returned to Aketaten.

He peered over to the general and wondered what then would be his next course of action when he found out what the rest of the council had done. Would he join them, or would he be a loyal instrument to Pharaoh Smenkare and have them all killed for treason and conspiracy?

I don't think he would let them harm Nefertiti—but her father and me, Horemheb reasoned, *he would have us executed.*

His gaze fell back on Nefertiti, and hers on him—or so he thought and maybe even hoped. He clenched his jaw and furrowed his brow as his thoughts drifted to her as she looked under the torchlight in the garden. He cleared his throat, took a wide stance, and clasped his hands in front of his stomach.

I am the Commander, he thought. *I will keep her safe from any more of Pawah's forthcoming schemes to get rid of Smenkare. I will not make her go through this again.*

❧ 9 ❧

THE TIME OF CONFLICTION

GENERAL PAATEN, VIZIER OF THE LOWER, NAKHT, AND Vizier of the Upper, Pawah, Master of the Pharaoh's Horses, Ay, Commander Horemheb, and Nefertiti sat in the council room looking at Pharaoh Smenkare under the sun's rays.

"Pharaoh, the Nubians have attacked our borders again," Paaten said. "The last time we sent one hundred—"

"Again?" Smenkare asked, and lifted an eyebrow.

Ay, Horemheb, and Nefertiti glanced at each other. After a moment's hesitation, Ay planned to take responsibility for this action; he didn't know what Smenkare would do, but knew he wasn't going to let him harm his daughter nor take away her chance at the throne by allowing him to remove her Coregent title.

Ay finally spoke, saying, "Yes, it was before your coronation. I brought the action to Pharaoh Akhenaten's Coregent. It was decided to barter a trade agreement with the Nubians: one hundred containers of grain for peace along our borders."

"I see. And how long of a peace did the one hundred containers buy?" Smenkare asked. The sun drenched his head and shoulders. He held the same long nose and round chin as Akhenaten did before him, and the sun's shadows fell just as they had on the late Pharaoh's face.

The scene evoked memories in Nefertiti—ones she wished she could burn.

"One season," Paaten said and peered at Ay and Nefertiti.

Pawah, seeing an opportunity to spread his influence over the young Pharaoh, cleared his throat. "And why wasn't Pharaoh Akhenaten's successor made aware of this border issue?"

"Because," Horemheb said, narrowing his eyes at Pawah, "Pharaoh Akhenaten's successor had not yet been crowned and his Coregent was available. The matter was urgent. But now that you are Vizier of the Upper, it will be *your* responsibility to field those border messages to Pharaoh."

Keeping his eyes on Horemheb, Pawah said, "So, my *son*, my Pharaoh"—he transitioned his gaze to Pharaoh Smenkare —"shall we cower behind a short-lived trade agreement, or put the Nubians in their place?"

Pharaoh Smenkare nodded. "The Nubians should remember that we are mighty Egypt and not test our patience. Use the one hundred containers of grain to pay soldiers and weapons. Advance upon Nubia and protect our borders."

"Perhaps you should send all three military commanders," Pawah suggested and gestured to Paaten, Horemheb, and Ay. "They aren't of much use here."

The three men wished they could snarl at this two-faced liar, but knew Smenkare favored him, so they simply sat still and glared at him.

"Yes, I agree," Pharaoh Smenkare said, and nodded again.

"Pharaoh Smenkare," Nefertiti said with a voice of honey, "there was a rebellion when your brother turned Egypt to the Aten, and Malkata was almost overrun had it not been for a few of General Paaten's companies there and Commander Horemheb sending his division. They were able to subdue the rebellion because they were close enough to be *of use*."

"There is no threat of rebellion," Pawah said to Pharaoh, sneering at Nefertiti.

"How can one be so sure?" Nefertiti gazed levelly at Pawah and kept her own sneer at bay. She did not need Smenkare to know how much she disliked Pawah, the man he adopted as his father. "The conspirators we tortured for information told us Aketaten was under constant threat of rebellion under Pharaoh Akhenaten's reign."

Paaten, Horemheb, and Ay nodded in agreement; then all gritted their teeth, wondering how Pawah was going to get rid of them now.

"Pharaoh," Paaten added, "they are a *real* threat, and their loyalty to their leaders transcends the torture we have put the known conspirators through."

"It was why the Pharaoh before always kept at least one division of men with him at all times," Nefertiti coached, seeing Smenkare's head bob in agreement with her.

"General, Commander," Pharaoh Smenkare ordered, "take your divisions to the Nubian border."

"We have borders at both the Upper and the Lower. To send the majority of the army to one border leaves the opposite border vulnerable and the capital relatively unprotected," Nefertiti crooned. "Should a border dispute arise in the Lower, it may be prudent to keep the divisions where they are."

"No!" Smenkare's cheeks blushed as he paused.

Nefertiti knew to quit speaking but was glad to see him taking a moment to think about what she said.

When at last he spoke, Smenkare turned to his three military commanders. "General, take all of your divisions. Commander, take a third of yours, and leave the rest here at

Aketaten. Master of Pharaoh's Horses, keep your divisions in the Lower."

"Very wise decision, Pharaoh," Pawah said with a pressed smile.

A beaming smile emanated from Smenkare's face.

"Thus Pharaoh says," Paaten said, nodding, and then Pharaoh Smenkare dismissed them.

AFTER THEY LEFT, PAATEN PULLED HOREMHEB ASIDE. Nefertiti eyed Horemheb in her peripheral vision as she walked past. She had been thinking about him since their encounter in the garden. Mostly she thought about the way he had tried to comfort her, and her urge to fall into his strong arms, letting the stress and burden upon her shoulders pour down in the form of tears upon his perfect chest. She chewed on her bottom lip, scolding herself for thinking such things only a season after her husband had died. Died? No —*murdered*. The truth gnawed at her insides and made her nauseated most nights, but her thoughts still lingered on Horemheb.

"They will come back to us," Ay whispered to Nefertiti.

"What?" Nefertiti stuttered, not realizing Ay followed her gaze after the commander. She turned to face her father a little farther down the corridor than Paaten and Horemheb.

"The General and the Commander." Ay's eyes smiled. "They will come back to us."

"Don't promise something you cannot know." Nefertiti glared at her father. "You make many promises." Her dagger of words cut him through and through. She particularly remembered the night Thutmose had been entombed, when her father had told her the plan to regain the power from the priesthood of Amun by temporarily turning Egypt to the Aten:

I promise no harm will come to you.

All will return to as it was.

Those were his words to his naïve thirteen-year-old daughter. She had believed his every word, and now he had broken his promises to her one by one.

Ay's voice dropped even lower as he leaned in toward her and whispered, "My daughter, had I known how serious Akhenaten's mind would fall, I would have done away with him myself the night of the rebellion at Malkata."

"Why?" Nefertiti shot back at him.

"To protect you, my lotus blossom."

She clenched her jaw and swallowed a hard lump; she hadn't expected her father to say *that*. Nor to call her by his pet name for her.

Taking a moment to readjust her collar, Nefertiti responded with a tart tone. "Well, too bad you were twelve years late, Father—and even then, you passed the job to me."

Ay's focus stayed on Nefertiti as he twisted his mouth into a grimace. "I'm so sorry, Nefertiti. I wish all your burdens on me. I want to take them from you."

Her stiff shoulders refused to relent. She drew a sharp inhale before snapping, "Well, you can't, can you?"

Horemheb and Paaten parted ways, and Horemheb glanced at Nefertiti and Ay. Nefertiti's blood coursed through her veins as she realized her own hypocrisy. She had forgiven Horemheb's involvement—had even thought about crying in his arms and releasing her burdens onto him—but her father, who had apologized, she could not come to forgive.

He is my father, she thought. *He should have protected me. He should have kept his promises to me. He should have loved me enough not to have convinced me to murder my own husband. He should have—*

"I want to," Ay repeated, interrupting her thoughts.

Nefertiti looked to her father and pinched her lips into a polite smile.

"But you can't."

Her façade fell, and she walked away from him, toward Horemheb.

HE STOOD WAITING FOR HER ONCE HE SAW HER APPROACH. He peered back at Ay, whose flat expression and pale face told him the conversation with his daughter had not gone well. He gave him a sympathetic grin. Ay dipped his head in gratitude and walked away.

Horemheb's focus drifted to Nefertiti as she walked toward him. He forced his gaze to stay with her eyes and not drop to the alluring sway of her hips. Just below her hard eyes, her pinched mouth told him contentment resided elsewhere.

"Walk with me, Commander." She did not slow down but kept walking past him.

"Yes, Pharaoh Coregent," Horemheb said, and fell in line a little behind her, as per his place.

He watched curiously as she turned her head slightly and examined the space beside her, then dropped her chin toward her chest.

Does she want me to walk beside her? he asked himself. She rounded into a more remote part of the palace and began to slow her steps. *I will see.*

He came up beside her and a slight smile crossed her face. "Commander," she said, then closed her mouth, seemingly unsure what to say.

Horemheb cleared his throat. "General Paaten plans to

leave at first light." He surveyed the empty corridor as they slowed to a stop.

"He doesn't know, does he?" she asked, turning to face him.

"About Pharaoh Akhenaten?" he whispered. He shook his head.

A glisten formed in her eyes. "I don't want him to find out the truth," she confessed.

Horemheb clenched his jaw. "I don't think it would be in any of our best interests if he found out the truth while Smenkare is on the throne. Smenkare would not be too fond of what we did, to put it mildly. Although he may spare you in his report, Paaten will carry out Pharaoh's orders to the best of his ability—even if it means killing for something he doesn't believe in."

"Or even if it means torturing known conspirators of a rebellious movement." Nefertiti shuddered.

Horemheb sighed, remembering her order of torture to find the leaders of the People's Restoration of Egypt. He hadn't agreed with her and had already known Pawah and Beketaten led the movement. But she had lost three daughters, her mentor, and her only friend, and she was still trapped in Akhenaten's conditional rule of coregency. She had to find out who was threatening the remainder of her family. Maybe he might have done the same? His gaze fell to the floor as he thought. She was only acting to secure power for Pharaoh's throne, as was the plan since the beginning. Rebellion against the throne is evidence of a weak Pharaoh. She had to keep power in Pharaoh's court and not let it slip back to the Amun priesthood. His stomach dropped at the realization of her abundant love for Egypt. He looked back at her with a renewed perspective. *She is such a strong woman, willing to sacrifice so much for her country. She has been a great ruler—a great . . . beautiful . . . Coregent.*

She shook her head to fight the tears.

"You did what you thought was right. We all are doing what we think is right—even Pharaohs Akhenaten and Smenkare."

"Yes, but it doesn't *make* it right," Nefertiti said. She looked at her hand; the skin had scabbed over from where she had hit Horemheb that night in the lotus garden.

Surprising even himself, Horemheb grabbed her wounded hand. His arm tensed for a second after he grabbed it, but at her lack of yell or scolding, he relaxed and pulled her hand closer to his chest. He smoothed his thumb over her soft skin and examined the wound.

"We all have our secrets. We have all done things of which we are not proud." His thumb found the scab. "Eventually, time allows us to make amends and move forward. We hope the wounds won't scar, but, regardless, they still shape our future. We can hide scars, display them, learn from them, or repeat them. They are with us forever, but it is up to you what you do with them. I try to learn from my scars."

She smiled at him as they shared their second moment of friendship in as many nights.

Horemheb added, "But I am not very smart, so I tend to repeat them from time to time."

A laugh burst from her lungs and she immediately covered her mouth. Her laugh bounced off the stone walls and filled their ears.

I love her laugh, Horemheb thought. *A deep, hearty laugh with a sweet ring to it.*

"Oh, you agree that I am not very smart?" he teased, but then realized he was speaking to her as if he were courting her.

She took a step forward, dwindling their personal space even further, and tilted her head to peer up at him. His heartbeat began to quicken.

I am already acting far above my status. I need to let go of her hand. I need to take a step back. I have a wife. Nothing can ever come of us—she is Pharaoh Coregent. I am Commander.

But still, he kept her hand in his, and still, he smiled at the gleam in her big, brown, almond eyes.

"I think you are very wise," she breathed, "and that is the second time you have made me laugh."

"It is such a rare treat. I want to hear it more often," he confessed, suppressing his thoughts further.

"My father says I have my mother's laugh. It reminds him of her." Nefertiti smiled at the memory. Even though she was mad at her father, she still loved him, and she still missed the mother she never knew.

"I would think she would be proud of the woman you've become."

"Yes . . . so *proud*," she snapped. Her face fell, and she tried to yank her hand away, but he kept a firm grasp on it.

"*Yes*, so proud, Pharaoh Coregent. You have had many hardships and endured many trials and persevered through many obstacles." It was true. She had endured more than any other woman he had ever heard or seen. "I am not lying," he said, watching her examine his face for his twitching eyebrow.

"I can see that," she responded and bit her lip in thought. "Why do you keep my hand in yours when I try to remove it?"

His face paled and a lump formed in his throat. He dropped her hand suddenly, his thoughts reeling.

I don't know why.

That is a lie. Her skin was soft, and I liked holding her hand.

I can't say that!

Finally, another thought came to him as she patiently waited for his answer. "You needed to know your mother would have been proud of you." He passed her lie test, but even though she found him telling her a truth, there seemed to be some disappointment behind her eyes.

"Thank you, Commander Horemheb," she whispered. Straightening her back and head and pulling her arms to her side, she let out a slow, shallow breath.

"You are welcome, Pharaoh Coregent," he whispered, mimicking her posture.

It is better this way. I could never court her, let alone marry her. Although she would make a stunning wife, and I would not take her for granted like her late husband. I would be good to her. What am I talking about? It can never be. I will be her friend because she needs a friend. That is all that I will do.

"I will be back in one and a half seasons' time," he said, changing the subject before he found himself thinking too much about a woman he could never be with.

Nefertiti bit her lip again as she peered up at him. "Fight well," she said and seemed to stop herself from saying more.

Horemheb nodded. "We shall." A weight set on his heart, wishing and hoping that whatever this was between them was not ending just as it had begun.

"Please go make preparations for your journey," she said. "I do not wish to hold you any longer."

"Should I call the royal guard to escort you wherever you were headed?" He still needed to make sure she was safe, even if there could never be anything between them.

"No." She shook her head. "I will walk by myself."

He nodded, took a step back, bowed at the waist, and began to walk away, but she placed her wounded hand on his bronze-scaled chest as he passed by her. They locked eyes over each other's shoulder.

"I am sorry I hit you, Horemheb."

Her shoulders fell again, and the apology and the lack of her use of his title made him think she did not want this to end either. He covered her hand with his as if by instinct.

"There is nothing to apologize for, my Pharaoh Coregent."

Every time he thought they would maintain their status, he or she would break it.

Her eyes held a glisten. "There are many things to apologize for." She half smiled. "Thank you for making me laugh in the midst of my sorrow."

"I hope to hear more when I return."

I am sure your father would too, but I am not going to say that, he thought as a soft pink fell upon her cheeks.

SHE LET HER HAND SLIDE OVER HIS SHOULDER AS HE walked away. Standing in the empty corridor, she watched him round the corner and saw him glance back, if only for a second. When she knew she was alone, she made fists and hit herself in the sides of the legs.

"Ah!" Her spine bent, and she thrust her head into her hands. "What am I doing?"

Dropping her hands, she pressed her back to the stone wall and slid down. The cool stone felt good on her neck and legs.

"Why him?" she asked herself. Society would never approve of a woman tempting a husband away from his wife, although not uncommon. Her head rested against the wall. "He is a friend, nothing more . . . a handsome friend who can make me laugh and has shown me more understanding than anyone in the past ten years. There are no judgments with him."

She closed her eyes, remembering the fallen look upon her stepmother's and sister's faces when she revealed to them what she had done. Her chest released a captive breath. She rubbed her thighs and then crossed her arms over her stomach, feeling the smooth linen between her hands.

Clearing her mind, a thought came to her: Horemheb was the first man to hold her hand since Meketaten journeyed west; she had tried to hold Akhenaten's hand then, but Akhenaten never returned her embrace. The last night they spent together was when she had returned from Waset, after he had banished her from Aketaten for pardoning his sister, Beketaten, so many years ago.

She huffed. *Which led to Tut,* she thought and rolled her eyes.

Akhenaten had lied to her, betrayed their bed, broke his promise she could bear the heir, and in Henuttaneb's demise, named Kiya as Tut's mother. She had put her trust in her husband per her father's words of wisdom: *Trust and truth are united in marriage.* Perhaps she should add to the saying: *with the right person.*

The morning's breakfast came to the top of her throat as she thought about what she had been through the past years.

I was so young when I fell in love with Amenhotep, and he was a good husband and father for a while and then this place, she looked around at the reliefs in the palace's corridor, *Aketaten, took him away from me, from us.*

He loved her as much as she loved him—but it wasn't enough to save him from his zealous obsession; it wasn't enough to keep their bed pure and his promises true; it wasn't enough to save him from a goblet of poisoned wine.

I tried. Maybe that's why I don't like Tut. He reminds me every day of my failure of my husband—a constant reminder that our love wasn't enough to save him.

A tear slid down her cheek.

Her thirty years in the land of the living had brought her to this point: crying alone in an empty corridor of a palace that spat in the face of Amun. She looked to her side and wished someone were there—even her father . . . but she wished more so that it were Horemheb. He had made her feel dignified again and helped her carry the weight of her burdens. He'd reached deep down inside of her and pulled out something she had buried long ago: happiness, even if for a brief moment.

She closed her eyes again, feeling once more the warmth of his hand upon hers, hearing his soft, deep voice, smelling his musky leather scent, seeing his muscular physique. His words, his *truthful* words, held so much meaning and sincerity, and she knew he had told her the truth by way of his facial tell. She chuckled at the memory of seeing it for the first time, and could not believe she had not noticed it before.

Well, she had been preoccupied.

She took in a long, deep breath and shook her head.

"I am sorry, Akhenaten," she said to his ka, his spirit. "I know I should mourn you for longer, before my thoughts begin drifting to another man, but you didn't touch me for seven years. Seven years! Even if he is beneath me in status, he talked to me like you used to when we were young. I think he cares for me. He seems to be a good man. He didn't go off with another woman when his wife could not produce a child, let alone an heir. I at least gave you six beautiful daughters."

Then a pang struck her heart.

Amenia . . . she thought. *I don't want to be the second wife.* She bit her lip. *As though I could even marry him. He is beneath my station! It is fruitless to even entertain the idea. Don't borrow heartache, Nefertiti. You already have had your fill.*

But even as she thought this, her eyes still watched the space where she last saw Horemheb in the corridor.

You have a budding friendship with the Commander. Nothing more!

She rubbed the middle of her forehead and closed her eyes.

"I need a friend."

Biting her lip, she repeated herself: "I need a friend."

Her hand moved from rubbing her forehead to her lip. "A friend who knows what to say to help me, who knows how to make me laugh, and who I can tell cares for me." She nodded. "A good friend, but nothing more."

She looked off to where he had rounded the corner, and she inhaled a sharp breath and stood up, still not resolved in her thoughts. She straightened her back and turned to go back to her chambers, but stopped. His last words floated back to her.

I hope to hear more when I return.

Glancing back to where she'd seen him last, she whispered, "Please return home safe, Horemheb."

✿ 10 ✿

THE TIME OF FRIENDSHIP

"WATCH THIS, ANKHESENPAATEN!"

Tut swung his wooden sword toward his tutor. Sennedjem blocked Tut's swing and thrust his wooden sword toward the boy's chest. Tut stumbled and fell over, his cane bouncing away from his reach and his sword sliding to Ankhesenpaaten's feet.

His cheeks flushed as red as the granite of the obelisks standing in Ipet-isut. He rolled over to his stomach and tried to crawl toward his cane, but his sidelock kept hitting his face.

"Young Prince Tutankhaten," Sennedjem said. "Your cane will not save you in battle."

Tut stopped crawling and looked to Ankhesenpaaten, who had grabbed his sword and stood over him, holding it out to him. He pushed off his chest and steadied himself with his one good foot, then took his sword from his half-sister, spinning around to Sennedjem.

"*I* will protect you, Ankhesenpaaten!" Tut yelled. "Get back!"

Ankhesenpaaten took a few steps back, but stayed guard in case he needed her help again.

His opposite arm levered for balance as he struck again. He began to advance, his club foot forward, but the weight of his body caused him to fall to his knee. He blocked a swing from Sennedjem as he pushed himself up. Hopping onto his good foot, he advanced.

"Good, my prince," Sennedjem said as he blocked a swing.

The block sent Tut back to hobbling again.

"Steady yourself. With practice, this will become second nature to you."

Tut flailed his arm until he regained control, gave a determined smile to Ankhesenpaaten, then swung again.

"Be in control of your weapon at all times," Sennedjem said as he blocked the surprisingly hard swing. "Good, good."

The sun could not compare to the beams of pride emanating from Tut's face as they ended their session. "Did you see, Ankhesenpaaten? Did you see?" Tut asked her as Sennedjem readied his cane for him to walk over to her.

"I did. You did very well, Tut," Ankhesenpaaten said, and gave him a hug, immediately drawing back from his sweaty body.

"I almost had Sennedjem!" Tut's eyes glittered at Ankhesenpaaten's smile.

"Yes, you did, Prince Tutankhaten," Sennedjem said, following them out of the harem palace's royal training yard.

"Do you think Coregent Neferneferuaten would be proud of me?" Tut asked, leaning toward Ankhesenpaaten.

"I am sure Mother would," she responded, nodding and forcing her lips together into a smile.

Tut beamed. He wanted to call her "Mother" as well, but the one time he had done so in front of the Coregent, he had received an icy stare. He vowed he would prove himself to her, so that instead of receiving disapproval at his endearment, she would grant a prideful smile—perhaps even a reciprocal "son."

"I can take him from here. We need to walk today," Ankhesenpaaten told Sennedjem as she flipped her wig off of her neck, having stood in the hot sun for the duration of Tut's lesson.

He nodded and left them to walk the palace corridor in the hopes the young prince's foot would eventually straighten out.

"I think you have walked with me every day since I *could* walk," Tut told her as he grasped the cane's inlaid golden handle in the palm of his hand.

"I think you're right." Ankhesenpaaten walked with her hands ready in case he fell. She spotted Nefe running up behind them. "And we always seem to have a tag-a-long."

"I am not a *tag-a-long*," Nefe said. "*You* are the tag-a-long!" She punched Ankhesenpaaten in the arm.

"Ow!" Ankhesenpaaten yelled. "Why can't you just leave us alone?!"

"Why can't *you* just leave us alone?"

The two sisters glared at each other. Nefe, three years younger than Ankhesenpaaten, stood her equal. The younger Tut just laughed—perhaps a little too young to understand why the girls were fighting with each other.

Ay suddenly appeared and gathered the two girls up in his arms, startling them, for it was a rare occasion their grandfather came to the royal harem.

"How are my two favorite granddaughters?"

Nefe giggled, not noticing Tut's sad smile. "What about Meritaten?" she whispered.

"Oh!" Ay's shoulders rounded about them as a sheepish grin crossed his lips. "She is a favorite, too, of course."

"Why are you here, grandfather?" Ankhesenpaaten asked as he lowered her to the ground.

"Vizier Nakht was to teach the Queen today about the affairs of Egypt, but he is taking care of some . . . issues . . . from the Libyans in the Lower, just as Vizier Pawah is taking care of some issues with the Nubians in the Upper. So, I am here to take Nakht's place. Pharaoh Smenkare thought it would be good for me to spend some time with the Queen as well." He patted Nefe's bald head and swished her sidelock affectionately. "It was good to see you young women, but I best not be late." He bowed to Prince Tutankhaten. "My Prince," he said as he stood. "Please take good care of my granddaughters."

Tut stood as tall as he could. "I have no greater pleasure."

Ay smiled at the sweet boy's demeanor and nodded as he took off toward the royal harem's library.

Tut began walking toward the Kap, hobbling along on his cane. Ankhesenpaaten and Nefe walked on either side of him. He kept his head down and focused on one step after the other.

After a moment's silence, Nefe asked, "What is wrong, Tut?"

Ankhesenpaaten draped an arm over his shoulder. "Yes, you seemed so happy, but now something bothers you?"

"I never met *my* grandfather," he said. "Or my mother."

The two girls bit their tongues, not knowing how to respond.

"And my father didn't even think highly enough of me to name me, his only son, as his successor." Tut's chin sunk lower to his chest.

"He didn't think highly of me, either," Ankhesenpaaten said. "He just married me because Meketaten was taken by the plague."

"At least he spent more time with you than me," Nefe said to her.

"Only when we were in the temple with Mother,"

Ankhesenpaaten shot back. "You know——" She shook her head and shrugged her shoulders, glancing around them. "We should not speak ill of the Pharaoh before."

The other two nodded their heads, but Tut, after some moments of silence, began again.

"I mean, I was his *son*, the Crown Prince. I know I've only just had my eighth year, but I also know that the Crown Prince takes the King's place when he journeys west. If he was ashamed of me, why are you friends with me? I won't ever be King. Now Pharaoh Smenkare's——"

"Tut, I don't think you had anything to do with his decision," Ankhesenpaaten said. "Father . . . well . . . as Mother said one time, he had his own way of seeing the world. Even Mother never really had time for us." She rubbed his back, but immediately wiped her hand on her dress to remove all of the sweat he had acquired in his daily fighting lesson. "In his own mind, it made sense. Just as in Mother's mind, it made sense for her never to be here with us. She was always at the palace."

"Don't talk about Pharaoh Coregent Neferneferuaten like that!" Tut yelled, and his hand curled into a fist. "She is *always* here for us! Always! You both are so lucky to have one to call 'Mother'!"

"Tut . . . Tut . . ." Ankhesenpaaten raised her hands to her chest, showing him her palms. He could become so angry so quickly. "I agree that we are lucky to have our mother with us, but you have to agree, she has never really been around us."

"Because she is devoted to Egypt!" Tut yelled, and raised his fist again.

It was Nefe's turn to try and calm him. "Yes, our mother is a very strong woman in the palace." She stroked his arm that held the cane.

"Yes," Tut said, and lowered his hand.

Ankhesenpaaten grabbed his hand and squeezed. "Tut, I was only trying to make you feel better. Your father loved you."

"He never *told* me he loved me." Tut's face fell. "He only loved the Aten." His shoulders slumped and his chin again dropped to his chest.

Ankhesenpaaten kissed his bald head, ignoring the sweat. "*We* love you."

Nefe joined in and threw her arms around him. "Yes, we do." Her nose wrinkled at his smell, but she too tried to ignore it as she released him.

"But I will never be King. Why love me?" Tut looked up to Ankhesenpaaten with tears in his eyes.

"Because we *like* you!" Nefe said, and threw her hands in the air in exasperation.

Ankhesenpaaten nodded. "Because you are our friend and half-brother."

A smile appeared on his face, and he chuckled.

"Now, enough of this nonsense," Ankhesenpaaten said as they reached the Kap. "Enjoy your studies, Tut."

Nefe began to step inside the Kap, but remembered she was now ten years old and had to go with Ankhesenpaaten to the temple to be taught by the priests.

***

WHILE ON THEIR WAY TO THE TEMPLE, ANKHESENPAATEN stopped and thrust her arm in front of Nefe's chest, halting her in her tracks.

"What is it?" Nefe asked with wide eyes, searching for the cause of Ankhesenpaaten's sudden stop.

"Look." Ankhesenpaaten pointed at the figure walking along the route from the temple to the palace. "It's Mother."

"Why does she walk like that?" Nefe asked, taking note of

Nefertiti's tilted head, heavy arms, and frown. "That is not how Pharaoh Coregent should walk."

Nefe peered up to her older sister for a response, but Ankhesenpaaten only shook her head. She had only seen her mother once since Smenakre's Appearance of the King ceremony, and it was to check in and see how she and her siblings were coping with yet another member of their family journeying west. Nefertiti stopped and looked to the north and then to the south, lingering toward the south as a gentle breeze flew into her face. Ankhesenpaaten turned to Nefe and nodded her head toward their mother. Then they proceeded to come near to her.

Nefertiti didn't notice her daughters until Nefe's voice snapped her from her thoughts.

"In peace, Mother," Nefe greeted Nefertiti.

"Oh, my daughters!" Nefertiti smiled, but her eyes remained dim. She opened her arms and embraced them both, and as she released them she ran her fingers under their chins, lifting their faces to her. "Are you headed to your lessons in the temple?"

Nefe's excited jitters were almost contagious, and Ankhesenpaaten smiled as her sister said, "Yes! Today we are to learn the methods Pharaoh uses to mediate between the Aten and the people."

"Oh, is that all?" Nefertiti asked with a sudden droop of her eyelids.

"Yes, for today," Nefe said, and flipped her sidelock.

"How have you been since I last came to visit you?" Nefertiti asked, rubbing the tops of their arms.

"We have been fine," Ankhesenpaaten responded rather quickly. "How have you been, Mother?" She added, before she could stop herself, "You seem sad."

"I am sad, my daughter." Nefertiti looked her in the eyes.

"But I do not want to burden you with my thoughts. You mustn't be late. Hurry to the temple."

There existed in her words a frightening apathy.

Nefe began to walk, but Ankhesenpaaten stood her ground.

"Will you come to see us again?"

A hard beat of Nefertiti's heart weighed on her nerves. She had not been to see them much at all since she acted in Pharaoh's place, and now that Smenkare was on the throne, she felt torn. He was now murdering his own people to purge Egypt of its heresy, and yet her daughters needed her so they would not fall victim to the brainwashing of the Aten, as Meritaten had. Time eluded her. She kept telling herself, *I must deal with this now, my children can wait. I will teach them later*; and now, looking upon Ankhesenpaaten, with her woman's wig, time was a dwindling asset.

"Of course, Ankhesenpaaten." She wrapped her in her arms once more and squeezed. "I will come to see you again."

Nefertiti bid farewell to her daughters and watched them enter the temple at the end of the path. She looked to the south again, toward Nubia, and wondered if the commander would be back soon. Her mind produced bouts of worry, but she would shake them away one by one, telling herself men were killed in battle all the time; the commander was no different. But the more she tried to convince herself she felt nothing for him, the more she did. She had been counting the days since he'd left, and his one-and-a-half seasons were almost up.

The last message they had received stated that relations weren't going as well as planned. To add to her burdens, Ay's men in the north sent a message to Pharaoh that the Libyans had heard about the Nubians' advance and had decided they would test great Egypt. But the most disheartening message: almost three thousand executions had been ordered since

Smenkare's edict. The people's screams filled the air of Waset and Men-nefer, even while, from the palace at Aketaten, all seemed serene.

Her hands were tied—unless she considered another murder . . . and she couldn't bring herself to think on it.

Nefertiti looked out again to the north, and then to the south, not knowing who to talk to or what to do.

Ay emerged with Meritaten from the royal harem's library and headed to the main palace. He looked her way. They connected their gaze. She reasoned that her father would be a good person to talk to about the state of Egypt—but at the thought, her jaw locked. She still had not forgiven him, and with an upturn of her nose, she ignored him. Out of her peripheral vision, she saw him dip his chin.

It was still too soon.

As she watched Meritaten's long linen dress flow with the slight breeze in her walk alongside Ay, dread encroached upon Nefertiti's heart. She wondered how long before the People's Restoration of Egypt would come asking for royal blood again.

This time, though, the chief royal wife would not be empathetic to their cause.

11

THE TIME OF PROTECTION

ALMOST NINE MONTHS HAD PASSED SINCE SMENKARE'S coronation, and his military officers had dutifully carried out his edict. The people continued to cry out from the streets, but their cries went unheard—until Sitamun could no longer bear it.

Smenkare sat on his throne and peered down at the woman who had borne him life. As daughter and royal wife of Pharaoh Amenhotep III, Sitamun did not bow.

"My son," Sitamun began.

"You will address me as Pharaoh," Smenkare huffed.

"Pharaoh," Sitamun said, lifting her chin, but her gaze intently focused upon her son.

Smenkare, she thought, *you hurt me. I lived in isolation for you. Raised you in secrecy until our father passed. I taught you the truth, and yet you reject Amun-Re and order the blood of those who believe in Egypt's gods and goddesses.*

She spoke again with the same boldness she was taught at Malkata. "Why has the Defender of Egypt done this? Egypt's land calls out to its appointed king with the blood of its people, slain by his edict." She tilted her head; her heart rate remained calm, although it wanted to beat as fast as the crocodile attacks. *I did not raise a murderer. I did not raise a tyrant.* "Does my son not love Egypt?"

"I love Egypt, woman!" Smenkare shot up from his seated throne. "It is precisely that love which forces me to cleanse Egypt of its heretic ways! I am purging the false gods from the empire. My brother and Pharaoh gave me that for my legacy."

The calm cage she had placed around her heart began to fracture as she took a quick inhale to repair it and decided against chiding her son for not using her title. "Pharaoh Akhenaten was my brother and your half-brother," Sitamun said; her voice flowed smoothly like the Nile, yet her brow furrowed at her son's disrespect.

Do you remember nothing, child?! You let my brother taint your faith with his mad ramblings and visions. After all I taught you, after all the sleepless nights worrying over you and your future, you disregard all that I have done for you because you let a false prophet into your mind and heart, she thought.

Her lip trembled, whether in sorrow or rage, it did not matter. "I am your mother," she said, praying to Amun-Re he remembered their bond, "and your mother pleads for the lives of your people."

"Your pleas are in vain," Smenkare said, and he motioned for the guards, who came and flanked either side of Sitamun. "Through all my days with you, you lied to me. You never told me who my father was. You robbed me of my right to the throne. You made me worship the false god Amun, along with your other heretic ways, even under Pharaoh Akhenaten's direct order to abandon those beliefs."

Sitamun looked to each guard by her side before looking back to the throne. "Yes. Something you did gladly, Pharaoh!" Sitamun pointed to her son as if he were a child that needed scolding. *If only you understood the full truth, the full pain, the full embarrassment of our father, you would know why I hid this from you,* she wanted to say but instead said, "I never told you my father was your father because he ordered me to silence. He already had an heir to the throne. You wished me to break the command of a Pharaoh?"

"You did with Pharaoh Akhenaten, why not with Pharaoh Amenhotep?" Smenkare said. "My brother showed me the true way. He revealed to me the truths of my past, and you tried to cover them up—picking and choosing which laws and commands to obey, which laws best suited your beliefs! You are neither obedient nor loyal, and so I disown you!"

Sitamun's jaw clenched. *You murder your own mother with your words.* Her tongue felt dry in her mouth as her royal training began to fail her in the midst of his declaration. Her heart broke from its cage and raced toward the edge.

Mother and son each held their stare, seeing who would break first.

"You disown me?" Sitamun finally croaked out. "You disown me?!"

Her voice reverberated from the stone walls.

Smenkare held his shoulders back and lifted his chin. "Pharaoh does not repeat himself."

She ground her teeth until she thought her jaw might crack, then she blurted out, "Do you not see that Pharaoh Akhenaten was *mad?* The people are tired of this! Whisperings of rebellion fill the streets of Waset, Men-nefer, and, yes, even Aketaten!"

Smenkare blinked but held his stare as she continued.

"The people lost respect for Pharaoh Akhenaten, as they will you. He told you many truths that I was not allowed to tell you, yes, but my father was a hundred times the Pharaoh my brother ever was. The stench of Egypt's rot reaches our enemies, and now, because of you, they can even taste its people's blood flowing from the Nile into the sea."

Her breath became trapped under an angry weight resting on her chest as she stared at her son's stone face.

His monotonous reply filled the room. "They only taste the purge. Soon we will rise up greater than ever before."

"People only worship the Aten because they are afraid of the sword. Amun will always be the premier god of Egypt, and Amun will always be on the hearts of the people, even if their lips praise the Aten. Why, O Pharaoh, are the temples of Aten all but empty? Yet praises and offerings filled the temples of Amun every—"

"Watch your tongue, woman," Smenkare said. "We no longer speak of the false god."

Her thoughts raged: *You spit in the face of Amun, son, and you will meet the same fate. I will warn you one last time. Your arrogance and your false belief will be your downfall. You will have to kill me before I ever say Amun is a false god. If Egypt does not kill you first, you will end up reigning over a poor, small empire, and die at the hands of an invading enemy.*

But she narrowed her eyes and rolled her shoulders back to ready herself for one last attempt to plead for the people's lives and, indirectly, that of her son. "Pharaoh Amenhotep worshiped Amun. He was Amun's divinely appointed. My brother was supposed to go back to Amun after he regained the power and recouped the prestige from the priesthood of Amun, but he didn't and instead has bled Egypt dry. Work cannot be found. Egypt cannot pay for everyone to be a soldier when the economy dies! Trade routes are drying up. Everything our father built is almost dead. You and my brother turn your backs on Egypt. Please—"

"No more of this," Smenkare said. His shoulders had risen to his chin as she spoke. His cheeks burned with every word. "Your father's reign is over. His commands are no longer valid. *I* am Pharaoh, and my word is law. Any who disobey me shall be executed."

"I would follow my father's command to my last breath," Sitamun said, giving herself as the last test of this Pharaoh's sanity.

"Then so be it," Smenkare said, and he snapped his fingers.

The guards on either side of Sitamun grabbed her arms.

She had wagered her life and lost.

"Imprison her and prepare for her execution. She shall be made an example for all of Egypt at the celebration marking the first year of Pharaoh's appointment. No one is above the law of Pharaoh . . . not even his mother."

A FEW DAYS LATER, PAWAH AND BEKETATEN MET WITH Horemheb, who had just returned from Nubia, Ay, and Nefertiti, to discuss the growing problem on the throne.

"We must do something about Smenkare," Beketaten began once they were all seated in the council room—before the sun rose, so as not to draw suspicion from a passerby. "He has even imprisoned his own mother and sentenced her to execution." Beketaten's eyes raged. "Though he decided to let her stay in prison for a while to give her some time to change her ways." Beketaten's gaze fell upon Nefertiti. "Even Akhenaten saved you, his wife, from the torment of sitting in a cold, damp, stone-walled prison pit. Why should my sister be any different? This is your doing." She pointed a long finger at Nefertiti. "If only you had made Akhenaten drink his poison before he could name Smenkare as his successor, people would not be killed in the streets and a great royal wife would not be due for execution."

"To the benefit of Nefertiti," Pawah began as he placed a hand on Beketaten's shoulders and lowered her pointed finger. "How could we have known he, of all people, who was raised by us and Sitamun, would be so Aten-istic? There was no way we could have known."

"But he is on the throne now. Worse than Akhenaten, if I do say so," Horemheb said. His return had been recent, the relations in Nubia not going as expected. The General still fought in the Upper, but due to relations with the Libyans in the Lower, Smenkare had ordered Horemheb to withdraw his third back to Aketaten and to be ready to go either north to the Libyans or return south to the Nubians, depending on where the need was the most. "We cannot change what happened. We can only plan for the future. All blame should be set aside." He eyed Beketaten.

Nefertiti looked to the commander, glad he had made it back safely. She missed him. She hadn't laughed since he'd left.

"You didn't know, Coregent?" Beketaten asked. "You spent all this time in the palace, and you didn't know about your own daughter and her husband? You are a horrible mother! Why didn't you teach your children?"

Horemheb put his hand up to silence her as Ay sat in the corner of the room with his arms crossed, unmoving. Nefertiti silently thanked Amun that Horemheb would stand up for her, even if her father wouldn't.

"The past is the past," Horemheb said.

Beketaten pointed her finger again. "This is *her* fault!"

"She was busy trying to patch your brother's mistakes!" Horemheb said with a sharp tone.

Nefertiti let out a deep breath as she watched her father in the corner. She knew he agreed with Beketaten . . . so then where was he as she went to kill her husband? He was supposed to protect his *lotus blossom*, but he had failed—just like he was failing her now in this room.

Horemheb came to her aid. His deep voice reverberated about the room as Beketaten's shrills overtook them—back and forth until Nefertiti stood up and looked at the two of them.

"*I* take responsibility for this," Nefertiti said, and threw her hands up. "Any great leader accepts failures as well as victories."

Her stab at Beketaten worked: the insinuation of her lack of leadership caused Beketaten's eye to twitch.

"Then correct your mistake. Correct the throne," Beketaten muttered.

Nefertiti brought her hands to her sides and released the tension in her neck by rubbing her thumb over the sides of her fingers. She could see Ay look at her, perhaps trying to read her reaction to this proposal.

"*Correct* it? Smenkare is young. He has many years left," Nefertiti said, dodging the weight behind the suggestion. Yet again, she didn't like where this was going.

"Coregent, Egypt won't survive many years," Horemheb said with pinched eyes and a half-grimace.

Nefertiti felt the stab of truth in her heart for his agreement with their common enemy. At least it appeared he didn't like where this was headed either. Her brow furrowed as fear of having to murder again crossed her mind. Her soul smiled when Horemheb seemed to read her mind with his next comment:

"But Pawah was the father Smenkare never had." Horemheb threw his head in Pawah's direction. "Perhaps *Pawah* should correct his own mistake."

Pawah narrowed his eyes at Horemheb and sneered, slowly crossing his arms over his chest.

"Well," Ay said, shaking his head, "something has to be done. Corruption is prevalent throughout the Aten priesthood, the military, the people. Starvation and poverty sweep Egypt's streets like the plague. The treasury reserve is almost gone . . . and then we will not be able to pay the troops, our last hope of survival."

"You will have a rebellion before then. I guarantee it," Pawah said. "If you want to not be counted as one of the targeted, I suggest you do something more immediate." His eyebrows arched over his eyes.

"Why don't *you* do it, '*Vizier* of the Upper'?" Nefertiti felt satisfaction when she saw that her comment caught him by surprise. "*You* will be targeted as well, Pawah."

"No," he said. "The people think I have only accepted this position to get close to Pharaoh. I will be safe from my own rebellion. But you see, I have not told them *you* are a true worshipper of Amun. They believe you are a follower of the Aten. And until I do, you will do what I say." He popped his knuckles and leaned back, smug in his victory. "Get rid of Smenkare."

"I do not have Smenkare's trust as I did with Akhenaten," Nefertiti said. "He trusts *you* more than he does me!" She pointed her finger at him, wanting to slap that grin from his face. She was Coregent; she had spent years building her name throughout Egypt and that of her allies. Nefertiti held much power, and yet this man held her life in his hands.

"Is your daughter for Amun or the Aten?" he asked pointedly. "Use Meritaten. He trusts her the most, as she is his only wife. We will even provide the hemlock, as we did with you."

"You shall not turn my daughter into a murderer!" Nefertiti shot a glare at Ay, whose shoulders shrank back. "That was my burden, as it is also my burden of having a daughter who worships the Aten because I did not teach her well enough."

"So you *did* know about Smenkare and Meritaten!" Beketaten thrust her finger toward Nefertiti a third time. "And yet you did nothing?! You liar! You enabler!"

"What was I to do? I didn't know he would name Smenkare as his successor. I thought his *son* would be the next Pharaoh. After all, he betrayed my bed to produce him —no thanks to you and Henuttaneb, you scheming demons! May Ammit devour your hearts!"

"Do not talk ill of the dead!" Beketaten's hands balled into fists.

Nefertiti remembered Henuttaneb's cold lifeless body on the floor after she birthed Tutankhaten. She knew Henuttaneb's heart was pure, only having been manipulated by Beketaten, and would not be eaten by Ammit in the afterlife. About her own, however, she often wondered.

Nefertiti's cheeks burned. "*You* were the one who got him drunk and enabled his obsessions by putting those visions in his head. *You* are the liar! You told me it was Kiya's doing! You took away my only friend, you miserable wretch!" Nefertiti's red cheeks burned up the tears she held back, remembering Kiya, at her last breath, telling her she was thankful Nefertiti was her friend, even though she had treated her so horribly after considering believing Beketaten's lies of Kiya sneaking off with Akhenaten and orchestrating the plan to bring a drunk Akhenaten his wives to further his chance for an heir.

"You—" Beketaten started.

"You could have killed him then, after Tutankhaten was born, but you left Aketaten like a coward, leaving me to believe Kiya betrayed me! Why did you not kill him then, Beketaten? Did you not wish to dirty your hands?" Nefertiti's pulse pounded in her ears and behind her eyes.

Ay's mouth twisted into a frown at his daughter's pain, and he closed his eyes, wishing her life had been with Thutmose instead. Horemheb stood unflinching, facing Beketaten and Pawah, standing behind every word of Nefertiti.

Pawah spoke at his wife's silence, his voice quiet. "She did not know how to kill Pharaoh Akhenaten," he responded. "We apologize for the inconvenience it caused you, but at the time, Akhenaten needed a male heir, and you only produced daughters."

Nefertiti gritted her teeth. She hoped one day they would find hemlock in *their* wine. "She took joy in watching my agony."

"Because you sent me into exile. *Exile!* We starved for years and . . ." Beketaten trailed off and looked between Pawah and Nefertiti, the end of her sentence unspoken—*and my husband desires you*—before she continued in a different direction. "You left me to die in a foreign land. You stripped away my title as King's Daughter!"

Nefertiti slammed her hand on the table. "I did no such thing! Your brother and mother wanted to kill you for treason —impalement in front of the temple! I *saved* you!"

Beketaten swallowed. Her skin flushed. "You speak ill of my late mother too? You liar . . . I hate you."

"Believe what you wish." Nefertiti shrugged her shoulders, throwing off her rage; she was done playing their games. "You will find a way to get rid of Smenkare, or I will tell the people that I witnessed the Vizier of the Upper devoting his life to the Aten by putting to death hundreds of worshippers of Amun—even some in front of me in the great hall. Since I am deemed to be a follower of the Aten, what reason would I have to lie about these happenings?"

Pawah's grin fell. "The people would believe *me*." His voice contained confidence, but his eyes held concern.

"Would they?" Nefertiti snorted. "False witness can go both ways, Vizier of the Upper."

Pawah tilted his head toward Nefertiti. "Well played, Coregent." Her power and wit struck in him a familiar chord of desire.

Some moments of silence passed as the four of them stared at each other. It was finally broken as Ay spoke.

"Then we are at an impasse?"

"No," Pawah replied. "I will see to it that Smenkare is removed from the throne. *I* don't mind dirtying my hands." He shuffled his hands together as an unnerving smile crossed his face.

"Don't enjoy it too much," Nefertiti said.

"I am willing to do whatever it takes to see power returned to the throne and Egypt. With Smenkare gone, *you* will be Pharaoh, Coregent Neferneferuaten . . . but we must act quickly before he names another his successor or removes you from his succession."

Pawah suppressed a smile. He had already planned to tell the people a woman Pharaoh is no Pharaoh after she succeeded Smenkare. Then she would be forced to marry Tut, whom he would kill, and then she would have to marry *him*, Pawah, the last living male royalty. The crown would be his. He rocked back on his heels and lifted his chin.

Nefertiti cringed at the name her husband gave her, but said nothing, because he at least used her title with respect. It was more than she would be able to garner from Beketaten.

Horemheb chimed in, leaning over the table toward Pawah and Beketaten. "You might be willing to do whatever it takes, but you must make Smenkare's journey west look like an accident."

"Agreed," Ay said with a tilt of his head.

"Of course, Commander and Master of Pharaoh's Horses," Pawah said, sneering. "I don't want to tarnish the position of Pharaoh. Future rulers are depending on his divine status." He thrust out his chest, envisioning himself on the throne. His plan was so clear now. He could almost taste his victory.

"And Pawah, you mustn't harm Meritaten," Nefertiti added. "She is not Coregent. She poses no threat."

Pawah and Beketaten nodded in agreement, and she nodded back, wondering what plan they would implement to kill Smenkare. Looking at her hand, she saw a little scar from where she had hit Horemheb almost a year prior, and suddenly remembered his words.

Am I reopening the same wound?

AY TOUCHED HIS DAUGHTER'S SHOULDER AFTER THEY LEFT the council room. Nefertiti knew his touch from anywhere, and she paused before turning to face him.

"My lotus blossom," he began as he looked to the floor. "I'm sorry this has happened."

"You were supposed to protect me," Nefertiti whispered, feeling her heart shrink inside her chest. "And yet you coaxed me into the lion's den and let me fend for myself. You've only continued to do the same today."

"You held your own." Ay raised his chin. "I did what I thought best for Egypt."

"What about your daughter? What about your family?" Nefertiti snapped, and she felt the sting that came with her father's lack of apology for again not standing up for her, not protecting her yet again.

"What about *your* family?" Ay cocked his head and wrinkled his forehead. "They would have been slaughtered in the pending rebellion, and if you had done it that night—" Ay drew in his breath.

"I know, Father. If I had killed him when I was supposed to . . ." Nefertiti trailed off and clenched her jaw. She shook her head, then found his eyes again. "Would you have killed Temehu? Would you have done the same if the roles were reversed?"

Ay's jaw dropped ever so slightly, and Nefertiti knew that

memories of his wife were flooding his mind. He had always told Nefertiti that her laugh mimicked Temehu's and that he missed it so. Her laugh made his heart whole.

"I don't know what I would have done," he finally said.

"Then don't pass judgment on me," she responded and pushed his shoulder to move him out of her way.

"I am not," Ay said as she walked past him.

"My lotus blossom," he called after her, but she rounded the corner.

⋙───⋘

As the sun began to sink, Horemheb found Nefertiti walking alone in the corridors, and smiled. He had feigned walking with a purpose around the palace, hoping to catch her alone.

He had managed to push her to the very back of his mind during his battles with the Nubians, but most nights, she would surface again. He often wondered how she would receive him when he came home. He had seen her watching him leave, so she must have seen him glance back at her.

Would his absence cause her to forget him or miss him?

He tried to keep thinking of Amenia when he thought of Nefertiti, because Amenia was his wife, but he had only seen her a handful of times in the past years. They wrote letters every now and then, but she was more of his head household steward than a wife or even a lover. He tried to imagine himself with her instead of Nefertiti, but he found his thoughts drifting back to Nefertiti and the way she had looked that night in the lotus garden. With Amenia, there only existed a mutual admiration of friendship between them. On her part, she admired him for not divorcing her and making known her infertility; he, in turn, admired her for not divorcing him for his absence.

But with Nefertiti, there was a longing in his heart.

He knew he should not entertain any interest in the Pharaoh Coregent, but she allured him. After the council meeting, he had nodded to her and had seen that Ay wanted to speak to his daughter, so he went on his way to let them talk. But his curiosity about her possible feelings toward him kept him walking about the palace throughout the day. He needed to know, so he could put to bed his thoughts; and if he found she did miss him, then, well, he would deal with it if it happened.

"The Pharaoh Coregent really should not be walking alone without an escort. There could be persons about who wish harm to her," he said while walking behind Nefertiti.

Her heart fluttered at the deep tone in his voice. Wetting her lips and thanking Amun for his safe delivery home, she said, "Perhaps I just needed some time to reflect," and peered over her shoulder. She had spent the greater of the last two seasons convincing herself she felt nothing for Horemheb, but at his footsteps behind her and the way he defended her in the council room earlier that day, she realized her toes and fingers tingled with excitement that he was home.

"Would Pharaoh Coregent prefer continuing her solitude?" He held his distance, in case her actions toward him before he left for war were only moments of weakness during a difficult time. The thought brought about a suspended disappointment that hung over his head.

She spun around to face him. "No," she whispered breathlessly. Her arms wanted so badly to wrap around his neck; she was so happy to see he was alive and well.

Horemheb smiled, finally letting go of the conditions he had put on his thoughts toward her. He watched the freshly lit torchlights dance in her eyes as the tension in his shoulders dissipated.

"I am glad you made it back to Aketaten." She tried to

hide the slight tremor in her hands. She clenched her jaw and attempted to quiet the flutter of her heart and the shakiness of her breathing.

"As am I," he said, and took a step toward her—a small step, yet still outside of his status.

"You were gone longer than one and a half seasons' time." She took a step toward him as well. His musky scent filled her airways, vividly evoking in her memories that had begun to fade over those seasons of absence.

"Yes . . . it took longer than expected to secure our border." He wanted to stroke her face and arms and tell her he missed her so. To keep himself from leaping outside of his status, every muscle in his arms and chest tightened.

Nefertiti's eyes followed the strain of his muscle fiber in his shoulders down to his biceps, but snapped to his face when she realized her eyes wandered. "Do you . . . did you leave . . ." Her words jumbled in her head as she tried to focus her thoughts, and she tried again. "Did you leave General Paaten in a good position?"

Horemheb suddenly stiffened, looking beyond her.

"Yes. The General should have the border secured within the year."

"That is good news." Nefertiti paused as she heard footsteps from behind.

A moment of silence came as a servant passed by. They did not know what to say to each other to keep wandering ears from reading too much into their conversation.

She looked to the floor, suddenly realizing her thoughts had been in vain. There would never be a chance she could ever be with Horemheb. She looked back up at him, reliving all the sleepless nights she told herself she was not attracted to him. *He is a friend,* she had thought, and she thought it again now; and as her mind cleared from the rush that accompanied his presence, the events of the day came back to her—along with the doubts of the plan to rid Egypt of Smenkare.

He saw her head drop and knew she thought the same: their status would keep them apart forever. He closed his eyes and took a deep breath, disheartened at the sudden dismissal of their excitement.

"Commander?" she asked, resolving her feelings toward him—at least for the moment. "May I ask you a question?"

"Always, my Pharaoh Coregent," he said, opening his eyes.

"Do you think me a fool, placing my daughter's safety in *their* hands?" she asked, hoping her wording to be cryptic enough to anyone who might overhear.

"They know you will not sit idly by if something happens to her," Horemheb told her.

"You didn't answer my question," Nefertiti said, shaking her head. "Am I a fool?"

Horemheb hesitated.

Nefertiti's brow contorted. "Be frank."

He studied her. Seeing how poorly she dealt and was dealing with her hand in Akhenaten's demise, another might tear her down completely; but if it were his daughter, he would do anything to guarantee her safety. He also knew Smenkare was not ill in the mind, unlike his predecessor, and it would be near impossible for anyone without a close relationship to him to get rid of him. If she were to be found out, it would spell disorder for the position of Pharaoh. Pawah was clearly the best choice.

"No, my Pharaoh Coregent," he said, and shook his head. "Never a fool."

She examined him for any sign of a lie, but found none; she let out a sigh of relief. "Thank you."

Horemheb knew he should drop the subject there, but he wasn't ready to let go of his nights dreaming of her. He added, "You are at an advantage."

She paused. "What do you mean?"

"You are able to ask me questions and know if I am truthful or not . . . but if I were to ask you a question, I would not know the truthfulness of your response." His tone turned into a playful, serious banter.

"Well, maybe you should learn to control your tell," she said, and smiled teasingly.

Horemheb chuckled and shook his head.

Nefertiti peered up at him. "What questions would you ask me, Commander?"

Horemheb took that as a sign she was not ready to give up on them either. But he wasn't quite ready to ask her the questions he held in his mind. "Many questions"—he smirked —"but perhaps for another time."

"How long are you in Aketaten? Perhaps another time can come soon . . . ?"

Horemheb's face fell. "Pharaoh has ordered me to leave with my divisions for the Libyan border in the morning."

She closed her eyes and let out a sigh. "But you just got back . . . for how long?"

"I do not know, Pharaoh Coregent. I must assess that when I get there."

"Please send a letter," Nefertiti said.

It was an odd request, since he would be sending a messenger to Pharaoh Smenkare already, but she wanted to know outside of the Pharaoh. And, to her surprise, he said he would oblige.

They stood in silence for another few moments as another servant passed by.

When they could no longer hear his footsteps, Nefertiti placed her hand on Horemheb's arm and said, "Promise me, Commander . . . promise you will come back."

Horemheb grinned, loving the touch of her on his body, and decided to step outside his place again. He loved her smile, and thought another fun comment would lift the weight of the situation. "I will fight like my life depends on it."

A half smile, followed by a slight narrowing of her eyes. "Don't play," she chided, and dropped her arm, looking around to make sure no one saw her. "I need you—" She bit her lip, debating if she should finish her sentence. "You are one of my council whom I value very much." Her eyes searched him.

I wish her eyebrow twitched when she lied, he thought. *It would be easier to read her . . . but nevertheless, I cannot court her, and so I shouldn't talk to her as if I am courting her. I should be standing behind her. I shouldn't even be this close to her. She is Pharaoh Coregent!*

"My apologies," he said, and straightened up as another servant passed by. "I will make a promise to fight and strategize, in order to bring home myself and as many men as I can."

Nefertiti nodded. "Very well, Commander. Thank you."

"I only do as I am commanded," he responded.

The servant's footsteps disappeared down the hallway.

"There is no other reason you wish to come back to Aketaten?"

"There is," he said. *And the reason is you,* he thought.

They shared a moment of looking into each other's eyes, trying to read each other's truth.

Nefertiti decided not to press him further. "Fight well." A soft tone accompanied her words.

"We shall," he responded and bowed his head.

"I will be expecting your letter."

"I will send it as soon as I know the duration," he said as he began to walk past her. They kept each other's gaze. "I shall return, my Pharaoh Coregent."

She held her chin up and pressed her lips together,

wanting to say more, but instead, she merely wished him well as she watched him walk off down the corridor.

"I shall miss you, Horemheb," she whispered.

He smiled, hearing the soft echo of her whisper on the stone walls. He did not turn around but only thought, *I shall miss you too*.

12

THE TIME OF SECRETS

A MONTH AFTER HOREMHEB LEFT FOR LIBYA, NEFERTITI summoned her stepmother and half-sister to her room and sat them down.

"What is wrong, my daughter?" Tey asked as Mut looked to Nefertiti.

She shook her head, not wanting to confess to the political conspiracies she had agreed to on top of already admitting to them her hand in Akhenaten's death.

Tey sat patiently waiting for Nefertiti to speak as she watched her wrestle with her thoughts. Mut leaned her elbows on her knees and placed her hands over her mouth as she held back her questions.

"Violence begets violence," Nefertiti started. Her hands lay clasped in her lap as she twirled her thumbs.

"Pharaoh Smenkare?" Tey asked.

Nefertiti drew in a deep breath, closed her eyes, and nodded.

"And Meritaten?" Tey's voice tightened, like flesh experiencing a chilly breeze after bathing.

Nefertiti's shoulders rolled back as she sat up straight in

her chair. "I will not let them hurt my daughter, no matter her beliefs. But I can do nothing for Smenkare. He sealed his own fate with the slaughter of those still loyal to Amun— even his own family."

"Yes, we heard about his mother," Tey said in barely a whisper. "When is she to be executed?"

"At the close of this season, when the Aten begins to give more light in the day. It will mark the first year of his coronation. He believes it will have special meaning to his vision for Egypt." Nefertiti shook her head and sighed. "His own mother. Oh, the nonsense Akhenaten must have filled his head with . . . and I can't bear to think about my poor Meritaten."

"Are you sure they will not harm her?" Tey asked again, wringing her hands in her lap. Then, answering her own question: "Ay will make sure."

Nefertiti huffed. "Yes, I'm sure Father will protect her." She bit her tongue; anger steamed in the back of her throat, venting through her nostrils. "Mother, he sat there during the entire meeting with Pawah and Beketaten and said *nothing*. He let them attack me like vicious dogs. I defended *my* family —a skill long forgotten by Ay, Master of Pharaoh's Horses. Perhaps his title has too long gone to his head."

Tey held up a finger to chide her daughter. "Nefertiti, do not speak of your father in that way."

Even as the mighty Coregent of Egypt, Nefertiti still felt the burn on her cheeks from Tey's scolding.

"What about Commander Horemheb? Is he for this as well?" Mut asked, clutching her hands, quivering. She hoped to Amun he had no part.

"Everyone was in agreement save General Paaten. I don't know where he stands in all of this. He carries out Pharaoh Smenkare's law, but I know he does not believe in it." Nefertiti looked to the ceiling as she drew in a sharp breath.

Mut's face fell somewhat at this.

"Why the frown?" Nefertiti asked Mut, suddenly bitter. "Did you think your commander mightier than me?" A bitter laugh slipped from her lips, remembering the night when he and her father talked her into becoming a murderer.

"I had hoped . . ." Mut muttered.

"You still have another year, maybe two, before you are of the age to marry. Think about loving younger men, sister."

"What?" Mut sucked in her breath and sat up straight. "I don't know what you mean."

Nefertiti nodded at her and bit her lip. It felt nice to tease her little sister and not have to think about the political power play at hand, but Tey wouldn't let it last for much longer.

"Daughter, you have to warn Meritaten that they are coming for Smenkare," Tey said as she looked to both girls to hush them.

"Why?" Nefertiti said. "Meritaten is safe—that is all that matters. They gave us their word. They might cross *me*, but not all three of us."

"The people . . . if they found out you knew and did nothing, they might think you wanted Smenkare out of the way, as you are Coregent and he has no heir." Tey wrung her hands and shook her head.

"Mother, you worry as much as I do."

"Well, I *am* the one who raised you," Tey said with a smile on her lips but concern in her brow. "At least *warn* Meritaten. I don't know what I would do if she were killed too."

"Mother!" Nefertiti bit her tongue, spotting her mother's subtle manipulation tricks like the snake spots the mouse. Her heart couldn't take another of her daughters being ripped from her life; but Ay and Horemheb were there—they wouldn't cross the both of them. Meritaten was Ay's granddaughter too, after all.

"They might go back to worshipping Amun if they knew their lives were in danger," Mut suggested. "I could even talk to Meritaten about it while I'm here. She did always like me."

"Mut, Smenkare ordered *his own mother's execution* just for speaking Amun's name. You must not say 'Amun' elsewhere, lest you befall the same fate. Do not wager your life for this. Sitamun did, and now she will lose it," Nefertiti warned.

Mut opened her mouth to speak, but Nefertiti cut her off.

"Mut, please. I beg you. Do not ask them to worship Amun. Do not go to Meritaten. She is confused. I don't know what she would do . . . but if Smenkare knew, he would kill you without any hesitation."

Mut hung her head. "So you are just going to trust the People's Restoration of Egypt to be true to their word and not harm Meritaten?"

Nefertiti closed her eyes.

Am I coward? A fool? Afraid for my own life more than that of my firstborn? she thought.

"Yes," she answered both Mut's and her own questions. "I am trusting my daughter's life to the rebellion."

Tey shook her head.

"Mother, I know I disappoint you in many ways. Please don't confirm it for me," Nefertiti begged.

Tey looked away as she clenched her jaw. "We best be leaving, Mut. The Coregent has no more need of us." She stood, popped her hands on her thighs haughtily, and turned to leave, not looking back.

Nefertiti didn't look up as she walked by. She knew this disappointment ran deep. Their trip to Aketaten was to comfort her in her sorrow of losing her steward, Merytre, and they had stayed for over a year. In that time, her mother and sister found her to be a murderer, a weakling, and a traitor. She guessed she would be disappointed too, if she weren't living through it.

Mut slowly stood up. She went to Nefertiti, who still looked down, and put her hand on her shoulder.

"Sister, I still love you."

Nefertiti let out a breath as she took Mut's hand in hers. Her misty eyes found her sister's.

"I love you too. Be better than me, Mut."

The door closed as they left Nefertiti alone in her room.

She stood up and walked over to the window; the sun warmed her face. Despondent, she looked to the sun, the Aten, wondering if Akhenaten was there, like he'd believed he would be, along with the Pharaohs before.

"Your legacy was supposed to be of greatness, my love . . . to restore Pharaoh as the true First Prophet of Amun, gaining strength from the priesthood . . . and yet only turmoil lays behind you as Egypt moves toward destruction," Nefertiti whispered as she looked out the window toward Akhe-Aten.

There were no tears in her eyes.

"What have you done?"

NEFERTITI RECEIVED WORD FROM HOREMHEB, SAYING HE thought it may be another season before the Libyans could be settled.

Sitamun may be dead by then, Nefertiti thought in despair. Then: *No . . . Beketaten would not let that happen. They would do away with Smenkare before that.*

She read his note—scribbled by his messenger, no doubt —as she lay in her bed, unable to sleep, like the many nights before.

> *In peace, Pharaoh Coregent. The situation with the Libyans appears*
> *less than that with the Nubians. I, Commander Horemheb, expect,*
> *at most, one season's time to settle this dispute.*

That was his letter.

Her heavy sigh filled the room. *It would seem odd if he put anything else, if the messenger read it, or the letter got intercepted,* she reasoned with herself.

Shaking her head and pressing her fingers to her temples, she closed her eyes. Her mind ran a never-ending race with everything that happened around her: Akhenaten's murder, Smenkare's assassination plot, the safety of her daughter, her feelings for Horemheb that she tried and failed to deny, this letter devoid of any feeling, the people being slain for their faith, the border disputes with the Nubians and Libyans . . .

The only reason they would rise up is because they perceive Egypt to be weak, she thought, and then her mind continued to race.

. . . the non-responsive Hittites, her father's lies, the ease with which royalty seemed to be murdered, her upcoming coronation once Smenkare was gone . . .

Would the people rebel? Would they come after me? Anyone who sat by Pharaoh? Anyone associated to me? Meritaten. Ankhesenpaaten and Tut . . .

She didn't like the boy, but also didn't want to see him harmed. Wanting to keep them safe, she decided to go to the royal harem and tell Ankhesenpaaten that when she was Pharaoh, she would distance herself out of necessity.

Outside her room stood Ineni, the royal guard. She asked him to escort her to the royal harem, remembering Horemheb's caution: there were people about who wished harm to Pharaoh and his Coregent. At least Ineni knew she was not an Aten worshipper, as he had been present when the People's Restoration of Egypt sent her to murder Akhenaten. She justified that he would honor his oath for her since they were at least of the same belief that Amun should be the premier god of Egypt.

Then why does sleep still elude me?

She came to Ankhesenpaaten's room, opened the door,

and watched her daughter sleep. Sneaking over to the bed, she sat on its side and rubbed Ankhesenpaaten's back, humming a song she remembered Tey humming to her when she was a child.

Ankhesenpaaten woke up and rolled to her side, looking up at Nefertiti.

"Mother?" She rubbed her eyes. "What are you doing here?"

"My daughter," Nefertiti said, holding her breath. But words escaped her, and instead of speaking, she just threw her arms around her daughter's small frame.

"Mother, what is it?"

Nefertiti could feel Ankhesenpaaten's heart racing.

"Is all well?"

"Yes, it will be." Nefertiti squeezed and stroked her daughter's back. She kissed the side of her forehead. Nefertiti pulled back to look at her daughter's face. She had her father's lips and long nose, but her high cheekbones and dark almond eyes belonged to Nefertiti.

Ankhesenpaaten took a breath. "What do you mean?"

Nefertiti shook her head. "I mean this: when I become Pharaoh, it will be dangerous for me." Tears filled her eyes, not wanting to lose yet another daughter. She rubbed Ankhesenpaaten's head. "It will be best for you if I distance you from me." She used her thumb to wipe under Ankhesenpaaten's eyes. "I will place you and Tut below Pharaoh's throne, on the lowest platform, for your own safety."

"I don't know what you mean, Mother. How . . ." She stuttered and held her mother's forearms. "How do you know you will be Pharaoh?"

"My sweet one . . ." Nefertiti pulled her close and kissed her forehead again. "There is much you will not understand right now."

"Mother, are you crying?"

"No," Nefertiti lied. She wished she could tell Ankhesenpaaten everything, but with her faith, she may betray her own mother to Smenkare. Instead, she just pleaded: "Ankhesenpaaten, no matter what happens, please know I have always wanted the best for you. I have always fought and did what I did for you and your sisters' safety."

"Mother, you are frightening me," Ankhesenpaaten said, and reciprocated her mother's hug. "Is all well?"

"It will be, my sweet one," Nefertiti crooned, and rocked with her now-grown baby in her arms. "It will be."

MUT FOUND HERSELF RESTLESS THAT NIGHT.

She looked to her mother, Tey, whose soft snores meant sleep had taken her. Mut turned to her side and swung both feet to the ground. She needed to do *something*, but wasn't sure what it should be. The cold stone made her toes curl as she stood, slipping into her sandals. She began to walk out of their guest quarters, but she heard Tey's voice.

"Mut, where are you going?"

Even in sleep, her mother knew her. Perhaps she was louder than she'd thought she had been.

"I need to tell Meritaten," Mut said. "It is the right thing to do."

Tey sat up in bed and glanced at Mut in the moonlight. "It is almost morning. She probably is not even awake yet. Come back to bed."

"I have thought on this all night. She needs to know," Mut whispered, turning her body away from the bed.

"I agree, Mut, but if Nefertiti thinks she will not listen—"

"We have to try."

"We will try in the morning." Tey yawned. "Come back to bed. They aren't going to do anything so quickly."

"How do you know?"

"Men like that must think it through strategically. No one is going to come in the middle of the night and stab them to death." Tey patted the empty space next to her. "Come to sleep. They are safe for tonight."

Mut obeyed; but when Tey's soft snores resurfaced, she quickly left the room and snuck away. She waited outside Meritaten's door as a servant went in to request her presence with Meritaten.

"She will see you," the servant said. "Be careful, young woman."

The whisper was low, and caused Mut to swallow the lump sitting in her throat. She couldn't tell if it was a threat or a genuine note of caution.

Mut watched the servant as she opened the door and led Mut into Meritaten's parlor of her bedchambers.

"Pharaoh is still sleeping," Meritaten said in a hushed voice as she yawned. "Mut, what is this about?"

"Pharaoh's life is in danger," Mut said.

Meritaten's face dropped, but then she shook her head. "Pharaoh's life is always in danger. Our enemies would smite him if they could."

"No, *Egypt* wants him gone. They are going to poison him because he follows in the footsteps of Akhenaten," Mut whispered.

A moment of silence came from Meritaten.

"You should be careful of what you say, Mut." Meritaten leaned over and put both of her hands on Mut's shoulders. "This isn't the place for made-up stories."

"But, Meritaten, I am not—"

"Mut, silence. I'll hear no more of it."

"The conspiracy, Meritaten. It's real, and Pharaoh's life is in danger. Yours might be as well."

"And how do you know all of this, Mut?"

"I overheard someone talking," Mut lied, and immediately felt the lie sink and gurgle its way down to her stomach; but she had to protect Nefertiti.

Meritaten's shoulders rose with a slight chuckle. "And who was speaking these words of rebellion?"

"I . . . don't know." Mut's eyes dropped to the floor.

"Oh, silly girl, with vivid dreams and imaginations." Meritaten patted her soft cheek. "If there were a conspiracy afoot, the Aten would have granted Pharaoh a vision."

"But the Aten is just a sun-disc, an aspect of Amun-Re," Mut whispered, to which Meritaten grabbed her jaw.

"You will not speak of false gods, Mut, or you will meet the same fate as those who do. Be this your only warning," Meritaten said and shook Mut's jaw before letting go.

Mut rubbed her jaw and took a step backward.

"Now," Meritaten said as she stretched her hands to the sky and arched her back. "Was there anything else?"

"No," Mut replied.

She had tried, and that was all she could do. Nefertiti was right. Thankful Smenkare was not there to hear her utter Amun's name, she took a half bow and requested to be excused.

Meritaten nodded. The servant, who had been standing not far off and heard the entire conversation, came to Mut and escorted her out, peering down at her with narrowed eyes.

Meritaten watched from the corner of her eye as Mut left, then muttered:

"Silly girl."

13

THE TIME OF SCORN

THE NIGHT BEFORE SITAMUN'S EXECUTION, THE COUNTRY
went to sleep wondering if Pharaoh Smenkare would actually
have his mother, the royal wife and daughter of Pharaoh
Amenhotep III, consume poison to end her life. And if so,
would he give her a proper burial so she could at least have
her body to journey to the afterlife?

During the three months she had been there, the prison's
stone pit had blistered Sitamun's body from the glare of each
day's sun and chilled her body at night. Other pits may have
had multiple prisoners, but Sitamun sat alone in one of the
deep pits of the prison. Her nails bled from having tried to
climb out and her feet and hands had callused from the
stone's edges. Looking up to the wooden grid that lay atop
the pit, a heavyset weight fell upon her heart.

*There is no way out. Even if I made it all the way, I could not lift
or squeeze through the bars.*

She shook her head and prayed to Amun that her son
would spare her life. The sun's shadow on the pit's stone walls
grew as it lowered in the sky. Her teeth ached from grinding
them as she agonized over her upcoming execution.

A hushed tone came from above as the wooden grid lifted:

"Great royal wife?"

The voice broke her trance, and she looked up out of the pit.

A rope fell.

"Grab it," the voice came again from above.

She took hold as she was instructed, and slowly, she began to lift from the ground as those above pulled her up. They helped her stand from the pit. A servant stood with clean linen and water for Sitamun to wash her face and hands. She looked to him and to the four jailers who had apparently helped her break free from prison.

"I thank you for saving my life," she said. "I am in your debt."

"Great royal wife, no debt is required," one jailer said.

"When they come in the morning and I am not down there"—Sitamun nodded toward her pit—"they will kill you, as is Egyptian law."

"Only me," a second jailer said. "This pit is under my purview. My life is a sacrifice I am willing to make to see Sitamun, great royal wife and King's daughter, not executed for worshipping the true premier god, Amun."

"No more blood shall be shed," Sitamun said as she washed her hands in the bowl. Pressing the linen to her face, she inhaled its fresh scent. With her exhale, she lowered the linen to look the five of them in the eyes. "I will correct my father's mistake." She handed the towel to the servant and told a guard, "Hand me your dagger." Receiving the dagger from the guard, she analyzed its blade. "Has this been sharpened?"

"Every day," the guard responded with a nod.

"Then it shall do," she said as she walked between the guards, who parted for her royalty.

"Hori and Khabek are standing guard at Pharaoh's chambers. They love Amun as well," the second jailer said.

She nodded and let out a breath.

One obstacle removed. Amun blesses my course of action.

"You are to speak of this to no one." She peered over her shoulder, then turned to look at them. "If any rise up with me, if any doubt the position of Pharaoh, let them know this: the title of Pharaoh is divinely appointed by Amun, and any Pharaoh who rejects Amun is no longer divine. Killing him, then, is like killing any other man. My blood runs through his body—let his slaying be on me. I brought him into this world, and I alone have the right—nay, the duty—to remove him, now that he has refused his divine appointment." Her chin raised to those standing before her, and they bowed their heads.

"As you command, King's great wife," one of the guards said. "We will do as you command."

"I will take whatever punishment there is for taking a life. It shall be recompense for my mistakes as a mother." She turned to go, hiding the dagger in the folds of her long linen and gold-lined dress, which was covered in dirt and bodily stains from being imprisoned for so long.

"We are in your debt, great royal wife Sitamun," the servant called after her.

THE ROYAL GUARDS, HORI AND KHABEK, STOOD SENTRY AT the door of Pharaoh's bedchambers. They peered into the darkness around them and saw the moonlight glint off a woman's white gown. The stench reached them before they saw her face.

"Is that . . . ?" Hori whispered to the other.

"I think so," Khabek responded.

As Sitamun approached them, they tried not to retch or cover their noses.

"Great royal wi—"

"Yes, it is I, Sitamun, great royal wife and King's daughter," she said.

Her bloodshot eyes stared them down, daring them to sound the alarm that she had escaped from prison; but instead they held their silence.

"What brings you to us?" Hori asked.

"It does not concern you. You will move aside, and you will not enter until morning light," Sitamun said to them, and let her hand fall to her side—her hand that held a knife in the folds of her dress.

Hori peered down at the knife in her hand, tilted his head in her direction, and sidestepped the door, giving his approval. "As you command."

Khabek opened the door for her, breathing a sigh of relief, and they resumed their position.

"About time," Hori whispered before the door closed.

Sitamun stood at the door for a moment to let her eyes adjust to the small amount of moonlight coming in through the window. She noticed the two figures on the bed beyond the open hallway. She pressed the dagger to her chest with the point down as she clutched its handle with both hands. She crept around to where her son slept. Her knuckles went white as she looked up and closed her eyes.

"Forgive me. I failed you."

She raised the dagger high and thrust it deep into his chest. No sound came from him, and as she pulled the dagger out, blood only seeped from the wound. She felt his cheek, and he was cool to the touch. She realized he had already left this life.

I've done something I didn't need to do!

She yanked her hand away from her son's face and shuffled back a step.

I didn't have to kill him. Praise Amun! Thank you!

But all of a sudden, her relief turned to a broken heart.

Ah, my son! My only son!

Her face twisted into a grimace as the murder of her son caused her world to stop.

Then Meritaten stirred in her sleep.

I've got to get out of here, she thought—

But it was too late. Meritaten awoke with a start, seeing the dark figure looming over her husband. Sitamun's body froze in her retreat.

"Go back to sleep, Meritaten," Sitamun said, her voice trembling. "Everything will be fine in the morning."

"What? Who are you?" Meritaten said in a loud voice. "Smenkare, wake up." She hit his shoulder but did not feel his usual warmth. "Smenkare!" she yelled, her voice growing frantic.

"Quiet, child," Sitamun said as she walked around to where Meritaten lay, still pushing Smenkare and touching his face. Sitamun's stomach fluttered, and her body tingled from adrenaline, as she waited for Meritaten to uncover Smenkare's fate.

"Is he gone? He's been killed . . ." She was speaking to herself, but now she glared up and thrust a finger in Sitamun's face. "*You* did this!" The rise in Meritaten's voice sent the hairs on Sitamun's body on edge.

"I said *quiet*, child!" Sitamun grabbed one of Meritaten's wrists and heard her racing heart pounding in her ears.

"Let go of me!" Meritaten's voice was louder now, and she was about to call for the guards when Sitamun pressed her other hand over the top of Meritaten's mouth, dropping the dagger on the bed. After a few moments, as her eyes adjusted to the dark, Meritaten whispered, "Sitamun?"

"Yes," she replied, hovering her hand over Meritaten's mouth to let her speak.

"How did you escape from prison? How are you here? What is that awful smell?" Meritaten said. "Did you kill Smen—"

"Go back to sleep, Meritaten." An idea struck her. "You are dreaming. Sitamun is not here. How could she be? She is in prison awaiting her execution in the morning."

Meritaten yanked herself back and fell onto Smenkare's lifeless body.

"No!"

An immense breathlessness overcame her as she tried to piece together the events of the night.

"I am awake," she finally expelled. "And you . . . you killed him. You killed my husband—your son! Your *son*! *You killed Pharaoh!*" Her hands rushed to her mouth and chest, clutching her nightdress.

Sitamun remembered her words to the jail guards. She had hoped to be able to rid Egypt of this Pharaoh who took innocent lives with no consequence, but with Meritaten as an eyewitness, she would face consequences. That thought sank like a rock to the pit of her stomach. Without thinking, Sitamun grabbed Meritaten by her head with both hands and shoved it into the linen-wrapped wool mattress.

"I told you to be *quiet*!"

Meritaten's muffled yell of "Help!" could barely be heard as Sitamun pushed her head further into the bed.

"Quiet! Child! Quiet!"

Meritaten flung her arms about, barely able to scratch her attacker. Sitamun stood and blocked her arms' movement from behind. Meritaten's legs were tangled up in the linen bedsheet and proved worthless as she found her mother-in-law to be quite strong.

Sitamun didn't register the moment when Meritaten's

hands stopped flailing. She continued to stand above her, pushing her head into the bed, telling her to be quiet, child, quiet, until almost morning light.

Finally, she lifted her hands and put them to her mouth, as her lungs had forgotten how to breathe, and inhaled a long, deep breath. She surveyed the room; nothing stirred.

"With Smenkare gone, the Coregent will have my head for taking her daughter's life," Sitamun whispered.

She paced a while until her nerves settled and her hands stopped shaking. Her mind came up with a possible way out of this. She rolled Meritaten over onto her back and put the dagger in her lifeless hand. Then she rolled her only son, Smenkare, to his belly, pulling his arms so his hands lay at Meritaten's neck.

"A lover's quarrel gone wrong," she whispered to herself, and took a shaky breath. Blinking back her tears, she stumbled backward and repeated to them and her god Amun, "I'm so sorry. Please forgive me . . ."

—until her heel touched their chamber door. She opened it and slid out as Khabek peered over his shoulder and nodded to her. She forced a smile in return—a smile of pity, not a smile of happiness—and ran to wake her stewards to take her back to her father's palace in Waset before the morning light uncovered her deed.

THE TIME OF THE
WOMAN KING

THE MORNING RANG OUT WITH NEWS THAT PHARAOH AND his Queen began the journey to the afterlife in their sleep; but those in the palace knew better; and even more so, Nefertiti knew Pawah must have had a hand in it. She had left Smenkare's murder in Pawah's malicious hands, and he had found a way to take Meritaten's life as well.

This was no "lover's quarrel." Whomever Pawah recruited to do his bidding will pay with their life, and when the time comes when I can arrest Pawah, he will pay mercilessly, she thought as she was crowned as Pharaoh Neferneferuaten.

Nefertiti watched the nobles at her crowning ceremony. She had named Pawah as her Vizier of both the Upper and the Lower, so to keep him close and under surveillance.

The nobles were happy but kept their emotions reserved, because the last pharaoh they had celebrated still made them tremble, even now in his tomb.

It had only been a year since she had taken her husband's life. Now she was where she was supposed to be—the wrong corrected—but Nefertiti sat on the throne, peering out over the nobles and officers, expressionless. Her cheeks sagged.

The corners of her mouth fell down, and her icy stare penetrated straight through the crowd and fixated on the wall behind them. She looked over to where Meritaten would have sat as a great royal wife. The heat from her ears gave her a headache, and the pain from her grinding teeth gave her the determination to find Meritaten's true killer.

She saw Mut and Tey there looking at the spot where Meritaten would have been sitting. Tey's eyes looked to her, and she felt her mother's blame cut through the crowd and slice through her.

She alone sat on the throne's platform. She had removed Ankhesenpaaten and Tut—to distance them from her, to keep them safe—but those in the great hall only saw a power-obsessed female Pharaoh.

Ankhesenpaaten peered up and over her shoulder at her mother. She still sat on a great royal wife's throne, but merely on the same level as everyone else. She looked to Tut by her side.

Shouldn't Tut be Pharaoh? He is the rightful heir, Ankhesenpaaten thought.

She peered up again at her mother and examined her aged face. She thought, for a woman who had lived only half her life, Nefertiti already carried a lifetime of woe in the creases on her brow and around her eyes. She wondered about all of the burdens she carried. Although her cheeks still rose as high as the great pyramids, her eyes as dark as the night sky, her dull skin and the loss of sparkle in her eyes drowned out her beauty.

Something weighs on her shoulders. She is hiding something. She didn't even cry when they told her Meritaten had journeyed west. . . . She knew it was going to happen—that's why she told me "when" she becomes Pharaoh, not "if"!

Her mind tried to recall that night her mother had come to her, but Tut broke her thoughts.

"I miss Smenkare and Meritaten. They let us be up there, beside them." He tapped his cane on the stone floor; the sound drowned out his mumblings. The corners of his mouth turned down as he crossed his arms. "I can't even *see* anything from down here."

"I wonder what the real reason was that made Mother move us from the platform," Ankhesenpaaten wondered aloud.

The horrible thought crossed her mind: *Does she think we would get in the way of her rule of Egypt?*

"No," she whispered to herself, but her thought shifted to Meritaten.

Mother wouldn't kill her own daughter . . . would she?

Ankhesenpaaten felt her muscles tense as she peered back up to her mother.

"What?" Tut asked.

"It's nothing. Mother . . . wouldn't do that."

Ankhesenpaaten's gaze shot to Tut as she struggled to get those last few words out, and she thought, *Wouldn't she? If I were in Meritaten's place, would I be gone too?* She peered over her shoulder again to the throne. *Did she have Meritaten and Smenkare killed so she could take the crown from Tut?*

"Do what? Oops!" Tut had dropped his leg of lamb to the ground before he was able to sink his teeth into the juicy meat. He laughed, scooted from the throne, and picked it up. Maia, his nurse, helped him back into his seat and took the leg from him before he could take a bite, a servant just as quickly replacing it with another.

Ankhesenpaaten looked at the young child. *He would be much too young to run a powerful nation such as Egypt.* She shook her head, missing her sidelock but glad to be wearing a woman's wig. *It's a silly thought, anyway.*

Ankhesenpaaten jolted from the suddenness with which Nefertiti stood and walked to the edge of the platform. The great hall silenced their whisperings to see what this Pharaoh would say. Was it to be doom for any who spoke Amun's name? Or liberation from their religious suffering? They leaned forward in anticipation, and she smiled, as if in knowledge of their fears and just what to say to allay them.

"As first order of this new crowning," she said, "Pharaoh of the Upper and Lower removes the decree made by the Pharaohs before. The divinely appointed of Amun-Re says this: No more blood shall be spilled for those who utter Amun's name. The temples shall be spared. The worship of our great empire's gods and goddesses of the past millennia shall continue. The people of Egypt may worship Ma'at, Anubis, Ptah, Isis, and all the others as they need, and, most importantly, Amun-Re shall be named the premier god of Egypt once again."

The great hall's celebratory cheers echoed off the stone walls and into the streets outside the palace, causing rumors to be spread like wildfire about the elated nobility in attendance at the crowning.

"Furthermore!" Nefertiti bellowed to quiet the crowd. "As Pharaoh, the solely divine of Amun to lead Egypt, the greatest of all, shall reinstate the priesthood of Amun and rebuild his temples. Being the true highest prophet of Amun, Pharaoh Neferneferuaten shows the people that Pharaoh alone has the power and authority to do this. A portion of all offerings to Amun will come to Pharaoh, as there are none greater."

The nobility applauded and began to chant:

"None are greater than Pharaoh! None are greater than Pharaoh!"

Under Nefertiti's smile was a sad thought: *Amenhotep . . . my love . . . this one decree was all that was required of you years before. Why didn't you just make it? Now, we have lost not only our people's respect for the throne but also the life of our daughter, Meritaten. Her murder is on your head.*

W<small>ATCHING</small> <small>FROM</small> <small>ACROSS</small> <small>THE</small> <small>ROOM</small>, P<small>AWAH</small>'<small>S</small> <small>MOUTH</small> curved into a wicked smile.

"She is perfect," he murmured under his breath, thinking this was his chance to marry into the Pharaoh position.

Beketaten heard him as she glanced between her husband and Nefertiti, and her heart hardened even more against this new Pharaoh.

She had helped arrange the murder of the last two Pharaohs . . . what was one more?

W<small>HEN</small> <small>THE</small> <small>CROWNING</small> <small>CEREMONY</small> <small>WAS</small> <small>COMPLETED</small> <small>AGAIN</small> in Men-nefer and then Waset, Smenkare and Meritaten were hurriedly buried and without much regard. Nefertiti had made the same declaration at each coronation, so the people loved her for her dedication to Amun-Re yet doubted her ability as a woman Pharaoh.

But Nefertiti's mission wasn't only to restore the priesthood of Amun; it was also to restore Egypt's prior glory and keep power in Pharaoh's court. With the reinstatement, however, Pawah received back his former title, Fifth Prophet of Amun, thus elevating him even higher in the eyes of the people than from his marriage to Beketaten and his leadership of the People's Restoration of Egypt. To counter, Nefertiti made sure the First Prophet could not self-appoint himself like Meryptah had under Pharaoh Amenhotep III. She acted quickly as the prophets squabbled over who would be First Prophet and took the traditional responsibility of Pharaoh, appointing Simut as the First Prophet of Amun to show none was greater than Pharaoh.

Pawah curled his top lip at her appointment and shook

his head. "Well done, *She-King*. Now it is my turn," he whispered under his breath. He left the appointment hearing and went to find Beketaten.

Nefertiti watched him leave as knots grew in her belly. The more she interacted with him, the more she realized one truth: he would do anything to get what he wanted. What scared her about this truth was the fact that he had caused her to push her beyond the limits of her own morality—twice. The second time had caused her to lose another daughter caught in the crossfire of political gain, and that thought caused a swarm of sickness to overtake her stomach as she dismissed all in her company.

As she stared distantly at the giant stone columns holding up the open roof of the throne room, debating the status of her guilt and dignity, a messenger came. Commander Horemheb and General Paaten had come to Aketaten with news of the border disputes. Her heart tried to spark a moment of happiness at the thought of seeing the Commander and the General again, but her mouth fell slack. Her daughter had been killed because of her cowardice and delay. Happiness was not deserved.

Horemheb and Paaten entered the throne room, bowing when they reached the lowest step of the platform. The sun-cast shadows deepened her sallow cheeks and circles under her eyes. She gazed at her old friend Paaten, and at Horemheb, the man she thought could save her from herself. A heavy breath escaped her lips as her voice lay limp in the air.

"What message do you bring the throne?"

Horemheb swallowed the lump in the back of his throat. When he had heard the news of Smenkare and Meritaten while in Libya, he wanted to scream out in heartache for Nefertiti. He had told her she was no fool for putting Meritaten's life in their hands for the betterment of the position of Pharaoh; and yet, Meritaten was no doubt murdered along with her husband. Now, as he looked upon her, he witnessed the true depths of the pain he had only imagined.

"The Libyan dispute has been resolved, to the glory of Egypt," he said.

The softness of his voice comforted Nefertiti's ears, causing her to find his eyes. His steady gaze gave her an unspoken comfort that nearly brought forth tears.

She quickly turned to Paaten. "And Nubia?"

"The Nubian threat has also been disabled." Paaten also possessed a soft tone. He shifted his weight as if trying to take some of her burden.

"Then we are now at peace . . ."—Nefertiti closed her eyes to keep them from glistening—"worshiping Amun-Re and with secured borders . . ." She opened her eyes, dry and dull. "But at what cost?"

She thought, *Amun still punishes me. I took the life of his appointed, why would he not?*

Both the Commander and the General stood still, knowing it mattered not what they said; it could not compare to the loss of Pharaoh's daughter.

"A great cost," Paaten finally murmured.

Nefertiti stood up. Stepping down to their level, she walked between and past them, and they fell in step behind her. Horemheb watched her shoulders roll forward and her head lower.

"Pharaoh, if I may speak?" he asked.

Nefertiti stopped walking. Placing her hands behind her back, she turned to face them, chin lifted high.

Horemheb drew in a deep breath. He didn't know what to say to her.

"I am sorry."

He was sorry for not taking more action, for telling her to

not take more action, for not preventing this death . . . but he left it at that—*I am sorry*—fully aware that Paaten did not know about the past two murder conspiracies.

Nefertiti clenched her jaw. She understood his apology, but she also understood that this was the second time that both he and her father had stood by, letting her take the brunt of the fall.

Paaten cleared his throat. "We are all sorry for your loss, Pharaoh."

"Thank you," she said, keeping her gaze on Horemheb, "General."

Surprised by his sudden, irrepressible desire to console her in her pain, Horemheb instinctively took a small step toward her—he wanted to pull her close; he wanted to forget his place. A hard stare from both Paaten and Nefertiti found him and pinned him where he stood, and he stepped back in line.

"You must be exhausted from your travels," Nefertiti said through her teeth. "I wish to be alone." She walked between the two again, imperceptibly brushing Horemheb's arm. She peered over her shoulder and said, "Thank you both for your continued dedication to Egypt and to the crown," and then continued walking toward her throne.

They bowed and left. As the door shut, Paaten pulled Horemheb aside. "Do not let the fact that Pharaoh is a woman obscure your judgment, Commander."

Horemheb looked back with a blank stare and slight shake of his head. "I don't know what you mean."

"I see the way your eyes dilate when you are around her. Do not play the fool. She is *Pharaoh*, and you are still Commander of her armies. Do not step out of your place again, or I will have you removed from your position." Paaten locked eyes with his subordinate. "Do you understand?"

"Yes, General," Horemheb said, and clenched his jaw, refusing to say more.

"Good," General Paaten said, turning to leave.

Horemheb rubbed his bronze armor as he watched Paaten walk away. Glancing at the closed doors of the throne room, he thought:

The General needn't know of my true desires.

THAT NIGHT, HOREMHEB WALKED ALONG THE HALLS JUST as he had before he left. He couldn't get her imperceptible brush of his arm out of his mind. Was it on purpose? Was it by accident? Did it mean she forgave him?

So easily?

He came upon Pharaoh's chambers and noticed only Ineni stood guard. He cleared his throat, and Ineni straightened up.

"Royal guard, where is Khabek? Or Hori? Should not at least two of you stand at Pharaoh's door?"

"Royal guard Hori is not on watch, and Pharaoh has dismissed royal guard Khabek," Ineni said, looking straight ahead.

"Why?"

Ineni faced the Commander. "She did not trust him."

"Has she been in any danger since the General and I have left?"

"No." Ineni shrugged his shoulders. "She came out of her chambers one night a month or so ago and said for him to leave."

Horemheb looked at the doors of her room.

If only I hadn't left to Libya . . . maybe I could have saved Meritaten. Maybe I could have kept her from further insomnia.

He debated entering. It would be a gigantic step outside of his position; he could risk the General finding out and stripping him of his title, possibly facing execution if Pharaoh commanded it. He rubbed his neck. But if she needed him and he didn't come, it could be just as bad for him.

He did want to see her and see how she was after the day. She mustn't have fared well while he was gone, with the murder of her daughter. He at least needed to give proper condolences and a proper apology for not being here when she needed him. If she became angry, he would only ask forgiveness, say that he foolishly misunderstood her kindness in the past as intrigue. Yes, that would do; and maybe, if he was lucky, he would come out still with his Commander rank.

He took a deep breath and grabbed the door handle to push open.

"I am sorry, Commander," Ineni said as he thrust his spear to block Horemheb's way. "Pharaoh has said she wants no company."

Horemheb puffed up his chest so his bronze armor sparkled in the torchlight. He bored into Ineni's eyes, staring at him until Ineni brought back his spear.

"You are to tell no one of this," Horemheb ordered.

"Yes, Commander," Ineni said, and returned to his dutiful guard position while Horemheb entered Pharaoh's chambers.

HE FOUND HER LOOKING OUT THE WINDOW. THE moonlight fell on every curve of her body but highlighted the sadness in her face.

"Pharaoh."

She'd heard him enter. At first, her heart raced upon hearing the door open, but then, hearing his deep voice, she sighed, relieved that it wasn't one of Pawah's pawns coming to kill her.

"I thought I told the guard no one was to enter," she said, still looking out the window.

Horemheb stopped in his tracks. "I used my rank to tell him otherwise," he admitted. "If Pharaoh does not wish to see me, I will leave. Let this error be on me."

"No . . ." She turned to face him as tears fell down her cheeks. "I want you to stay."

He took a few steps toward her, but she turned to look out the window again, and he stopped, unsure what to do.

"Why did I ever want to be Queen and now Pharaoh? I was such a stupid young girl," she confided. "Akhenaten always told me—or rather, *Amenhotep* always told me—that he never wanted to be Pharaoh. Now I know what he meant. People want to kill you, and you can't always have what you want without there being an equal cost. But I am Pharaoh now . . . and it still does not matter."

Horemheb approached with caution, not letting his heart make the decisions. He came to stand behind her, peering down at her as she looked out the window.

"I have lost four daughters, all at the hand of my own carelessness. I brought home the army from diseased lands that sent plague across Egypt. I killed Setepenre, Neferneferure, and Meketaten, with that decision, and then I foolishly gave Meritaten into Pawah and Beketaten's safekeeping." She shook her head. "I am a failure as a mother."

Horemheb wanted to rub his hands along her arms and turn her to face him, but he silenced his want with tight control of his limbs. "No, Pharaoh, you are not. I am your Commander. I should have been here. I should have stayed and protected Meritaten."

"No. My father, who ranks higher than you, stayed in Aketaten. Meritaten was his granddaughter, and he did nothing. I do not blame you," she whispered. "I blame myself." She drew in a long breath. "I loved Akhenaten. He gave me six beautiful daughters. But I also hated him. I hated him for making me choose between him and Egypt. I hated him for betraying me." She slammed her fist on the window sill. "I wish I had never become his Queen—and yet, if I had not, I would not have had my children. My children, whom I have failed." She fell to her knees and wept, pressing her head against the sill.

Horemheb knelt down and placed a gentle hand on her back.

She wrenched away. "I don't deserve your kindness, Commander. Please leave me—" Her brittle voice shattered in the moonlit darkness.

He stayed kneeling beside her and, after debating whether she really wanted him to leave or not, decided to go against her wishes. He justified to himself that if she had indeed brushed him on purpose earlier in the day, then she wanted him there with her.

He lowered his hand back down on her shoulder. This time she didn't pull away. He rubbed a circle on her back and then finally took his other arm underneath her and pulled her close. She let go of the window sill and fell into his embrace.

"I killed the king," Nefertiti said between sobs. Horemheb kept silent. "And then I let someone kill my own daughter." She grasped his arm harder. "What mother would do that?"

He stroked her arm and across her forehead as she pulled on him still tighter as if trying to claw herself from her despairing abyss.

"Hasn't Amun punished me enough? Have I not paid for my transgressions? What more do you want from me, my god?! What more can I *give*? Do you want my blood? Then take it! Spare my two living daughters this grief. *Spare them!*" she yelled up through the window with a fist in the air.

Horemheb clasped his hand over her fist, not wanting her to further anger the gods, and crumpled her arms over her chest, whispering in her ear, "Breathe with me . . ." He took a deep breath, making her body rise and fall with his own.

When he had helped her gain control, she whimpered, "Have I not been punished enough?"

"No one knows your pain," Horemheb said, trying to hold back his own tears, internalizing her screams and cries. He could feel the intensity with which she held to him, drawing blood on his arm. "Cast it upon me. I will take your pain. I will suffer in your place. I am to blame."

She released his arm. "No, I alone am to blame." Lying limp in Horemheb's arm, her energy spent, she could not even lift her arms to raise herself from his lap. "I alone shall bear this burden."

They stayed on the floor for some time while Horemheb stroked her arm and face, until Nefertiti, exhausted from grief, fell asleep. Horemheb lifted her in his arms and took her to the bed.

As he laid her down, she found the strength to grab his chest strap as he pulled away, and she drew him back down to her.

"You are a good man, Commander, and I am thankful you are here with me."

"I care for you in many ways . . ." He had already stepped out of his place and disobeyed several direct orders from her thus far—what was admitting his forbidden feelings now?

"I do not deserve your care," Nefertiti mumbled; sleep had begun to take her again, and it appeared she did not fully understand the depth behind his words.

"For you, I would do anything." In a rush of impulse, he brought his lips to her cheek—but he halted himself right before they touched and instead whispered in her ear, "Know this . . . I wish your pain on me."

She smiled at him with sorrow on her lips. "Some wishes are never granted." Then she closed her eyes. "Commander, will you please stay . . . so I can feel safe while I sleep?"

"For you, I would do anything," he repeated and pulled a chair next to her bed.

NEFERTITI AWOKE THE NEXT MORNING TO FIND HOREMHEB standing by the window.

"Thank you, Commander."

He nodded. His eyebrows drew together as he watched her rise from the bed: her body aching, she rubbed her neck and stretched her back. He debated overstepping his line again and going to rub her shoulders, but decided against it. This woman, maybe only needed him in her sorrow of the previous night, but today was a new day, and perhaps she was ashamed of acting this way with her subordinate. He watched her, nonetheless, wishing he could help her.

"Commander," she said, drawing near to him as the night came rushing back to her. She peered up at him. Her eyes held so much sorrow, but as the sunlight came upon them, they revealed a growing fire. "Someone will answer for Meritaten."

"As they should," Horemheb responded. Her anger became his.

"Will you please call a meeting of council with Pawah and Beketaten?" Her muscles tensed as a weight grew on her chest.

"I will." Horemheb stood back, bowed, and began to walk away.

"Commander—" She turned her shoulders to him. "I will not forget your kindness shown to me last night, and the risk you took in coming to me."

He dipped his chin and swallowed. "I would risk it again," he said. "For you, my Pharaoh."

He bowed slightly at the waist and left to carry out her command.

Nefertiti watched the door close and began to cry. Her hatred of Meritaten's murderer, her growing fondness of the Commander, her self-loathing, her failure as a mother—all were too much to bear.

Eventually, she gathered herself enough to call her stewards. She would meet her council in her best and make Pawah and Beketaten pay for the murder of her daughter.

15

THE TIME OF REVEAL

LATER THAT DAY, GENERAL PAATEN, HER FATHER, MASTER of Pharaoh's Horses, Ay, and Commander Horemheb sat across from Pawah and Beketaten, with Nefertiti at the head of the table in the council room.

The sun shone overhead, drenching Nefertiti in its light. She called over a messenger and whispered, "At first light tomorrow, I want plans for the roofs of the council room and throne room to be covered from the Aten's rays."

"As Pharaoh says," the messenger said, and went out of the room, presumably in search of the royal architects.

They were now left alone. The others in the room waited for Nefertiti to speak, but she only glared at Pawah and Beketaten. Neither Pawah, too confident to be intimidated, nor Beketaten, too enraged with jealousy to notice, shifted in their seats.

"Pharaoh Neferneferuaten." Paaten leaned over to Nefertiti. "Perhaps we should begin with the reason for why we have assembled."

"Of course, General," Nefertiti said. She rolled her shoulders back as she sat up straight in the gold-enthroned chair. Then she said: "Arrest Pawah, Fifth Prophet of Amun, and Beketaten, King's daughter, for treason and inciting rebellion against Pharaoh. They are the leaders of the People's Restoration of Egypt."

Pawah stood up with a smug smirk.

You stupid woman. You cannot arrest me, he thought and pointed a long finger at Nefertiti before he spoke.

"You murdered Pharaoh Akhenaten! *You* should die as well!"

Paaten stood up, along with Horemheb, and he yelled, "You dare to make such lies against our Pharaoh Neferneferuaten?!"

"It is no lie!" Pawah yelled, his ears simmering at Paaten's accusation, and then focused his snake-like eyes on Nefertiti.

I have you in my hands. You will be my puppet.

"The people will believe me. I will be your undoing— either in life or in death!"

"Do you think the people will believe *you,* the vizier to Pharaoh Smenkare—"

"Who we killed to save Egypt!"

Paaten thrust a finger in Pawah's face. "So you confess to killing the divinely appointed?"

Horemheb clenched his jaw as he eyed the General and then peered at Nefertiti.

Pawah, seeing Horemheb's reaction, chuckled, and said to the others, "He doesn't know?"

This keeps getting better and better.

"Egypt's highest-ranking military officer doesn't know what Master of Pharaoh's Horses and the Commander and even Pharaoh herself agreed to?" He laughed, shook his head, and leaned toward Nefertiti with both hands on the table. "O how the three of you like to keep secrets!"

Paaten looked at Nefertiti, the color draining from his face. His eyes pleaded for it not to be true, but Nefertiti did not give him any such indication. Only guilt lived in her eyes as they held their stare.

Pawah continued to speak, reveling in the betrayal of it all. "Ah, the great General Paaten, the soldier who carried out the Coregent's word at great cost of Egyptian life, torturing men to find the leaders of the rebellious movement. Yes, *we* are the leaders of the People's Restoration of Egypt. Yes, you have us here—but you cannot arrest us. The truth will come out, trust me, and the beloved Pharaoh Neferneferuaten will be known as a traitor and a liar—so much for her divine appointment. Vanity all of it! Can you imagine the repercussions?"

His smile stayed plastered to his face. He might have pitied her a little if the whole situation wasn't so fun to witness.

"You see, General, Horemheb and Ay struck a deal with us, to poison Akhenaten, but we couldn't give him the poison because Akhenaten would have noticed the cupbearer not drinking the wine. They convinced our *noble* Neferneferuaten into bringing him the hemlock-laced wine herself."

He saw Ay's gaze fall to the floor and knew then to squeeze out a few more blood drops and do a bit more damage to the so-called *loyal* relationships in the room.

"And Ay . . . *Ay*," he said again, to get Ay to look up at him, "he was very convincing, believe you me, using her dead mother as guilt. Well done, Ay, well done." He mockingly applauded Ay's efforts as Ay's jaw clenched, his brow furrowed, fists tight, swallowing against a dry throat.

Nefertiti broke her stare with Paaten and sent a glare to her father.

Horemheb clenched his fist so hard it cracked his knuckles as he bared his teeth. His hand lingered near the handle of his khopesh, and his fingers twitched.

Pawah glanced at him, and a wide grin spread across his

face as he thought: *I dare you.* Pawah licked his lip toward Horemheb and knew he had them all right where he wanted.

"So you see, General Paaten, Nefertiti—or should I say, rather, Pharaoh Neferneferuaten—is a murderer as well. Now, how would it look if Amun's divine killed another of Amun's divine, or, worse, we told the people how she killed Smenkare and his bride as well. What would the people think? She refuses the crown to the rightful heir, the boy Tut, and she murders her own daughter? Tsk-tsk."

Nefertiti slowly rose, lowering her head like a wolf about to attack. Her muscles were taut, veins straining against her skin.

Pawah continued, "Smenkare was a fool and didn't even know that cupbearers are meant to taste the wine before handing it to royalty. It was easy to slip him the poison, easy enough for the Coregent to see her opportunity for full glory."

Nefertiti slammed her fists into the table. "Curse you, Pawah!"

Pawah's wicked smile returned, enraging Nefertiti further.

I am right, he thought. *She knows she can't touch me.*

"You will pay for what you did to my Meritaten," she hissed. "I will make you pay."

Ah, but she still threatens. He cocked his head to the side. *If it weren't in vain, I might actually fear you, Pharaoh.*

"Ah She-King, I love the commitment, but with your hands as dirty as mine, I don't see you making anyone pay for anything." To show his complete lack of respect for her as Pharaoh, Pawah examined his nail beds as he spoke. "And I know you prefer to blame us rather than Smenkare for killing Meritaten. He was the one who strangled her—must have been a lover's quarrel."

"Do you dare insult Pharaoh's intelligence?" Nefertiti spat.

Beketaten said through clenched teeth, "We swear we only put the hemlock in Smenkare's wine. He should have died that night. We are not responsible for Meritaten. Even as much as I hate you, Nefertiti, I would never kill your daughter."

Nefertiti peered at her over the bridge of her nose. "Would you not?"

"We know how they were found," Beketaten said, dismissing Nefertiti's accusation with a wave of her hand. "Smenkare strangled her, and she stabbed him as a last struggle before his hands around her neck took her life away."

"Do you think me a fool?" Nefertiti yelled as a sudden flush overcame her face. "It was a *jailer's* dagger. Where would Meritaten have gotten a jailer's dagger in the middle of the night?"

Their eyes met, as though they both realized what must have happened. The mysterious yet overlooked disappearance of Sitamun played a key role in the Queen's murder.

"Sitamun . . ." Nefertiti murmured through the heaves of her chest.

All eyes fell on Nefertiti in her revelation. The sun's rays fell upon Nefertiti's shoulders and head and appeared to steam off of her skin. Sweat gathered on her brow as her lips stretched into a scowl.

Beketaten tensed. "If you harm her, I will kill you," she threatened. Her fingers pressed hard into the wood table, making her knuckles white.

Horemheb pulled his dagger and pointed it at Beketaten's face.

"You will not threaten the throne!"

Paaten squared his shoulders to Pawah and Beketaten, but appeared to debate in his eyes on deciding to arrest her for threatening Pharaoh.

"People die for such statements," Nefertiti hissed, but her gaze darted between Paaten and Beketaten.

Pawah still needed his wife—for now—and at least with no witnesses to his wife's threat, outside of this guilty group, they still couldn't arrest her; it would be his word against theirs, something Nefertiti couldn't wager. He pushed Horemheb's hand away and out of his wife's face. "We can do whatever we want . . . unless the She-King wants to jeopardize the power of Pharaoh and risk her own life?" Pawah peered at Paaten and noted his lack of action, his decision apparent.

Ay leaned over and whispered to Nefertiti, "And the people love the King's daughter and the great royal wife of Pharaoh Amenhotep III. You will have done yourself a disservice in her execution. If we want to say they were not murdered to keep the throne divine, you will be killing an innocent woman of royalty."

Silence filled the room. They were at an impasse. They each held secrets about the other. Each had their own advantages, but both dared not touch the other, as they each had tied themselves to the boulder of sin.

"Mark my words," Nefertiti said at last. "When this is all said and done, Sitamun will be hunted down—"

"And *if* this is all said and done"—Beketaten rose, and now they all stood around the table—"I will be right there with a knife to your heart."

Pawah grinned; he liked the vengeful side of these two powerful women in the room. His wife would serve him well —if his first plan to marry into the Pharaoh's position did not come to fruition.

PAATEN REQUESTED A PRIVATE AUDIENCE WITH NEFERTITI A few days later. She accepted; however, she wished she did not have to speak with him so soon after he had learned of her deception. They met privately in the throne room. She watched him with a shaky eye as he entered, and everyone else left. It appeared disappointment still dripped with every step, but the sting of betrayal in his eyes at least looked as though it had been reduced.

"My Pharaoh," he said, and put his right hand over his heart and bowed his head.

Nefertiti stood and walked down the platform steps to him.

"Shall we walk?" she asked. There was much to say and much to forgive.

He nodded, and they walked about the great throne room first in silence, but Nefertiti soon peered over at him.

"Don't look at me like that, General," she said, averting her eyes. "My mother and sister already do. My friend and confidant . . . I cannot bear the same look from you as well."

"Thus Pharaoh says." General Paaten's voice strained.

Nefertiti just looked upon him with sad eyes, then blurted, "I am sorry, General."

"Pharaoh does not apologize," he reminded her.

She stopped, still looking at him. "Perhaps in the public setting. But we are—"

"Friends? Confidants?" he suggested, and he stopped as well. He stood straight, unmoving, with a tough exterior, but the slight upward tick in his voice suggested he had a soft spot—a soft spot she felt she had stabbed. He looked as if he were going to apologize for his curtness, but then refrained.

"And I betrayed that friendship. I betrayed that confidence," Nefertiti added and then held her breath.

They both sensed time stop.

Her eyes eagerly searched him for any presence of forgiveness.

"Pharaoh had her reasons," General Paaten finally said after a hard swallow.

"Of all those I've known for the greater part of my life, you are the only officer who truly stands beside me." Nefertiti graced his arm with her hand. "Thank you."

"I took an oath to the gods, and for each Pharaoh, I will stand beside." His stiffness proved he had not quite given his complete forgiveness, if any.

"No, General, it is more than that. I considered you my friend and advocate. I knew I could trust you with my daughters' lives. I asked you to protect them should a rebellion come. Do you remember?"

"Of course, I remember." His voice fell flat as Nefertiti noticed his eyes drift to the carvings on the pillars of the throne room. He observed one of the royal daughters. "My word remains the same."

They continued walking in silence.

Nefertiti felt a little of the burden release from her shoulders. At least her daughters would still be under his care, even if his respect for her was gone. That last, however, would eat at her like a disease. She knew how her mother and sister felt about her; she knew how the Commander and her father felt about her. Now, she wondered which way the General would lean; and so, in the privacy of their meeting, she summoned the courage to ask.

"Do you think less of me . . . now that you know the truth?" Nefertiti's eyes closed, bracing herself for the response that she thought might come.

General Paaten's response was quick: "It matters not what I think."

"It does to me," she said, and peered up at him. Now that he knew she had murdered Pharaoh Akhenaten, had agreed to stand aside for the murder of Pharaoh Smenkare, Nefertiti felt a part of herself die. She wanted to so desperately cling to that innocent girl with the auspicious future ahead of her, not this tragic excuse with a life that seemed to be dwindling in front of her eyes.

He took a deep breath, and his eyes narrowed as he pieced words together. "In war, we kill many men. We execute many strategic plans to gain a new territory, and we kill kings who do not surrender." He stopped, pressing his lips together to signal he had nothing else to say.

"You did not answer my question," Nefertiti said.

"As Pharaoh, I will never think less of you," he said.

"But as Nefertiti, do you?" Nefertiti's eyes pleaded, needing to know the truth.

"May I speak freely?" The question seemed to light a familiar admiration in his eyes.

Nefertiti nodded and fidgeted with her dress. "I am asking you to."

Paaten began a slow pace back and forth with his hands behind his back. "I understand why you did what you did . . . but look at the damage it has done to the position of Pharaoh; the situation it has put you in with Pawah. If the people do not like a Pharaoh, they can just orchestrate a murder. Look how quickly Smenkare was killed. How much time do you think will pass before they come after you? Will the title Pharaoh even be honored in a hundred years?"

"Look at the damage Akhenaten did," Nefertiti said, throwing her hand in the air like it somehow defended her actions. "He was not without his followers. They ignored the downfall of the economy and Egypt's allies. They mourned him. They mourn Smenkare. Pharaoh is still revered even when—"

"They will come for you, Pharaoh. *He* will come for you. Pawah. I have seen men such as Pawah. They are manipulative men. If it is in a rebellion or a coup, he will make sure you are out of his way." Paaten stopped in his pace, shoving his arms to his sides as if resisting the urge to push a finger in Nefertiti's face. "When you keep a man such as Pawah from his plans—" He shook his head and changed his tone. "He speaks on behalf of the people, he will usurp that power out of the hands of the people, and he will kill you if you don't do as he says."

Nefertiti let out a heavy sigh as tears wet her eyes. "I know . . ."

Paaten cleared his throat. "Though he may be your vizier" —he raised an eyebrow—"keep him close and under your nose."

"That is precisely why I named him Vizier." Nefertiti hung her head. "Can I still trust you, not only as Pharaoh but as Nefertiti too?"

Paaten bowed his head and stood straight, placing his hand over his heart. "Till the end of my days, I give my life protecting Pharaoh . . . and my friend, Neferneferuaten-Nefertiti."

Nefertiti sighed as a slow smile crept across her lips in relief at his forgiveness. "Take Ankhesenpaaten and Nefe with you should I be killed or the people attack. Take whatever you need from the treasury to make it so. Protect them." She repeated her plea from years ago. "Protect them."

General Paaten placed a heavy hand on her shoulder. "What about Pawah and Beketaten? What will you do?"

"I don't know." Nefertiti shrugged; she needed another confirmation regarding the safety of her daughters. "Promise me."

"I have already promised," General Paaten said and gave a gentle shake of reassurance.

"Promise me again," she said. "I need to know they are safe."

He ducked his head to look her in the eyes. "I promise."

She let out a sigh of relief. She closed her eyes and nodded her head in thankfulness. "Take Aitye with you as well if time allows," Nefertiti said. "She has been more of a mother to them than I have been."

"You mustn't say things like that. You are a perfectly good mother for them."

"No. My stepmother, Tey, was a perfect mother, and I'm sure my real mother would have been too. But I have not upheld Tey's example. I have let others raise my children. I let a foreign Queen be their mother in my absence. Royal wife Kiya . . . she knew nothing of Egypt's ways, yet she loved them as I should have." Nefertiti drew a quick inhale to soothe the stab to her soul. "She was good to them. She was good to me."

"Royal wife Kiya was a warm and caring person, that I agree." Paaten nodded and looked off as if remembering her interacting with the royal children—teaching them to paint, playing with them in the courtyard . . . "But *you* are their mother. There is no one who loves them or cares for them more."

"I wish I could believe you. I have failed them in so many ways—and even worse, they see me in my actions without understanding the reasons behind them. It is why Meritaten was murdered. I failed her. I will not fail Ankhesenpaaten and Nefe."

"Meritaten knew about Amun. She was your oldest. She watched as Egypt worshipped Amun for the first part of her life. She made her own choices, as do we all."

Nefertiti bit her lip. "I still failed her. I'm her mother. I should have protected my child."

"*I* should have protected her. I should have protected *Pharaoh*," Paaten said, pressing a hand into his chest; he

LAUREN LEE MEREWETHER

clearly wanted to take away Nefertiti's guilt. "Blame me. Don't blame yourself."

Nefertiti wiped away a tear. "I could never blame you. Despite what Beketaten says she will do in retaliation, I will find Sitamun, and she will pay with her life."

"My friend, keep watch over yourself. Do not become the enemy. Stop now. Don't continue on this path."

"She killed my firstborn." Her voice filled with a chesty growl.

"Revenge blinds a good eye," General Paaten murmured.

But Nefertiti's focus was not on his words.

LATER THAT MONTH, NEFERTITI FINALLY KNEW SHE HAD TO confront her mother and sister about what happened, and so Mut and Tey came to Nefertiti's room per her request. Nefertiti dismissed the servants so they could talk. Tey sat in her chair with her hands folded on her lap and her eyes downcast. Her lips set in judgment without saying a word. Mut wiped away a tear as Nefertiti also sat in her chair in the same way as Tey.

"I tried to warn Meritaten," Mut finally confessed.

Nefertiti and Tey both shot a glance at her, but slowly their gazes drifted back to the floor.

"She wouldn't listen to me," Mut continued as she cried further. "You were right, Nefertiti." Tears streamed down her face now. "She wouldn't listen, and she threatened to have me killed for speaking Amun's name. I'm sorry . . . I'm so sorry."

"You have nothing to apologize for," Nefertiti said in a hushed tone. "I should have warned her."

Tey nodded her head in agreement, but said nothing. She knew Nefertiti's guilt was already great; if there were any more guilt placed upon her shoulders, her back might break.

"I should have protected her," Nefertiti whispered. She lifted her head. "You are better than me, Mut." She gritted her teeth as she watched her mother and sister come to their own emotional acceptance of Meritaten's murder. "But this I swear to you . . . the one who killed her will pay with their life."

16

THE TIME OF EXECUTION

LATER THAT SEASON, A MESSENGER CAME AND BOWED before Nefertiti. "We have found Sitamun, who stays at Malkata."

Hearing her name, Nefertiti's blood boiled, the heat coloring her skin red. "Bring her to me," she commanded. She tilted her head back against the back of the throne and stared off into the distance. The pressure from the grit of her teeth caused her to draw a quick inhale.

Now, how to make her suffer? I cannot arrest her for killing Pharaoh and his Queen. How will I right this wrong? How will I be able to execute a seemingly innocent woman? How will I bring justice to my daughter without endangering the throne even more?

Her mind raced as she thought of scenario after scenario, until she finally rested on one and drew her mouth into a smirk. The consequences, she would deal with later.

A FEW DECANS CAME AND WENT. SITAMUN ARRIVED AT Aketaten with her royal guards. They accompanied her into the throne room, where Nefertiti sat in her long golden robes. Ankhesenpaaten sat along with Tutankhaten off to the side of the platform. Nefertiti's guards lined the walls of the throne room.

"Great royal wife Sitamun," Nefertiti began. She waited to see if any guilt crossed the woman's face, and when none did, she added, "King's *daughter*."

At the mention of her royal title, Sitamun's face fell.

"Your disappearance from prison and your execution date were overlooked as we mourned the passing of your son and his Queen." Nefertiti peered at her down the length of her nose. "Now comes the time to correct this error."

"I commanded the prison guards to release me—" Sitamun proclaimed.

"And to give you a *jailer's* dagger?"

Nefertiti's question lingered in the air like the hot air on an arid, summer day.

Sitamun's gaze fell with a twist of her mouth. "He was my son, too," she said, looking back at Nefertiti.

"The country thinks they passed in their sleep," Nefertiti said. "But we know better, do we not?"

"For the good of the kingdom—for the good of Pharaoh and everything *my* family went through to regain Pharaoh's power—we must move on," Sitamun said. "I only meant to correct—" She hesitated. "But Queen Meritaten, she . . ." Sitamun faltered as tears welled in her eyes.

Ankhesenpaaten's jaw dropped at the implication of guilt in Sitamun. "You killed my sister?" Her whisper went unnoticed.

"She saw you, didn't she?" Nefertiti said, her voice raising.

"I am sorrowful," Sitamun said. "I never meant for it to happen that way. You must believe me."

"Oh, I believe you, Sitamun," Nefertiti said, stripping the

use of her title as if to give her a preview of her punishment. "But I do not forgive you."

Nefertiti snapped her fingers; the guards lining the walls stepped forward, lowering their spears to Sitamun and her company.

"What are you doing?" Sitamun asked, her tears evaporating from her hot cheeks. "If you charge me with the royals' murders, all will have been in vain!"

"I am not charging you with the royals' murders. I am simply executing the last order of Pharaoh Smenkare, which was to have you drink poison for your disobedience to his edict," Nefertiti said, leaning forward in her throne.

"The people will see you as carrying on his and Akhenaten's tyranny!" Sitamun's shoulders raised in panic. "You will be the next one to be killed! The people will rise up again on behalf of my execution!"

"Ah, a threat to the throne!" Nefertiti smiled. Now she had her. "Sitamun, royal wife of Pharaoh Amenhotep III and King's daughter, has threatened the throne—an offense which has been and always will be punishable by death!"

Sitamun yelled to Nefertiti as her guards laid down their spears and Nefertiti's guards surrounded her and dragged her off.

"Nefertiti! Curse you and your children! May you be forever forgotten! May you be hidden forever in the sands of Egypt!"

Her cries trailed off down the corridor, and the great throne room's door shut out her predictions of doom, replaced by a ringing silence in the great palace of Aketaten.

***

WORD OF SITAMUN'S ARREST AND ORDER OF EXECUTION traveled quickly.

Beketaten burst through the throne room doors.

"Nefertiti!"

The head royal guard, Jabari, scowled and corrected her: "Pharaoh Neferneferuaten."

"*Pharaoh*," Beketaten said. "Release Sitamun at once!"

"There are none greater than Pharaoh," Nefertiti said, refusing to look at her.

"I told you I would—"

"Ah-ah-ah," Nefertiti interrupted her. "Would you dare to threaten the throne and join your sister in death?" Nefertiti shut her mouth and shook her head; she regretted warning her. *Ignorant fool!* she chided herself.

Beketaten's tongue rolled behind her shut lips as her face narrowed in hatred. "I am asking you, Pharaoh, pleading, begging you, to spare her. She did nothing the rest of us wouldn't have done. Queen Meritaten was in the wrong place at the wrong time. Sitamun should have come to us first. We had already held up our end of the bargain."

"And for her actions, she will die," Nefertiti said, finally deciding to look at Beketaten. "Unofficially, of course."

"You are pitiful." Beketaten spat at the first stair leading to the platform where Nefertiti sat.

"A life for a life," Nefertiti said, blinded by her grief and rage. "My daughter's life."

"Are you really going to impale her and burn her body afterward so that there is no chance of her journeying to the afterlife? Would you take that away from her?"

"Impalement and disposal of the body is the written punishment for threatening the throne."

"Not for royalty! Not for my sister."

"I cannot change the laws that have held our country together for millennia," Nefertiti said calmly. "Or else the country might think me as mad as Akhenaten and Smenkare."

"Please . . ." Beketaten fell to her knees in her last attempt to plead for her sister's afterlife.

"No, she—"

Ankhesenpaaten had risen from her throne and walked up the side of the platform beyond her mother's focus. She touched her arm before she could finish her sentence. Ankhesenpaaten whispered in her mother's silence, "I loved Meritaten too . . . but I don't want my aunt Sitamun to have no afterlife because of her. You are Pharaoh . . . make an exception in this one case."

The wet glisten from Ankhesenpaaten's cheeks softened the callouses in Nefertiti's heart. She lowered her head and glanced at Beketaten and then back at her daughter. Pressing her lips together, she patted Ankhesenpaaten's hand that graced her arm. "You are wiser than me," she whispered. "Be better than me, Ankhesenpaaten."

Nefertiti returned her hand to her leg and took a deep breath as Ankhesenpaaten took her seat again.

"Because Sitamun is a royal wife and King's daughter, the punishment shall be amended." Nefertiti thought about her own deeds regarding Akhenaten. She did not want to be impaled, if ever that came out to the public, and they demanded her death. "The punishment shall be suicide by poison. Sitamun's body will be prepared for royal burial and the afterlife, as is her right as a royal wife and King's daughter."

Beketaten took a deep breath, thankful Sitamun could still journey to the afterlife and not experience much pain in her death. However, she would not give Pharaoh the satisfaction of a "Thank you" for giving Sitamun this small reprieve, so she turned and left, vowing to avenge Sitamun, her last remaining sister.

⚜ 17 ⚜
THE TIME OF NEW ALLIES

A CARAVAN ARRIVED FROM THE HITTITES, ACCEPTING AN alliance and bringing gifts of jewels and medicine to Egypt. It had been three years since Nefertiti had sent the offer of alliance under Pharaoh Akhenaten's name. Paaten, Ay, and Horemheb all agreed this was still what was best for Egypt since Egypt's allies had all but stopped trading with them.

Nefertiti accepted their caravan, then mumbled to herself, "Three years . . . better late than never."

"The treasury at least is growing again," her daughter, Ankhesenpaaten, said as she came from the shadows to her mother. "Though I hate it to be at the generosity of our enemy."

"Ankhesenpaaten—" Nefertiti motioned for her to approach. "The treasury grows because of the portion we receive from the priesthood of Amun as well."

After a moment of silence, Ankhesenpaaten tilted her head and swung her arms behind her back. "Mother . . . may I ask you something without you becoming angry?" Her long, thin body swayed in the gentle breeze of the throne room. Beads of sweat trickled down her brow as she stepped into the sunlight. The throne room's roof sat partially covered; even decrees from Pharaohs still took time to implement. Her shallow breathing followed the rhythm of her racing pulse.

Nefertiti cocked a half-grin. "Of course, my sweet one."

Her mother had always called her the sweet one; she didn't know why.

"Mut and I were speaking the other day—"

"What did Mut say?" Nefertiti's stern voice equaled the straight edge of her back.

"Mother!" Ankhesenpaaten threw her hands at her sides. "You promised you wouldn't become angry."

Nefertiti held up her hand. "Please, continue."

Ankhesenpaaten lowered her chin. She didn't want to confront her mother outright with her suspicions regarding the strange night Nefertiti had come to her, quickly followed by the murder of Meritaten, so she began with Mut just as she had rehearsed. "Mut told me you were sad . . ."

"Why wouldn't I be sad, daughter? Meritaten was killed. Meketaten, Neferneferure, and Setepenre were all taken by the plague—royal wife Kiya as well. My husband . . ."— Nefertiti drew in a sharp breath and closed her eyes momentarily—"journeys to the afterlife. Our country, although making strides back to greatness, almost bore the burden of poverty. There are many things that make me sad. One day, if you are to be Pharaoh as myself, or even chief royal wife or Coregent, you too will see sadness, and then you will understand."

Ankhesenpaaten drew nearer to her mother. "But, Mother, they were my father and my husband. My sisters. Have I not lost too?"

Here is my leading question. I cannot turn back now, she thought as her fingers trembled.

"Your smile is elusive. Mut tells me you talk as if you see

the end. Are you not happy that you and Nefe and myself are still among the living?"

"Of course I am, my sweet one," Nefertiti said, and she jumped up and threw her arms around Ankhesenpaaten. She acted as if she wanted Ankhesenpaaten's arms to rise around her waist, but Ankhesenpaaten kept them rigid by her body.

It is time to confront her, Ankhesenpaaten thought. *No more hiding.*

"You wish us killed as well," she whispered, holding her gaze with her mother.

Nefertiti's jaw hung ajar. "Why would you say such a thing?" The words flowed on the gush of her breath.

"All my life, you have taught us to worship the Aten . . . and then you reverse Father's and Smenkare's decrees. You allow the worship of false gods. You wish us killed like Meritaten, don't you?" Ankhesenpaaten whispered as her heartbeat increased with her growing courage to ask the woman who bore her about her deepest desires. "It is the real reason why you remove me and Tut from the throne. It is why you knew you would become Pharaoh."

Nefertiti squeezed her shoulders tight. *"Silence your tongue."* Her hot breath carried her words in a hushed flurry. "I removed you from the throne to *save* your life. These are very dangerous political times, *daughter.*" She shook Ankhesenpaaten's shoulders. "You would do well to distance yourself from me. I will try to undo the damage your father and Smenkare did, so that when I am gone, you and Nefe will have a life of *peace*, not of paranoia and conspiracy." Her nostrils flared. "My father always told me that one must never assume anything when one is given authority. Doing so will be your downfall."

After a moment of reflection, Ankhesenpaaten continued, "Even if I *did* believe you . . . why the false gods, Mother?"

"Daughter . . ." Nefertiti sighed. "O daughter, forgive me!"

She placed a hand on her cheek and found the back of her neck with the other. "I have taught you by my example, and that I cannot take back. But know this—Amun-Re is and has always been the premier god of Egypt."

Ankhesenpaaten took a step back and pushed her mother's hands away. "The Aten is the only true god." Her brow furrowed as it shielded her eyes from the sun's rays overhead.

"You will realize that your father was mad," Nefertiti said, clenching her fist in anger—at her father or at her, Ankhesenpaaten wasn't sure. Nefertiti went on, "I'm not asking you to believe it now at this moment, but in time you will know it to be true."

"My father was not *mad*. He *loved* me—"

"And I did not?"

Ankhesenpaaten bit her tongue as she drew farther away, choosing her words carefully.

"You were never there."

She turned and left the throne room, leaving Nefertiti speechless.

It was as if someone had kicked her in the chest as Nefertiti struggled to draw in a breath. A tear fell, and she chewed on her tongue to stop the flow. Finally, Nefertiti put her hand to her forehead as she whispered to the spot where Ankhesenpaaten was standing:

"One day you will understand . . . I sacrificed so much for the greater good of Egypt."

She looked to the door where her daughter had left as her hand dropped, defeated.

"I hope you can come to appreciate that . . . and I swear upon my life you will never have to do the same."

NEFERTITI WALKED TO THE COUNCIL ROOM WHERE Horemheb, Ay, and Paaten waited for her. Each step weighed her down, until finally, when she thought she would not make it any farther, she reached the door and opened it. Their faces drew more weight on her feet until she sat in her throne. They sat afterward.

"Pharaoh," Paaten began. "I bear the burden of informing you we have additional concerns . . . the people do not accept a female Pharaoh, especially after the execution of Sitamun. You must marry the Crown Prince Tutankhaten. He is the last of Pharaoh Amenhotep III's line."

At hearing this, Horemheb's ribs seemed to crush his lungs, but he kept a straight face.

I knew this would come. Why did I ever entertain the idea of being with her? If nothing else, she knows I care. The past year has been so hard for me to keep my distance, and yet I have failed in doing so, growing more and more in love with her.

He dreaded her marriage to the boy because it meant he could truly never have her as his own—even though he knew, deep down, that it was only a fantasy.

Why did I ever try to comfort her that night in the garden?

He answered his own question: *Because she needed you.*

Nefertiti looked at Horemheb and read his eyes: he agreed with Paaten's pronouncement, but sadness lay behind them. Then she shot a look to her father, who said nothing.

"Do you agree, Ay, Master of Pharaoh's Horses?" she asked coldly.

He pushed his lips together as he sat with his hands folded on the table in front of him. Leaning his weight into his elbows, his eyes darted between Horemheb, Paaten, and Nefertiti. Finally, he said: "The people are already wary of you because of your connection to both Akhenaten and Smenkare. For the past two decades, they have been forced into a new age for Egypt that to them was bleak and depraved. To suddenly thrust upon them a female Pharaoh, which is not of the old ways, may be too much to ask of an unwilling empire." Ay then chewed on his lip and sat back.

"I never asked for this," Nefertiti said as she tapped her fingers on the table and brought her other hand to her forehead. The thought of marriage to the young boy, even if just ceremonial, tore at her soul. "You told me we would go back to Amun as soon as power was regained from the Amun priesthood," she spat at her father.

"That was the plan, but Akhenaten became ill in the head, as you well know," Ay said as he pressed his hands into the table, clearly annoyed his daughter still had not forgiven him. "What is done is done."

"Pharaoh, just marry the boy. You can act in his place until he reaches an age of understanding," Paaten offered.

Nefertiti shook her head slowly. "And be doomed to a life of what? Loneliness?" She looked at Horemheb again. His eyes had fallen to the table: he did not like it either. Her gaze went back to Paaten. "How is Tut any different than me? He is just as connected, if not more so, to Akhenaten and Smenkare. He is their blood! I am only related through marriage."

"Queen Tiye was my sister," Ay pointed out. "You are still blood related, and you are a woman."

"The boy is young," Paaten said to mitigate the fierce look Nefertiti shot at her father. "The people still think him innocent enough not to have learned a great deal from his father."

"So what is it, then?" Nefertiti yelled at the three of them. "Am I an old, biased *coward* to them?!"

The room remained silent.

Nefertiti tapped her fingers harder, then slapped her palm down on the table. "If they want a male Pharaoh who is truly not influenced by Akhenaten or Smenkare, I need to marry someone else." Nefertiti crossed her arms as she thought.

"Who would you marry?" Horemheb asked, knowing it could not be himself—although he wished desperately that it were true. "All are beneath you. There aren't any other male Egyptian royals."

"Pawah is," Paaten muttered. "But only by marriage to Beketaten, and I would not."

"My brother Anen only had living daughters," Ay said, shaking his head.

"What if we use our newly formed alliance with the Hittites?" Nefertiti said, squeezing her hand into a fist. She did not want to marry a nasty, hairy Hittite who only bathed once a week or less, but she'd rather that than Tut.

Ay tilted his head to the side. "What are you saying, daughter?"

"I ask for a Hittite prince to marry." A sheen of sweat appeared on her brow and cheeks as she flexed her fingers before pulling them back into a fist. "I can keep the crown, and the people . . . the people will have their *male* Pharaoh."

"No—absolutely not," Paaten blurted out. His chest puffed in agitation. "The people would see that as treason. They would see you giving away the Egyptian empire to the Hittites. Surely then you would have a full-blown rebellion on your hands, putting everything that we have done in vain."

"I refuse to marry Tut!" Nefertiti pounded her hand down on the table, looking the three of them in the eyes one after the other. "If I am pressed, I will ask the Hittites to send a prince."

"Why not Tut, Nefertiti?" Ay asked.

"You know why! He is the product of Akhenaten and Henuttaneb!" Her heart raced as a red glow burned her cheeks. The words stung her heart. Even after all this time, the betrayal of her husband's promise to her still left a fresh wound, and Tut would forever be a visual reminder of her shortcomings.

"Your pride rivals the blindness of Akhenaten's zeal for the Aten," Ay said, shaking his head. "I cannot protect you if you do not do what the people ask."

"You *will* not protect me," Nefertiti corrected and saw the same hurt cross his eyes as she saw in the corridor after Akhenaten's funeral procession.

"Marry the boy," Horemheb pleaded. "Give the people what they want. They have been deprived for so long. The military cannot withstand all of Egypt rising up against you, my Pharaoh. This is the only viable option." He couldn't bear to see her killed. If she married Tut, at least she'd be alive.

Nefertiti stood up like an arrow released from the archer's bow, locking Horemheb's gaze as the color drained from her face. Her eyes shimmered with unspoken words: *Not you, too.*

She swallowed the lump in her throat. "We are dismissed."

THAT EVENING HOREMHEB FOUND NEFERTITI WALKING the halls alone again. He shook his head in silent disapproval, knowing she took a chance with her life being by her lonesome like this. At least she was close to her chambers.

If it weren't for me, would she take such a risk? he wondered. *I did come looking for her like I do most nights I am in the palace. It must stop. It is not worth Pharaoh making unwise decisions. She has made so many, first with Sitamun, now with Tut.*

He realized he had gotten too close to her. The echo of his footsteps gave him away. She stopped and turned toward him with a thin grimace.

"Does sleep still evade you, Pharaoh?" Horemheb asked with a bow, hoping to evade her scrutiny.

"Does it you?" Nefertiti asked as she crossed her arms.

"Yes." His gaze shifted to the floor between them.

"You told me to marry another." She narrowed his eyes. "I thought you cared for me. You told me. You come find me every night you are here to speak to me." Her voice turned breathless. "You held me in my sorrow."

Her whisper pricked his heart, and her hot glare burned his chest as his eyes lifted to face her. "Yes, my Pharaoh." Her full lips and big, almond eyes allured him, but he stood his ground. Soon, if she married Tut, he could no longer entertain any thoughts of her, for they would only drive him mad or cause him to commit the crime of lying with another man's wife.

"Why? Why would you do that?" she whispered through her teeth.

Her question stabbed his heart. *Because we can never be!* he wanted to yell. *You are Pharaoh! I am the Commander! I am sorry for ever stepping outside of my status.*

She paused before asking her next question, knowing that after the question left her lips, their entire relationship would change one way or the other. She gathered her courage and rationalized that even if his answer was yes, she was still Pharaoh and he was still the Commander. They would act like civilized adults and carry on their responsibilities without incident—or so she hoped. The desire to know overtook her mind in her time of vulnerability, so much so that she opened her mouth to speak and cast off the consequences.

"Did I misinterpret your actions? Were they truly only out of kindness?"

He found her eyes. "No."

"Then why?" She pressed her jaw together, bracing in anticipation for his response; and yet her heart felt half of its burden fall away, relieved he did in fact feel the same way about her.

The corners of his mouth fell, and he shook his head. "You know why, my Pharaoh."

Her chin trembled as she pushed away the sinking feeling in her stomach.

"It's not fair," she whimpered.

Her shoulders crumpled, and Horemheb took a few steps forward, wanting to sweep her up in his embrace and wrap her body in his. He stopped when she raised her hand to halt him.

She took a deep breath, regaining her composure. "Will you escort me to my chambers?"

"Yes, my Pharaoh," he said, and let her lead the way as he walked slightly to the side and behind her. She said nothing while they walked, and, following her lead, he kept silent. When they reached her chamber doors, Horemheb noticed Ineni was not outside.

Seeing him notice, she said, "I dismissed him. I don't trust him to keep me safe. I prop a chair against the door at night and try to stay awake to hear it as I lie in bed . . . I haven't slept well in a long time."

"Pharaoh, you need sleep. Without it, your mind dies." Horemheb bowed and said, "I will stand watch at your door."

"You don't understand. I'm afraid, Commander." Nefertiti placed a hand on her door. "I'm afraid of eating and drinking. I'm afraid of sleeping. It seemed so easy to get rid of Akhenaten and Smenkare and even . . ." Tears filled her eyes as she thought of her innocent daughter. "How much easier would it be to get rid of *me*?" A tear slid down her cheek as she looked down the hallway, making sure no one was there. "Will you again come inside with me? It was the only time I felt safe."

"I will do whatever you need me to do."

She saw in his eyes that Horemheb meant the words he said.

"Thank you," she whispered and opened the door. He walked in and she closed the door behind him and moved the chair to the door—just as she had done every night since Horemheb had stayed with her. "Can you check the chambers and make sure no one is here?" she asked with a gesture around her room. "I usually do it . . . but it scares me."

"Yes, my Pharaoh," Horemheb said, and he began to walk around, pulling his dagger from his chest belt. He searched the entire chamber and reported that it was indeed empty. He pulled the sheet back on her bed, gesturing for her to climb in. "You need to sleep. I will stay up and keep watch for you."

"Thank you, Commander," she said as she slipped past him. She let her hand rest on his chest. She found his eyes. It had been a long time since she had been alone with a man in her chambers—at least when she was in a sound mind. The last time Horemheb was in her room alone was almost a year ago; she had not forgotten his kindness in her agony.

"Sleep now, Pharaoh. I am always loyal to you and to Egypt. You will never have to doubt me," Horemheb said as he covered her hand with his.

The candlelight flickered. His gaze fell to her lips and his mouth parted. He so badly wanted to kiss her, just as he had wanted to every night they had met in the hallways for the past year, and even in Libya and Nubia several years ago and in the lotus garden of the palace that night of Akhenaten's funeral; but this time, it was stronger than he'd ever felt before. Maybe it was because he knew in a short while, when she had to marry someone else, the idea would be dead.

But it isn't dead now . . .

In a heady rush, he leaned forward, kissed her cheek, and let out a breath on her neck. He reached around her and took the candle by her bed. He pulled back to see the glisten in her eyes.

"I'm sorry, my Pharaoh." He closed his eyes. "I should not have done that."

Her hand still stayed on his chest. He took a step back, letting it fall.

"I will stay here and keep watch while you sleep."

He hinged at the waist and went to sit down in a neighboring chair.

She stared at him for a moment, wishing he hadn't stopped with a kiss to her cheek; but she knew why he hadn't dared go further.

He watched her watch him until she fell asleep. He removed his heavy bronze armor and placed it on the ground and put his khopesh on the table next to him as he watched the door.

IN THE NIGHT, NEFERTITI SCREAMED; HOREMHEB JUMPED to his feet with his dagger aimed ready to strike, but then realized Nefertiti was only having a nightmare. He sheathed his dagger, rushed to her bedside, and woke her as she beat on his chest.

"Pharaoh, it's me. It's me, Horemheb. You are safe. You are safe with me," he said over and over again.

Her eyes adjusted in the dark, and she began to cry. Putting her hand up to shield her eyes, she shook her head vigorously. Horemheb sat next to her on the bed and rubbed her back until she settled down. She took a deep breath and let it out slowly, then placed her hand on Horemheb's knee.

"I dreamed everyone I cared about left me to be killed," she confided.

Letting go of his inhibitions, he guided her head to his chest with one hand and grasped her hand on his knee with the other. "It was only a dream. Your daughters, your father, your mother, your sister, myself . . . we would never leave you." He turned his nose into the perfumed skin of her forehead. "*I* will never leave you."

Her fingers crept up to his neck as she lifted her face to his. Her eyes fell to his lips, and she pressed her chest against him, allowing herself to be pulled into his embrace.

"I will keep you safe, my Pharaoh," Horemheb whispered to her as he wrapped his strong arms around her. His heart beat hard in his chest as he wrestled in his mind what to do.

She is Pharaoh—she will marry another, so kiss her now while it is still legal! he told himself. *And risk whatever Paaten does to you.*

"Call me Nefertiti," she breathed as their faces drew closer, "in times like these."

He smiled in the darkness.

It had been a long time since he had held a woman in bed, but never such a beautiful woman as Nefertiti. She drew the back of her hand around his face. He grasped her hand and kissed it.

"Nefertiti, I more than anything want to touch you . . . to love you."

He paused.

"But . . ."

Tears filled her eyes, for she knew what he was going to say.

"We shouldn't complicate things more. They will force you to marry, and it won't be to me." He dropped his forehead to hers. "I'm sorry. I'm so sorry I did this. I let this happen."

She closed her eyes, pressing out hot tears. "Then at least stay with me. Hold me so I can feel safe."

"For you, Nefertiti . . . anything," he whispered, and pushed her back into the bed. He removed his chest belt and laid down next to her, wrapping her in his arms.

"What if someone enters?" she asked, her voice muffled against his chest.

"I am a light sleeper. I will hear if someone enters," he reassured her, keeping his chin on her forehead.

"If I was not Pharaoh, would you have stayed and kept watch for me?" Nefertiti whispered.

"Yes," he answered.

"If I was not Pharaoh, would you have kissed me?"

Part of her needed to know she was still desirable; but part of her needed him, wanted him, cared for him, loved him, and she hoped he would confirm that for her, that his feelings for her were more than just lust.

Horemheb didn't know how to answer. Of course he wanted to kiss her, but she was still Pharaoh. Instead, he caressed her face.

"I am a servant of Egypt—and of you, as Pharaoh. I am not worthy to be your lover, but please know that I admire your courage, your wit, your passion, your loyalty to Egypt, your conscience, and your stunning face and body that rivals that of a goddess. If you were not Pharaoh, I would have asked to marry you a long time ago."

A tear slid out of Nefertiti's eye. "Would you marry me now and be the people's male Pharaoh they so desire?"

Horemheb entertained this possibility for the briefest of moments, but then shook his head. "It is Prince Tutankhaten's place first, and then Pawah's. Even after that, it would never be mine."

"Would you doom me to a life of loneliness?" she asked; both she and Horemheb knew she would never entertain a marriage to either of those men.

"You are not alone, Nefertiti," Horemheb said. "There are many—"

She put her hand on his shaven cheek, shushing him. Burrowing her body further into his embrace, she guided his face closer to hers. "I am going to kiss you . . . ?" she whispered, more as a question than a command, still lingering back in case he wanted to stop her. "As a woman, not as Pharaoh."

Her lips hovered above his. She watched his face as he made no attempt to stop her. And so she laid a soft and gentle kiss upon his lips and pulled away to gauge his response.

He studied her face and brought her close again. "You can't deny who you are, Nefertiti." His lips brushed past hers. "You are still Pharaoh."

"I trust you with the empire." She ran her hand down his cheek and to his chest and rubbed his thigh with her leg, and in a commanding voice she said, "Become Pharaoh and marry me."

Horemheb hesitated. "I shouldn't be here."

"You are here because I asked you to be here. Akhenaten has been gone for years now, and it was even longer still when last he touched me. I—"

"Are you wanting me to satisfy a desire, love you, or just be a means to an end?" His dark eyes pleaded with her for honesty.

"All of them," she replied as her eyes glistened. "I see the way you look at me, Horemheb. I never knew if it was lust or love, but either way, I have come to take comfort in your presence, and I care so much for you. I trust you enough to let you stay in my bedchambers while I sleep. I trust you with my armies. I would trust you with the crown. The people press me for a husband. You would be a fitting husband and a strong Pharaoh."

"Nothing between us will ever be accepted. I will have to watch you marry another," he said, shaking his head. "Even Paaten told me he would strip my rank if I let myself get too close to you."

"Then *marry* me." She ran her hands over his large arms. "I am Pharaoh. I can marry whomever I wish."

He shook his head, resisting her touch through taut muscles. "You must marry royalty, and I . . . I am the son of a soldier."

"Please, then, just kiss me," she asked of him. "We can think on it later."

"Nefertiti," he said in protest, yet still brought his lips close to hers again. "I shouldn't." But his hand betrayed his words as it ran up her body's curves in the moonlight.

"I know, but I need you right now," she whispered, and she brought his face closer still.

"Nefertiti, I . . ." he began.

But she pressed a finger to his lips. She removed it and waited for him to kiss her. She needed him to want to kiss her.

"You tempt me." Horemheb swept his arms around Nefertiti and rested one hand on the nape of her neck, the other on her lower back. He pressed his lips to hers and pulled her closer to him as he deepened the kiss, running his tongue across her bottom lip.

He pulled away, leaving her breathless. She grabbed his face and kissed him again. She pressed her body against his harder still as his hands roamed up and down her back and his mind screamed for him to stop, that this would have ramifications, but his hands found a way to keep his thoughts at bay at least for a moment.

He pulled away a second time, trying to slow his beating heart, and said in a husky voice, "Nefertiti, you are the most beautiful woman a man could ever ask for. I am humbled you have directed your affections toward me, but we should end this before it is too late." He tried to regain control of his breath. He pulled himself out of her bed and bowed before her as she rose to her knees, not wanting him to go.

"Nefertiti, if you were not my Pharaoh, I would stay. But I am the commander of your armies. We should not blur the lines any more than we already have, and for this, I am to blame. Accept my deepest apologies."

"Horemheb, please," she begged. "Don't do this."

"I will stand guard at your door, so you may feel safe. I will always protect—"

She reached for his hand and drew him back to her. "Please stay with me. Just hold me so I can sleep. Please, Horemheb." She wrapped her arms around him and buried her head in his chest, breathing in his musky scent. "Please."

Her whispered plea tore down the small barrier he had put up, and he knew without a doubt that she meant it. He guided her to lie in the bed, slid in, and wrapped her up in his arms. She pressed into his warmth as her tears and Horemheb's understanding hands moving across her back eventually lulled her to sleep.

WHEN MORNING CAME AND NEFERTITI OPENED HER EYES, she was glad to find that Horemheb had not left her. She closed her eyes and rubbed her cheek on his chest, pulling him closer. He returned her embrace. They lay in silence for a moment, not wanting the coming day to force them to leave each other.

"Did you sleep well?" he finally murmured, pressing his cheek to the top of her head.

"Yes." Her hot breath on his chest made him squeeze her a little harder. Lifting her chin, she smoothed her hand over his arm. "Horemheb, do you not wish this to be every morning? Will you not marry me?" Her eyes danced as they searched his for a response.

He traced the outline of her face before gently touching

his forehead to hers and giving her the lightest of kisses upon her lips. "I do wish this to be every morning . . . but it is not my right to marry you. Nor is it yours to choose a man of non-royalty."

As the morning sun's beams crept from the window to the bed, he pulled himself away from her. As he donned his bronze armor and khopesh, they kept each other's gaze, their thoughts turned inward. He came near to the bed to grab his chest belt; he wrung the leather belt in his hand as he squeezed the dagger's sheath. Her dark eyes looked up to him as his deep but soft voice spoke:

"Nefertiti . . . I want what I cannot have."

Nefertiti's face fell. "As do I," she whispered.

He let out a loud breath and slapped his sheathed dagger in the palm of his hand. The thought crossed his mind of just throwing his uniform to the ground and wrapping her up in his arms, come what may, but instead, he turned and walked to the door. He buckled his chest belt across his shoulder and lingered by the door, knowing this was the last time he would be in her bedchambers. Looking back at her with the same yearning with which she looked upon him, he opened her door and left.

LATER THAT MORNING, NEFERTITI SAT ON HER THRONE, and with a shaky voice ordered all to be dismissed and then commanded the scribe to write a letter to King Suppiluliuma of the Hittites requesting a prince to marry because she had no one to marry among her own people. She then ordered the scribe to silence.

"If the country rebels, then so be it," Nefertiti muttered to herself after the messenger had turned to leave with the letter. Part of her wanted to be killed anyway—at least she could reach immortality with her daughters who had gone before.

She debated ordering the messenger back, but her soul was compromised. She buried her head in her hands as she bent over in the throne, forcing her mouth shut, wishing she could marry whom she wanted. She heard the throne doors close just as the crown upon her head nearly toppled off, but she caught it with her hand. Sitting back up again, she looked at the now-almost-covered ceiling.

She closed her eyes. "If anything, this will be the true test of Pharaoh's power."

Ankhesenpaaten walked in to take her place on the throne sitting on the lower platform and nodded to her mother as she sat. Nefertiti watched her fidget with her fingers until she finally turned around and looked at her again.

"Mother," she said as she stood up and walked up to the platform. "Did I hear you ask for a prince?"

"You must keep it to yourself," Nefertiti warned, her voice a harsh whisper, shaking her head. *You sly daughter, eavesdropping after I had ordered everyone to leave.*

"But, Mother, from the *Hittites?*" Ankhesenpaaten asked, tilting her head.

"You won't understand," Nefertiti said, watching her daughter's eyes avert from hers.

"You keep telling me that, so tell me so I *do* understand," Ankhesenpaaten said, lifting her gaze to her again. At her mother's silence, she blurted out, "Do you even *miss* Father?"

"No." She surprised Ankhesenpaaten and herself at how fast she responded. Nefertiti chewed her lip, debating how much she should tell her daughter. "Ankhesenpaaten . . . your father ruined this country. I am trying to put together the pieces."

"What do you mean?"

"I will tell you when you are older." Nefertiti waved her on and looked forward to the doors of the throne room. She watched from the corner of her eye as Ankhesenpaaten licked her lips, wrung her hands, and took a shaky breath, as if wondering if she could muster the courage to keep probing.

"I *am* older," Ankhesenpaaten mumbled, and then straightened her back and said, "I am almost of the age of marriage."

"Yes, you are," Nefertiti said, and her body relaxed as her lips curled at the corners.

"Why are you smiling?" Ankhesenpaaten's face fell into a scowl.

Nefertiti chuckled. "You."

"What *about* me?" Ankhesenpaaten's voice became shrill as her cheeks flushed.

"I remember when you were a little girl and you were too shy to ask Aitye for some more beans at dinner. You made Meketaten do it for you." Nefertiti laughed and smiled at the fond memory of her two girls, then suddenly became despondent at the thought that one of them wasn't there anymore. Shaking her head to get rid of the sad thought, she continued, "And now look at you—standing up to your mother, Pharaoh, demanding to know her innermost thoughts and motives."

"I am g-grown up now," Ankhesenpaaten said with a stutter. Her shoulders caved a little at her mother's laughing.

"And so you believe you should know everything?" Nefertiti sighed. "My daughter, you don't want to know. I am trying to keep you safe—sheltered from the crocodile's teeth, for there are many snares as Pharaoh."

Ankhesenpaaten closed her eyes as she reflected on her mother's words, but Nefertiti could see the doubt come to the surface again. Her daughter asked, "Are you sure you keep the truth hidden to just keep us safe?"

Nefertiti's eyes narrowed. "What do you mean, am I sure?"

Ankhesenpaaten's heart raced as she drew shallow breaths, inflating her courage as she dared ask her mother the question that had lingered on her mind for over a year. Last time she insinuated the act, she never received a straight answer. This time, she would not walk away with any confusion over her mother's actions. Ankhesenpaaten crossed her arms, defending herself from whatever answer her mother gave, and asked bluntly, "Did you kill Smenkare to take his place?"

Nefertiti drew in a shaky breath and pushed her lips together. She shook her head and closed her eyes, leaning forward in her throne. How to respond? She opened her eyes and straightened her back. "No," Nefertiti answered, but felt her heart drop into her stomach at the half-truth. She watched her daughter's unmoving arms and her quivering jaw, signifying her struggle to accept the answer. "And to think—if my own daughter assumes as much, it makes me wonder what the rest of the people think." Nefertiti leaned back in her throne and propped her head up with one elbow. "Ankhesenpaaten, the people rejoice in the streets because they are gone. Your father, too. They are happy to worship Amun-Re again, as it should be. As it has always been."

"I *saw* the mourners! The people were sad they were gone —*all* of them!" Ankhesenpaaten yelled, her arms still crossed.

"Ankhesenpaaten. The mourners are *paid* to be mourners." Nefertiti took in a deep breath. "I know it pains you to hear—"

"You are a liar. No one is happy they are gone." Ankhesenpaaten's hands dropped as her face fell and a swift coldness seeped into her bones. "The Aten is the true god."

Nefertiti blinked, not anticipating this response from her daughter. "When you become a royal wife, you will learn you mustn't say things like that or else end up like your father and sister."

"Why? If *you* aren't around to kill me—"

"The people will," Nefertiti cut her off as her breathing grew labored. How to get her daughter to understand? "And they will send those who can to do their bidding."

"But Pharaoh is all-powerful. One who kills the Aten's divinely appointed is forever lost and will not be able to journey to the afterlife."

"*Amun*'s divinely appointed." Nefertiti threw her hand toward the door. "Go to Malkata. Go to Waset, child. Learn for yourself the truth."

"I am not a *child*," Ankhesenpaaten retorted, bringing her hands to her hips in a pose that, to Nefertiti, was nothing but childish.

"You wanted to know the *truth*? You claim to be mature enough to understand? Then quit believing like a child!" Nefertiti yelled at her. "There are consequences if you don't worship the true god, Amun-Re. If you be like your father and sister, Egypt will cease to exist!" She stood up from her chair and began to pace. "Do you know how close we have come to bankruptcy? Do you know how close we have come to *rebellion*? We have lost our allies. The economy was failing; the royal treasury and grain houses was the only thing to keep the nation afloat for these past ten years—all because your father chased after his own selfish desires and took the whole of Egypt with him into his despairing pit of madness!"

"Don't talk about Father that way," Ankhesenpaaten muttered as she clenched her hands by her sides, her cheeks flushed from the scolding her mother gave her.

Nefertiti marched up to Ankhesenpaaten, who cowered in her presence. "Open your eyes, Ankhesenpaaten!"

"If I *do* believe you, then why the Hittites?"

Ankhesenpaaten drew in a hot breath as she waited for her mother to respond.

Nefertiti gritted her teeth, narrowing her eyes; her mind flashed to the morning as she watched Horemheb leave her room. "The people want a *male* Pharaoh," Nefertiti said at last. "To be as it has always been. Thanks to your father, once again, the people are paranoid of change."

"But, Mother, why the Hittites?" she asked again.

"I must marry royalty." Nefertiti straightened her back and walked toward her throne.

"*Tut* is royalty! And Pawah is royalty by marriage." Ankhesenpaaten presented the facts to her mother with a swing of her hand. "Can't you marry *them*?"

"Ha. Pawah. Never trust that man." Nefertiti peered over her shoulder. "Keep him close so you can see what he is up to, but *never* trust him, like your life depends on it." She reached her throne and sat down. "And I would never marry Tut."

"Why not? Tut is sweet and kind." Ankhesenpaaten smiled at the thought of his daily fighting class, at his yelling he would protect her.

Nefertiti noticed her smile and bit her tongue, shaking her head in disgust. She rubbed her forehead. "Why am I still being punished?" she whispered to herself.

"What?" Ankhesenpaaten leaned forward, trying to hear what her mother said.

Nefertiti looked up. "You wouldn't understand."

"Just tell me. I might. I am old enough to understand these things."

Ankhesenpaaten's whiny, shrill voice sent Nefertiti's blood boiling. "You wouldn't understand—I tried telling you about your father and you reject the truth!"

Ankhesenpaaten's nostrils flared. "Tell me, Mother! Tell me!"

Nefertiti yanked herself from her seat again and shot a finger in the air. "You will not yell at Pharaoh!"

Ankhesenpaaten's barrage of unsaid words hit her closed lips. Swallowing them down, they fueled the fire in her eyes.

Nefertiti's hand dropped, as did her chin. "You wouldn't understand, my sweet one." Nefertiti's quiet voice contrasted with the last remnant of echo from her outburst.

Seeing her mother's sadness extinguished Ankhesenpaaten's anger as she came near to her mother's side. Hesitant fingers wrapped around Nefertiti's arm.

Nefertiti took a sharp inhale as her body stiffened. "I will not marry your father's son and give up the crown to a boy who should never have been born."

Ankhesenpaaten's eyes pleaded, *Why?*, but the question lingered in her throat. Maybe there was more to the woman she called mother than what she gave her credit for. "Something happened with Father, didn't it?"

"I hope you never have to understand," Nefertiti whispered. She caressed Ankhesenpaaten's cheek and kissed her forehead. "I'm sorry I was never there for you. I am sorry I put my responsibilities over you and your sisters."

Ankhesenpaaten's heart skipped a beat. Out of sheer impulse, she threw her hands around Nefertiti's shoulders and squeezed. She had only wanted some acknowledgment from her mother about her absence all these years; even if she did still feel she wasn't being completely truthful, in this moment, she felt something for her mother that she hadn't felt before.

Nefertiti wrapped her arms around her daughter as they shared an unspoken connection. It was the first real embrace Ankhesenpaaten had given her in a long time.

☙ 18 ☙

THE TIME OF DEMANDS

Pawah and Beketaten requested a council with Nefertiti. She invited Ay, Horemheb, and Paaten to join her in the council room with the leaders of the People's Restoration of Egypt. Beketaten sat before Nefertiti reached her throne, but the others remained standing, as was custom, until Nefertiti sat down.

"The people demand Tut now more than ever," Pawah began. "Especially after the execution of Sitamun, who was innocent in their eyes."

"I am Egypt," Nefertiti countered. "She was not innocent."

"Just like you and me," Beketaten said. "The only innocent one in here is General Paaten. Perhaps he should arrest us all and force *us* to drink—"

"Silence, Beketaten," Pawah said; he moved his hand in front of her mouth when he observed the faces around them grow grim.

"The sins of the hypocrite come to fruition," Beketaten jabbed one last time.

"Egypt wants a male Pharaoh," Pawah said, raising an

annoyed eyebrow at his wife. "Tut is your only option . . . other than me."

Beketaten's head swung toward her husband; she crossed her arms as she leaned back in the chair. He did speak the truth.

"I will not marry. There are none greater than Pharaoh," Nefertiti said. "The people may demand a male Pharaoh, but I will wear the Pharaoh's beard and wear the Pharaoh's crown. If they want a man, I will *dress* like a man."

"Daughter," Ay whispered. "Just marry the boy."

"Master of Pharaoh's Horses, you have done enough to convince me of a great many things in my life, all of which I am not proud," Nefertiti shot back. "It is time to do what you do best and let me fend for myself."

The dagger in the air drew blood as Ay felt his heart bleed.

"There will be no marriage," Nefertiti continued to the room. "Let them come. They will be put to death as well, and"—she looked to Beketaten—"there will be no exception to the law this time."

"My brother Akhenaten put to death the rebellion that came upon Malkata and sent us to exile," Beketaten gently reminded her. "And you see what happened to him."

"The people's bellies are full again and their hands do not lay idle," Nefertiti retorted, "their faith reestablished, their lives not in danger for uttering Amun-Re's name. I have corrected all that your brothers have done."

"We shall see." Beketaten pressed her lips into a wicked smile. "I hope you sleep well tonight, Pharaoh, for it may be the last."

Nefertiti raised an eyebrow. "Are you threatening Pharaoh? We all know what happens to those who threaten the throne."

"Nonsense. I am merely *warning* Pharaoh." Beketaten's

shoulders emphasized her intent with an innocent shrug, but her eyes glowered at Nefertiti.

Nefertiti narrowed her eyes in response. "I should have asked your brother and mother to kill you when you rebelled against Pharaoh. I *saved* you from execution."

"You sent us to exile!"

Nefertiti sat up straight, ready to defend herself. "I didn't send you to exile. Akhenaten did. We have already had this discussion, and I will not have it again."

Beketaten sent a fist into the table. "Because of you, half of my siblings are dead. You—"

Paaten jerked out of his chair and threw his dagger into the table between the two women. "What is done is done." He looked to Beketaten. "We can either live in the past, continually righting every wrong done to us in our own minds, or . . ." He picked up his dagger and sheathed it in his belt. ". . . we can move forward, accepting that each side has lost, and work together to rebuild Egypt." He smoothed the splinters from the wood that his dagger had created, brushing them back into the table until the mark was hardly noticeable. "What say you?"

He fixated on Beketaten, as did Horemheb and Ay.

"One does not simply walk away from murder," Beketaten muttered through her clenched teeth.

"Words for you to remember as well." Horemheb's gaze bore into Beketaten and Pawah. Horemheb stood. "We stand with Pharaoh. She has spoken—there will be no marriage to Prince Tutankhaten, nor to you, Pawah."

Horemheb puffed his chest, which drew a slight peer from Nefertiti. Why couldn't Ay have defended her like Paaten and Horemheb? *Coward,* she thought.

"Now leave." Horemheb's voice boomed off the stone walls.

Beketaten opened her mouth to speak, but Pawah stood

and grabbed her arm, yanking her out of the chair. "Remember, the four of you, we will follow your wishes . . . for now. I cannot ensure the people will comply." He pushed Beketaten in front of him, urging her to the door. She shot daggers back at him as she turned to leave. "Power is fleeting when you are a woman. Use what you have left wisely," Pawah said as he followed Beketaten and slammed the door behind them.

"Well, I think we got to Pawah," Ay said, looking at his clasped hands on the table.

"We?" Nefertiti asked, and her eyes danced in annoyance. "Thank you, General and Commander, for defending your Pharaoh."

They each bowed their head in reverence.

"Daughter," Ay started, but Nefertiti spoke over him.

"General and Commander, please let me speak to Master of Pharaoh's Horses in private."

"As you command," Paaten said, and the two men left Nefertiti and Ay alone.

Nefertiti knew the General thought less of her now that she had taken her revenge with Sitamun, and she had not spoken to Horemheb alone since he stayed with her that night. She couldn't bear to look at him. She would not marry; or, if the Hittites responded to her impulsive request, she would have to marry a nasty Hittite, or risk breaching their alliance. Both of those thoughts made her sick, for her heart belonged to Horemheb, even though he refused it.

"My lotus blossom," Ay said, looking deep into her eyes. "Don't wager your life with this nonsense. Please, my love. You tie my hands."

Nefertiti shrugged away her father's stare. "You convinced me I would thrive when Thutmose passed from his illness, and I was to marry Amenhotep instead. You convinced me Amenhotep would love me when he turned me away after our marriage. 'Trust and truth are united in marriage, my daughter'—those were your words. You convinced me I could help Akhenaten come back from his madness. You convinced me to stay true to him, that he would relent with his obsessions with the Aten. You convinced me to *murder* him! Now you want to convince me to marry his son? To what end? To see me in more pain? More anger? More sadness?" Her words flew out faster than she could take in the breath to say them.

Ay sat mute for a moment and closed his eyes. He let out a slow breath. "I did convince you of a great many things. A father is never perfect. We never claim to be. All we want is what's best for our daughters and our sons. I convinced you of those things because—"

"You were afraid to stand up for me, to protect me," Nefertiti said.

"No . . ." He pleaded with his eyes. "I thought I was protecting you." He buried his head in his hands, and then she took his gaze once more. "I thought I was doing the right thing: protecting you from the greater, more pressing threat. Even now, as I urge you to marry Tut, I do so hoping the ceremonial marriage will be enough to appease the people's concern, and that they do not try to kill you like Akhenaten and Smenkare. I love you, Nefertiti." His shoulders fell as his heart poured out against the wall she had barricaded herself behind.

Nefertiti's cheeks flushed hot with rage. "I would rather die than see that boy Tut as Pharaoh!"

"Please, Nefertiti," Ay said. "Don't say such things. He is just a boy. You will still be the ruler behind him."

"I don't care about that," Nefertiti said; although the weight of the crown upon her head did feel good, the motive drew its source much deeper.

"Then why, Nefertiti?"

"Father! He promised me! He *promised* me!" Nefertiti yelled as her tears smudged the kohl under her eyes. "I was to bear his son! I was to be the mother of the next Pharaoh! He betrayed me because I wasn't *enough*. I couldn't help him. I couldn't bear a *son*! His stupid visions! I hate him! I *hate* him, Father! I hate his son!"

Ay only sat with his shoulders slumped as he watched his daughter, his beloved, his lotus blossom, still suffering from the actions of the man he should have done away with years before.

"The boy has done nothing wrong," Ay tried to calm her.

"Can't you see? I hate that boy! I hate hearing his name— I hate even *looking* at him!" Nefertiti slammed her fist into the table. "He will never be Pharaoh so long as I live!"

"My Nefertiti." Ay stood and came near to his daughter. "Please, I am sorry." He put a hand to her cheek and guided her to him. "I am so sorry." He pulled her head into his chest. "Please forgive me. I have failed you." A tear rolled down his cheek. "I have failed you. Please forgive me."

She wasn't listening to her father anymore, only absentmindedly reaffirming that she could not marry Tut. "I can't . . . not right now . . ." Horemheb's impassioned kiss filled her mind as her eyes glistened from the memory, knowing she could never be with him. Her mind shifted to her first kiss with Amenhotep under the moonlight—before he became Akhenaten. The sweetness of his kiss filled her with one last longing for her late husband; but then, thinking of his son, her blood boiled—his son, who embodied the sum of his betrayal of everything she had done for him. The heat from her anger caused her tears to dissipate.

"Please," Ay begged. "These past years have been worse than when I lost your mother, knowing that I have lost you too, even as you still live." He rubbed her back. "Please, my lotus blossom. I have stayed away, trying to let you come to your own acceptance, but I see that was wrong of me."

"Father, I still love Akhenaten, despite all that he did . . . but with the same breath, I hate him," Nefertiti gurgled from her chest, ignoring Ay and focusing on the proposed marriage to Tut. "I cannot marry Tut. I will not marry Tut."

She pushed away from his chest. "I won't."

"Nefertiti, please. I cannot protect you. I will die trying to protect you, but if you don't marry Tut and make him Pharaoh, Pawah will make *sure* the people act." Ay dipped his chin, pleading with his daughter to make the wise choice. "Especially after Sitamun."

She drew her eyebrows together and scowled. "Then *distance* yourself from me, Father, so that when the people do rise up, you are not caught in the crossfire!"

She stormed out of her own council room.

Unbeknownst to Nefertiti and Ay, Pawah stood behind the wall of the open-roofed council room, listening to their conversation, and smiled, knowing all he had to do was bide his time.

NEFERTITI SAW HOREMHEB UPON LEAVING THE COUNCIL room. He had stayed behind to see Nefertiti, but feigned some official reason to the general. His time with her as an unmarried woman was swiftly dwindling, and if they were to have another moment of weakness, at least they would not be punished—or rather, *she* would not be punished; he may still have his rank stripped.

She looked at him with a slack face, and instead of walking toward him, she walked away. He attempted to follow her, but she turned and shook her head.

"I can't," she whispered, rubbing her palm over her chest as if to protect her heart from him.

He watched her walk away, silent and forlorn.

Ay, who had been watching him from the council room, came out to him and then looked down the hallway at Nefertiti, who eventually turned a corner.

"She needs a guard with her," Horemheb said, realizing Ay was standing next to him.

"She has never been the same since . . ." Ay trailed off. "The sins of the father ripple throughout a child's life."

"She is your daughter," Horemheb said, still looking to where Nefertiti had rounded the corner. "Forgiveness will come in time."

Ay looked back to Horemheb. "You care for her?"

Horemheb fell completely still as a knot grew in his stomach. He clenched his jaw. *Is it that obvious?* He peered over to Ay, then dropped his gaze to the floor and back to where Nefertiti had disappeared.

Ay patted his back. "Your secret is safe with me." He turned to leave, but then stopped and laid a knuckle on Horemheb's shoulder. "I wished Nefertiti could have been with someone like you," he whispered.

Horemheb dipped his chin and swallowed the lump that had formed in his throat. "Thank you, Master of Pharaoh's Horses." The two men locked eyes for a second. "I will always protect her, regardless of who she marries."

"You are a good man, Commander." Ay knocked his knuckle on Horemheb's shoulder as he began to walk away. "You are a good man."

PAWAH STOOD WAITING FOR HER OUTSIDE HER bedchambers.

"Pharaoh Neferneferuaten," he said with a deep bow.

"Vizier Pawah—or do you still prefer Fifth Prophet of Amun?" Nefertiti rolled her shoulder away from him in a defensive stance.

"Tsk-tsk." He shook his head. "Are you still wary of me?" He took a step closer, narrowing his gaze. "After everything we have been through?"

"You mean rebellion, conspiracy, and murder? Yes, of course, I am still wary of you." Nefertiti planted her feet; she suddenly wished she had not dismissed her guards, but she did not falter in her stare.

Pawah chuckled deeply, replying with a smug tone, "And yet you still keep me as Vizier?"

"I keep my enemies close," Nefertiti said through her teeth. Pawah chose just then to lean an arm on the wall beside her head, drawing closer as if to challenge her words. She wanted to shuffle backward, but she instead stood unflinching, refusing to let slip she was afraid of this man.

Why didn't I let Horemheb walk with me?

"Then maybe you should marry me," Pawah proposed, wetting his lips. "I am the only other royal male left, and then . . ." He leaned into her unamused face and whispered, "You could keep me *really* close."

She stared straight ahead, repulsed by his advances. He did have a handsome face, strong jaw and nose, but she knew who he was and wanted no part.

"You would be aligning Pharaoh with the priesthood of Amun," he said, his intense glare burning her face. "Really seal in the power you and Akhenaten tried so hard to regain."

"Or handing it *back* to the priesthood," Nefertiti shot back, turning her head to look him in the eye; but, to her dismay, his lips were that much closer, almost brushing against her own.

"The great beautiful Nefertiti . . . as your late husband

described, 'the most beautiful woman in all the world.' Your lips as full as the blossoming lotus flower—isn't that what your father calls you? Lotus flower?" He touched her under her chin.

"Lotus blossom," Nefertiti muttered as she swatted his hand away and looked straight ahead again, turning her lips from his.

"Oh yes . . . *my lotus blossom*," he murmured in her ear.

Only my father calls me that, you wretch, she thought.

Pawah mistook the blush of her cheeks as an invitation rather than a brewing rage.

"Eyes as dark as night and cheeks that rise to the heights of the gods . . ." He paused to see if his sultry voice had any effect on her, then continued tapping his foot in annoyance. Raising his hand to her neck, his fingertips barely graced her skin. Again he whispered in her ear, "A long, slender neck . . ." His hand fell to her chest. "And—"

Nefertiti took ahold of his wrist and squeezed. "I would rather die a thousand times than marry you. I would marry *Tut* before I would ever marry you." She spat at his neck and thrust his wrist away.

"You need a husband to be Pharaoh," Pawah said, straightening up, his voice becoming harsh and sharp. "Choose me. I will see to it you are not harmed."

"No." Nefertiti's voice dropped as she strung out the word to emphasize her point.

"No one tells me no," Pawah threatened.

"I'll arrest you," Nefertiti quickly responded, more fearful of this power-seeking man than ever before.

"No, you won't." Pawah chuckled and rubbed his hands together, tossing her threat to the wind. "You only get one mistake as a woman Pharaoh—and you decided to use it on the execution of Sitamun. Any more, and you will for sure have a rebellion on your hands, and then the *boy* will be Pharaoh."

Her ears turned hot.

"If I were you, I would have chosen *me*," Pawah said as he showcased his face. "Beketaten talks a lot, but she wouldn't harm anyone. Now, *me* . . . I might." Pawah winked at her. "I do what needs to be done."

"You disgust me." Nefertiti gagged.

"No, I *resemble* you." He took a deep, hearty laugh. He shook his head and wagged his finger at her. "I think that is why I am drawn to you. You are a powerful woman, Nefertiti." He touched the under part of her chin with a flick of his finger. "You do what needs to be done, just like any man, but it might just take you a bit of coaxing."

"I don't trust you," Nefertiti said through pinched lips. "I will never trust you."

"Just think on my offer. Marry me—I have Beketaten for my pleasures, you wouldn't have to touch me since I disgust you so. But, as Pharaoh, I would make sure you live to see an old age. Remember—I, too, hold the people's best interest at heart."

Nefertiti cocked an eyebrow. "Or your own."

"That hurts," Pawah said as he drew back, mockingly caressing a false wound on his chest. "Maybe one day you will think better of me, *She-King*."

"Perhaps one day *you* will keep your manipulations to yourself. I do not need a husband. I will not marry Tut, and I will not marry you," Nefertiti said with a fervid glare. "Even if you were the last man in Egypt."

"You will regret that." He raised his hand to slap her, but refrained and instead brought his hand to her cheek and patted. "Because I can be quite the charmer."

Nefertiti jerked her head away from his touch. "Charm is illusive."

"And beauty is brief," Pawah replied as he drew his finger under her chin and down to her shoulder. Shrugging his own shoulders, he pulled away and said, "Your loss. We could have made a great team."

" 'Team'?" Nefertiti gave an exaggerated eye roll. "Rather, I would have just handed you the crown. You think you are so suave, but I can see right through you. You are nothing but an evil, conniving master manipulator with a heavy heart!"

"A heavy heart?" Pawah pushed his hands to his chest in melodramatic sarcasm. "So you condemn me to eternal suffering?"

"I condemn you to mediocrity," Nefertiti said, staring him down. "You will never share my bed, you will never share my crown, and you will never share my power."

His hand clenched her shoulder. "Now *that* you will regret, Your Majesty." He wrenched her shoulder before letting go and turning to leave. "There is always Nefe and Ankhesenpaaten."

"I will kill you before you can get your dirty hands on my daughters," Nefertiti called after him as he left her seething outside her chambers with a fearful, racing heart.

PAWAH TOOK ONE OF HIS LITTLE-KNOWN SHORTCUTS ACROSS the palace, muttering to himself. "She will suffer for her words. She doesn't understand what she just lost. *She* is an ignorant fool not worthy of the crown, and *I* will do Egypt a favor by seizing my own right to rule." He stopped in his tracks upon seeing Pharaoh Akhenaten's only son, Tut, doing his daily walk around the palace. An idea slithered into his mind and pushed forth an evil grin on his face. "If she will not let me marry into the throne," he chuckled to himself, "then I will make it so I am named Hereditary Prince once I do away with her."

He stepped out of the shadows and said, "My dear Prince."

Tut's nurse, Maia, tended to him to make sure he didn't fall as he hobbled around with his cane and club foot.

"Vizier," Tut said with a smile.

Pawah shooed Maia away, saying, "I will tend to him."

The nurse nodded and went on her way.

"Now tell me, Tut," Pawah said as he took a slow step and waited for Tut to catch up. "How old are you these days?"

"I will soon be nine years," Tut said as he puffed up his chest, not realizing his lack of title.

"Ah, almost a *man!*" Pawah winked at him.

Tut nodded and said, "Yes! I will be a man soon!"

Pawah turned to look at him. "And then you will be *Pharaoh.*"

Tut pushed out his bottom lip so that it was even with his overbite. "Pharaoh Neferneferuaten still has a long life ahead of her, and she may name another successor."

"I see," Pawah said. "Tell me—do you *want* to be Pharaoh?"

"I could never be as great as Pharaoh Neferneferuaten," the boy said, and his cheeks blushed.

"Oh? Is that so? How is that?"

"Because she is wonderful and great and pretty and speaks well," Tut said. His eyes gleamed with adoration.

Pawah's stomach churned at the boy's worship of Nefertiti. "I see," he said again. "What if she said she *hated* you? Wished you were *dead?*"

"What?" Tut asked, stopping his tracks. Then he started to laugh. "No, no. She would never say that about me!" Shaking his head, he said, laughing, "You are funny, Vizier Pawah!"

Pawah stood with a stone-cold face. "I do not imagine this, my Prince."

Tut lowered his chin and his neck shrunk into his shoulders. "You are a liar."

"Furthermore, she said she will do anything to keep you from your rightful place as heir to the throne," Pawah continued in a low voice. He stood with his hands clasped in front of his body, gently swaying front and back as he spoke, as if he were simply reciting an old history lesson from his youth.

Tut shook his head and tried to walk quicker with his cane to get away from perceived lies.

But Pawah stopped him with a hand on his shoulder. "Son," he said, and bent down, so he was eye-level with Tut. Putting a hand on his shoulder, he searched his eyes.

Tut felt an immediate heat sweep over his body. *Son . . . no one had ever called him that before.* But the realization of what Pawah was saying sunk in and he decided to ask, "Why do you tell me this now?"

"Because now that she is Pharaoh, she has to think about the threats to her throne . . . and that includes you." The lie slid easily from Pawah's lips.

"But she is a good person. She . . . she demands perfection because she is p-perfect," Tut stuttered in defense of the only woman he could ever really call "Mother."

"And yet, here you are. Will *you* ever attain perfection?" Pawah said as he gestured toward the boy's leg and severe overbite.

Tut blinked back tears. "She may not accept me, but she would never kill me. She likes me—I'm her daughters' friend."

"My Prince, O my Prince! She hates you." Pawah pursed his lips and nodded his head in a façade of sympathy.

"She doesn't hate me! She has no reason to hate me," Tut said, and pushed Pawah's hand from his shoulder.

"She hates you because she could never give birth to a son. Your father betrayed her to have you. I know these are subjects for men's ears, but you are almost a man. I'm testing you, to see if you are ready for manhood. If you can't accept these truths, then perhaps you shall stay a boy who hobbles with a cane and speaks with a slur." He shrugged a shoulder and shook his head. "A boy you might stay."

Pawah began to walk away, but Tut called after him.

"No, I will *not* stay a boy."

A sly smile crossed Pawah's face. "Then, son, let me tell you about the one you want to call 'Mother.' "

Tut bit the inside of his mouth as he nodded his head and wrenched his eyes closed, anticipating the emotional beating he was about to receive.

"Pharaoh Neferneferuaten is jealous of you," Pawah began.

"Why?" Tut asked.

"Because the people demand you as their Pharaoh, and not her."

"Why?" Tut asked again with a shrug of his shoulders, shaking his head in disbelief.

"Because they are afraid of her—she killed her own sister-in-law, royal wife Sitamun, for nothing, and she has been striking deals with our enemies the Hittites, losing our allies. When the time comes, she will hand Egypt over to the Libyans and the Nubians. No one trusts her."

"*I* trust her. She wouldn't do any of that, and if Sitamun was executed, then she did something to deserve it."

Pawah shook his head. "No, no. She did nothing, and now Pharaoh wants to get rid of *you*."

"Why are you even telling me these things?"

"Because the people want you as their Pharaoh, and you are the only one who can get rid of her," Pawah said.

"Me?" Tut asked.

"Yes, you."

"How?"

"Because if the people back *you*, they will not back *her*. You could take the throne by forcing her to abdicate," Pawah said.

"But why would I do that?"

Pawah grabbed Tut by the shoulders and shook him. "Because the people want *you*! *You* will be the new Pharaoh!"

"I don't know . . ."

"Prince Tutankhaten, Pharaoh Neferneferuaten wants you dead. She has already asked me to kill you, but I will not do it, Tut, I won't." Pawah released his grip as he mustered the most pitiful look he could imagine to try and win the boy's trust. Tut's eyes swelled with tears, and Pawah knew he had him. "She cares nothing for you." Pawah paused, watching the boy's face fall into sadness. "I am the only one who cares."

"No! Nefe and Ankhesenpaaten care about me!"

"Do you really believe so?" Pawah asked, lowering his chin and wrinkling his forehead. "Are you sure they aren't pretending, so they can get close to you and kill you when you fully trust them, as their mother has asked of them?"

"No, they wouldn't do that . . . ?" Tut said, but it was more of a question than a statement.

"Ask one of them if they love you and see if they would marry you," Pawah suggested.

"What would that prove?"

"That they are lying!" Pawah touched Tut's cheek to turn his face toward him.

"How so?"

"Look at you! Prince, yes—but you are a weak, fragile young boy who still wears a sidelock. Ask Ankhesenpaaten.

She is already a woman of marriageable age. If she says yes, then you know she is lying, she is only gaining your trust. Why would she wait and disgrace herself to marry you when she could marry one of the able young men who are also of marriageable age? She is a royal wife of Pharaoh Akhenaten and King's daughter! Would she not marry one of the noble young men her own age or older?"

Tut shook his head, not wanting to believe him, but he could not deny the man's words made sense. "She would say yes . . . Ankhesenpaaten and Nefe are my best friends."

Pawah drew in a deep breath and took a knee, so he was eye-level with the boy. "Tutankhaten, do you honestly believe you compare to a fully able-bodied man?"

"Yes . . ." But Tut's darting eyes gave away his insecurity.

Pawah lowered his eyes to him as if to say, *Are you sure?*

Tut paused and answered again: ". . . no."

Pawah nodded. "Ask her and see."

"So what? Even if it is all true, then what?"

"Then you can trust me. I will be there for you, Tutankhaten. Always. I will never lie to you and I will never pretend with you. I will keep you safe for all my days. You will then know your true friends, your true allies."

"But Ankhesenpaaten—"

"Is nothing but a pawn from her mother to kill you after she gains your trust."

Tut shook his head.

"Ask her to marry you. See what she says," Pawah suggested again. "If she says anything other than a firm yes, then you may call me a liar for all my days."

Tut pushed his lips together as he thought about it.

Pawah extended his hand. "Do we have a deal?"

Tut nodded slowly and clasped Pawah's forearm with his own.

"Good boy, Tut."

Just then, Ankhesenpaaten came running up behind Tut, calling for him.

"Tut! Tut!"

Tut smiled at the sound of her voice, but, observing Pawah's face of concern, his smile disappeared.

"Vizier Pawah," Ankhesenpaaten said as she approached, halting beside Tut.

"Royal wife Ankhesenpaaten," Pawah said as he bowed his head. "I was just leaving." He stood and bowed again, this time from the waist, to both Tut and Ankhesenpaaten.

He left with a lingering stare at the boy, their eyes locked.

"What was that about?" Ankhesenpaaten asked Tut once Pawah was gone.

"Nothing," Tut said, and he resumed his walk, debating the deal he'd just made with the intense vizier.

"What was it?" she asked again. "You know I hate when you keep secrets from me!"

I am not the one keeping secrets, he thought, but smiled anyway. "We were talking about marriage."

"Marriage?" Ankhesenpaaten stopped in her gait, her expression showing how silly an answer she thought this was. "Why?"

"He was just wondering if I was going to ask someone to marry me, since I am crippled." Tut looked out to the columns, unable to meet her eyes.

"Oh, all right," Ankhesenpaaten said. "You are only eight—"

"Almost nine."

"Yes, and people can see past the cane!"

They walked in silence a bit more until Tut finally turned to her.

"Ankhesenpaaten, will you marry me?"

She looked at him for a moment, and then, without hesitation, threw her arms around him.

"Yes, I will!"

He raised one arm to return the embrace, the other gripping his cane to support his weak frame. His heart tingled with joy, but also with a burning, with the truth Pawah had given him. A tear rolled down his cheek as he thought of the façade Ankhesenpaaten had given him all this time.

I wish I didn't know, he thought. *Life would have been easier.*

Pawah heard her response from behind a hidden connecting corridor that he used often to slink from place to place. Smiling at his accomplishment, he set off to find Beketaten. He had much to tell and much to plan.

❦ 19 ❦

THE TIME OF THE COREGENT

AFTER PAWAH'S ADVANCE, NEFERTITI HAD THE CHIEF ROYAL guard, Jabari, and his subordinate Ineni escort her daughters wherever they went, and she had Horemheb escort herself. It had been a year and one season since she had become Pharaoh, but it already seemed like a lifetime.

She and Horemheb walked in silence most of the time, knowing the days drew near when she would have to make a decision on whom to marry; the people pressed harder and harder. She'd asked Horemheb to stand guard by her bed while she slept, but he insisted he would stand by her door instead, along with Khabek, whom she'd commanded to guard her door again. She relented and let him do what he felt he needed to do.

And yet, she still felt tingles in her fingers and her toes each time he drew near to her, and she cherished that little bit of secret joy . . . but she wondered if he still felt that way about her as well.

For all that it mattered—she would have to marry someone else soon, whether it be the boy Tut or the Hittite prince if they ever responded and sent one. The other alternative would be to give up the crown altogether, which would only reduce Pharaoh to an elected figurehead instead of Amun's divinely appointed, something Horemheb would not stand for.

He dutifully kept his distance; even when she would slow down whenever they walked into more quiet areas of the palace, he would keep behind her instead of walking beside her as he did before. He would only whisper, "Pharaoh, I can only protect you," although he longed to reach for her hand and pull her into his arms. The sadness in his voice and his rejection of the opportunity she gave him caused her heart to break each time.

Soon she stopped her advancements, knowing when he said *I can only protect you*, he was trying to protect her from heartache when the time came to marry another.

———

SOON AFTER THESE NEW MEASURES OF ESCORT BEGAN, MUT found Nefertiti in the corridor one day. Tey had just given her a woman's wig, as she had turned twelve years old. Her eyes lingered at Horemheb, who stood off behind her sister. He smiled at her, thinking she looked a lot more like Nefertiti with her woman's wig. She smiled back halfheartedly, knowing he was part of the plot to kill Pharaoh Akhenaten—but then again, so was her sister, whom she admired regardless.

Nefertiti turned to see Mut standing there. She blinked. "Mut? What is it, Mut? What's wrong? Why aren't you in the royal harem?"

"Nothing, I . . ." Mut suddenly lost her voice, quelled beneath Horemheb's gaze.

"Do not stutter, Mut, it is not dignified," Nefertiti told her. "Tell me what is wrong."

"Nothing is wrong. I just wanted to tell you what Ankhesenpaaten told me."

"And what is that?"

"She . . . she wants to marry Tut."

A grimace passed over Nefertiti's face. She stood up straight and began to pace with her hands folded behind her back. The silence that had risen between the three of them suffocated any stray comments, until Nefertiti finally let out a sigh. The idea came to her as if in a dream.

"I will order Ankhesenpaaten to marry Tutankhaten"—her shoulders fell—"and name him Coregent. That should appease the people."

She looked to Horemheb, who returned her gaze. They held each other's eyes for a long time, each trying to think of a way they could still be together; but in the end, they both came to the same conclusion: Pharaoh does not abdicate. Pharaoh has *never* abdicated. The next Pharaoh only takes the crown when the current Pharaoh dies. There would be no hope for a life together—maybe an affair in secrecy, but nothing real, nothing that could be allowed to flourish with time.

Mut's smile disappeared as she noticed Horemheb and Nefertiti's intense gaze upon one another. Her eyes darted between them, as they had seemingly forgotten her presence. Her stare eventually fell upon Horemheb's face: his furrowed brow, his wanting eyes, his sad half-smile. All for her half-sister. She wondered what had taken place between them, if anything; certainly he cared for Nefertiti. But *Mut* was a woman too now, even wore a woman's wig. She chewed her bottom lip. Would he ever look at her the same?

SOMETHING SEEMED TO BE ON TUT'S MIND THE NEXT DAY. He had failed to counter any attack from Sennedjem and a scowl replaced his usual smile. At Ankhesenpaaten's request, Tut's nurse left them alone. She held Tut's hand like she'd seen her mother and father do when they were happy.

He wrenched his hand away from hers. Ankhesenpaaten hurried and stood in front of him with her hands on her hips. "Tut, tell me what's wrong?"

"Nothing." He hobbled around her.

"I don't understand you, Tut," she said, going to stand in front of him again. "First you ask me to marry you and then you act like you want nothing to do with me."

He thinned his lips and averted his eyes and proceeded to walk around her again.

"No—" Ankhesenpaaten blocked his path with her arm. "Tut . . . did I do something to anger you?"

His eyes filled with hot tears. "No!" he yelled at her. "Just leave me alone!" He quickly hobbled around her and off toward the Kap, repeating, "Leave me alone."

"Tut!" Ankhesenpaaten called after him. He didn't turn around, so she sped up until she was by his side again. "Tut, please tell me."

He stopped and looked at her, searching her eyes for something—but what? He opened his mouth to speak, but then Nefe called after them as she ran up behind them.

"You don't ever wait for me!" Nefe huffed as she approached them.

"We were having a private conversation," Ankhesenpaaten said as she turned her shoulder to her sister. Nefe grabbed Ankhesenpaaten's shoulder and yanked it back toward her. "Ow!" Ankhesenpaaten yelled looking at the scratch mark on her skin.

"Would you both just leave me alone!" Tut screamed at

them. "Just go to the temple already!" With that, he turned and hobbled his way to the Kap.

Nefe muttered, "What did I say?" Then she peered up to her older sister in accusation. "What did *you* say?"

"I didn't say anything." Ankhesenpaaten jumped at the touch of a hand on her shoulder. Looking up to see who it was, she gave a guarded smiled. "Oh . . . it's you." Her mother's warning of Pawah rushed to the forefront of her memory.

"I think a little more enthusiasm would behold a vizier," Pawah said as he patted the two girls' shoulders.

"Why are you here?" Nefe said, crossing her arms.

"I have come to talk to the Crown Prince," Pawah said. "Something it seems the two of you do not do so well."

Nefe's jaw dropped. "I didn't say anything!"

"He was fine the other day," Ankhesenpaaten protested, shoving Pawah's hand from her shoulder.

Pawah's face was smug. "Why the hostility, my young royal wife?"

Ankhesenpaaten crossed her arms and narrowed her eyes at him, believing more and more in her mother's warning about this man. "Every time he talks to you, Tut is mad at us! What are you telling him?"

Pawah let out a chuckle and pressed his lips together. Looking them up and down, he said, "You are a keen girl," then patted her wig, adding, "or perhaps . . . a young woman of marriageable age?"

Ankhesenpaaten swatted Pawah's hand away from her head. Her stomach gurgled at his touch. She huffed, "Tut asked me to marry him."

"He is only but nine years old. Are you sure he knows what marriage truly entails?"

Ankhesenpaaten threw her hands in the air. "I was married at seven! *I* knew what it was."

"Yes, you were," Pawah said, tapping his finger on his lip as if in consideration. "It seems to me that you will be passed from Pharaoh to Pharaoh."

"Tut is not Pharaoh." Nefe put her hands on her hips when she spoke.

"Ah, but the people *want* Tut to be Pharaoh." Pawah leaned forward. "But—"

"Well, he is *not* Pharaoh. My *mother* is Pharaoh." Ankhesenpaaten crossed her arms again, defending herself against Pawah's lies per her mother's warning. Never before had Ankhesenpaaten wanted to stand up for her, but something inside her knew this man had told Tut something to drive them apart.

"Hmm . . . yes, well. We shall see for how long she stays Pharaoh," Pawah said, his lips curling into a smile.

"What does *that* mean? Are you threatening Pharaoh?" Ankhesenpaaten tapped her foot, trying to keep the rest of her body from trembling. It was a bold accusation for a young woman to make against the vizier—albeit against a man who was fully capable of twisting her neck without so much as a notice from any guard.

"No, I am not." Pawah straightened his back. "But think about it, royal wife Ankhesenpaaten: to be a chief royal wife at such a young age . . . to be able to run the entire royal harem by yourself at age thirteen—"

"I'm *fourteen*," she snapped.

"Yes, well . . ." Pawah shrugged off her correction. "It would be some accomplishment. Wouldn't you like that?"

"Yes . . ." Ankhesenpaaten thought about the privilege she could carry as chief royal wife. "But that won't be for many years, and only if Tut becomes Pharaoh and names me chief royal wife."

"Well"—Pawah bounced his head as if weighing options—

"I could make sure that was your future . . . but you would have to get your mother to abdicate the throne first."

"Why would she do that? She's Pharaoh. Pharaoh doesn't abdicate the throne—it is a divine appointment," Nefe said, rattling off the lesson she'd learned in the temple the prior day.

"For her own good. The people want Tut as Pharaoh, and when the people feel something is amiss, the people rise up." Pawah shrugged casually.

"No, they don't. To do so would be certain death," Nefe said, adamantly shaking her head.

Pawah ignored Nefe. "You were only a babe, royal wife Ankhesenpaaten, but the people have rebelled already before. They stormed your grandfather's palace at Malkata."

"The people would never do such a thing to the Aten's divinely appointed!" Nefe yelled, furious at being ignored.

Pawah gave a pitying *tsk-tsk*. "It is actually *Amun's* divinely appointed. Your father led Egypt astray to the Aten."

"That's what Mother says, too." Ankhesenpaaten chewed on her lower lip, trying to accept the truth about her father; maybe her mother was right on all accounts.

"In that regard, she is right . . . but if she stays on the throne, the people will rise up again. You must do what you can to save her," Pawah said, leaning toward her and shaking his finger. "If she is killed, you will have to live knowing you didn't try . . ."

"Why should I believe you?" Ankhesenpaaten took a small step back, trying to distance him from her.

"I am Vizier. I know many things. You would do well to trust me." His *s* came out like a snake's hiss—*trussst*.

That will be the last thing I do if Mother is right, Ankhesenpaaten thought. *If . . .*

"Now, if you'll excuse me, I must find our young prince Tutankhaten." With that, Pawah left Nefe and

Ankhesenpaaten in the corridor of the royal harem, the latter replaying the conversation over and over in her mind.

"Where did he go?" Nefe asked.

The long corridor didn't have any connecting corridors that they knew of; they should have still seen him walking down the path. Ankhesenpaaten looked after him—but he'd already disappeared. She shook her head, silent.

"Do you trust him?" Nefe asked quietly. "I don't want Mother to get hurt."

"I don't know," Ankhesenpaaten muttered, shaking her head. "I don't trust anybody right now . . . well, except you, I guess." She playfully pushed her sister's bald head.

Nefe smiled and grabbed her sister's hand.

Ankhesenpaaten looked to Nefe. "I'm glad we are sisters. I know we fight, but I still love you."

"I love you, too." Nefe squeezed her hand.

Mut had told Ankhesenpaaten about Nefertiti's initial reaction upon hearing about Tut's proposal. Her mother "grimaced and paced in frustration," per Mut's words.

Ankhesenpaaten marched back and forth in her room, debating whether or not to be mad at her mother, fuming that she *still* didn't know the whole truth. Her mother kept secrets from her, and Pawah was filling in the gaps. But she wasn't to trust him . . . right? He was the enemy . . . right? She let out an angry breath as she sat on the edge of her bed. She had to find out who was telling the truth and why her mother disliked Tut so much.

An idea struck her: Maybe she should act as if she believed Pawah to see what her mother did or said in response. Maybe *that* would coax the full truth out.

Nefertiti stood at the edge of the dais in her throne room.

"Pharaoh Neferneferuaten decrees: the royal wife Ankhesenpaaten, King's daughter, shall marry the Crown Prince Tutankhaten, thus securing his claim to the throne. He shall be Pharaoh's Coregent."

She had hoped this would quell the rumblings in the street. Even though it ate at her stomach that she had ordered her own flesh and blood to marry the embodiment of her husband's betrayal, a small part of her was not ready to be ousted from the throne; on top of this, she knew abdicating would only show Pharaoh's weakness, something Horemheb would not want her to do—nor any of her council, except perhaps for Pawah.

Ankhesenpaaten entered the throne room just as the scribe took down her last decree. Having not heard the final words, she asked, "Who shall be Pharaoh's Coregent?"

Her presence startled Nefertiti, as she thought Ankhesenpaaten would have been in the royal harem at this time. "Oh! My daughter!" Nefertiti opened an arm wide to embrace her, but Ankhesenpaaten stood where she was and repeated her question.

"Who shall be Pharaoh's Coregent?"

Nefertiti dropped her arm with a thud. Last time she was with her daughter, Nefertiti received a genuine hug of sympathy from her and thought maybe things would be different between the two of them. Perhaps she was wrong. With a defeated breath, Nefertiti responded to her daughter's question.

"Your soon-to-be new husband, Tutankhaten."

"Pawah told us all about your schemes." Ankhesenpaaten

put her hands on her hips. "You are ordering us to marry so you can keep the crown."

"Silence yourself," Nefertiti snapped, and rose a finger. "Don't trust a word that man says."

"He says to not trust you." Ankhesenpaaten crossed her arms and dropped her chin.

Her daughter's words echoed in her heart as it began to race.

"So, as of now," Ankhesenpaaten said, "I trust him more than I trust you."

"Daughter, you will come to regret your choice." Nefertiti shook her head and returned to her stately position on the throne.

"He said you won't abdicate the throne, potentially causing the people to rise up against Pharaoh," Ankhesenpaaten uncrossed her arms and held them at her sides. "Maybe you will regret your choice."

Nefertiti blinked with an exaggerated sigh. "Think what you will, but know this—in the end, you will be chief royal wife, and who you trust will decide your fate. That goes for the boy as well."

"His name is Tutankhaten, *Mother*. Think what you will of Father, but *that 'boy'* has done nothing to you except show you the respect and honor deserving of his own mother." Her arm sliced through the air. "A horrible mother you turned out to be." The last part slipped out before she could shut her mouth, wishing she could take back her words.

"Silence your tongue, Ankhesenpaaten!" Nefertiti slammed her fist into the throne's arm. Her eyes filled with rage—not at her daughter, but at herself.

The two women glared at each other. Nefertiti waited to see if Ankhesenpaaten would say more. Ankhesenpaaten seemed to wait to see what her mother would say. At the scribe's clearing of his throat, Ankhesenpaaten's shoulders relaxed, and she leaned back from her enraged stance. Her face fell solemn.

Nefertiti's hand still grasped in a fist, she muttered, "I have already apologized for not being there for you. I pray to Amun you will be a better mother than me."

"I will be," Ankhesenpaaten whispered, but Nefertiti chose to ignore her.

"May you produce a son, so your husband does not have to go to another wife's bed to get an heir," Nefertiti said, and she relaxed her hand. She closed her eyes and turned her head toward the throne doors, away from Ankhesenpaaten. Opening her eyes, her shoulders once again fell back into rigid alignment with the throne's back as she brought her chin parallel to the floor.

Ankhesenpaaten crossed her arms. "Tut has done nothing wrong. He has done *nothing* to you."

Still ignoring her, Nefertiti went on: "We all make choices. Some of which we are not proud, but we make them anyway. The true test of your character"—she looked over her shoulder to her daughter—"is whether or not you can accept the consequences of your actions, good or bad."

"Tut didn't have a choice," Ankhesenpaaten said as she walked around to the front of the throne, forcing her mother to look at her. "But you do. Why can't you at least call him by name? You are disgusted to think I would marry him out of my own will, so you use us to your advantage to keep the crown and quiet the people. You have made a lot of choices, Mother, and they affect more than just you."

"Yes, I have. It is the lot of Pharaoh. I must make the hard choices." Nefertiti stood, still a head taller than her daughter. "I chose Egypt over my family, even when I have gained nothing in return."

"You gained the crown," Ankhesenpaaten muttered.

Nefertiti clenched her jaw. "Hate me if you will, but I did

what I thought needed to be done, and I deserve the right to choose whom I like and dislike. I have chosen to dislike the male child of Pharaoh Akhenaten."

"Why? Because Father slept with another one of his wives?" Ankhesenpaaten shrugged her shoulder as if to show how inconsequential she thought this.

"He *promised* me, Ankhesenpaaten!" Nefertiti yelled, stepping closer to her.

"Mother! Father is *with Re*, and has been gone for years now. Tut is nine years old. This happened a long time ago." Ankhesenpaaten threw her hands in the air, taking a small step backward from her advancing mother. "Get past this!"

Nefertiti grabbed Ankhesenpaaten's shoulders. "You do not understand!"

"You keep saying that! But I *do* understand!"

Ankhesenpaaten wrenched one of her shoulders free, but Nefertiti took hold of it again.

"Despite everything your father did to me, despite how crippled and pathetic a child that boy is, despite yours and Nefe's friendship with him, I cannot like that boy. I can barely even look at him. He disgusts me!"

"Why? What did he do?!"

"Nothing. The boy did *nothing!*"

Nefertiti released a large breath at this realization as the truth she had denied for so long fell from her lips. She dropped her hands.

"He did nothing . . ."

With the throne room still partially uncovered, the sun chose that moment to fall into Nefertiti's eyes. Sitting back down, she shielded her face. The Aten drained her energy. She'd begun to see visions, too, and knew she would become her late husband if she didn't do something.

"I am *not* Akhenaten," she whispered to herself.

She lifted her head and yelled to the scribe: "Cover the throne room roof! I want it covered by first light!"

Ankhesenpaaten snorted at her mother's refusal to deal with the issue at hand.

"How long have I had the crown now, Ankhesenpaaten?" Nefertiti whispered, looking back up at her.

"A year and two seasons, Mother," Ankhesenpaaten said, shaking her head in clear pity.

"No—I have had the crown since we moved to Aketaten. Your father never was a good Pharaoh. His son will be no better." She let her hand fall from her eyes. The sun was so bright. "Maybe I don't like the boy because I know he will become his father."

"That is the most foolish thing I have ever heard," Ankhesenpaaten said.

"I'm tired." Nefertiti shooed her daughter away. "I must prepare for the crowning ceremony."

"If Tut disgusts you, then *you* disgust *me*," Ankhesenpaaten's face held a grimace.

"Learn, or you will *become* me." Nefertiti stared at her daughter, unblinking. "Be better than me, Ankhesenpaaten."

Ankhesenpaaten crossed her arms again. "Why can't *you* be better?"

"It's too late for me," Nefertiti said. "I have made my decisions. They will decide my fate."

"Don't be silly, Mother. You have many years left. There is still time."

Nefertiti smiled at her naïveté. "Perhaps," she said, and rose to stand again. She patted her cheek and wrapped her arms around Ankhesenpaaten and, to her surprise, her daughter let her hug her. Cupping her head in her hand and wrapping her arm all the way around her, she squeezed. "Remember, daughter, we all must make choices. Some are wrong. Some are right. Some make sense. Some don't. But in the end, whatever choice you make, you own the consequences." She pulled back to look her in the eyes, and her voice dropped to the barest of whispers. "I fear my future. I have made many choices. Choices that were wrong and full of folly."

Ankhesenpaaten shook her head and put her mother's head between her hands. "Then make the right choice, Mother."

"I don't know what is right anymore, my sweet one," Nefertiti confessed to her beloved daughter.

ANKHESENPAATEN STOOD BEHIND TUT AS THEY BOTH TRIED to recall what they were supposed to do once the drapes were pulled back and they walked down the aisle to be crowned. Ankhesenpaaten had done it once before when she married her father, but that was half a lifetime ago.

"Tut," Ankhesenpaaten whispered.

His head half-turned, but he whipped it forward again, ignoring her.

"Tut," Ankhesenpaaten whispered again, some spit flying out from the force of her whisper.

Tut peered over his shoulder, narrowing his eyes. "What do you want?"

"Why are you mad at me?" Ankhesenpaaten asked. "We are about to be married and crowned Coregent and his chief royal wife. But why are you mad at me? Tell me."

He spun around with his cane as his center of weight. "I want the *real* reason why you are marrying me." His eyes were hot, his mouth a scowl.

"Isn't it obvious?" Ankhesenpaaten shrugged. "Because I love you."

He narrowed his eyes at her again. "Why should I believe you?"

"I have been your friend since you were born. I would never do anything to cross you or hurt you . . . because I love you, Tut." Ankhesenpaaten's shoulders fell, as if dropping her heart before him.

"There are others who say you and your mother just want to kill me since I am the rightful heir to the throne," Tut said. "Get close and then strike." He punched the air with such a force he almost knocked himself over, but he quickly regained his balance.

Ankhesenpaaten chuckled and shook her head. "Who says that? That is the most ridiculous thing I have ever heard."

"Very important people," Tut said, and leaned toward her. "I am watching you."

"Be careful of where you place your trust—"

Ankhesenpaaten shut her mouth. *Those are my mother's words,* she thought.

"*You* should be careful, too. If I find you are conspiring against me, I will order your execution," Tut threatened.

Ankhesenpaaten's half-smile disappeared. "Tut, I would never conspire against you. I can't make you believe me . . . but please know I would never hurt you."

Tut huffed and spun back around just as the curtains opened.

Simut, Pharaoh's appointed First Prophet of Amun, stood at the end of the aisle, his hands clasped over his belly, waiting on the second step of the throne's platform. The second and third prophets stood on either side, holding the ceremonial Pshent crown for Tutankhaten and the Modius crown for Ankhesenpaaten.

They walked down the aisle. All eyes watched the Crown

Prince hobble—with an impressive speed for a boy with a cane—and his older bride step gracefully behind him.

When they reached the steps, Ankhesenpaaten went up halfway and Tutankhaten continued upward, careful not to fall.

Simut took the great red copper-and-white papyrus crown from the Second Prophet of Amun, Maya, while another lower priest of Amun recited the language of the gods, granting the crowning of a divine King.

The crown fit perfectly upon his head—after all, they had fitted him for it the day before. He slowly turned around to face the hall, careful the double crown did not topple.

Tut's brow held no sweat as he spouted the words he'd painstakingly memorized—his oath as the divinely appointed. "I swear by Amun-Re to fulfill my divine purpose to lead the Upper and the Lower of Egypt boldly into prosperity."

"People of Egypt," Pharaoh Neferneferuaten bellowed as she stood from her throne, "presented to you: Pharaoh Coregent Tutankhaten, having divine selection to lead the unified nation, both the Upper and the Lower, to a more prosperous future,"

And the people cheered for their new leader.

"Now shall be named chief royal wife of Pharaoh Coregent, Ankhesenpaaten, to stand with Pharaoh." Nefertiti motioned to her daughter.

The people cheered again.

Simut took the blue-and-gold Modius crown from Maya as Ankhesenpaaten walked up to the step beneath him, and he placed it upon her head.

The people cheered a third time, but Ankhesenpaaten could only think of Tut's threat, and, wondering who spread those lies, settled on the only possible person: Pawah. Even as she considered all the possibilities, a tiny voice in the back of her mind wondered if her mother truly wanted Tut gone.

20

THE TIME OF BROKEN OATHS

As Nefertiti's second year as Pharaoh almost drew to a close, Horemheb found himself in each sleepless night wrestling with a future without her. The people seemed to not accept only a Coregency, and he knew the time would come when she would be forced to marry. His mind raced. She had stopped her advances and she had stopped peering over her shoulder. Perhaps she no longer felt the same as he— and that would be for the best, he reasoned. But then she'd look at him in the council room or in general conversation, and there was still something behind her eyes.

He pushed it from his mind.

In the past, he'd forced himself to sleep when he was not on watch, but the days grew long and the nights short; he was desperately afraid she would be killed as he slept. But every morning, he'd force his heavy eyes open. He'd promised her and her father that he would protect her. She had asked him to stand guard for her and to be her escort, and she had not changed that order. So, in his present duty as guard and escort at Pharaoh's command, he had placed his troop commander, Paramesse, his

SECRETS IN THE SAND

comrade he knew he could trust, as Commander in his absence.

A morning came when General Paaten came up to Nefertiti and Horemheb in the hallway. "Pharaoh Neferneferuaten," he said with a half-bow. "Commander." He turned to Horemheb and his eyes fell to the man's feet, making sure they were behind his Pharaoh. Paaten's face, seemingly flustered, held a red hue and his eyes were ablaze.

"What is wrong, General?" Horemheb asked, keeping his face as set in stone. He wasn't going to let the General know any more than he already did about his feelings for Nefertiti. The tryst was behind him, and he needed to look to a future without her—however bleak it may seem.

"I have just received word that we had to put down some small riots in Waset and Men-nefer," Paaten said. "Pawah." He gritted his teeth. "He actually did it, the cursed fool. The men we arrested said this was only the beginning." General Paaten shook his head. "Until Egypt is fully restored."

Nefertiti bit her lip. "They still demand a male Pharaoh?"

Paaten nodded.

"I hate this," she said and threw her hands in the air.

Horemheb planted his feet on the ground and looked around, glaring down at any servants who dared to stop and stare at their Pharaoh.

She put her hands on Paaten's shoulders. "I know I have asked much of you in the past. If the time comes, will you keep your promise to me?"

Horemheb's eyebrows raised. *What promise?* he wanted to ask.

Paaten drew in a deep breath, ignoring Horemheb's confused stare. "Indeed, my Pharaoh. You need nothing more than my word."

"Take all who will go with you," she said.

"As you wish." General Paaten nodded. "What about you?

241

You could come with me. I would keep you safe." He put his hands on her shoulders as well, deepening Horemheb's confusion.

"General," she said as tears welled. "There are no second chances for me."

Horemheb cleared his throat again, wondering what was meant by asking Nefertiti to come with him—to keep her safe? Was he not privy to some secret between them?

Paaten dropped his hands as he shot Horemheb a reproachful look. Horemheb stepped back, keeping his eyes on the man, until Paaten believed he was no longer in earshot. He saw Paaten's lips moving as he continued the conversation and Nefertiti shaking her head and touching his cheek. The closeness of their faces gave his heart a good squeeze.

What promise? Paaten is much older than me. He shook his head at his own implication. *Nefertiti wouldn't do that to me. Trade a commander for a general? Maybe she and Paaten were something before I came along.* He raised his eyebrow again. *Maybe that is why the General warned me so harshly . . . because he has had to stay away all this time? No. No. No. I refuse to believe that.*

But as he watched the tears fall from Nefertiti's face, he wondered even more.

Paaten lowered his head to speak to her, so any passersby could not hear.

"The choice is yours, Pharaoh. If you come with me when I take your daughters should the people rise up, I will keep you safe."

A silence arose between them as Nefertiti considered a life in exile, with no one but the General and her daughters to keep her company. Would safety be worth never seeing Horemheb again? At least if she did marry either Tut or the Hittite—if they ever responded—she could at least still be in his presence. A lonely life either way.

She touched his cheek as she shook her head. "General Paaten, you have served me loyally all of my days in the palace, even when I was not loyal to you. I thank you for that. Now I must ask one more favor."

She paused.

"I want Pawah dead," Nefertiti said through her teeth.

A tear slid down her cheek. She had killed Akhenaten and let them kill Smenkare—what was a lowly life such as Pawah's worth to her dignity? There was no more depth to which she could fall.

Paaten stared at her, bowed his head, and whispered, "Pharaoh?"

"Can we order his execution for crimes against Pharaoh?" Nefertiti asked General Paaten.

"The men I trust have told me the people do look up to him. He is their '*savior*.' He did, in fact, gather up the people, and they were going to rebel that night you brought Akhenaten the poison." Paaten stopped at Nefertiti's stare. "When I learned of what happened, I sent my own intelligence men to validate and verify. Everything Pawah threatens is true. If we arrest him and he says you killed Akhenaten . . ."

"They would believe him." Nefertiti's gaze fell to the floor. "This would not only wage war against me, but against the position of Pharaoh. The last twenty years would be in vain. If people think they can kill Pharaoh and nothing happens as a consequence, well, what purpose does divine appointment serve?" She put her forehead between her finger and thumb. "There would be complete anarchy. At best, the country would be yet again divided."

"Brother would kill brother. It wouldn't even be the Upper and the Lower," Paaten said.

"I want him out of the way, General. Do what you must to make it look as though he journeyed west due to natural causes," she ordered him, letting her hand fall to her side.

He lifted his eyes and found hers. "Do not become the evil you wish to kill."

"Only evil can kill evil, General." Her stare was hard. "I ordered the torture of seventeen men to find information about who threatened Akhenaten, and you carried it out. Do this again for me. Pawah threatens the throne. It is no different."

He dropped his chin and lowered his gaze. "Thus Pharaoh says."

Paaten walked away, staring Horemheb down as he passed by him.

"IS THERE SOMETHING I SHOULD KNOW ABOUT BETWEEN you and the General?" Nefertiti asked as Horemheb watched Paaten walk down the hallway.

"No, my Pharaoh." Horemheb turned to look at her. He wanted to ask her the same question, but he kept his mouth shut. It was not his place.

She studied him for a while and, at the jerk of his jaw, she pressed her lips into a small smirk and dropped her gaze.

"It was several years ago," she began, her eyes peering down at his frame and his shuffling feet.

A muscle in his neck twitched, but he stayed in his dutiful position. "Pharaoh . . ."

How did she know my question? Am I that obvious? First, the General threatens me for my implied feelings, then her father guesses I care for her, and now she sees my jealous curiosity.

She walked a little closer, her hips swaying with her graceful saunter. He tried to keep his eyes on her face.

If there is something between them, why is she walking toward me in this way? His body grew rigid as she peered up at him and licked her bottom lip. *Is she remembering her time with the General?*

"We were in the council room," she started again.

Why is she telling me knowing how I feel for her? I can't hear this.

"Pharaoh, I don't need to know," Horemheb said, wondering if she loved Paaten or was just toying with him, but he shook the thought from his mind. It wasn't his place to know, regardless.

"You don't need to know? Or you don't want to know?" Nefertiti whispered. Her eyes searched him.

"I don't need to know," he said finally, and turned his face away. Even though he had been working on his tell, he still couldn't control it all of the time.

She smiled at his twitching eyebrow, although much more controlled. She touched his arm just for a second. "In the council room, we were discussing the People's Restoration of Egypt. I made him promise to leave this place and take my children to safety by whatever means necessary."

Horemheb drew in a breath of relief and let it out slowly.

Why did I think that? She made it seem . . .

He turned to Nefertiti again, who held a coy grin on her lips. His cheeks grew a slight blush. He'd been had.

"There is nothing between us," she reassured him as a small laugh escaped her.

It had been a while since he'd had the privilege of hearing her laughter, and he was glad he could once again be the cause of it—even at his own expense. The laugh passed as quickly as it had come. Her face fell solemn as she traced the outline of his face.

"Just like there can be nothing between you and me . . . isn't that right, Commander?"

His desire for her burned through his body as she was just within his grasp. If only he could marry her. Why did he continue to entertain the idea of her when it was all in vain? "Yes, my Pharaoh."

"You can only protect me." She chewed her lip and lifted her chin.

He nodded. "Yes, my Pharaoh."

The day waned, and the sun was almost set behind the Nile. As the shadows of the evening fell, the dark circles under his eyes from the countless nights he had stood guard by her bedchambers became more apparent and signified his dedication to her. Nothing had happened thus far to her, and all three military leaders—her father, Paaten, and Horemheb—were in Aketaten should she need them. The riots were in Men-nefer and Waset, and they were put down. Perhaps she should let him sleep this night.

She put a hand on his armor. "Let Khabek and Hori guard my door tonight. You need your sleep."

"I will stand guard at your door," he said, turning his shoulders to her. "You said you don't trust them."

"But you are tired. I can see it in your face. You have lost your appetite too," she said, looking at his thinner frame.

"Food does not taste as good as it used to," he admitted.

His furrowed brow told her she was not going to get her way this time. "All right, Commander." She tilted her head. "Will you guard my door tonight with Khabek?"

"For you, I will do anything," he whispered.

She smiled, outlining his face once again with her eyes before turning to go to her bedchambers.

When they arrived, he opened the door for her. Her steward, Aitye, and lesser servants stood waiting for Pharaoh to enter.

"Sleep well, my Pharaoh."

"Thank you, *my* Commander."

He smiled at the hidden meaning. They held each other's gaze for a moment.

She entered, ready for her bath.

As Horemheb stood outside her door waiting for the servants to leave her bedchambers, his eyelids drooped. Finally they came out, and Aitye, the last to leave, told Horemheb, "She preferred to be alone tonight. There are no others with her."

He only nodded in response.

Soon Khabek came to the door for his post as Horemheb tried to hide a yawn.

Khabek cleared his throat. "Tired, Commander?"

"Aren't military men always?" he responded with a smirk as Khabek stood next to him.

Khabek dropped his spear before scrambling to pick it up again. Rubbing his neck, he cleared his throat again.

"Something on your mind, Khabek?" Horemheb asked, eyeing his movements.

"No," he said quickly.

There was a tightness around the young guard's eyes, and Horemheb noticed Khabek had not made eye contact with him that evening.

"Do you—"

"I don't want to talk," Khabek huffed, and looked off down the hallway. He shrugged, muttering by way of explanation: "Lady problems."

Horemheb snorted and nodded. "Don't we all?"

The soft crackle of the torchlight slowed the blink of his eyes after a while.

"Commander, sit down and rest for a while," Khabek offered. "You are awake for most of the day and night. I will keep watch and wake you should I see or hear something."

Horemheb shook his head but sat down anyway. Leaning his head against the doorframe, he looked up to Khabek and said, "Can I trust you?"

"Always, Commander," he said.

Horemheb was too tired to see the sweat forming on the man's hands.

Losing control, Horemheb fell asleep.

He awoke with a start.

There'd been a faint clash. He jumped to his feet.

Khabek was nowhere to be seen. Looking around, Horemheb decided to open the door to Nefertiti's room to check on her, and to his surprise, saw a figure looming over her bed. A ball of nausea dropped hard in his stomach as he thought he had lost his love at his own negligence. Grief muted him as he ran to the figure and knocked him to the ground. Horemheb pulled out his chest dagger just as the man grunted and sprung to his feet.

Horemheb heard Nefertiti coughing and struggling to breathe.

She's alive! he thought as he slashed at the man, churning up more vigor in his attack.

The man jumped back, grabbing a spear that lay nearby, and thrust it at Horemheb. Turning, he leaned away from the spear tip as it sliced through the air by his chest, barely knocking his bronze armor. Horemheb grabbed his khopesh with his other hand, and the next time the spear jabbed at him, he spun and hacked off the tip. The attacker looked to his disabled weapon, then broke the spear's handle across his thigh into two pieces of wood that he held in each hand. He swung them in front of his body as if to ready himself for another clash.

"Wood against bronze makes for no fight," Horemheb declared.

In answer, the man threw one handle at him and turned to run.

After knocking the piece of wood away, Horemheb saw the man had nearly escaped and without a further thought he threw his dagger, nailing the man in the back. The man fell into the hallway, coughing and struggling to breathe.

Horemheb glanced at Nefertiti, who had curled up on her bed, watching him fight her attacker. A breath escaped his lungs, relieved she was alive; then he went to end the assailant. Keeping his foot on the attacker's hand, Horemheb pulled the dagger from his back and turned him over.

Khabek stared up at him.

"You?" Horemheb asked with a cold stare.

"You are lucky you fell asleep, Commander—they paid me to kill you, too, if you stayed watch—" Khabek coughed up blood.

The urge to destroy him caused Horemheb to shove his dagger in Khabek's chest. "You disgust me. You took an oath." His lip curled as he grabbed a fistful of Khabek's tunic at his neck, lifting him bodily off the ground.

"She is not Amun's divinely appointed . . ." His voice trailed off, and then his life left him.

Horemheb pulled his dagger out of Khabek's chest and let him fall to the ground with a thud.

Nefertiti's soft cries pulled him away from his anger toward the royal guard.

A servant's eyes grew big upon turning the corner and seeing the dead guard.

"You there," Horemheb barked. "Go inform General Paaten and Master of Pharaoh's Horses, Ay, that one of the royal guards broke his oath."

The servant shrunk into the stone wall behind him, his sights glued to the bloody man on the floor.

"Go now!"

The servant looked at Horemheb and the bloody blade in his hand, then sprinted off down the corridor.

Horemheb used the dead man's tunic to wipe the blood from his dagger before returning it to its sheath. He stood staring at Khabek and shook his head in disgust. Then he turned and entered back into Pharaoh's chambers.

"My Pharaoh?" he asked as he drew near to her bed.

The full weight of Nefertiti's body slammed into his as she threw her arms around him. Her tears fell on his neck and her quick, shallow breaths dropped on his chest.

"You are safe now, my Pharaoh," he said, rubbing her back. "You are safe, my Nefertiti," he whispered in her ear, breathing in her freshly perfumed scent, not knowing what he would do if he had been the reason she was killed. The only light came from the hallway, and the partially opened door kept them in the darkness. His hands roamed over her body, making sure she was not hurt, greedily feeling her warmth under his fingers.

"Where were you?" Her shaky voice and body reverberated to his touch.

He couldn't bring himself to answer her. "I'm here now," he said instead. "I'm sorry." He turned his head into her neck. "I'm so sorry," he repeated, hating that he had succumbed to his need of sleep. He calmed his own heart and breaths so it could be easier for her to feel safe beside him.

She pulled away from him, letting her lips slide by his. "Horemheb," she whispered, desperately holding on to him as her source of strength, "thank you for saving me."

"Always," he said, pulling his hand up to caress her face.

"He . . . he had his hands on m-my face and n-neck," she stuttered, trying to keep the memory from coming, and leaned forward, pressing her forehead to his. "I knocked the candle to the floor hoping you would hear."

"I did," he said, nodding to reassure her, pulling her body closer to his, realizing how close he'd come to losing her. "I'm sorry, Nefertiti. Please forgive me. I nearly failed you."

His heart raced as he cupped the side of her face.

"But you didn't." She leaned forward again and placed a soft kiss on his lips. "You saved me."

Horemheb parted his mouth and leaned into another kiss, which she received with an open heart. In the darkness, they could be whatever they wanted.

Clamor in the hallway made their kiss draw to an end. Their shoulders pulled back, but their faces remained close. Horemheb smiled; he could feel the smile upon her face with his hand. He picked her up and let her stand on the floor.

Drooping down, he spotted the scattered candle in the light coming from the doorway. He picked it up and lit it and then placed it back on the nightstand just as Ay and Paaten came rushing in, letting the full light of the hallway fall into the bedroom. Chief royal guard Jabari, behind them, looked over Khabek and kicked the dead man in the head, cursing beneath his breath.

"Are you hurt?" Ay said as he rushed to his daughter.

"No, I am fine. Horem— . . . Commander Horemheb saved me just in time," she said as she peered over to Horemheb.

"Thank you, Commander," Ay said as he pulled his daughter into his embrace. "Oh, my lotus blossom, I don't know what I would have done if I had lost you too."

"Father, I'm fine," Nefertiti repeated, and shrugged him off.

"What happened?" Paaten barked at Horemheb, advancing toward his subordinate.

"Khabek attacked her—tried to suffocate her. I attacked

him, and he tried to flee. I killed him in his escape. He said he was paid—I assume by Pawah," Horemheb said matter-of-factly, standing in a soldier stance face-forward.

"That cursed Pawah." Paaten clenched his jaw, looking down at the dead man. Then his hot glare landed back on Horemheb. "How did Khabek get in her room and try to suffocate her without you knowing in the first place?" Paaten leaned forward in Horemheb's face.

Ay pulled Nefertiti close, continually asking her if she was hurt to try and distract her from Horemheb's answer. Horemheb's cheeks flushed; he knew the dark circles under his eyes gave him away. "I thought we could trust Khabek."

"Trust no one." Paaten sent a finger into Horemheb's chest. "Take the night, Commander. I will resume your watch." Then he turned to Jabari. "Get that mess cleaned up."

"I have already sent for the servants," Jabari replied.

Paaten's gaze fell back to Horemheb. "I said take the night, Commander."

"Yes, General," Horemheb muttered, and began to leave, stealing one last look at Nefertiti before he passed through the open doors. He'd thought he would never taste her lips again, and yet there in the aftermath of the chaos in Khabek's assassination attempt, he did. He smiled.

Maybe the universe might bestow upon me a life with her, after all . . . somehow . . . in some way.

LATER THAT NIGHT, AS HOREMHEB LAY IN BED, A messenger came to him.

"Pharaoh thanks the Commander for saving her life." The messenger reached out and handed him something.

"What is this?" Horemheb asked as he tried to make out the trinket.

"Pharaoh says it is the ring her father gave her when she became a woman. It was her mother's," the messenger said. "She gives it to you as a token of appreciation."

The messenger left before he could respond. He rubbed the golden ring and felt a jewel in it. He placed it on his pinky finger, the only finger it would fit.

"I will cherish it always, my Nefertiti."

HOREMHEB AWOKE REMEMBERING THE NIGHT BEFORE. THE thought of him losing Nefertiti swarmed his mind, but, looking to his hand, he saw her ring on his finger and closed his eyes in relief. Then he smiled, remembering her kiss. He rubbed her ring and let out a breath.

"If nothing else, I have this to remember her by."

Pulling himself from bed, he brushed his finger on his bottom lip. He could almost taste her again. But then he hung his head. Unless Pawah and Tut were out of the picture, he could never marry her.

I would gladly get rid of that Pawah, he thought.

"But the boy . . ." He shook his head and drew a deep breath.

If I got rid of Pawah, then maybe I could talk to Tut. Maybe he would allow us a secret marriage. He adores Nefertiti. Maybe. It's the only chance I have.

He pulled on his leather tunic and bronze armor, tied his belts, and left his room to start the day with a new mission in mind: he was going to find someone to get close enough to Pawah to kill him—and make it look like an accident so the people did not rise up against Pharaoh for the slaying of their perceived savior.

21

THE TIME OF LOVE

Two seasons passed, and General Paaten requested a private audience with Nefertiti.

"Has any progress been made with Pawah?" she asked as she stood and walked down the platform steps to General Paaten.

"We are having trouble . . . it is hard to tell whose loyalty is unbroken or whose is willing to break." Paaten scratched the back of his neck. "Commander Horemheb seeks opportunity as well." He refused to tell Nefertiti her father was also scouring his contacts to find some way to get rid of Pawah.

"Is there no one loyal to the throne anymore?"

"There are many who still remain loyal, but Pawah pays those around him. He knows exactly where his men's loyalties lie. We are at a disadvantage." Paaten looked away from Nefertiti, not wanting to fail her, but doubted his own ability —his first instance of doubt in a long time.

"Why can't we just put hemlock in his drink like he orchestrated with Akhenaten and Smenkare?" Nefertiti whispered, and peered up at General Paaten.

"Who among our allies can get close enough to him to do so?" Paaten asked. "We've tried that many times. Once he even made his servant, whom we had paid more than what Pawah was paying him, drink his cup when the servant wiped the cup with a hemlock-laced cloth after tasting. We've lost many men in our attempts, and the more we lose, the more Pawah's loyalties grow stronger. They see him thwart our attempts and he grows larger than life to them. The more he kills our assassins, the more afraid those loyal to him become, and they are less likely to aid us."

"Do not strike until you know it will be successful," Nefertiti ordered.

"All the previous times, we thought it would be," Paaten softly said. "It would be so easy to have one of my archers just pick him off—" He flicked his thumb and finger together in imitation of a bow releasing an arrow, but then looked to Nefertiti and regained his composure. "But, in the current situation, we would be hard-pressed to do even that, especially since we don't know who all is loyal to the throne."

"General, I tasked you with his death. See to it that he dies and does not cause a riot. Do not strike until you are certain death will follow."

"Thus Pharaoh says," General Paaten said, and bowed to her before leaving the throne room.

NEFERTITI PACED BACK AND FORTH IN HER ROOM AS THE sun waned. The General was no closer to Pawah than he was when he'd started. The morning's messages raced through her mind. She dreaded Horemheb coming to stand watch by her bed and, knowing she couldn't hide this from him, having to tell him what troubled her.

After her servants had left for the night, the door creaked open.

"In peace, my Pharaoh," Horemheb said as he entered.

He began with his official report, as he had done in all the nights previous since her attack. "Royal guards Hori and Ineni stand watch for your daughters, and chief royal guard Jabari stands guard outside your door. I stand guard by your bed, per your command."

The door closed behind him, and they were both happy to slough off the formalities as the sun set.

For the last two seasons, Horemheb had felt as if a burden had been lifted from his chest as he had come to her room every night and slowly the barriers he had put between them dwindled; he became more hopeful that Tut would allow him to be with Nefertiti—and if not, he resolved that he would cherish this time with her regardless the outcome. Behind closed doors and with the servants dismissed, they could be together—no one dared to accuse Pharaoh and the Commander. For all they knew, he did indeed stand guard by her bed.

He pulled the nearby chair against the doors just in case Jabari decided to renege on his oath as well. The past season Horemheb had tried at every turn to get rid of Pawah, working with Paaten—it seemed an impossible task—but he put it out of his mind for tonight. He turned around and saw her pacing come to an end. He rushed to her, pulled her into his arms, and embraced her with a lingering kiss.

"What bothers you, my Nefertiti?"

Tears welled in her eyes. "Our time together is limited."

Her whisper soured his stomach.

"Pawah?" he asked as he settled his hands on her waist.

"No." Her body rocked slightly, afraid to tell him what she had done. "I . . . made a mistake."

Horemheb tried to think what her mistake might be that

would limit their time together—a mistake that did not have to do with Pawah? His mind raced, brining up every conversation, until he landed on a small, insignificant memory.

"The Hittite prince?"

She closed her eyes and nodded. "He comes after the next harvest." She clutched his leather tunic. "I sent a letter the morning after the night I thought you would never hold me again . . . the morning you left."

He clenched his jaw; his shoulders curled forward.

"I'm sorry, Horemheb. Part of me thought they wouldn't respond. What have I done? I can't refuse him now. It will only make things worse. The alliance will be over before it started." She shook her head and pushed Horemheb away. Bringing her hands to cover her face, she let out a heavy sigh and said again, "What have I done?"

Horemheb stood looking at the floor. He had no words, no advice. Vainly, he'd thought their time could potentially go on forever, and now there was a hard stop: the next harvest.

"What should I do?" she whispered through her fingers.

Horemheb found her eyes. Words eluded him.

"What should I *do?*" Her voice shook. Her hands trembled.

Horemheb opened his mouth, but only a small breath escaped.

"If I am already married by the time he comes, then he can be on his way because they took so long to reply," she thought aloud. "But I don't want to marry Tut, and I will never marry Pawah." She began to pace again, rubbing her temples in agitation.

"Marry Tut," Horemheb finally said. "Marry Tut before the next harvest." His voice was low and filled with a lack of enthusiasm.

"No, Horemheb, I don't want to marry Tut. I want to

marry you," she said, coming near and placing her hands on his bronze armor.

"Nefertiti. I am not a royal. The people would not accept me. There is an heir. I cannot be named Hereditary Prince. No matter how many scenarios I think of where we may be together, the only one I can maybe see is if you marry Tut and we get rid of Pawah, and somehow Tut lets us be together." Horemheb rubbed her hands. "Marry Tut."

"Don't make me marry him." She shook her head. "Please."

"Nefertiti, I am not making you marry him. Just know that whatever you decide, I'll be here for you, and I will protect you at whatever the cost," he said, rubbing her arms.

"They will find out we are together in time. Tut will be forced to carry out the law under pressure from the people . . . I can see the people thinking, 'If Pharaoh cannot defend his bed, how can he defend Egypt?' You will die for laying with Pharaoh's wife." She turned from him, one hand on her hip, the other covering her tears. She spun around again. "Marry me, please."

"Nefertiti, even if I did"—he emphasized his words with his hands—"the people would not accept me either."

"Why?" Softly, she hit his chest with both fists.

"You know why," Horemheb whispered. He gently grabbed her wrists and placed his forehead upon hers.

Nefertiti slid her hands up to his face and he laid a kiss on her palm as she looked upon him with wet eyes. "I love you."

She chuckled.

She had said it many times before to Thutmose, to Akhenaten, but now, as those words passed her lips, her heart became alive as her tears embodied her happiness and not her sorrow. She drew in a shallow breath and whispered again, "I *love* you."

In the dizzying whirlwind of their racing thoughts, they

became engulfed in each other. His body rushed into hers as he pressed his parted lips onto her mouth. He enclosed her in his arms and pressed her close to him to imprint upon his memory her savory scent, her warm touch, her sweet taste . . . for after the coming harvest season, they would be separated forever.

LATER AS THE MOON ROSE TO ITS FULL HEIGHT IN THE night sky, her head rested on his bare chest.

She whispered, "Should I give up the crown?" She asked the question one more time, already knowing the answer. They'd had this same conversation many times before. Her mind drifted to their lives together if she could abdicate. She could live in his house in Waset and bear his children. She could even give one to his wife, Amenia, in Men-nefer, if Amenia pressed him for his philandering—even though what he did wasn't a crime. He did not owe Amenia anything. A simple life didn't seem so bad now.

Horemheb rubbed her shoulder with one hand and her fingers with his other. He stared off into the darkness of the room, only lit by a dwindling candle on the table by the bedside. "Pharaoh is Amun's—"

"I know," Nefertiti said, and buried her face into his chest. "Everyone wishes to be royalty," she murmured bitterly. "They say, 'Oh, look at their luxury, look at their privilege, look at their full bellies!' " She turned her face to Horemheb's. "I told you long ago, as a young girl, I wanted to be chief royal wife so much." She chuckled in sorrow, then took a deep breath as she rose up to give Horemheb a soft kiss on his lips. "But I believe what I've always wanted was love. Illness took Thutmose. The Aten took Akhenaten. And now the crown keeps me from you." A tear slid down her cheek as

Horemheb took ahold of both her shoulders and sat up, placing his forehead against hers. "Will I ever just have love?" she cried as her eyes met his.

He took his thumb and wiped away her tears. "My most magnificent Nefertiti, you have my love," he whispered to her as he studied her face.

"As you have mine," she said, running her hand over his. "But we can never be."

His lips pressed into a grimace. He wanted to retort her argument, but she spoke the truth. He could not even comfort her with a lie, for his eyebrow would twitch, giving him away. "We—" he started. "I—" He held his breath, trying to find the words he wanted to say. A tightness set in his chest as he watched her hope die in her eyes. "Nefertiti—"

"You were right all along," Nefertiti whispered, placing a hand upon his cheek. "We should have never let this go any further than it did. It is too much for me to bear." She kissed his mouth and drew back slightly. Her tears made the kohl around her eyes streak down her cheeks. She looked from his lips to his eyes and then pulled away further.

"Nefertiti, I would never trade this time with you. *I* was wrong. All that time spent refusing you, rejecting you . . . that was time I could have been with you. *Years*, instead of only two seasons—I could have been with you. It could have been more time for us." He pulled her back to him and repeated, "*I* was wrong."

"No—because it is all in vain. I will be pressed to marry Tut if I don't marry the Hittite when he comes."

"Before the Hittite comes, and I must watch you marry another," Horemheb said as the perfume of her neck invited a kiss, "I want you to know . . . I will regret every day being the son of a military man instead of that of a king. I forever want you as my wife." He ran his hands up and down her back and let out a deep breath.

She pushed up to look him in the face. "Then *marry* me, Horemheb," she pleaded one last time. "You refused my last request, so I sent a letter in my grief to our enemy to ask for a prince." She shook her head at her own stupidity. "The next time I may hand Egypt to Nubia." She chuckled, more in sorrow than in truth.

"Please don't hand Egypt to Nubia." He smirked, but both of their mouths curved down soon after.

She thought about running away to a life of exile with him, but her daughters would not approve, and Egypt— even though it had given her nothing in return, she could not abandon Egypt to Pawah, and she knew Horemheb would never turn his back on his country. Pushing that alternative to the side, she rubbed her neck and thought again.

"What if I *did* marry Tut? I am Pharaoh. Pharaoh has many wives. Couldn't I have many husbands?" She chuckled again, knowing the ridiculousness of such a scenario.

"One would think." Horemheb smiled sadly. "But if the people aren't going to accept a woman Pharaoh, I don't think they would accept a woman Pharaoh with multiple husbands. And even if you could only marry Tut, it's a crime to have another man's wife, and Tut . . . like you said—if it were ever found out, he would probably be forced to have me killed for laying with you."

"I will never share a bed with that boy." Nefertiti rolled her eyes in exasperation. "If Tut and Pawah were out of the picture, would you marry me *then?*"

"Tut and Pawah are the last living male royals. Without them, I think you could choose your own husband." Horemheb leaned back to look at her.

"Tut is already sickly," Nefertiti said, but stopped, realizing what she had implied, and dropped her head, shutting her eyes. She shook her head, lamenting the same vicious cycle. She was out of ideas and knew he was too. There were no solutions where happiness was shared by all.

Rolling over in her bed, she pulled the sheet over her shoulder.

Horemheb softly bumped the back of his head on the stone wall as he finally found his breath again. "We are wasting our time together discussing the same points that always lead to the same outcome. We both know this will have to end." He looked up to pray to the gods one more time that this be not the case—but they did not owe him anything.

He looked over at her and brought a hand to her shoulder.

A soft whisper came back: "Please leave me."

Horemheb kept his hand on her shoulder. "Nefertiti, you and I both know you don't want me to leave." He rolled her over to face him again. He couldn't fix the situation, but he could say something he knew was truth. "I love you, Nefertiti." He leaned down to her and kissed her forehead and then her full lips.

"Don't think about it anymore." Horemheb put a gentle hand on her jaw and guided her into another kiss. "We have a few more hours until the sun breaks." He moved her underneath him and kissed her neck. "Be here with me now."

22

THE TIME OF TRUTH

"PHARAOH NEFERNEFERUATEN," PAWAH SAID WITH A NOD of his head as she entered the council room.

She did not even peer at him, but rather took her seat at the head of the table, hating the fact she was early enough to arrive before Paaten and her father. Now she had the burden of speaking with Pawah and Beketaten on her own.

"You, my Pharaoh," Pawah said with a *tsk-tsk*, "are an extremely stubborn woman."

"The People's Restoration of Egypt demands the boy King," Beketaten said. "Abdicate the throne to Coregent Tutankhaten. It has been over a year since he has been crowned Coregent, and the people no longer want a woman ruler. A true divinely appointed King is a *man*, just as it has always been."

"Well, that is one way to start a meeting of council." Nefertiti smiled at the little bit of evil that tugged at her soul. "When Pawah tried to seduce me into marrying him 'for the good of my own life' "—she watched the fury build in Beketaten's eyes—"I assumed he had other motives." She stood, pushing her hands on her hips. "But I know master

manipulation when I see it. I could smell it on his breath."
Sitting back down, she leaned back in her chair and lifted her
chin. "O great Vizier Pawah, formerly Fifth Prophet of
Amun, how do I know you truly speak on behalf of the
people? Is this not just another manipulation to get the
crown yourself?"

"O great Pharaoh . . ." Pawah chuckled. "Don't flatter
yourself. We are *both* master manipulators, you and I. If I
truly wanted the crown, wouldn't I just kill you and take it?"

"No, because the crown would then go to the boy,"
Nefertiti answered, speaking rather quickly so as to shoot
down his attempt to intimidate her. "But I wouldn't put it
past you to kill both of us, *and* Vizier Nakht, so that you
would be Vizier of the Upper and of the Lower, husband to
the King's daughter, and a former priest of Amun." Nefertiti
took a quick breath. Her eyes narrowed as the final goal of
the man who sat in front of her came to her mind. Her
mouth became dry and a lump formed in her throat, realizing
his full conspiracy. Nausea kept her mouth closed for a
moment, until her whisper finally leeched out: "You could
easily slip into the throne whether the people wanted you
there or not."

A hesitant smirk appeared on Pawah's face; she had
figured it out. His wife spoke first.

"Be careful, *Pharaoh*," Beketaten said. "You will not
insinuate such things about *my* husband."

"Why are you even here, Beketaten?" Nefertiti scoffed at
her. This woman was not a member of Pharaoh's council, and
Nefertiti was done with her empty threats. "You hold no
officer's title. Shouldn't you take your rightful place in the
royal harem with the rest of the women and children?"
Nefertiti said as she threw some nonchalant fingers toward
her. "Be gone." Nefertiti commanded a guard to take her
away.

Beketaten chewed her bottom lip as she kicked her chair out of her way to stand. Pawah stayed seated, allowing the guard to take his wife from the room. Beketaten pulled on his shoulder, but he ignored her as the guard helped her along. Beketaten's eyes fell upon Nefertiti. "You will wish you had not done this . . . any of it!"

If there were other witnesses to her threats, I would kill her like her sister, Nefertiti thought to herself, but her eyes stayed locked with Pawah's.

Beketaten slammed the door behind her.

Silence fell over the room.

Pawah sat in his chair, slightly beguiled by Nefertiti's show of power. "She is right, you know," he finally murmured.

And if the time comes when I can kill you as well, I will seize it with every passion. Nefertiti smacked her lips trying to regain the moisture in her mouth.

"She is only jealous because you tried to marry into the throne."

Pawah chuckled and leaned his head back. "Which you so rudely rejected." He clasped his hands over his belly. "You will learn, Pharaoh, one way or another, where your place is."

"I know the power of Pharaoh."

"Do you know?" Pawah shook his head. "For you, it should be by my side, with me as your husband. It's your last chance, lotus flower."

Her cheeks burned. She knew he'd said that just to get under her skin, so she calmed her anger. "You failed at your last attempt to marry into the throne, and you will fail again."

Ay walked in and stopped short, with Paaten behind him. Ay set Pawah ablaze with his glare. Paaten put his hand on Ay's shoulder and guided him to his seat.

"How did you try to marry into the throne?" Ay spoke through his teeth to Pawah, as if he thought the man had tried to violate his daughter.

Pawah seemed to absorb the tension in the room—almost as if it empowered him, emboldened him. With a sly smile, he responded, "Now I cannot go sharing *all* of my secrets with you, Master of Pharaoh's Horses."

Ay slammed his fist on the table. "I'll have you killed for those words!"

Nefertiti stared at Pawah, not showing the happiness in her soul that her father had come to her side after his hiatus.

"Try it, Master of Pharaoh's Horses," Pawah said, a hand on his chest.

Ay stood up as if ready to kill his daughter's greatest adversary. Pawah's cool, unflinching body and growing smile enraged him even further.

"Sit down," Paaten commanded. Ay stood still. "Sit *down*," Paaten instructed again, and this time Ay obeyed.

Pawah chuckled. "Do your men obey you, Ay, as well as you obey the General?"

"Ay," Paaten said. "He will have his day. For now, we are tied to this devil."

"Yes, listen to your General. He knows best for all." Pawah's attention turned back to Nefertiti. "Wait until the people hear about Pharaoh Neferneferuaten's latest act of glory. First, the execution of royal wife Sitamun, and then the banishment of Pharaoh Amenhotep's last remaining daughter to the royal harem."

"I didn't banish her. That is where she is *supposed* to be."

He laughed. "My dear Pharaoh, no, no. That is not the story the people will hear."

"If you spread false rumors about Her Majesty," Paaten started, "then—"

"Then what? You will arrest me? *Kill* me?" Pawah questioned with a sneer, and kicked his feet onto the table. "No. We are back in that same dreadful cycle again." At their silence, he plopped his feet back to the ground. "You see, you can't do anything. Your hands are tied. You can't touch me." He stood, his lips pulling into a victorious grin. "I also know something that the two of you don't," he said, pointing between Paaten and Ay.

They sat there, unamused, as Nefertiti closed her eyes and held her breath, bracing for the shame that would come over her when he said it. Her mind raced—what did he know . . . about Horemheb, about the Hittite? Or both?

He will tell and force me to marry him.

His voice rose with an evil ring, almost like the sound the wind makes right before a sandstorm, and he said: "A foreign prince is coming."

Paaten and Ay turned to look at her. Nefertiti opened her eyes and let her captive breath escape into a shameful huff of air. Part of her rejoiced that he did not know about her and Horemheb—or at least he had chosen not to reveal that he knew—but as she stared at Pawah, feeling her father's and the General's heavy gaze upon her, she wished nothing more than to curl up and die. *Now* what to say?

Pawah's gleeful eyes beamed as he struck his prey. "So, *Pharaoh* Neferneferuaten, are you not marrying the boy, seeing as you requested a foreigner? The boy would be the better choice—it would be easy to sway him and tell him what to do, especially since he adores you. Well . . . adored you."

"No, I'm not marrying Tut." Nefertiti shook her head. "And what do you mean, '*adored*' me?"

"Oh, nothing. It's just . . . he now thinks you hate him and want him gone like his father."

"Why would he think tha—"

She stopped and slowly pulled her jaw closed as a sneer grew on Pawah's face. Her stomach tightened into a knot and forced her breath out.

How have I let him get away with all of this? How much has he done to undermine me?

Her lips pulled back in disgust. "You are truly evil, Pawah. May Amun curse you for your nefarious acts of treason against Pharaoh and Egypt."

"Your god *Amun* will honor me for always working. And sooner or later, one of my many works will get me what I want."

Silence. The council was astounded at the lengths Pawah had taken to end Pharaoh's rule. But before they could react to his comment, Pawah set the focus back on Nefertiti's mistake.

"And what about this next Pharaoh?"

Nefertiti dropped her chin and narrowed her eyes at Pawah. "I had no choice."

Paaten turned to the enemy in the room. "Leave, Pawah."

"Or what?" Pawah asked. "I'm interested to hear who my next Pharaoh will be, and as a part of this council, I have a right to know."

Nefertiti looked to Paaten and then her father, knowing they could not make him leave—and part of her feared that if he *did* know about Horemheb then he would tell them if she forced him out. He would be witness to her failure. Seeing she could not change the outcome, she finally spoke.

"I have asked for a foreign royal to marry."

"Mitanni?" Pawah asked in a façade of curiosity. His eyes grew wide at the anticipation and dread filling the room, his smile plastered on his wicked face.

"No," Nefertiti said through her teeth, lowering her chin.

He is enjoying this. I have never wanted to kill a man so much as I do right now. She envisioned leaping across the table and squeezing her fingers around his neck.

"I should think they wouldn't send anyone, after you sent

back poor King Tustratta's daughter as a childless corpse." Pawah's eyes laughed.

Nefertiti sneered at his contempt. "Royal wife Kiya was the most beautiful person and friend. What you did to her sickens me."

"Me? I had no part in Beketaten's doing. I wanted to do away with Akhenaten as soon as possible, but she wanted to make sure he had a male heir—no thanks to you."

Nefertiti's lips pulled back as she imaged what he and Beketaten did and discussed behind closed doors. "You and Beketaten, always meddling and caring only for yourselves, never anyone else."

"Yes, yes. You made your disgust perfectly clear, dear Pharaoh, when I proposed a marriage between the two of us." Pawah drummed his fingers on the table. "But I am most definitely waiting to hear who was so much better than me to be the next Pharaoh of Egypt."

"I requested a Hittite prince to seal our alliance," Nefertiti declared as she sat back in her chair, shoulders tall and chin lifted. A quick strike to end the pain she was causing to her father and the General.

Ay and Paaten said nothing, but Pawah laughed with his belly, a deep, menacing laugh. "Hittite?!" Swinging his head from shoulder to shoulder, he laughed until his lungs emptied of air. He leaned an elbow upon the table in exaggerated mirth. "The people will finally know their woman Pharaoh is giving Egypt to the enemy! This will be sure to endear them to you, Nefertiti."

"We are allies now!" she rebuked him.

"We can never be allies with the enemy! The people will believe *me*! Not you, chief royal wife of Pharaoh Akhenaten, the heretic King! He betrayed us to the Aten, and you betray us to the Hittites!"

"Enough!" Paaten shot from his seat as he stared down

the slender former prophet of Amun. His large frame and suddenness did give Pawah's neck a visible pulse for a moment.

"Have they responded?" Ay asked in a soft voice to Nefertiti.

"Yesterday morning. Over a year since I sent my request."

"What was the response?"

Nefertiti drew in a slow breath of reluctance. Her gaze went to her hands and she shuffled her feet. She looked to the spot where Horemheb would be seated if he did not have other matters to tend. Then she replied:

"Prince Zannanza is due to arrive after the next harvest."

Ay's glance dropped to his hands. His chest rose and fell as he drew in dry air.

"Your reign will be short," Pawah said, voicing the thoughts of Ay and Paaten.

"The people are not to know," Paaten ordered the room.

Pawah chuckled. "Or what, great General?" He picked himself up from his chair and strode to the door.

"Vizier Pawah," Nefertiti said as he reached for the handle.

He stopped, but did not turn to look at her.

"I know you desire the crown," Nefertiti said. "You will not get it."

"I wouldn't be so sure," Pawah said. "Royals are just men —" He turned to look at her. "And women, who can be . . . removed from *divine* appointment." He exited the council room before she could respond.

The three of them sat in silence for a few moments.

"Well, the Hittite prince does not help matters," Paaten whispered.

"It is done. Everything is already done. We cannot go back. We must march to whatever future fate has set for us." Nefertiti's shoulders dropped. She turned to the General, her friend. "Has no more progress been made on my order?" Her eyes darted to her father, not wanting him to know she had ordered the assassination of Pawah.

Paaten clenched his jaw. "We have tried many things, Pharaoh. We are still trying. Commander Horemheb tries as we speak."

"May Amun be with us," she whispered, hoping that their hearts would not be too heavy from her deeds upon this land when it was weighed in the afterlife.

NEFERTITI OPENED HER BEDCHAMBERS DOOR AND WAS surprised to find Mut standing there, waiting. Aitye tended to the bedchamber, as was her duty.

"Mut . . . what are you doing here?" Nefertiti asked. She peered to both sides of the hallway before she closed the door.

"Is it true?" Mut crossed her arms, arming herself against the inevitable answer.

"Is what true?" Nefertiti asked as she glided across the room to her, dreading the shame that was to follow.

"Ankhesenpaaten told me you were marrying a *Hittite*," Mut said, uncrossing her arms and placing her hands on her hips. "Why would you do that?" she demanded.

"Mut, if you ever become royalty, you may be forced to do things you do not want to do," Nefertiti said as she patted her head.

Mut pushed her hand away from her head. "I am not a child. I am thirteen, a woman of marriageable age!"

At the sight of Mut's red cheeks, Nefertiti stopped and placed both hands on her shoulders, pressing into them. "Sit down, Mut." Nefertiti sat down and Mut followed.

"You were worried before that you couldn't trust anyone.

Now, marrying a *Hittite?* You can guarantee no one will trust you," Mut started. "I can—"

"Mut." Nefertiti sighed. "It was either that or marry Tut or Pawah."

"What's wrong with Tut?" Mut said. "I know you'd never marry Pawah."

Nefertiti shook her head just as a knock came at the door.

Aitye answered it. "My Pharaoh, your father and Master of Pharaoh's Horses, Ay, requests a private audience with you," she said, and bowed.

"Yes, let him in," Nefertiti said as she stood to greet her father once Aitye let him inside.

"Nefertiti," Ay said. The muscles in his arms strained—clearly his desire to embrace his daughter had been met with an icy chill in the air around her.

"Father!" Mut ran to him and threw her arms around his waist.

"My dear Mutnedjmet," Ay said, returning her hug. "I've missed you so. I'm sorry I never come around the royal harem, and when I do you are not there." Mut smiled up at him and he down at her. His face fell as he looked to his firstborn. "Nefertiti, I need you to reconsider this decision." He pulled Mut's arms away from his waist and sidestepped her.

"The decision has already been made. Prince Zannanza is on his way here as we speak," Nefertiti said as she also stood up to be eye-to-eye with her father.

"No—there is still time. Marry Tut and make Pawah look the fool. We could end his influence over the people."

Nefertiti bit hard with her back teeth. Her nostrils flared. "I will not marry Tut."

"Daughter, let go of your pride. It—"

"No!" Nefertiti said. "It is not pride that keeps me from—"

"Nefertiti! Do this for yourself. Think of your children. Think—"

"We are done here!" Nefertiti yelled, and began to walk past her father toward the door.

"Marry Tut," Ay said as he blocked her path. "If you marry the Hittite prince, the people will rise up. Pawah will make sure of it. Tut is just a boy. I know you could still rule in his place. Save yourself from the people's wrath, daughter."

"I'm long past saving, Father. I am not worth anything to you now. You got what you wanted from me, and now you have washed your hands of me." Nefertiti tried to sidestep as she pushed on his chest.

"Don't say that, Nefertiti!" Ay grabbed his daughter's wrists to pull her to his side.

"Let go of me!"

"Nefertiti, please. My lotus blossom." Ay tightened his grip.

She ripped away from him. "Once I stood by your side and you promised me you would keep me safe—"

"And I am still trying to keep you safe, Nefertiti. Marry Tut and you will be safe."

"Marry Tut—" Nefertiti shook her head and shrugged helplessly. "The words fall so easily from your mouth." Tears welled in her eyes. "After all, you think, he is only ten years, almost eleven, right? Not so much a boy in a few years—his father became Coregent at fourteen when he married me. I guess that is when the little boy becomes a man, is it not so?"

"Please, daughter—enough of this nonsense. Marry Tut and save yourself."

"Yes, save myself—because you won't! Look at what I have become. I ordered Sitamun's death. In exchange for my daughter's life, I took hers. I ordered Pawah's assassination—what was one more? I'm beyond saving, Father. You had your hand in my undoing. You should save yourself . . . I am not worth it anymore."

Ay shut his eyes.

Nefertiti clenched her jaw, realizing she had just revealed her involvement with Paaten and Horemheb's secret assassination attempts.

He seemed to ignore it as he opened his eyes and took a breath. "But you *are* worth saving, Nefertiti. I'm sorry for what Akhenaten did to you. I'm sorry I led you in the wrong direction with my advice regarding him, and I'm sorry for what I have asked of you."

Nefertiti's head bounced back and forth. "I just don't want to feel anymore. I don't want to think anymore. I killed a man"—her voice dropped—"and not just any man, but Pharaoh." She drew a quick breath. "Am I the only one who cares? And all the while I have to tell myself it was justified, it was excusable. But why should I be the one to live? Why should I be the one to not have to pay for my sins? What makes *me* so special? This is why Amun punishes me. This is why my daughters are taken from me. This is why I am forced to marry someone I don't love. This is why I must even marry the son of my husband to save myself. He punishes me, Father! Amun punishes me!" Her arms squeezed her sides as she felt her insides collapsing in on themselves. Her body ached. Her teeth ached. Her eyes ached. Tiredness crept over her. Tired of fighting. Tired of speaking. Tired of trying.

"Daughter—"

"But aren't you proud of me, Father? Isn't this what you wanted for your little girl—to be forever remembered as the living image of the ruler of Egypt carved in its mighty stone? A stone immortal!" Nefertiti threw her hands in the air and lifted her face to the ceiling. "Aren't you proud?!" She let her hands drop as she once again brought her eyes to her father, who stood with a grimace etched on his face. "Aren't you proud?!" Tears formed in her eyes as her voice shook.

Ay rushed to Nefertiti, throwing his arms around her, and she couldn't hold back the tears anymore. She buried her head into his chest and wept like her ten-year-old innocent self. Ay kissed her forehead and whispered nothing but, "My dear lotus blossom, I'm so, so sorry," over and over again.

Mut stood off nearby, her presence forgotten by her father and his favored daughter. Aitye half-rubbed a cleaning cloth over the bed frame as she watched the three of them.

"My love," Pawah crooned to his wife, seated in her newly designated wing of the royal harem.

"Don't you do that." Beketaten swatted at his face and turned her shoulder to him. "After what you did to me."

"My golden grain, I did nothing," Pawah whispered in her ear, and rubbed the shoulder she presented to him as her sign of dismissal. Planting a kiss there, he found her eyes. "I only proposed marriage to Nefertiti so I could align Pharaoh with the priesthood of Amun." The half-truth slid easily from his lips.

"Part of you desires her." Beketaten looked away and turned her nose up. "Don't lie to me."

"Beketaten—"

"I knew you desired someone else when we were in exile, and all you could do was talk about her beauty and her power. I knew all of the sweet whisperings in my ear were nothing but lies!" Beketaten wrenched her shoulder from his hand and stood up.

"They were not lies," Pawah pleaded. "My sweet, beautiful Nile reed, the one to whom I pledge my undying loyalty and love . . ." He stroked a stray hair from her wig out of her eyesight. "Know this: I married you for a reason."

To get closer to the throne, he thought, but he said:

"Because when I saw you, out of the entire royal party, who assisted your father in his yearly sacrifice to Amun, I knew you were the only one for me."

She crossed her arms and pressed her lips into a grimace. "Liar!"

He rubbed the sides of her arms until she finally released her stance. "That's better," he murmured as he pressed his nose into the side of her face.

She let out a little squeal. "Stop it!" She pushed him away. "I'm still mad at you."

"Why?"

"Because you never told me you were going to try to marry Nefertiti," she huffed. "She is the enemy. You said so yourself."

"I never said such things about our Pharaoh."

"Yes, you did."

"My sweet flower, I have never lied to you."

She tapped her foot and placed her hands on her hips. "How do I know?"

"Because I love you. I would never lead you astray. Are you going to believe *me* . . . or Nefertiti? She, the one who ordered Sitamun's death?" He stroked her face. "Nefertiti only said those things to try and upset you—to drive a chasm between us."

Beketaten's eyes narrowed, and she gnashed her teeth. "That cursed woman!"

Easily deflected. Gullible. Short attention span. Perfect for my wife.

She paced the room a little more. "Curse her and curse her children," she muttered. "I will make her pay for her sins . . . blood for blood."

An idea for a new plan presented itself in Pawah's mind after hearing Beketaten's passing thought. He said casually, "She is spitting in the face of Amun by not marrying a male of Egyptian royal blood."

Beketaten paced some more, nodding. "She is so power-hungry, she wants the crown all to herself!"

"No, she is marrying a Hittite prince," he said, hiding his smug smile.

Beketaten stopped and stared at Pawah, her jaw dropping. "She is doing *what?*"

"You heard me."

"This is great news!" Beketaten said. "We can use this to outrage the people!"

Pawah nodded slowly in agreement. "She is giving Egypt into the hands of the Hittites."

"We mustn't let her marry the prince—that would not be good for Egypt."

Or good for me in my quest for the crown, Pawah thought.

Pawah jumped up, grabbed her shoulders, and squeezed. "We must act now."

"But how?"

"We hold a good deal of the military in our hand. Let's use them to keep the prince from reaching Aketaten." Pawah rubbed his hands down her arms as he spoke.

"And Nefertiti?"

"Leave her to me." He smirked openly.

"No, no." Beketaten pressed her body into his. His smirk whenever he thought of a genius plan always drew her near. "We will not have another situation like that again," she said, referring to his marriage proposal to Nefertiti. "You will take me with you—what do you want me to do?"

"When the time is right, and when I tell you . . . strike," he said and handed her a dagger he had requested from one of his loyal guards. "You will be able to take your revenge for

Sitamun. If they can successfully cover a dagger to Meritaten's heart, they can cover a strike to Nefertiti's."

She smiled but chewed her bottom lip.

"I know you've never taken a life before," Pawah said, covering the dagger with his hand. "But no one will know." At her silence, he continued: "She did kill Sitamun."

Beketaten's stare upon the dagger hardened and she pulled it from his hand. "It is for my sister. A life for a life," she murmured under her breath.

"Yes . . . that's my good wife," he said as he pushed the wig from her eyes and brought his lips to hers. As she fell weak in his arms, he knew he'd won her over once again with his charm and irresistible kisses.

❧ 23 ❧
THE TIME OF CONSOLATION

ALMOST FIVE DECANS HAD COME AND GONE SINCE THE Hittites' response, and Nefertiti suddenly found herself carrying Horemheb's child. The Hittite Prince Zannanza would arrive in one season's time. Her father stood guard at her door with chief royal guard Jabari, as it was the Commander and General's night to sleep. Her father would have stood guard inside her bedchambers, as she also now asked of both Horemheb and the General, so that no one would think it strange when the Commander emerged from her room in the morning; but tonight, she asked him to guard outside.

She paced the room, mumbling to herself, "What am I to do? The people will know. I will be killed. I don't know what to do. . . . The prince will know it is not his child. What am I going to *do*? Do I tell Horemheb? What would he say? I could tell him he would finally be a father. Only, if the Hittite came today, I could have the child and Amenia could raise the baby as her own. No, no—the prince would think it was his . . . but no one would know the difference, would they? I'm not ready to marry the Hittite. I don't want to marry a dirty, hairy

Hittite . . . but if I were already married, I could just blame a messenger who'd died in route—just one big misunderstanding—" Her breath caught in her throat; that was the only possible way out of this situation. "Or else I insult our new allies and bring war to our borders." She pounded her fists into her legs as she paced. "Or they are insulted regardless and bring war to our borders." She shook her head like a horse ridding itself of flies. "I wish I could take back my letter. I wish he weren't coming . . . but then what? I'd have a baby and no named father? It would only incite the people even more. 'Whose child is this?' The Commander's, I would have to say. 'But he is not royalty. Kill him! Kill the child. Kill everyone!' " Her hot, whispered breath shook with panic. She pinched her lips together as her eyes lifted to the heavens. "Amun!" she yelled. "Why do you punish me still? Have I not returned your people to you? Have I not reestablished the ways of old? O why do you punish me so? What have I done wrong?" At the silence, she yelled, "Tell me!" She raised a fist to the air, but shortly thereafter fell to her knees, her hands limp. She knew why he still punished her: she'd taken the life of Pharaoh. "But he turned from you," she whimpered as she looked above. "Why does *Pawah* not suffer? He forced my hand. He slew Smenkare. Why does punishment only befall *me*?" Her hands covered her face. "What have I done?" she cried. "What have I done . . . ?"

A knock came at her door, and it opened. Her father entered, closing the door behind him. "Nefertiti? My lotus blossom? Is all well? I hear your screams."

"Yes, Father. Please leave me," she muttered.

Ay's heart lit at her calling him "Father" again. He took a few steps forward.

"I said *leave*!" She wheeled to look at him, on the ground

like a wild animal. The candlelight was lost in the smudged kohl around her eyes.

Ay came near and knelt beside her. He put his hand on her back, which soon rocked from her sobs. "Come, come, my daughter," he whispered, and pulled her into his chest, wrapping her in his arms.

"I hate this, Father," she whimpered. "I have done it all to myself."

"No, my Nefertiti—"

"*Yes*—I pushed Akhenaten further in his obsession with the Aten, I brought him his poisoned wine, I let Pawah kill Smenkare and condemned Meritaten to murder in the process, I executed Sitamun for revenge and further incited the people, I did not teach my children about Amun, I refuse to marry Tut, I asked for a Hittite prince, and I fell in lo—"

She cut herself off and took a breath while Ay pondered the rest of her sentence; he guessed she had fallen in love with someone she couldn't marry; but at her next words, he dismissed it.

". . . and I let myself fall."

"We learn from our mistakes, my daughter, just as I learned from my mistakes with you. I thought your marriage would be as mine and your mother's or mine and Tey's, but it was not. I told you Akhenaten would return to you if you just gave him all of your love, and look what it has done."

"No, Father, I cannot blame you anymore. I have done this—I have done all of it. It is why Amun still punishes me. How can you still love me? How can anyone still love me?" She buried her head into his chest.

"Look at me, Nefertiti." He raised her chin, gently but firmly. "All I see is my innocent baby girl, my lotus blossom, whose laugh and smile stole my heart when I thought I could never love again." Ay stroked his daughter's face. "My lotus blossom, I love you. Nothing you can do will ever take away my love for you."

She smiled and kissed his cheek, her lips slick with her own tears. Her voice trembled. "I'm sorry I have pushed you away and blamed you for the last three years."

"No, no. All is in the past. We cannot change it. We can only push onward with what we have and make the best of it."

She found his eyes. "Should I abdicate?"

"No. It would lessen Pharaoh in the people's eyes—more so than just marrying Tut," Ay said as he traced her face. "Please, my lotus blossom . . . marry Tut."

"I cannot." She brought a hand to her belly and closed her eyes, thinking of a life without Horemheb; she wasn't ready to stop fighting. "For many reasons, I cannot marry Tut."

"Whatever you do, do not abdicate and do not marry the Hittite."

"But I must be married before the Hittite comes—"

"Nefertiti, your army is growing again. It fell slack under Akhenaten, but we have made soldiers of the boys who came to us for food when the economy suffered. Should you refuse the Hittite and they declare war, your army will fight."

"But Pharaoh is the defender of Egypt, and I will have brought war upon it," Nefertiti said. "I cannot do that to Egypt. I must be married by the time he comes."

"That is soon—most likely within the season. Who will you marry?"

Silence, then: "Must I marry Tut?"

"He is the rightful heir," Ay said. "He is your only option for marriage."

"If Tut and Pawah were gone, who then would I marry?"

"Maybe someone of the noble class? I would think it would be your choosing. But that is nonsense. Pawah, we are working on removing . . . but Tut, he hasn't done anything wrong. Marry him, daughter."

"And live my life alone? I will never share a bed with him."

Ay's face fell at the dismal future. "It is the only way."

She turned from her father and crawled to her bed and into its embrace. She inhaled Horemheb's scent from the linen sheets and wrapped her arms around herself.

Ay stood and drew near. "Perhaps Tut will not live much longer. He is a sickly child."

"Tut was not supposed to live *at all*. They said he would journey west soon after birth. Sickly, but resilient," Nefertiti said into her bed.

"Nefertiti." Ay knelt by her bed and leaned with both elbows so he was beside her face. He kissed her forehead.

"Why can't I just have love?" She rubbed her face into the linen sheet, as if scrubbing her father's kiss away.

"You have my love," Ay said, and caressed her shoulder.

Turning her face to him, she said, "I know," but her eyes were dim.

He kissed her cheek and stood up. "Whatever you decide, my lotus blossom, General Paaten, Commander Horemheb, chief royal guard Jabari, and myself will stand with you." He covered the candle. "Get some sleep, my daughter. I will stand guard at your door."

Her heart longed to tell him about Horemheb and his child, but she chewed on her lip before releasing the words, "Thank you, Father." It was all that would come.

As soon as the door closed, she turned her face back to the linen sheets, and the memory of Horemheb next to her flooded her senses. "A child. I bet it will be a male child." She grimaced, even though her heart grew. "After all these years, I will finally have a male child, and for a man I love yet cannot marry."

She cried at the irony. Her tears finally exhausted her to

sleep.

NEFERTITI RAN DOWN THE CORRIDOR CLUTCHING HER BABY TO her chest. Horemheb's baby. The Hittites and the people rose up against her and they chased her with fire and spears at every turn. She felt herself surrounded as her heart raced and sweat poured from her brow. Her baby boy screamed at the clamor around his mother. The corner in which they had her pinned grew teeth above and below her and began to crunch down as the men's spears jabbed at her, killing her baby, Horemheb's baby, and at the last jab, struck her in her heart while Egypt burned around her. Then, as she breathed her last, her eyes made out against the smoke a towering form: Pawah, standing and smiling at her agony.

NEFERTITI AWOKE WITH TREMBLING HANDS AND A palpitating heart. Her fingers frantically touched her chest and felt her belly—still smooth, still pregnant, no blood. She looked to her side: she was alone. She looked at her door. Four shadows came from underneath it, signaling both her father and Jabari still stood guard.

Tears welled in her eyes. She could feel the stab of the spear; she could hear her baby's cries, even now as she was awake. The warmth of her child against her chest as she ran was still there, she swore it was. Drawing her knees close to her chest, she wrapped her arms around her legs and tried to catch her breath.

After some time, she went to the door and asked her father to send for papyrus and ink.

She sat at the table, reed brush still in its ink well, papyrus blank in front of her, until the words came.

My dearest Horemheb,

I hope this letter finds you in peace. I am so happy you are in my life and for the moments we have shared, but I have had a dream where I have seen the end of Egypt should I not marry the Hittite and with no husband already. I must marry, and I must marry soon. My father said he would fight a war if I refused the Hittite with no husband, but my love, I carry your child.

She stopped writing. Her mind went blank. How to put all of this into a letter?

After some time, she resumed:

Thus, I have resolved to marry Tut, so the people may think it is his child, so our child may not be outcasted or his life endangered as a potential threat to the throne's heir. If it is a daughter, perhaps Tut will allow you to take the child to Amenia. My one request is that Amenia allows me to know this child, that I may redeem myself as a mother. If it is a son,

She stopped again. What would she ask if it was a son? She had seen his death and her own. But she shook her head. It was only a dream . . . or was it a vision?

"Even Amun wants me to marry Tut," she whispered.

Tut may want to claim him as his own, should he have no other sons. I am sorry this has happened, but please admire your son from afar while staying near, and should Tut have a son of his own, I don't know what will happen.

All I know is this: I love you and wish our lives had been different so that we could have been together. Our time dwindles. I saw my death in this life as a dream, and Pawah waiting for me to travel to the Field of Reeds. If this is a vision from Amun, my love, I make final requests:

Make sure Pawah never seizes the crown. Once I'm gone, he

would only have to get in close with Tut and then push the poor crippled child down the stairs. With no heir, Pawah ranks as the next male relative and takes the throne. Akhenaten might have put Egypt through torture, but Pawah as Pharaoh would be the end of Egypt altogether.

Please take care of Mut for me. She is a woman now. I ask you to request marriage to her and keep her safe in one of your houses. Be good to her, as you are to me. She is still smitten with you.

Please take care of Ankhesenpaaten and Nefe should the General fail in his promise to me. Keep them all safe from Pawah and Beketaten. Where I have failed them, teach them about Amun.

Counsel my mother and father in their sorrow. They have many children, but my father only has me from my mother, whom he loved greatly. Should I become one with Re, my journey west will be hardest for him.

I have so much guilt, my love. It weighs my heart. Pray for Ammit not to devour it when placed upon the balance in the afterlife. Eternal unrest is more than I can bear.

No matter the outcome, I will wait for you in the afterlife. You have given me joy and happiness in this time of darkness. I will always remember your caring touch, your patience, your taking of my burdens, your protection, your loyalty, and your love. I loved Thutmose, but it was a young love. I loved Akhenaten, but it was more because I needed to feel loved. However, the love I have for you, Horemheb, is mature and selfless—one I will never forget. Every night as I go to sleep as Tut's wife, I will remember you and dream of life as yours and yours alone.

Love, Your Nefertiti

She read it over and realized how little words would ever

be able to truly say. Closing her eyes, she blew the ink to dry it. Then she sealed it and wrote *Commander* on the front.

EARLY THE NEXT MORNING, ANKHESENPAATEN CAME TO her room.

"Mother . . ." Ankhesenpaaten's voice shook a little. "Mother, may I come in?"

Nefertiti lifted her head at the sound of her daughter's voice. She sat up straight in bed and cleared her throat. The pain from trying to silence her own tears in the night had strained her voice. "Come in, Ankhesenpaaten."

The door opened enough for Ankhesenpaaten to slide inside. Nefertiti lit the candle next to her bedside, as the early morning light barely lit the room. Ankhesenpaaten walked to her mother and as they looked upon each other's faces, they both let out a chuckle seeing the smeared kohl around the other's eyes. Nefertiti opened up her arm and drew Ankhesenpaaten into an embrace, sitting her on her bed.

"What causes your tears, my sweet one?"

Ankhesenpaaten let out a breath and pressed her eyes closed, forcing the last remnant of tears from her eyes. "Why would Tut ask me to marry him if he thinks I want to kill him? He hates me, Mother."

Nefertiti rubbed her daughter's back. "Tut is a young boy. Boys his age are not married, and there is a reason for that. I am sorry, Ankhesenpaaten, that I forced you to marry so young. Life has not been fair to you." Nefertiti thought back to what Akhenaten did to Ankhesenpaaten, as well: marrying her at seven years old—outrageous! "You were forced to grow up so quickly. Now, you are caught in the mess your father and I made. For that, I am sorry."

Nefertiti bit her lip as her daughter's eyes searched her for sincerity.

"But why, Mother? At my age, you already had two children! And Tut, he won't even look at me."

"He is eleven and his mind has been swayed by Pawah." Shaking her head, Nefertiti drew her hand into a fist and placed it on her lips as she debated reiterating her father's advice on marriage. "My father always told me, 'Trust and truth are united in marriage,' my sweet one."

Nefertiti hesitated but thought, *She is sixteen years old, she needs to know.*

"I thought I could save your father from his obsessions, but I was not enough. Trust and truth must go both ways. Tut does not trust you, so you continue to live your life in the most truthful way possible, and if he never comes to his senses, at the end of your life, at least your heart will not be heavy, and Ammit will not devour it when you journey to the afterlife."

Nefertiti clutched her own heart, knowing her ways had not always been truthful even though the motivations behind them might have been justified. Would it be enough for the balance when her heart was weighed? She didn't know the answer, and a cold chill of uncertainty passed through her body.

"You want to journey west, Ankhesenpaaten, knowing your heart is not heavy, that there is no question. Eternal restlessness is not something to take lightly. I know I never taught you about the other gods of Egypt, but learn them. The Aten is a lie, and has always been a lie, a deceiver of your father," Nefertiti warned as she found her daughter's eyes. "I will not lie to you."

Ankhesenpaaten opened her eyes. "I know, Mother. I see now." She placed her hand in Nefertiti's and squeezed. "Why do you cry?"

"Oh, daughter, for so many reasons, I cry," Nefertiti whispered.

"Tell me." Ankhesenpaaten squeezed Nefertiti's hand again.

"I cry because I wanted to be a good mother, but I was not. I cry because I lost your father and your sisters. I cry because I lost my friend, Kiya, my Mitanni sister-wife who never betrayed me. And now I cry because I love and cannot have what I love. All I have ever wanted was to be loved."

"You have *my* love, Mother." Ankhesenpaaten leaned her head on her mother's shoulder. Nefertiti drew her into a side embrace, as Ankhesenpaaten continued: "I'm sorry I do not know what you have gone through . . . and part of me does not want to know."

"Part of me does not want you to know either." Nefertiti closed her eyes, chuckling bitterly. "But I think you should." She tipped her daughter's chin so her face was to hers. "I will start from the beginning."

Nefertiti told her daughter all that had come to pass since Queen Tiye asked for her hand in marriage to Thutmose. "I loved him. He was my friend." She remembered her childhood. "Illness took him, so the crown fell to his brother —your father. He loved our uncle Anen's daughter, Kasmut. Anen was the Second Prophet of Amun, and given the state of power between the priesthood and Pharaoh, Pharaoh Amenhotep III and Queen Tiye would not allow him to marry her . . . so he married me instead. He did not love me at first, but we grew to love each other. He took care of me, and despite his father's loveless attempts to mold him into the man he wanted him to be, he became something better in his own eyes. We had Meritaten, Meketaten, and you, and then . . . he decided to denounce Amun—which was part of the plan—but he also planned to move the capital of our empire to here, Aketaten. The people rebelled, almost killing me and you and your sisters in the process, but we were able to subdue them. Your aunt Nebetah—you know her as Beketaten—and her husband Pawah led the rebellion. Your grandmother and father wanted to kill them for their conspiracies against the throne, but I urged them not to, to choose exile instead. I saw then in Nebetah's eyes, as she was exiled, that she was furious. She still holds that against me, always will. I took it all from her: the crown, the palace, the luxury . . . well, she took it from herself." She shook her head. "She should have just married her brother instead of Pawah."

Nefertiti looked out the window, wondering how different life would have been; but she found her daughter needing more of the past, and so she continued.

"Your father fell more and more into his obsessions with the Aten disc and forbade all worship of any other god, which was not planned. Once we had regained power over the priesthood of Amun, he should have reinstated Amun's priesthood and taken control of it. Yet he did not. He forced the people into poverty, as much of their work was dependent on the worship of other gods. We began amassing everyone into the army and we found we couldn't pay them what they should have been paid. He forced the people into loyalty for Pawah. He and Beketaten led a movement called the People's Restoration of Egypt. Your aunt came out of exile, changed her name to Beketaten, asked for pardon, and because I was on the throne due to your father's negligence, I granted it. Your father exiled me from Aketaten, and when I found that I was with his child, he allowed me to come back, but it was after some time. Come to find out, Beketaten had made him drunk so that he lay with his sister, Henuttaneb—Tut's mother. We had our children around the same time: I, another girl, and she a son. Royal wife, Kiya—"

Nefertiti stopped, seeing the fondness in Ankhesenpaaten's eyes at the mention of Kiya.

"Yes, Kiya . . . she was more of a mother to you than I ever was, and I'm sorry for that, Ankhesenpaaten. I left a foreign queen to care for my own children. I could not teach you about the true ways, and she could not either." Nefertiti laughed as tears welled in her eyes. "It took her a long time to learn how to pronounce 'Amun.' "

Ankhesenpaaten smiled and placed her hand on her mother's knee. "I still love you, Mother."

Nefertiti wrapped her arms around her daughter and kissed her forehead. "I love you."

"What happened after?"

"Kiya comforted me. She loved you children so much. She was my friend, even though I treated her with contempt at times. If you strive to be like anyone, be like Kiya." Nefertiti released her daughter and slid her hands down her arms. Before Ankhesenpaaten could soothe her, she spoke again, not wanting to be placated by her daughter. "Soon after, I ordered our armies home from the Mitanni and the Hittite lands, as disease was spreading. They brought the plague back to Egypt." Nefertiti shook her head. "You were only seven. The plague took three of your sisters, your grandmother . . . and Kiya. I felt so numb after that. I had been the cause of my daughters' deaths. I hadn't thought it through. And then your father, lost in his own mind, only descended deeper into his madness, marrying you, neglecting Egypt every day. The movement ran deep, and General Paaten, at my command, tortured men to find the leaders and discover what they were planning, until eventually the People's Restoration of Egypt came to Horemheb, my father, and myself. Then I knew Pawah and Beketaten led the movement. They threatened rebellion that night if I did not bring poisoned wine to your father—"

Nefertiti heard Ankhesenpaaten's gasp before she saw her eyes dim.

"So I did . . . to save our lives and to save the position of Pharaoh. I couldn't quite bring myself, though, to make sure he drank, and during that time between leaving him the wine and him finally drinking, he announced Smenkare as his successor. It was my fault." She let out a breath and then shook her head with an ironic, sad grin. "And Smenkare was worse than *he* was. Ordering the slaughter of Egyptians for their beliefs?" Nefertiti shook her head again. "Of course, Pawah and Beketaten came to me again. I told them I could not. I was not close enough to either Smenkare or Meritaten, and Meritaten believed as Smenkare did. Pawah poisoned Smenkare, but Sitamun, in her haste, and unknowing of Pawah's doings, went to kill Smenkare herself. She killed Meritaten."

Nefertiti swallowed her guilt. "I should have protected her." Her mind raced back to the pain of losing Meritaten, again at her own negligence.

"And now, even though I have lifted the ban of worship, seized control of the priesthood, given power back to Pharaoh—somewhat . . ." She closed her eyes. "The people still hold influence. I am not Amun's divinely appointed in their eyes because I was your father's wife. They want Tut, the young child who can be molded. But Tut is the embodiment of my failure as a wife and a mother. His father failed him, as I have failed all of you." She opened her eyes and wiped her tears. "In my grief, I asked for a Hittite prince to marry. A mistake. A mistake that will cost much. Pawah knows no bounds. He wants the crown, Ankhesenpaaten, and he will do anything to get it."

Her hand went to her belly. She'd left out her affair and love for the Commander.

Some things are better left unsaid.

After Nefertiti spoke, Ankhesenpaaten was at first silent, taking in everything that had happened. She opened her mouth to speak but said nothing. Tears welled in her eyes and then she threw her arms around her mother's neck and kissed her cheek.

"I will not doubt you again," she whispered in her ear. "I love you, Mother."

Nefertiti wrapped her arms around her daughter and pressed her body into her own. "I love you too, my daughter."

Ankhesenpaaten wiped the tears from her eyes and looked to the window, which now poured out the full sun's rays upon the floor. "A new day means new beginnings."

"That's right," Nefertiti said as she took her hand to help them both stand. "Remember, Ankhesenpaaten, all you can do is love Tut, live truthfully, and pray he one day opens his eyes."

Ankhesenpaaten nodded. As she turned to leave, she noticed the letter to the Commander on Nefertiti's bedside table. "I can take this to the Commander, Mother."

Nefertiti thought it might be safer with her than with a messenger she may or may not be able to trust, but then her father opened the door to check on them.

"That's all right, Ankhesenpaaten," Nefertiti said. "I'll ask my father to give it to him."

I'll ask him to give it to Horemheb when I announce my marriage, but I will wait on the announcement. I need more time. No, I want more time.

Ankhesenpaaten smiled and nodded. "All right, Mother. I shall go get ready for the day."

Nefertiti kissed her daughter's forehead.

"A new day," she whispered.

"A new day," Ankhesenpaaten whispered back, her eyes gleaming in the morning sun.

24

THE TIME OF DESPERATION

"A RUMOR IS GROWING." PAWAH PRANCED DOWN THE HALL alongside Nefertiti and Horemheb. "A nasty little rumor it is, too. Is Pharaoh giving Egypt into the hands of the Hittites? A prince is at Egypt's borders coming to the throne in all haste. He will be here in a few decans' time."

Nefertiti stopped in her gait and turned to Pawah. "Your lies cannot faze me."

"Well, Your Majesty," he said with a faux bow as Horemheb stepped between them. "The people still demand Tut, and I have Tut believing you and your entire family want him gone. He will remove you all if you don't abdicate. I will make sure of it." He talked over Horemheb's shoulder.

"You are showing your hand, Pawah," Nefertiti said as she lifted her chin. "One day, the people will see you for what you really are."

"Leave," Horemheb said through his teeth and pulled his dagger from his chest belt. *It would be so easy to kill him here,* he thought. His knuckles went white around the dagger's handle. The past two seasons had been nothing but heartache for him, one attempt to kill this man after another failing. He wished he could just stab him like he did Khabek, but he knew there were supporters in the palace who would tell the people the truth, which would result in a mass riot on their hands.

"Ah, the ever-loyal Commander protects his Pharaoh," Pawah teased, and put his finger on the dagger's flat edge, guiding it away from his face.

Horemheb pulled it back up to Pawah's neck. "I will kill you. When you fall down, knowing you are going to die, I want you to think of me."

"Oh, Commander. Your threats mean nothing to me. How many of your little 'attempts' have failed now? I know of at least thirteen." He chuckled. "Go ahead. Spill my blood right here, right now. See what happens to your beloved Pharaoh. My loyal supporters are everywhere. You can't be awake all the time, can you now, Commander?"

Horemheb leaned forward and pressed the blade into Pawah's neck as his nostrils flared and his grip tightened on the blade's handle. He gripped Pawah's collar with his other hand, which shook as his muscles tightened, restraining himself from pushing anymore. Blood began to seep onto the blade. He clenched his jaw and finally pushed Pawah away from him.

"Not today, Pawah, but I will end you."

Pawah chuckled. "Yes, Commander. I'm sure." Then he peered over at Nefertiti as he wiped the blood from his neck. "One last chance to quell the people's thirst—marry me, Nefertiti." He threw his arms wide, but Horemheb stepped toward him.

Nefertiti's eyes narrowed at him. "I would rather die."

"Careful with the words you choose," Pawah muttered under his breath. His eyes darted between her and Horemheb, then he slunk back into the shadows from whence he came.

"THERE ARE MORE RIOTS IN THE STREETS OF WASET AND Men-nefer every day as the Hittite gets closer to Aketaten," Ay told Nefertiti. "Pawah feeds the people's rage with your planned marriage to Prince Zannanza."

"So I have heard," Nefertiti said indifferently, then turned to the General. "Is Pawah any closer to death?"

He grimaced. "Commander Horemheb is attempting this as we speak. He will be absent tonight, along with Ineni. I will stand at your door, and chief royal guard Jabari and Hori will stand guard for your daughters, until they are able to resume. It is your father's night to sleep."

She bit her lip and let out a breath. Every time Horemheb led an attempt, she wished safety on him and hoped they would have at least one more time together. The Hittite prince was due any day now. "General, I want *you* to stand at my daughter's door. Should the people attack, you need a way to keep your promise to me."

"I insist, Pharaoh. Let me stand at your door," Paaten pressed.

"No. Protect my daughters, General." Nefertiti's stare signaled that the topic was not up for debate.

Paaten nodded in agreement.

"Very well," Nefertiti said, moving on. "What else should I know?"

"There are reports of people who pray to Amun to reject your divine appointment," Paaten said. "They want Coregent to be the sole regent."

Ay sighed. "The people are many, and they follow the word of Pawah. I do care about the position of Pharaoh, but I care for you more. Marry Tut before the prince arrives."

Nefertiti's heart smiled at her father's words, but her face fell. "Then it would seem, after all this time, everything we have done is in vain. The people do not fear Pharaoh. Pharaoh has not regained power at all." Nefertiti's disgust sank into the stone walls of the council room. "The stench from our failure burns my soul."

"It was not all in vain," Paaten said after a moment. "Pharaoh now has more power than the Amun priesthood."

"I do not think so," Nefertiti said.

"It is true. Pharaoh restored the priesthood as the divine ruler. Therefore, Pharaoh reigns over them. You appointed the first prophet, as it is supposed to be. Pharaoh Amenhotep III could not even do that. It was not all in vain, my Pharaoh." Paaten smiled at her, but it felt forced, and they all knew it.

"But they still demand from Pharaoh a boy, Tut, the crippled child, to be their King. The son of the man they hated," Nefertiti muttered. "They don't care he is Coregent."

Paaten nodded.

Nefertiti took in a hot breath through her nose as she rolled her anger in her mouth like a fireball. Then she released it, standing, her cheeks red. "Why? What have I done that makes the people dislike me so? I have done nothing to them. I have given them everything! Their bellies are full, their hands are working, their heads are praying . . . I have done nothing to harm them!"

"They want the boy even more so than Pawah. He is young and can be molded. He is not jaded like you."

"I am not jaded."

"The people think that you are. You were married to Pharaoh Akhenaten, and there are plenty of reliefs that show you with him worshipping the Aten with your children. Tut is not in those reliefs because you are not his mother, and he was crippled. As vain as Akhenaten was, he ended up being like his father, shunning the less-than-perfect son," Paaten said with a smirk of pity for the dead.

Nefertiti gritted her teeth. "I haven't done anything. In fact, I was the one who *rid* them of him, and they cast me out. Me! This is how they show me gratitude?"

"My lotus blossom, please, let it go, get past this," Ay begged. "Pawah will kill you, just like he did with Smenkare, or he will find someone who can get close to you and kill you like he did with yourself and Akhenaten."

"No." Nefertiti's voice fell low. "I will show them."

"How?" General Paaten asked. "What will you do?"

Nefertiti looked off to the wall. "You are certain your strike will result in Pawah's death?"

Paaten nodded.

"And after Pawah's death, I will still be forced to marry Tut?"

Paaten nodded again. "Or enrage the people and marry the Hittite. Or don't marry either, and then for sure, with or without Pawah, you will have a rising on your hands, both domestic and foreign."

"I will not marry either. I will not be forced. I will not have war. I will not have an uprising."

Nefertiti lifted her chin, resolved in her path forward. She would marry Horemheb, bear his child, and that child would be the next heir; but that meant removing Tut in the equation as Paaten worked to remove Pawah. *But what was one more?*

"I will show them they cannot simply make me disappear . . . one way or another."

NEFERTITI THREW OPEN THE DOORS OF HER BEDCHAMBERS, strolling inside. "Aitye!"

Her servant rushed to her as the doors closed and bowed. "Yes, my Pharaoh."

She kept her voice low so Jabari, who stood just outside, would not hear. "I want you to do whatever it takes to get rid of Coregent Tutankhaten."

Aitye swallowed a large ball of fear. "Get—get rid of . . . ?"

"Yes. I want him gone," Nefertiti whispered as she began to walk past her.

"Has he done something against you?" At Nefertiti's silence, she asked, "Why?"

Nefertiti turned and smacked her across the cheek. "I am your Pharaoh. Do as you are told." Her ring caused her cheek to bleed.

"My Pharaoh, please, may I speak freely, as I once was given that privilege?" Aitye's words came on shallow breaths as she fell to her knees, silently begging her master to not let this demand fall into her hands.

"No." Nefertiti's coarse voice evidenced her throat closing up on itself. "I don't want to change my mind. With him and Pawah gone, the people will have no recourse. They will quit their complaining, and I will no longer have to marry either one!" Nefertiti knocked a candle from the table. "Get rid of Tutankhaten tonight. Make it so, Aitye."

"My Pharaoh, he is only a boy," Aitye whispered, but Nefertiti stormed off to take her bath in pure distress. "Why have you fallen from your grace, our lady of the two lands?" Aitye asked under her breath. "I warned you. I warned you so."

AITYE WATCHED THE LESSER SERVANTS TEND TO HER AND felt the breeze from the window, which cooled the tears in her eyes. Her gaze fell to the neatly folded thick wool blanket she had placed at the foot of Pharaoh's bed. She squeezed her eyes shut, not wanting to imagine having to push it over the

Crown Prince's head, but her feet took her near to it, and her arm obediently reached for it.

Pharaoh wanted it done tonight. There is no time to have someone else do it; it must be me, she thought, and pushed the blanket up to her own face, trying to inhale, but found it difficult.

Lowering it to her chest, she whispered, "You are Pharaoh." Bowing her head, her tears wet the blanket. "I will do as you command me to, and I pray that at the end of my life my heart hangs well on the scales of Ma'at, for this deed I pray be on you, Pharaoh."

With the blanket still held fast to her chest, she turned and went to the royal harem, asking Tut's guard to let her into the room on account of Pharaoh. He eyed her but followed Pharaoh's secondhand command and let her in, closing the door behind her.

She clutched her heart as she watched Tut sleep, the blanket she held smashed between her arms and her body. She feared her shallow breaths would surely wake the sleeping child. She held the folded blanket over his head for an interminable moment, not touching his face. Licking her lips, she told herself that it would be so easy to just hold it over him until he quit moving. He would be helpless without his cane, delirious from his sleep, maybe think it was a bad dream.

Murderer, the breeze whispered to her as she held her chosen weapon suspended above Tut's head.

He let out a soft snore, and she brought it back into her arms. *What I am I doing? I cannot do this. Pharaoh was not in the right state of mind. She will come to regret this.* Shaking her head and dropping the blanket, she backed up until she found the door and walked out.

"No, no, no, no," she said over and over again until she reached Nefertiti's chambers. She entered and saw all the other servants attending to Nefertiti as she lay in bed, humming a deep and enchanting melody that Tey used to hum to her.

Aitye approached her and bowed. "May I be so bold as to request a private audience with Pharaoh Neferneferuaten?"

"Yes, Aitye," she answered. "Leave us," she told the others. When she heard the doors close, she ordered Aitye to speak.

"My Pharaoh," she began. "I have served you every day you have been my master to the very best of my abilities—"

"Is it done?" Nefertiti asked impatiently, a nervous rattle to her teeth.

Aitye formed words, but no sound came out. She finally uttered, "I could not."

Nefertiti rubbed her temples as tears streamed down her cheeks.

"I stood there, but I—I have never taken a life," Aitye said with her breath caught in her throat. "Even at the order of my Pharaoh, whom I love, I could not do it."

Nefertiti put her hand on Aitye's bowed head, saying nothing.

Aitye wiped her tears, thinking she would be cast out for not following Pharaoh's command, but Nefertiti never gave the order. Aitye knelt at her bedside, keeping her head bowed.

Nefertiti laughed, and tears gushed from her eyes. "To think I was willing to have that boy killed." She took in a deep breath through her nose. "Who am I? What have I become?"

"A momentary loss of judgment, my Pharaoh," Aitye whispered.

"I just don't know anymore, Aitye. I no longer have a soul. When I was an unmarried girl, I knew what was right. There was a clear line. But now . . ."

"There still is," Aitye said.

"No. No, I've blurred that line. Perhaps I should give up the crown? Maybe it is for the better."

"It is *your* crown, my Pharaoh."

"Aitye, be honest with me. Pharaoh Akhenaten was a threat to Egypt, and that is why he was removed. Am I a threat as well?"

"The Hittite prince makes you seem like a threat, but I know you. You would never put Egypt in harm's way. I trust you."

"Be careful who you trust, Aitye." Nefertiti's response was almost instinctive, but after mulling over Aitye's words, she continued, "It is too late to send the Hittite prince back. It would do more harm than good to our newfound allies. We have a very shaky foundation, but I am with—" She dared not reveal her pregnancy with her servant. She was lucky she was not showing already. With her last daughter, she had an unmistakable ball under her dress at this point. Right now, it looked as if she had just had a little too much to eat.

"You know what is best for Egypt," Aitye said at Nefertiti's continued silence. "I trust your judgment."

"My judgment was to kill my stepson for my own selfish reasons," Nefertiti said through clenched teeth, thinking of her foolish justifying thought, *What was one more?*

"You carry many burdens," Aitye said.

Nefertiti rolled to her side and took Aitye's hand. "Aitye, never speak of what happened. It is too much for me to bear."

"Yes, my Pharaoh," Aitye answered.

❧ 25 ❧

THE TIME OF DEATH

WITHOUT WARNING, THE DOORS TO NEFERTITI'S bedchambers were thrust open and Jabari, chief royal guard, stood in their shadow. "Pharaoh, forgive me," he said with a long exhale. "The people . . . the people have risen up. They have killed the Hittite Prince Zannanza. They march to our gate."

Nefertiti swung her feet to the floor.

"Aitye, go get General Paaten and my daughters. Now."

"There isn't time," Jabari said as he rushed in and pulled Nefertiti to her feet. He bowed in apology, but urged her toward the door. "We will retreat to the council room. It is at the center of the palace."

"Aitye, go quickly," Nefertiti ordered, ignoring Jabari as he continued to usher her away. "Have them meet us in the council room. Go! Now!"

Aitye rushed from the room. Jabari appeared to be flustered, but continued to half-pull his Pharaoh down the winding corridors.

"I don't see or hear anything," Nefertiti whispered to Jabari.

"The fighting takes place on the other side of the palace. It is only a matter of time before they encircle it. The Commander's men are holding them back, but we need to get you to safety." He grabbed her wrist.

Nefertiti dug in her heels and yanked her wrist back. "I would go to safety if I were a royal wife, but I am Pharaoh, defender of Egypt. I must fight."

Jabari snorted and pulled a dagger, tossing it to her.

Nefertiti clumsily dropped it and picked it up.

He pulled out another dagger.

"Kill me," he ordered her.

Heat rose from her collarbone to her jaw, choking her.

He doesn't think me capable, she thought. *I've only had a few trainings . . . at that dreaded rebellion in Malkata I almost held my own, but General Paaten saved me.*

"Kill me," Jabari said again, jarring her from her thoughts.

Nefertiti lunged, but Jabari blocked it and knocked her down.

"You have no skill," Jabari said, helping her up. "You would die on the first attack. We don't need another departed Pharaoh." He sheathed his dagger and picked up hers.

Nefertiti dusted off her linen dress as shame flooded her cheeks. If she were a man, he wouldn't talk to her in this way; but she also would have been training her whole life.

He sheathed the second dagger. "Let's keep moving."

They crept along the walls, silent in the night.

"Are you sure there are attacks on the palace?" Nefertiti whispered to him; she imagined there would be more clamoring, like there was in the rebellion at Malkata all those years ago.

"Like I said, the Commander's men are holding them off."

"But there are no torchlights in the dark, no shouts, no sounds of battle," Nefertiti observed as she followed Jabari.

The pounding of feet came toward them just as they

turned the corner. General Paaten, leading Ankhesenpaaten and Nefe, with Aitye close behind. They all met at the council room doors.

The bleary-eyed General growled at Jabari, "Why wasn't I notified of the attack? I've sent Hori to tell Ay and Horemheb."

"It all came about very suddenly. I sent a messenger, but perhaps he was detained," Jabari spouted off, and threw open the door, hurrying the women inside first.

"Why are we in the council room? There is no means of escape." Ankhesenpaaten was frightened. The moonlight barely showed through the almost-completed ceiling, leaving little light to make out the figures in the room.

"Is there a torchlight in here?" Nefertiti asked over her daughter.

Jabari closed the door. "No. We do not light anything, for they may see the light through the unfinished roof."

"You suggest we hide," Paaten asked him, "like cowards?"

"I suggest we take Pharaoh and her family to safety, away from this place. The people have killed the Hittite Prince Zannanza on his journey here, and one way or another she will abdicate," Jabari said with a bow to the leader of the Egyptian military.

"Why wasn't I informed of the Hittite's death?" General Paaten asked him, pushed his shoulder as his subordinate. "Why am I the last to know any of this?"

"As I said, General, it came about so suddenly. The messenger I sent you . . . he must have been detained." Jabari regained his composure. "There is a secret way out of the council room—" He used his hands along the wall, feeling for the tiny burst of air. "Ah, here it is." He pressed on one of the stones, opening a half-door to a dark tunnel. A scrim of sand blew in from the night breeze in the tunnel.

"I didn't know there was an escape passageway in here," Nefertiti said. "Why didn't I know of this?"

"This was a design for the royal guard, in case we needed to get Pharaoh to safety if he were injured in battle. They are all over the palace. The doors only open from the inside. Once it is closed, no one can open it from the other side." Jabari stood and dusted his hands on his legs. "You must always have an escape route in your fortress."

"So, what now?" Nefe asked.

"You leave." Jabari placed his hands on Nefertiti's shoulders. "Probably never to return, for your own sake."

She wrenched back from his grip, but Ankhesenpaaten grabbed her arm.

"Mother, what about Tut? He will be killed!"

"We aren't going anywhere until I know the threat is real," Nefertiti said, looking over to Jabari. "Where do your loyalties lie, chief royal guard?"

Ankhesenpaaten crossed her arms and looked toward Jabari's silhouette. Nefe followed suit. General Paaten puffed up his chest and stood behind Pharaoh.

The moonlight did not penetrate the room enough to make out Jabari's reaction, but his voice was clear: "My loyalties are with Pharaoh."

Silence lingered in the room, and something caused General Paaten to stir.

"Jabari, light a torch," Nefertiti ordered.

"But, my Pharaoh, the rebels will see the light and come to attack," Jabari reasoned.

"I did not hear any rebels," Nefertiti snapped.

"Neither did I." Paaten's hand fell to his dagger.

"Believe what you will, but I was told the Hittite prince was slain, killed by the very riot that tears down the gates of the palace." The moonlight silhouetted Jabari's hand gestures as he spoke.

"I don't know . . . something does not seem right." Paaten walked toward the sound that caused his hairs to stand on end. He turned to Pharaoh and whispered, "I don't think we are alone in here."

A glint in the moonlight—and Jabari went down.

Ankhesenpaaten screamed as warm blood splattered her face. Nefertiti felt the droplets as well, but instinctively grabbed her daughters and pushed them to the escape tunnel.

"General, remember your promise!"

Nefertiti's voice bounced off the stone walls as the moonlight glowed brighter in the room and she saw a torch on the wall. Aitye screamed and she jumped away from a flesh wound to her arm. Nefertiti grabbed the torch and thrust it into Aitye's arms and pushed her into the escape tunnel with her daughters.

Paaten drew his dagger and swiped at the air in front of him, trying to make his old eyes adjust. He slowly backed to the entrance of the tunnel, waiting for Nefertiti to go inside. But out of the darkness, a kick to his chest sent him flying into the tunnel before her.

WHEN THE GENERAL VANISHED BEHIND THE WALL, Beketaten grabbed Nefertiti from around the waist and threw her on the ground as Pawah shut the door. Nefertiti staggered to her feet only in time to trip over Jabari's collapsed body. He struggled to breathe and tried to keep the blood from coming out of his neck. Nefertiti screamed. Hearing her, Jabari tried to hand her his dagger, but Pawah kicked it from her grasp. Beketaten lit a torch and Pawah grabbed Nefertiti by the collar and pushed her into the wall.

Sliding a dagger from inside his shendyt, he whispered to

her, "I took the lives of Thutmose, Anen, Akhenaten, Smenkare—and now you, great Pharaoh."

Her eyes grew wide as she struggled, trying to keep him from bringing the dagger closer.

You killed Thutmose? You killed all of them! Her thoughts raced in rage.

He overpowered her and thrust the dagger through her ribcage and into her chest wall. She let out a short grunt, clutching onto his arms. The immense and sudden heaviness in her chest depleted her breath as he pulled the dagger out.

"And I take every pleasure in doing so," he said as he stepped aside, letting her fall to the floor.

Jabari choked, "This wasn't the plan . . . she was supposed to run away."

Beketaten stepped on his neck. "You fool. You thought we were going to let her live?"

His eyes found Nefertiti's as she lay on her side, as if to say he was sorry, before he breathed his last. Her gaze drifted up to Pawah, who stood over her, and then down to the dagger in his hand, streaked and dripping with her blood.

Hardly any blood seemed to have come out of the stab wound in her chest; but on her inhale, sudden pain ripped through her chest and out through a screech in her throat. A slow, shallow exhale followed with the same penetrating pain.

"You—" she barely squeaked out as she tried to take a few surface breaths.

"For Amun and his priesthood to reign supreme," Beketaten said for Pawah. He sauntered over to Beketaten, who had picked up Jabari's spear. The stone hallways from outside the council room echoed with the sounds of a small crowd approaching. "Shall I finish her, my love?" she asked.

He smiled at her as he took the spear from her hand. "No, *I* shall," he said as he placed a hand on her shoulder. "Beketaten, you have always stood by my side, but your place there is no longer needed. You shall serve a higher purpose."

"I don't under—"

He rammed the spearhead into her heart.

Her mouth contorted, and her eyes longed for an answer.

Pawah's black eyes were the only response she received as he watched her slip away.

Nefertiti watched them as she struggled to sit up against the wall. The door sat across the room. If she could only reach the door, she perhaps could live. Her unborn would never be if she didn't make it to the door. With each breath, a heavier weight drew upon her chest. She pulled her leg under her as she leaned forward, but to her dismay she couldn't stand. Her daughters at least escaped. She knew they were on the other side of the passageway, heading toward a life free from the threat of violence and political turmoil. She placed the palm of her hand on the wall behind her.

"Live, my daughters," she whispered through her struggling breaths.

She could hear them calling her—but maybe she only imagined it.

PAATEN WAS UP FAIRLY QUICKLY FOR HIS AGE, BUT NOT before the door slammed shut. He banged on the stone wall and its well-constructed hidden door, throwing his shoulder into it, but even as he did so he knew it to be of no use.

"Light the torch so I can see!" he yelled to Aitye.

"I'm t-trying," she cried; she had been trying to light it since she got into the tunnel; finally, using the flint that attached to its base, she was able to get a spark, and the torch lit.

Paaten grabbed it and pressed his hand against the wall,

trying to find some sort of weakness. But he knew he struggled in vain. It was not built to be opened from the outside. He took a sad step back and dropped his head, knowing he had ultimately failed his Pharaoh, his Nefertiti. They were one day too late—for Horemheb and his men sat waiting to grab Pawah as he entered his room for the night; they had planned to hold him down and suffocate him so that it looked like he passed from natural causes. But Pawah had no intention of entering his room that night.

To pay off his guards took a mountain of time and effort, he thought, *and it was all a waste, for Pharaoh is slain. Pawah wins. Why didn't I stand guard at her door? I thought we could trust Jabari.*

His words to Horemheb came back to him: "Trust no one."

His chest caved around him, but the soft cries behind him made his mind stop. He turned to look at the two remaining daughters of Pharaoh and her servant.

It is out of my hands now, for I made a promise to you, Nefertiti.

"Your mother wanted me to take you to safety. Live a life of anonymity, where no one will know you are royalty, so you can be safe. Follow me."

Nefe was in too much shock to argue, and let Aitye lead her after Paaten's footsteps. But Ankhesenpaaten's heart still raced.

"We are to do nothing?" she asked.

Paaten stopped and looked back. "We cannot do anything more. I made Pharaoh a promise that if anything should happen to her, I was to save you."

"What about Tut?"

"If they came after Pharaoh, they probably have come after him too. He is a much easier target." Paaten wished he could take back his last sentence as the firelight danced on

Ankhesenpaaten's horrified expression. "Come now. We need to cover much ground."

He turned and Aitye and Nefe followed the light of the torch. *I'm not even sure where this leads,* he thought.

Ankhesenpaaten, however, lingered in the growing darkness and felt her way back to the door. She tried to open it, but there was no handle; she pushed, but nothing. And then she heard a *thud* on the other side. Pressing her ear to the door, she could hear very little—but she heard her mother's scream, dying . . . being murdered.

"No!" she yelled. Ankhesenpaaten banged on the stone door. *"Mother!"* she yelled. "MOTHER!"

She rammed her shoulder into the door, but it did not move, not even a shake. She thought she could faintly make out Pawah's voice talking to her mother and she tried to ram the door again. "Pawah, I'll kill you," she screeched out through her teeth.

The noise caused the General to turn back, leaving Nefe and Aitye where they stood in the tunnel in the dark. He came upon Ankhesenpaaten. "Forgive me, chief royal wife," he said, and picked her up.

"No, General Paaten! He is killing her! Pawah is *killing her!*"

A tear formed in his eye, but the door only opened one way. She kicked and beat his back as he lifted her upon his shoulder.

"General! No!" she yelled again. "HELP HER!"

"I cannot save her, chief royal wife Ankhesenpaaten," he whispered, and took off running down the tunnel with her on his shoulder.

"Mother!"

She reached toward the wall she couldn't break down as it disappeared in the dark. They reached Nefe, who was also crying, hearing her sister's cries. Aitye was little condolence, as she too was still in shock.

He let Ankhesenpaaten down. "My ladies of the two lands," he whispered as he gathered the daughters of Nefertiti close. "These are dark times." He looked specifically to Ankhesenpaaten. "Your mother knew this was a possibility and so made me promise her that I would take her daughters to safety—perhaps even beyond Egypt's borders. I have carried on me at all times gold for barter, from the treasury, at her command, should the day ever spring upon us. As it has today."

Ankhesenpaaten dropped her head and sobbed. Nefe rubbed her sister's arm helplessly.

"Ankhesenpaaten," he whispered. "Your mother will live through you."

Then he touched Nefe's cheek. "And through you."

He wrapped his arms around the girls, as they had nearly filled a void in his own life through the years. Now, as he held the two crying girls, he looked forward to their life together, away from all of the political upset and constant paranoia.

Ending their embrace when Ankhesenpaaten's tears subsided, he whispered, "We must go." He nodded to Aitye.

As soon as they exited the tunnel by way of another hidden door at the tunnel's end, a dark figure appeared in front of them; soft, scattered light emerged in the predawn sky behind him. Paaten stopped in his tracks as he made out the figure of a man with a hooded cloak.

Reaching up, the man uncovered his head.

"You are not Egyptian," General Paaten said, drawing his dagger.

"No, I am not Egyptian, but a friend to Pharaoh Neferneferuaten," he said with a bow of his head. "There is no need for a weapon, General Paaten. My name is Atinuk. Come with me."

"Pharaoh never mentioned a friend named Atinuk to me," Paaten said, lowering his sword just a fraction.

"She did not know me."

General Paaten raised his sword again, debating whether to trust this foreign stranger. "Then how are you a friend?"

"I loved the one known to you, royal wife Kiya," he answered as he swished his cloak to reveal his Canaanite attire.

Paaten's face warmed at the memory of such a sweet woman. He let his defense drop.

"Her last request of me was to look after the daughters of Nefertiti. With the riots and rebellions, I knew it was only a matter of time before I honored her wish." Atinuk gestured to the northeast. "I have land in Canaan. They will be safe there. The sun is about to rise, and we shall do well to leave now under the cover of darkness."

"Agreed," Paaten said, and they followed Atinuk out.

All except Ankhesenpaaten. She stayed in the tunnel as she watched the three of them leave and not look back. She knew who killed her mother. If only she had grabbed her and pulled her into the tunnel with them, she'd be alive. Shaking her head, she pushed the thought away.

"Pawah," she said through her teeth. "They will know you killed her because I will tell them."

She watched them run to the palace wall as she felt her mother's ka in the light breeze.

Did she know she was going to be murdered?

Closing her eyes, she thought back to the last time she was with her. She had indeed known the end was coming. Even Paaten told her that just now; that was why her mother had pushed her away. A tear slid from her eye.

"I understand now, Mother."

A breath escaped her lips.

"You will not be slain in vain."

She looked around her and knew they were still behind the city walls, close to the royal harem. She peered out, watching the four shadowy figures climb over a wall.

She clenched her jaw. "Tut." An image of his mangled body flashed in her mind, and she turned to go to the royal harem to find him. If she didn't do something, he would be defenseless.

She stopped, though, and looked back. The early lights before the sun showed that Paaten sat atop the wall now, and he nodded to her and then jumped off to the other side, toward a life unknown. Her heart dropped to another level. She knew she would never see her sister again.

"My family is gone," she whispered. "I am the last remaining royal save for Tut, and if Pawah got what he is after, he will kill him too."

She blew a kiss to the wind and prayed to Amun or the Aten—whoever was premier—that they keep vigilant over Nefe on her way to Canaan. And then she took off toward the royal harem and her husband.

✣ 26 ✣

THE TIME OF GRIEF

NEFERTITI USED THE MOVEMENT OF HER HEAD TO LUNGE her body toward the door. She fell on her arm, and the pain radiated from her chest wound in all-consuming waves. Still, she hopped on her arm and tried to crawl.

For my baby, she told herself. *I must live for my baby.*

From the corner of her eye, she saw Pawah lower Beketaten to the ground and place the dagger in her hand— the dagger with Nefertiti's blood. She heard the sounds in the hallway and hoped this meant Paaten had sent word to Ay and Horemheb.

Pawah kicked Jabari's foot as he walked past him. "Ignorant fool. You were only supposed to bring *Nefertiti*, and we wouldn't have this mess." He paused, listening for the echo of footsteps; having apparently calculated that he still had a few more moments with Nefertiti, he sent a toe into her shoulder, knocking her to her back.

After the pain subsided, she asked him, "Did you ever— love her?" The agony with each breath cut into her words.

"She was useful," he said casually. "But I cannot be the one holding the weapon used to murder Pharaoh."

"Why?" She tried to turn on her side and resume crawling toward the door.

"It was more humane to kill her fast with the spear than have her die a slow death from impalement in front of the temple of Amun." He shrugged his shoulders as he went and picked up Jabari's dagger and hid it in his shendyt. "Because it would be my word against hers, and I am the vizier and the former Fifth Prophet of Amun. When the boy becomes King, I will be there to lead him into subservience to the priesthood. I will be named the First Prophet of Amun, and when I am done with the boy Pharaoh, I will have become the most powerful man in all of Egypt—not by some *divine* appointment, but by careful and dedicated action."

"You . . . appall me . . ." she sputtered, bent over from the searing agony in her chest. The door seemed so far, and the dwindling hope of a future which she held for her life and her baby's life fell upon her.

He cocked a crooked grin as he knelt next to her. "The priesthood's greed for power is the appalling thing, my blossom flower. But little do they know, when they least expect it, they will die by my hand. With the ruling elite, such as yourself, out of the way, and the boy King under my purview—whom I assure you will die young without an heir and me named as successor—I will have what I want."

The echoes from the hallway grew louder moments before Horemheb threw open the door and stood in its threshold surveying the dead guard, then Beketaten, and finally coming to rest upon Pawah bent over Nefertiti. At seeing his love on the floor bleeding from the chest, a fire coursed through his body; his ears pounded and he stared unblinking at the man who stood over her.

"I'll kill you, Pawah!"

He drew his dagger as he ran, but Pawah also drew his dagger in secret.

Nefertiti envisioned Pawah taking Horemheb's life as well. She collapsed on the floor. The burn seared the inside of her chest, but she had to warn her love.

"*Dagger—!*"

Pawah tried to undercut Horemheb, but Nefertiti's warning caused Horemheb to parry his strike at the last moment. Pawah's blade bounced off Horemheb's bronze armor and cut his arm; at the same time, Horemheb sliced Pawah on the side of his shoulder, just missing his neck. Pawah tripped Horemheb as he ran and then fled for the door.

Regaining his balance and seeing his only chance, Horemheb let his dagger fly; but through his rage-filled eyes, his dagger sailed past and barely nicked Pawah's ear, landing with a *thud* into the doorframe just as Pawah got to the entrance of the council room.

Pawah turned and laughed. "You missed your chance."

Horemheb stood by Nefertiti. "I swear to you, Pawah, before Ammit has your heart I shall rip it from your chest."

Pawah laughed again. "You are the one who failed her, *Commander*." He disappeared into the dark hallway—only to run into Hori and others loyal to the crown.

"What happened?" Hori asked, holding Pawah at spearpoint.

Pawah was quick to fake panic. "I tried to save her! Jabari—he rushed the Pharaoh. I killed him and got his spear, but it was too late . . . Beketaten—accomplices, they were—she had already stabbed Pharaoh. I had to kill my own wife to stop her attack." He dropped his head, bringing his hand to shield his eyes as if the sacrifice was too much to bear. "Beketaten," he said, pointing to inside the room, "she has had vengeance on her mind since the exile . . . even more so since Pharaoh ordered her sister Sitamun's death."

Pawah peered through his splayed fingers. Hori kept his spear upward and pursed his lips, clearly not believing him.

A WAVE OF NAUSEA OVERCAME HOREMHEB AS HE KNELT AND lifted Nefertiti's head, pulling her close to him. "Nefertiti . . ." he whispered, and her eyes opened. At the sight of him, a light smile graced her lips. His face contorted as tears welled in his eyes.

Nefertiti knew she could only say a few more words before her breath was gone forever. She still had so many things to tell him and her father and her sister and her daughters. A tear slid down her cheek as words raced through her mind; she tried to fight time in determining her last words, hoping they held some meaning, hoping not to waste them.

Some wishes are never granted, she thought. *Some words are better unspoken.*

"Nefertiti," he whispered again. "I love you." He pressed his forehead to hers, hating himself for not doing away with that murderer long before and living with the consequences. Swallowing the painful lump in the back of his throat, he leaned forward and kissed her. "I'm so sorry. I've failed you."

She shook her head. "No—" She tried to inhale. "You made . . ." Her exhale carried with it a thousand knives coursing through her chest.

Horemheb's lips trembled and his jaw clenched; his body felt as though it was caving in on itself, every muscle holding his utter agony inside.

"You made me—feel alive." Her eyes danced in the dwindling torchlight as she smiled once more. Then she breathed her last and the dance in her eyes ceased.

AT THAT MOMENT, AY RUSHED IN, MUT CLOSE BEHIND HIM. A guttural yell escaped Ay's lips. The guards standing outside the council room were cut to the heart at Ay's yell, and knew their Pharaoh was gone. Ay fell to his daughter and pulled her away from the Commander and close to his chest. No words accompanied Ay; only yells of disbelief and pain.

Horemheb let his hands drop to his side. He became lost in his own thoughts, wishing he were the one to have been killed. Ay's screams finally broke him from his fog, and he laid a hand on Ay's shoulder.

Mut stepped forward to see her sister laying on the floor, Nefertiti's dead eyes peering up at her over Ay's shoulder. She fell to one knee as she clutched her heart, unable to yell, to breathe, to feel. Then she looked to Jabari and Beketaten and her scream, at last, escaped at the sight of all the blood.

Horemheb jolted up toward Mut, covering her with his body. "No woman should see this," he whispered, holding her and blocking her view. She screamed again as tears fell down her face, and he pulled her closer, swallowing his own hot burn of shame.

I let this happen, Horemheb thought, feeling Mut's trembles. *She was killed because of my failure.*

"No, no, no," Ay mumbled as he drew in shaky breath after shaky breath. He pulled back so as to look at Nefertiti's face. After a few moments of silence, he whispered, "You are worth everything to me, my lotus blossom," and pressed his cheek into her forehead.

THE GUARDS LET PAWAH GO BECAUSE THERE WAS NO evidence on which to arrest him.

"He killed her, didn't he?" Mut asked Horemheb, overhearing the conversations in the hallway. She had shrunk in the corner of the room, unable to look at the death surrounding her.

"He says he did not, but I know he did," Horemheb said through his teeth. He had to hold in his grief in front of Ay and Mut. He was Commander to them, not Nefertiti's lover. With every breath, a fire raged inside of him as he tried to quell his grief for the time being.

"He killed her, he should die a murderer of Pharaoh . . . impalement in front of the temple . . . his body burned so he cannot journey to the afterlife—"

"Mut." Horemheb knelt beside her and put a hand on her shaking shoulder. "The position of Pharaoh is unstable. Are we prepared to say the Pharaoh was murdered? Both of them? All three of them?"

"What do you mean?"

Horemheb licked his bottom lip and rubbed his forehead. "Pharaoh Akhenaten was—"

"I know that. Nefertiti poisoned him, and you did your part." Mut's voice sank lower and lower, as did her naïve young soul as it perished little by little.

Horemheb blinked slowly. "We all did our part. Pharaoh Smenkare was murdered much the same way, and now Pharaoh Neferneferuaten as well. That makes three. Three divinely appointed Pharaohs, murdered at the hand of one man."

"So what are you suggesting? That the council will just do away with Pharaoh?" Mut asked, her jaw-dropping.

"No . . . Mut, I know how it seems, but a lot has happened. We all knew the plan when Pharaoh Amenhotep III traveled to Re, and we were all prepared to sacrifice whatever we must so that the position of Pharaoh could once again become all-powerful, even against the priesthood of

Amun. You were not even born when this all happened. I know it is not fair to you, but Egypt must come first . . . and that means securing Pharaoh as a divine, all-powerful ruler."

Mut's eyes filled with tears. "But he killed her."

"Be strong, Mut. Be strong. I know we are asking much of you. Telling the people would have a detrimental effect on the power and position of Pharaoh. We cannot let the people know. Pharaohs Akhenaten and Smenkare passed in their sleep, and Neferneferuaten . . . Nefertiti journeyed west from—"

"She was *murdered*," Mut said as her father, Ay, still clung to Nefertiti's lifeless body. "Either by Beketaten or Pawah, she was murdered. They need to face the harshest sentence Egypt has to offer." Tears streamed down her eyes as her brow furrowed in hatred. "The priesthood of Amun was behind this—you know it to be true!"

"Silence, my daughter," Ay whispered. "See where greed and hate have brought your sister." He looked at her with tear-filled eyes. "I cannot lose you too." He gripped Nefertiti's body one last time in a firm and lasting embrace before laying her back on the floor. He placed her hands gently on top of each other, over her chest to hide the ghastly wound. Tracing her high cheekbones with his forefinger, he sighed and closed his eyes, trying to remember the sound of her laugh—but it had been so long. With the last memory of his daughter, so he lost the last memory of his precious first wife, Temehu. Inhaling a deep breath through his nostrils, he looked to Horemheb. "You are right. They cannot know the last three Pharaohs were all murdered."

"Father—"

"It would have meant your sister lived in vain. We cannot let the power of Pharaoh fall to the priesthood."

Mut stood. "Then one day I will see justice is done for her, if you choose not to."

"One day, daughter, you will see why we can never have justice for her." Ay stood up with the help of the nearby chair. He had aged ten years in the last hour.

Horemheb stayed by Mut. He reached out and grazed her arm. Her eyes shot back at him. "We all want justice, Mut," he said, not adding, *More than you know.* "But for the greater of Egypt, we cannot have justice. Pawah would have been the only one to have the strength to kill both women at once. I have no doubt he killed your sister, and one day he will die— your father and I will see to that. But until then, we cannot reestablish the position of Pharaoh if we tell the people now."

Mut's eyes drifted downward and saw, at the last blow of the wind through the almost-closed roof of the council room, the sand dust had begun to cover her sister's blood drops. "A time will come when all secrets are revealed," she whispered.

"Mut, this secret must stay buried," Horemheb said.

"One day we will make Pawah pay for what he has done. Make sure Tutankhaten trusts you," she said to her father and Horemheb. "You will make sure Pawah pays for this."

Horemheb nodded.

"Promise me!"

"I promise," Ay said.

Mut nodded. "Good." She turned and left that room filled with death. She would leave the story of what happened to them with her father and Horemheb; she did not want any part of the lies.

ANKHESENPAATEN RUSHED TO THE ROYAL HAREM AS FAST AS her legs would carry her. She found Maia near the entrance. "Quick, Maia!" She grabbed her wrist and Maia fell in step beside her. "Where is Tut?"

"Uh—" Maia spluttered, horrified at the blood splatter across Ankhesenpaaten's face.

"Maia, where is he?"

"He is with Sennedjem—in the training yard," Maia said at last.

Ankhesenpaaten let go of her wrist and ran to the training yard. Her heart had never beat so fast in her life. Her lungs burned within her chest, and she bent over, dropping her head into her chest, trying to catch her breath. She looked up and found Tut doing a good job against Sennedjem. She tried to call his name, but nothing but a gasp for air overtook her lips.

She looked around: life at the royal harem seemed fine; in fact, she hadn't seen one rebel in her haste to get here. She caught her breath and stood with a sore and dry throat.

Pawah . . . I know now for certain that this is his doing, she thought. She walked out into the training yard and held up her hand to stop Sennedjem. He stopped and bowed to her, and Tut turned to see who it was that interrupted his training.

"Oh . . . it's you," Tut said, and threw his wooden sword on the ground. "What do you want?" His eyes grew wide at the red splatter on her face.

"Tut, Pawah entrapped us. He has killed my mother. I came to warn you."

Ankhesenpaaten wrapped her arms around his body, but Tut pushed her off of him.

"Lies are your specialty, chief royal wife. Pawah told me you were a liar—just like your mother. He told me you both had conspired to kill me, and guess what my guard told me when I awoke from the sound of the door closing? Pharaoh's steward went into my room while I slept—and I found a thick blanket by the door. I guess she couldn't do it. She couldn't smother a helpless person in his sleep like a coward.

LAUREN LEE MEREWETHER

So I got up and ordered Sennedjem to teach me to defend myself against you and your mother's assassination attempts!" Tut said as he swiped his cane at Ankhesenpaaten's leg.

"Ow!" The sting from his cane traveled up to her knee and hip. "Tut, I do not know what you are talking about, but Pawah killed—"

"Pawah told the truth. You both want me dead." Tut hit her again on the shin.

"Would you stop doing that?!" Ankhesenpaaten stomped her foot. "If I wanted you dead, Tut, I would have killed you already. You have done nothing but tear at my heart for the last two years."

Sennedjem stood awkwardly in the back, his eyes going back and forth between the two royals.

"But Pawah—"

"Pawah has murdered my mother!"

"Oh, yeah, and how do you know? Are you trying to lead me outside so you can strike me when no one is around?" His voice cracked as puberty encroached on his years.

Ankhesenpaaten growled and turned her hands into fists. "Tut! He ambushed us—we made it through an escape tunnel, but I heard Pawah through the door. He cut her off from us."

"Who is 'us'?" Tut raised his cane as if to stop her and demand an answer.

"General Paaten and Nefe and—"

"Where are they? Why don't they come and tell me the same thing?" Tut crossed his arms.

"They left. General Paaten made a promise that he would take us out of Egypt so we could live peacefully, but only Nefe and Aitye went with him. I stayed behind so I could warn you because—because I love you . . . you are my husband and my friend, and I—I was afraid Pawah would come after you as well."

"Hmm . . ." Tut hobbled around Ankhesenpaaten, sizing

her up. "It is an elaborate story, chief royal wife." He stopped and looked to his tutor. "Sennedjem, what are your thoughts?"

Sennedjem bowed. "Coregent, I have no thoughts. Chief royal wife Ankhesenpaaten always speaks truth to me. I give no direction."

"Your reputation might save you," Tut said as he rubbed his chin and eyed her.

Ankhesenpaaten let out a sigh. She wanted to scream. "Don't believe me and let him kill you too, then," she said, and walked away. She got to the entrance of the royal harem and debated leaving the city of Aketaten to try to catch General Paaten. But as soon as she took a step east, her mother's words came back to her.

Pharaoh's place is defender of Egypt.

"If Pawah kills Tut, there will be no one left to defend Egypt," she whispered to herself. The desert wind whipped through her wig, westward, as if the gods were asking her to stay.

Her body wanted to fall against the wind, but her mother's scream through the stone planted her feet to the ground. Finally, the wind settled as she became resolved to stay.

"Goodbye Nefe," she whispered to the east. "I love you."

Then she went to find her grandfather, not noticing that Tut had left the royal harem in search of Pawah only moments after her.

MOMENTS LATER, ANKHESENPAATEN FOUND HERSELF surrounded by the royal guards, being escorted through the hallways toward the council room. She almost ran away, knowing Pawah lay in wait for her there—she also knew she couldn't trust the royal guards around her—but then she saw

Mut emerge from the room with bleary eyes and a hardened brow.

"Mut!" she called. The guards pointed their spears at her when she walked toward Ankhesenpaaten. "Oh, stop it! Put those down!" She pushed her way through their barricade and Mut rushed into her arms.

"Mut, Mut, is it my mother?"

"She's gone," Mut cried. "Father and Horemheb want to —" She stopped short.

"They want to what?" Ankhesenpaaten asked as she pulled her back to look at her.

"You will have to go ask them," Mut said as she straightened up and wiped her tears away. "You have something on your face," she mumbled as she pushed her away and continued down the hallway.

Ankhesenpaaten watched her leave and then wiped her face, remembering the warm blood of Jabari. A cold chill crawled up her spine, and she drew in a deep breath. Turning her attention to the council room, she braced herself to see her mother's body. No telling what that horrid Pawah did to her mother.

Her feet took her to the door and she went in. Holding her breath, she walked around to the other side of the table, unnoticed by Horemheb and Ay, who both knelt beside Nefertiti.

Her eyes grew wide and a whimper escaped her lips. The two men turned to look.

"Ankhesenpaaten!" Ay said, and Horemheb stood.

"Let me see her," she said with a calm tone.

"My queen, why is there blood on your face?" Horemheb asked her.

Ankhesenpaaten took a step forward and looked at her mother's body. Her jaw clenched. Her eyes set on the chest wound; the blood dribble from the corner of her mouth.

Horemheb repeated his question, drawing her from her focus.

"It is Jabari's blood," she said, and motioned to his body. "I was here. I heard Pawah kill her through the wall." She pointed in the direction of the secret tunnel.

"Where?" Ay asked, looking to the stone.

Ankhesenpaaten proceeded to recount the entire horrible story of what happened, down to the last few moments. At the end of it, both men stood with chin in hand, lips pursed, eyes closed.

"I'm sorry you had to hear him do such unspeakable harm to your mother," Horemheb said at last.

She nodded. "What are we to do now?"

"Pawah cannot be charged with murder. It would show the position of Pharaoh as weak in the people's eyes," Ay said, hoping the older Ankhesenpaaten would understand more than Mut.

Ankhesenpaaten nodded solemnly.

"Coregent Tutankhaten will be sole Regent—Pharaoh—and he will not believe Pawah killed his stepmother. But he is young, and he can be convinced in time," Horemheb said, crossing his arms.

"What makes you so sure?" Ankhesenpaaten asked.

"The older a man gets, the wider their eyes become," Horemheb answered.

She nodded again. "Pawah remains his vizier—the only vizier. How will he ever open his eyes, especially when Pawah undoubtedly wants to kill Tut too?"

"We all need to persuade our new regent that he needs two viziers and offer Ay up for appointment," Horemheb suggested.

"I agree," Ay said. "Now that General Paaten has left us, it would fall to me, but I think my position would better be served as vizier, and yours would be better served as General."

"And what do we tell Egypt about her Pharaoh?" Ankhesenpaaten looked at her mother and took in another breath.

"She began the journey to the afterlife peacefully in her sleep." Horemheb spoke through thin lips.

"No. The people wanted her to abdicate the throne. Tell them she gave up the crown and journeyed west from a broken heart because her people abandoned her," Ankhesenpaaten said. "This was the people's doing. They should feel some remorse."

"You are the chief royal wife," Ay said. "We follow your order." But she saw in his eyes that he agreed—the people of Egypt should be made to pay.

"No," Horemheb said, taking a longing look at Nefertiti. "Pharaoh does not refuse Amun's appointment. Pharaoh is Pharaoh until he journeys to Re. Anything short of that is weakness."

Ay let a tear fall. "Commander Horemheb is right, Ankhesenpaaten. It was why she did not abdicate in the first place. If we tell the people she did, she would have been killed in vain."

"She could have been happy," Horemheb whispered, thinking of the life he had envisioned with her.

"Yes." Ay paused before turning to Ankhesenpaaten. "Come, granddaughter. You are much too young to be in a room filled with so much death."

He guided her out, she trying to wipe the rest of Jabari's blood from her face and he trying to wipe his tear-stained kohl from his cheeks so the guards outside would not see.

HOREMHEB, LEFT ALONE IN THE COUNCIL ROOM, STOOD looking down at Nefertiti's body. He knelt once more and lifted her head to his.

"In the next life . . ."

He paused and kissed her forehead. He could not finish his thought. He wrapped his arms around her and held onto her for one last moment, remembering her sweet laugh, and its memory rang in his ears. For one last time, her body pressed against his.

"I was too late," he finally murmured. "I should have been here. I should have protected you." His voice cracked as his agony finally burst forth. "I was supposed to save you . . . but instead, you, in your last breaths, saved me from Pawah's cowardice in attack." He buried his head in her neck as hot tears burned his cheeks, wrapping her up into his body as if trying to cover her death from those who might have passed by. "How could I let this happen?" he moaned. "I was supposed to save you." He nuzzled her face with his. "I'm so sorry. I will never forgive myself. I will . . ." His breath hitched as he whispered in her ear: "I will *never* forgive myself."

He softly lay her down to the ground as the men outside began to whisper. Part of him did not care anymore, but another part knew that to retain the respect he needed in order to kill Pawah, he couldn't let the whispers continue.

He studied her face: her cheeks still rose as high as the mountains and her lips were still as full as the blossom, but the pale mark of death had already begun to accompany her face. He sat back on his heel and held her hand. Closing his eyes, her laugh still rang in ears, but his countenance remained blank.

"I will always love you, my Nefertiti," he whispered.

The thickness in his throat made swallowing difficult. Holding in the night's dinner, he stood, never taking his eyes off of her.

The whispers in the hallway halted his grief as he resolved

that he would not rest until Pawah was dead. He wiped his face with his arm, and with a sunken stare, he walked out to face his men. He grabbed his dagger from the doorframe. Yanking it from the wall, he noticed a small trail of blood down his arm where Pawah had nicked him. In his rage and his despair, he had missed his chance to kill the man and instead let him leave a scar upon his life, and now also upon his arm. The lasting scar would always remind him in an ironic twist of fate that the woman he planned to save had instead saved him after he was too late—an eternal reminder of his failure.

He turned to Paramesse, his comrade, and studied his contorted face and knew then: Paramesse could guess the reason for his heartache. But at least Horemheb knew his secret would be safe with Paramesse, his lifelong brother-in-arms. Horemheb then turned to the others.

"Pharaoh was murdered, but you are to say she passed in her sleep. The position of Pharaoh depends on it. If you do not, Pharaoh Neferneferuaten will have been killed in vain, and we will have been to blame, each of us, for a broken oath, and we will be subject to execution. Is that what you wish for Amun's appointed and for yourselves?"

The men one by one shook their heads, not wanting to die an embarrassing death, not wanting their Pharaoh to endure any more pain.

"Then we are agreed." Horemheb swallowed his heart into his stomach, but stood as the Commander should. "Guard Pharaoh's body until the priests of Anubis come to take her for burial preparation." He nodded to Hori and Ineni.

"Yes, Commander." Hori nodded, and he and Ineni took a post next to the council room.

Horemheb looked to Paramesse and the remainder of the men. "Crown Prince and Coregent Tutankhaten will be Pharaoh. We serve him now."

27

THE TIME OF THE BOY KING

"She was with child," Beset, the priest who oversaw burial preparations, whispered to Ay.

Horemheb overhead and snapped his head toward him. A fine sweat took shape on his brow as he dug his nails into his curled fists. "She was with—?"

Beset pulled Ay closer, attempting to cut Horemheb off from overhearing any more of the conversation. "A male child," Beset said to Ay as he pressed his lips together, peered over at Horemheb, and shook his head. "You are her father, and she had no husband. I did not know who else to ask this, but what shall we do with her son?"

Ay bit his lip as he looked over to Horemheb's contorted face, then looked to the floor before he responded: "Prepare him alongside his mother."

Beset nodded and turned to leave.

Ay continued, "And Beset . . . tell *no* one."

Beset bowed to Ay and left to tend to the rest of Nefertiti's preparation for the afterlife.

Ay shook his head, remembering back to his last moments with Nefertiti—what was it she'd said? She had "fell in lo—"

He closed his eyes; now he knew the rest of what she was going to say. Perhaps she had fallen, yes . . . but at least she had fallen in love.

"My poor lotus blossom. Denied love and a child . . . forced to marry another," Ay muttered under his breath. His gaze fell upon Horemheb and he clamped his teeth. "She was in love with you, wasn't she? Her child was yours." Ay let out a breath of peace. At least he knew Horemheb was a good man and had treated her with love in the last times of her life.

Ay's words fell on deaf ears. Horemheb's heart raced through his chest and his breath couldn't decide to stay in or come out. His brow beat out sweat of anger and of vengeance against Pawah. He took not only Nefertiti, but their child as well! His firstborn. His love's only son. A child he could never have. He took his dagger from his chest belt and let out a warrior yell and turned to the door.

Ay grabbed his arm, and when he found his eyes, he said, "Commander, I loved her too, and I wished nothing more than for her to bear a son. But we cannot act now."

"Pawah! He took *everything*," Horemheb said through his teeth, and lunged toward the door; but Ay, in his elder years, still held him back.

"Yes, he did, Pawah did this, and one day we will make sure he pays for his transgressions. But for now we must stay silent." Ay's heart broke at the words he said—he wished he could let Horemheb go kill the monster, wished he could allow himself to join in avenging his daughter's death. But Egypt did not need a civil war right now. If the people see and respect Tut as Amun's divinely appointed and Pawah kills him, then would be the time to strike to minimize bloodshed. All would see Pawah for what he was—a murderer, a liar, a schemer.

"He took . . . he took . . ." Horemheb's spine slumped, and his eyes vacated as he thought:

The gods punish me for my infidelity and my part in removing Akhenaten. O my Nefertiti, and my son! His cheeks burned as his heart filled with the grief of a thousand men. *What would you have done?* he called out to the gods in silent plea. *What would you have done? Now you take my son from me as well as the only woman I have ever truly loved?*

"Yes, Pawah took everything." Ay found his eyes and put a hand over the handle of his dagger. Pushing it down, he said, "Revenge will come soon enough, Commander. Revenge will come."

TUT WANTED TO HASTILY BURY NEFERTITI, MAD AT HER FOR sending Aitye to kill him and not caring about Ankhesenpaaten's feelings in the matter; but of all people, Pawah convinced him not to. He was no fool and knew if Tut had not named him as Hereditary Prince before he passed, Ay or Horemheb could easily steal the throne from him, and so he needed Tut on his side and he needed the people to honor Tut so as to honor his named successor. He would just make sure Tut never had children who lived.

"The people believe they caused her passing," Pawah told Tut as he stood in front of Tut's throne. "They mourn her becoming one with Re. They didn't want her as Pharaoh, but they didn't want her to journey west either."

Ankhesenpaaten sat behind Tut as Pawah spoke to him.

"My *son*, bury her as a Pharaoh, give her the honor the people want for her," Pawah said. "I know she conspired against you"—Tut cut a stare to his wife as Pawah continued —"but you must give her a proper send-off to the afterlife or risk the people demand you abdicate the throne as well, and who would be left to rule? You have no children."

"Fine," Tut said, and crossed his arms petulantly.

"No one conspired against you, Tut," Ankhesenpaaten said, but Pawah cut her out of his view.

"Don't listen to her," Pawah said. "She is only trying to save herself. But in due time the liar that she is will reap her reward."

The whisper only partially made its way back to Ankhesenpaaten, but Tut nodded in full agreement. "I'm married to a liar," Tut whispered. "First she told me she loves me, and then she tells me you killed her mother." He shook his head. "Liar."

"Like mother, like daughter," Pawah said with a sneer.

"Yes." Tut hugged his arms tighter across his chest. His eleven-year-old body had grown stronger as his lessons with Sennedjem progressed over the years, but he still needed a cane to walk.

Pawah smiled. "That is my good son." He stood up straight, turned to Ankhesenpaaten, and then back to Tut. "My work here is done. I shall make preparations for Pharaoh Neferneferuaten's burial. I shall be back, Pharaoh," he said, and bowed to the young King, then left.

Ankhesenpaaten got up from her throne and marched out after him. She caught him in the hallway. "Pawah, you snake!"

Pawah bowed his head as she approached him. "My Queen, what have I done to deserve your wrath?"

"You know what you did." Ankhesenpaaten threw her hands on her hips. "You turned Tut against me. But I plan to protect him and Egypt from the likes of you!"

Pawah burst out in a laugh. "You?" He shook his head in disbelief. "You can't even get your own *husband* to believe you! You know, he told me what you said in the Kap training yard. Clearly the rants of a deluded woman." His eyes lingered in victory.

"You murdered my mother and you seek his throne,"

Ankhesenpaaten said to his face. "I heard you through the wall."

"Perhaps I should have done away with all of you," Pawah said as he rubbed his chin. "Fewer loose ends to tie up."

"You are despicable." Ankhesenpaaten spat at the floor between his feet.

Pawah rolled his eyes, remembering Nefertiti's similar action. "The ambitious always are." He sidestepped her insult and walked around her. "You see, my precious Queen, your husband, young and stupid, trusts me with his life, and he will always choose me over you."

Pawah's sneer almost caused her to lose her dinner. "Would you bet your life on it?" Ankhesenpaaten snapped back, crossing her arms.

"I certainly would."

"Careful, Pawah. Pride goes before the fall."

"Ah, your mother and I played this dance. Are you taking her place?" Pawah chuckled and made a gesture of a dancer.

"You forced my hand."

"Yes, and don't you forget it." Pawah leaned forward and hit his hand on the wall behind her head, making her jump. His eyes bore deep into hers and then he left.

The stone's chill crept up her spine as she watched the door shut behind him.

"I wish my mother were here," Ankhesenpaaten whispered.

AFTER PHARAOH NEFERNEFERUATEN'S BURIAL, THE PEOPLE seemed placated. Pharaoh Tutankhaten now sat where Nefertiti once sat in the council room with Master of Pharaoh's Horses, Ay, Commander Horemheb, Vizier of the Lower Nakht, and Vizier of the Upper Pawah at his table.

"Now it is time for you to appoint viziers," Horemheb said, his face fallen, his voice monotone.

"I appoint Pawah," Tut said, pointing, and smiled.

"You may want to appoint a second, for Egypt is a large nation."

"Do I have to?"

"No, my boy, you don't have to," Pawah quickly interjected.

"Pawah's hands will be very busy. Perhaps a second vizier would be prudent. The four Pharaohs before you all had two viziers, at least in the beginning," Nakht said, leaning forward, partially blocking Tut's view of Pawah. "I suggest Ay, Master of Pharaoh's Horses. I am tired, as I have been a vizier for a long, long time. He knows the military and has held many offices for Pharaohs before. He is more experienced than all of us, including that of Pawah."

Pawah shot Nakht dead from the daggers in his eyes, but Horemheb added, "Yes, Pharaoh Tutankhaten, Ay would serve a most loyal and valuable vizier." He drew the attention away from Pawah, meeting the young Pharaoh's eyes and nodding in agreement.

"Well, then, Ay will serve as Vizier of the Lower," Tut said. "And Pawah will serve as Vizier of the Upper."

"Thus Pharaoh says. It is settled then. Horemheb will take command of your army as General, and Horemheb has appointed Paramesse as Commander, and I will serve as Vizier of the Lower," Ay said, and placed a hand on Tut's shoulder. "We have much to discuss, including who will take my place as Master of Pharaoh's Horses. Please walk with me, Pharaoh Tutankhaten."

"Very well," Tut said, and he got up to leave with Ay.

Once they left, Pawah leaned back and crossed his arms, looking at Nakht and Horemheb.

"Two can play your game, Pawah," Horemheb said. "Or in our case, three."

"Careful, *General*. Your numbers dwindle. Paaten and Nefertiti are gone. I was even able to buy off the chief royal guard, the late Jabari."

"There are still those loyal to the true crown of Egypt," Horemheb said, matching Pawah's stance. "And as long as one of us lives, we will do whatever it takes to make sure it stays out of your hands."

"Then let the game begin . . . again," Pawah said as he stood up and leaned his hands on the table. Horemheb and Nakht followed suit until Pawah leaned back and walked to the door. "I shall get the next move," he said, and left.

"And we shall get the last," Horemheb whispered.

28

THE TIME OF WAR

ONLY A FEW DECANS AFTER THE GREAT FUNERAL procession for Pharaoh Neferneferuaten, Tut sat upon his throne, Ay and Pawah standing beside him. He listened to messengers and followed his step-grandfather's advice in each response. A particular messenger came in, out of breath, and bowed.

"Speak, messenger," Tut said.

"Pharaoh—" The messenger bowed again before opening and reading the papyrus scroll: "Suppiluliuma, King and Lord of the Hittite people, writes to this nation of Egypt: 'Be prepared for your slaughter as cowards. You deceptive people! You feign alliance and kill our Prince Zannanza. Blood for blood!' " The messenger's hands shook as he lowered the scroll. "We also have word from our northern border . . . the Hittites have attacked. This message does confirm they retaliate for the slaying of their Prince Zannanza."

Tut peered to Pawah—the only action he was able to do, for his body was frozen in fear. "What do I say?"

Ay interjected before Pawah could speak. "Pharaoh, we

must send reinforcements to the northern border at once so the Hittites do not invade Egypt."

Tut ignored him, still looking at Pawah, who sneered at Ay. "I would agree, young Pharaoh."

Tut chewed his lip and turned to face his throne room. "Pharaoh says to send reinforcements to the northern border at once!" The small crack in his voice signaled his age.

"Pharaoh, this is an opportunity for you to go to war to show the people their King defends them," Ay whispered, thinking that if it was at war, he would at least be protected by Horemheb and the army and out of Pawah's grasp. "Your great successors, Pharaohs Thutmose and Amenhotep, all did the same. They gained great respect and honor."

Tut looked again to Pawah, who reluctantly nodded. He could not argue with that.

"I would suggest leaving me to your affairs, as I have served many Pharaohs in this capacity," Ay said, knowing Pawah would take this time to seize every opportunity.

Tut looked to Pawah, who shook his head. "Tsk-tsk," he said, and cocked an eyebrow to Ay. "Vizier Ay is Nefertiti's father. Are you sure you would like to leave Egypt in the hands of the man who bore the woman bent on killing you?"

"No, I do not want to do that."

"Then send Ay to war as well, since you are presently missing a Master of Pharaoh's Horses. You only need one vizier right now," Pawah's snake tongue whispered.

But before Tut could speak, Ay did. "Pharaoh, to further bring respect and honor to your throne you need to show the people you are Amun's divinely appointed. Let me go and make preparations to move the capital back to Waset. Move the palace back to the palace of your grandfather: Malkata. Leave this place devoted to the Aten. It will secure your right to rule with the people." He needed to stay close, and Waset was close enough; but in doing so, it left Ankhesenpaaten alone in Aketaten. Tut sat back and thought about it some. He looked at Pawah, who shook his head, and Ay jumped in again: "The last Pharaohs did not last long in Aketaten. The people resent them. Do you want the love of the people?"

Tut's head turned to Ay. "Yes."

Ay lowered his chin and set his focus on the young boy. "Then, as the vizier with far greater experience, I would recommend Pharaoh move back to Waset, where the temples of Amun abide."

Tut looked to Pawah again, who shook his head.

"But I do want the people to love me . . ." Tut said, and Pawah's head stopped shaking and his lips began to move as his mind raced to find the words. "But, Vizier Ay, I am afraid to battle. I still have a club foot and I must walk with a cane." Tut rubbed his deformed leg. "How will I survive war?"

Ay knelt down and placed his hand on his shoulder, turning him so Pawah was completely out of view. "General Horemheb is an outstanding teacher, and the northern border is a long journey. He will teach you. Your army took an oath to protect Pharaoh and to defend Egypt with their very lives. Your army protects you, my Pharaoh. There is no reason to fear."

Ay's reassuring smile prompted a sigh of relief in Tut. "Then I will go to war. Vizier Ay will go to Waset, and Pawah will tend to affairs—"

"My Pharaoh—" Ay coughed. "Usually the chief royal wife tends to Pharaoh's affairs while he is indisposed. That has been the custom for many generations."

"No!" Tut said, and wrenched his shoulder away from Ay. "I will not have Ankhesenpaaten tend to anything. She is her mother's daughter!"

Ay felt as though Tut had hit him in the chest with a club, and his eyes fell upon Pawah, who came into view behind

Tut's head. He held a wicked smirk as he chewed on a piece of grain.

"No, no, no." Tut waved his hands in the air as he scooted his backside fully into the throne seat again. "I will go to war, you will go to Waset, and Pawah will stay here and tend to the affairs of Pharaoh in my absence."

Ay stood, keeping his eyes on Pawah, who shrugged and mouthed, *You win some, you lose some,* then made a motion toward the very spot on his chest where he had stabbed Nefertiti.

IN THE NEXT DAYS, HALF OF EGYPT'S ARMY CAME TO THE northern border's aid. Tut was already on the royal barge, headed with Paramesse down the Nile, and Horemheb waited on the dock by his own barge. He had stayed to plan out the border defenses against Libya and Nubia should they attack again, since Tut had not yet appointed someone as Master of Pharaoh's Horses.

Ay came up behind him. "She wanted you to have this on the day she announced her marriage." Ay held the sealed letter to Horemheb's waist. He looked at it and grasped it, but Ay held on. "You keep that boy safe. You pit him against Pawah. Do not let my daughter be murdered in vain."

Horemheb nodded. "Yes, Vizier."

And Ay released it. "I know you loved her, but I was her father. You promise me." He laid a finger on Horemheb's armor. "You get close to the boy and you turn him against Pawah."

Horemheb turned to find his eyes. "She was the mother of my only child. I promise you."

Ay rolled his shoulders back and let out his breath. "Fight

well, General. I shall be in Waset. Send a trusted messenger should you need me."

"I will. Make sure Pawah doesn't kill Ankhesenpaaten. Keep her as close as you can."

"Pharaoh will not let her leave the royal harem." Ay got into the boat to go to Waset. "She will be on her own for a while. I have tasked Hori and Ineni with her safety." He grimaced. "I pray to the gods Pawah does not get to them as well."

Horemheb nodded in agreement as he watched Ay leave. Rubbing the scar on his arm where Pawah had sliced him, he grimaced as he remembered holding Nefertiti's smooth and soft hand in his, rubbing his thumb over the scar on her hand. His own words came back to him. *Eventually, time allows us to make amends and move forward. We can hide scars, display them, learn from them, or repeat them. They are with us forever . . .*

"Next time, Pawah will not be so lucky," he muttered to Nefertiti's ka, but let out a breath amidst his anger soon after. "I miss you."

He studied the letter in his hand as he boarded his boat: *Commander*, it said in Nefertiti's handwriting. He dropped his head and looked to the collar laid over his bronze armor to signify that he was now the General of Pharaoh's Armies.

"I will always be *your* Commander, my love."

He held the smooth papyrus in his hand and debated opening it and reading it then, but instead put it in his shendyt. He would read it on an especially dark night when his heart needed to be reminded of her.

✣ 29 ✣
THE TIME OF REFLECTION

PAWAH OPENED THE DOOR TO THE ROYAL THRONE ROOM, only populated with a few servants cleaning the grand pillared hall. The King's throne sat empty as he slinked up the platform steps to it. He ran his hand along its inlaid golden arm.

"So close," he whispered. He gripped the end of the arm as he swung his body in front of it and eased into its seat. "Ah . . . in a few more years this will be mine, as soon as that boy and girl are out of my way." He tightened his hand into a fist and slammed it on the throne. "Curse you, Nefertiti, in your afterlife. You have made me spill so much blood." He stopped to admire the intricate craftsmanship of the throne and the plushness of the seat cushion on which he sat. "But for this" —he looked out to the grand throne room—"I would do it all again."

Talking to Nefertiti's ka, he muttered, "Your wretched daughter will not ruin it for me. I am hoping the battle will do away with the cripple boy King and his General. Then that leaves your coward father and nosy daughter. If they don't stay out of my way, they will meet the same fate."

343

He heard a gasp behind him. Turning to look, he found Ankhesenpaaten standing there with her hand over her mouth.

He stood up. She took a step back.

His back stood straight as a pin, and the corners of his mouth curled into a menacing smile. "My Queen." He nodded his head and took a step to the side. "Your throne." His hand showed the path to it.

Her hand dropped to her side. "I know what you did." She lifted her chin and pulled her shoulders back.

"Yes, and should you utter a word—" He lunged for her, grabbing her neck and slamming her against the back wall.

A servant stood up to come to her aid, but two others restrained him, their families' homes filled with briber's grain. She looked at first at the servant, and then to Pawah, and her eyes grew with fear.

"That's right, Your Majesty. Even your own throne room is not yours." His eyes dropped to her bosom under her translucent linen gown. Her body and face rivaled her mother's; hopefully, this girl would play by his rules and he would not have to do away with such beauty. "Such a pity your mother couldn't see you now."

She slapped his face and his hand grew tighter around her neck. He leaned his face in and planted his lips on hers with a violent rage. Yanking his head back, he then thrust his lips to her ear.

"Should you utter a word again, chief royal wife Ankhesenpaaten, I will have my way with you under the eyes of all those in the palace who are loyal to me, and when I am done, I will slice you up like I did to the great Nefertiti. And I will know if you utter a word, Your Majesty, because I have ears all over Aketaten, Men-nefer, and Waset."

"When they see who you really are, they will turn back to

the true royalty of Egypt!" Ankhesenpaaten rasped, and she spat in his face.

His eyelids dropped as he wiped her spit off his cheek. "Who will see? Who will they believe? You tried to tell your own husband, and did he believe you?"

She averted her eyes and her nostrils flared.

"No." He clicked his tongue behind his teeth. "He trusts me more than you. It is why he left me to run Egypt while he went to battle."

"He went to battle with General Horemheb, who knows you killed my mother. He will come back knowing the better," Ankhesenpaaten said as she pulled at his tightening hands around her neck.

"Yes, but to a country I have already pitted against him. He should have listened to his dear old step-grandfather not to leave me in charge." He smiled again, then released her neck a little. It amused him to watch her struggle for life again and again and he alone could give it back. It made him feel like the gods he didn't believe in. He laughed as he squeezed again. "Your father made it so easy to make promises to a destitute people. He robbed them of faith and food. I am their savior. I give them food in exchange for their loyalty."

"You mean you *steal* from the royal grain holds. You deceive and lie. It isn't your food to give." Ankhesenpaaten breathed, getting her fingers between her neck and his grip.

"It will be, my dear." He grabbed her around the waist. "In due time." He swung her into his arms, still keeping his puppet-hold on her neck. "And when that time comes, it will be your choice—to stay by my side as my wife and Queen, or to die with what is left of your family." He pushed her hips into his and tightened his grip around her neck. Her whimper sent a thrill through him. "I do miss having a wife," he said as he grabbed her buttock.

"Let go of me," she whispered with the small amount of breath she could muster. Pulling at his fingers wound tightly around her neck, she was finally able to take in a breath.

His countenance fell and his eyes narrowed as he pushed her away from him, throwing her on the ground. "Have it your way."

She fell down the platform steps and rolled toward the door. A cut above her eyebrow bled, but she stood anyway, despite her foot ripping her dress.

"Pawah, I will not utter a word, but before the day I journey west I will—"

"Careful, my Queen. Your mother uttered those same words, and, well, look what happened . . ." Pawah shook his finger at her.

She bit her tongue as a smug smile overcame his face. "One day you will get what you deserve."

He laughed. "I *deserve* the throne." He plopped down into the mighty chair and threw up a leg over the armrest as he leaned back in its generous embrace. "Now begone, Ankhesenpaaten, and remember you have a choice: forever my Queen . . . or early travels to the Field of Reeds." He shooed her away and ordered Amenket, a guard obviously on his list of bribes, to take her back to the royal harem where she belonged.

Amenket grabbed her arm and forced her out of her throne room. Before the doors closed, however, she glared at Pawah and muttered under her hot breath:

"Before I journey west, you will."

BACK AT THE ROYAL HAREM, ANKHESENPAATEN FOUND Sennedjem, with a single thought burning through her mind:

If Pawah imprisons me here, I will make use of my time before his ultimatum comes due.

She placed her hands on her hips as Sennedjem stood up from cleaning a training blade. She reached down and tore a slit in her long linen dress, from the tear made when Pawah pushed her, for her legs to move with greater agility. She grabbed a wooden training stick that rested on the wall as he bowed to her and rubbed his chin, observing her odd actions.

"Sennedjem, Overseer of the Tutors." She pointed the stick at him. Her voice was steady and low; she readied her muscles with a calm, clear focus on her subject.

"Yes, chief royal wife?" Sennedjem straightened his back, but kept his chin lowered out of respect for her.

She placed one foot behind the other and bent her knees, as if ready to defend herself. Her unwavering gaze met his, and she tapped her stick on the ground.

"Teach me to fight."

"Yes, my Queen," he said, and grabbed another stick from the wall.

Ankhesenpaaten set her jaw and gave a curt nod.

"Teach me to kill."

Sennedjem nodded. "Let's begin."

EPILOGUE
THE TIME OF REMEMBERING

First Prophet of Amun, Wennefer, slowly stood during Pharaoh Horemheb's silence after his last recounting. The sun had already begun to dip behind the great horizon. Servants attempted invisibility as they lit the torches in the room.

A weight dropped to Mut's stomach; she had not realized Horemheb had fathered a child with her half-sister. He had told her he loved Nefertiti as a Pharaoh, but never the extent. She had assumed it was an admiration; she never had reason to suspect otherwise. Mut looked to her own growing belly and peered over at him. Was she only a replacement for her sister?

"My Pharaoh and his Queen: we, the Amun Priesthood, do not agree with what the former Prophet of Amun, Pawah, did, nor with what the people demanded, nor with what Pharaohs Akhenaten and Smenkare believed. So, as we all are in agreement"—Wennefer looked around to make sure his fellow prophets' heads were nodding with him—"we all know very well what happened to the two Pharaohs after Pharaoh Neferneferuaten. Perhaps now

Pharaoh can sign the edict before the sun sets on this second day."

Pharaoh Horemheb looked around to those in the room and stood as well.

"No. *All* of the Pharaohs deserve their account to be retold for the last time. We will honor them before we rid them from our historical records."

"My King——" Wennefer began.

Horemheb held his hand out to silence them. "None are greater than Pharaoh."

Wennefer bit his tongue and took a deep breath; the other prophets did the same.

"We shall continue the recounting at first light." A few grumblings made their way to Horemheb's ears. "Honor the slain," he commanded. The grumblings ceased. "Remember their legacy before we rid them from our children's memory." The two guards behind him stepped forward as he raised his voice. "First light." He pointed a finger in the air.

Mut stood behind him. Her feet ached from standing all day, but so was her place as her husband spoke of the family who would never be remembered. Silence came from the priesthood, so she spoke. "Your Pharaoh has commanded first light, or do you speak treason against Amun's true First Prophet, his divinely appointed King?"

"No." Wennefer nodded his head in reverence to the position of Pharaoh, but he spoke through clenched teeth. "There are none greater than Pharaoh."

"Then we shall resume at first light," she said with her back straight and her hands to her sides.

They agreed and left for the temple.

Horemheb turned to Mut after their exit. His eyes held her pain. She had tried in the days before, pleaded with him for another way, begged him on her knees, but there was nothing else he could do. He closed his eyes and dropped his head. She put a hand on his shoulder. He looked up to find tears streaming down her face.

"I know why you must do this. I see the way they question you. The future people of Egypt can't know about this period of time, or else the divine crown will always be questioned," she said as she wiped her eyes and her nose, realizing now, after all these years, why her sister did the things she did—she loved Egypt more than all else. "But it doesn't take away the pain."

"Be strong, Mut," he said as he cupped her cheek with his hand. "You are courageous. It was why I fell in love with you."

Nuzzling her nose into his palm, she breathed a sigh of relief at his reaffirmation that his love for her was not a replacement; but yet, as her gaze focused on the gold-and-blue lapis ring upon his pinky finger that she now knew was Nefertiti's, she wondered more. "I am trying."

He brought her into his chest and kissed her forehead.

"May Amun be with us," Horemheb whispered to her.

Mut looked up at her husband with a wary eye. "May Amun give us strength."

THE STORY CONTINUES
SCARAB IN THE STORM BOOK III

Scarab in the Storm Book III

Egypt is divided and conspiracy runs deep—the boy King Tut inherits a nation of chaos, and his wife, Queen Ankhesenamun, is desperate to earn his trust.

Pharaoh must decide Egypt's path amid political turmoil and corruption while Ankhesenamun struggles to convince Pharaoh that their lives are at stake.

With truth shrouded in mystery, doubt attacks the royalty as a power mercilessly pursues the crown. Egypt's fate is determined by Pharaoh's and Queen Ankhesenamun's success or failure in the coming storm.

"Ah, my Queen," Pawah sneered, and he looked her body up
and down.

Ankhesenpaaten crossed her arms to avoid his
penetrating gaze. To the forefront of her memory came the
stench of his breath, the feel of his hard lips pressed against
hers. She too well remembered his threat to her life in the
Aketaten throne room. The motivation to never feel that
again made her mind flee to the training yard. Her fingers
slipped unseen under her belt and grasped the handle of the
small dagger Sennedjem had given her.

"What do you want?"

The ache in her hand made her realize how hard she
gripped the handle. The desire to yank it out and stab Pawah
in the chest right then and there, just as he had done to her
mother, almost caused her hand to do what it willed, but the
paralyzing effect of fear kept it at bay. His height and weight
outsized her in every way. Her strength waned from
yesterday's practice, and her lack of training with a dagger
finally succeeded in stilling her hand—even if she did attack
him, he could probably wrangle it away from her and kill her
with her own weapon. But she still kept her fingers wrapped
around it. All she needed was one good strike if he came too
close to her.

A slow smile crossed his lips, as though reading her mind.
"Aketaten belongs to me now," he reminded her. "When your
precious husband comes home, I will do away with him, and
you will choose me or death."

"And if I choose death, will you kill me in secret like you
did my mother?" Her stomach twisted inward on itself as she
spoke, but she forced her voice to stay strong.

I will not be weak.

I will not be a victim.
I will not die defenseless.

"No, silly girl." Pawah ran the tips of his fingers down her cheek; she jerked her face away from his touch and he clenched his jaw from the blow to his ego. "I will have you executed for your crimes against Amun and Egypt's people. The masses will love to see vengeance on the family that set food upon Aketaten's eight hundred offering tables to spoil in the sun for the Aten disc while the people endured starvation. The family that depleted the royal treasury of its grain on extravagance while turning their backs on the people . . . finally gone. A day of celebration."

"If you were so keen on taking the crown, why didn't you just kill Tut when you had the chance after my mother's murder? Why not just kill me now?" Her fingers tightened around the smooth bronze of the dagger handle.

"A mistake I will not soon forget." Pawah's lips enunciated each word and he lowered his gaze to hers. "I thought I needed more supporters. But now, all of Egypt stands behind me."

"Not all," Ankhesenpaaten whispered, knowing at least her mother's family in Waset, General Horemheb, and maybe Sennedjem still fought for her and Tut. "My mother allowed the worship of the gods again. The people have no reason to hate us now. You need a reason for them to fight for you. I know that is why you have not killed us. My mother watched out for us. She knew you and your ways."

Pawah curled his lip and shuffled a step backward. Then he widened his stance and leaned forward. "The people will follow me. They believe what I tell them, just as they have done in the past."

"They will see through the lies, and when they know the truth, when they know you took the life of a divinely appointed ruler, they will see you impaled per the law. They will demand it." Ankhesenpaaten's eyes flared as she narrowed her focus on him.

He only chuckled and shook his head. "You will watch what you say, *Queen*. The only reason you are still alive is because I want a warm body in my bed when I am Pharaoh."

Her full lips peeled back in disgust, and she let out a gagging breath.

He chuckled again. "If the other does not go the way I need it to, all I have to do is marry you. I offered the same deal to your mother, but she refused me." His voice became innocent and soft, but took a hard turn. "Maybe you will not be as foolish as she."

Ankhesenpaaten felt her heart beat out of her chest as she stood up straight and rooted her feet to the floor. "You will never touch me again."

"I will get my satisfaction, one way or another." Then he peered over to Hori, who stared him down, and Ineni, who played with a rock with his toe. "Tell me, Queen . . . do you trust your guards at night?"

Ankhesenpaaten set her jaw. "I trust no one."

Pawah smiled and patted her cheek. "You are already smarter than your mother. It might keep you alive long enough to see my coronation."

"I will tell Pharaoh Tutankhaten what you have done here in his absence, and he will—"

"If you say one word, my Queen, I will *rip* your throat out in front of my supporters and label you an adulteress to the throne." Pawah saw the flinch in her eye and smirked. "Haven't you been with Sennedjem while your husband is away? There are many who saw you with him. You enjoyed his touch and his kiss and his—"

"Those are lies!" Ankhesenpaaten slammed her fisted hands to her side in a rush of fury.

"Oh, my dear little girl . . ." Pawah laughed and waved his hand in dismissal.

Her ears turned to flame. She was nearing sixteen—a woman old enough to bear children and have a family of her own. She was no little girl.

"Anything can be truth when multiple people say the same thing." Pawah pursed his lips. "What do you think your husband would do to you and Sennedjem if he found out about your little transgressions?"

Ankhesenpaaten growled at him. She rolled her shoulders forward, ready to pounce.

"Better yet, if you say anything, I will make you out to be an adulteress and see you executed along with your lovers. I know those still loyal to the throne. Those men will have been with you too. Most all have seen it." Pawah smiled. "And then, when the young King dies from an unfortunate tumble off his balcony, who shall take the throne?"

"You're a monster. He hasn't done anything to you. He is still a boy."

"He was *born*, Ankhesenpaaten, and that is enough. If it weren't for him, I would be marrying you right now and claiming my place on the throne."

"I would never marry you. And if you kill me, you have no right to the throne."

"Ah, you do hold a point there . . . but you see, I am the closest male relative, and seeing as the people did not want a female Pharaoh, I do not need you in order to become King of Egypt. I just need enough people to want me as their leader to not cause a riot when the throne is left empty."

"You are despicable."

"I know." Pawah smiled. "It is one of my best qualities."

Ankhesenpaaten wondered why he didn't try to take advantage of her. Perhaps he feared someone still loyal to the throne. Was it Hori or Ineni? Hori was an intimidating man, standing a full head above Ineni and holding an athletic frame.

"So," Pawah said, breaking her from her thoughts. "You will not say one word."

"And sit idly by while you plot a way to kill Pharaoh?"

"I only need him to name me Heredity Prince. When he does, there will be no bloodshed in Egypt because I will then be not only the closest living male relative but also the named successor." Pawah clasped his hands together in front of his chest, as if satisfied that everything would happen as he said it would. "You see, I am not so despicable. I do care if there is bloodshed in Egypt."

"That didn't stop you from spilling the blood of my mother and my husband—"

"And your father, dear."

Ankhesenpaaten knew what her mother had told her, but for some reason it did not phase her until now. Her body grew numb. This man killed her parents. He'd orphaned her. She wet her lips in the desert heat and her eyes focused on his mouth as he spoke:

"Tut will be removed one way or another, but if you keep silent and help me, you can be my wife and we can save much Egyptian blood. Hasn't there already been enough spilt?"

"You disgust me, Pawah."

"Believe me, you have made that very clear. But no matter. I am a very forgiving man." He winked at her. "I tell you what . . ." A half-smile grew on his face as he looked to her breasts and then back to her lips. "Even though our young Pharaoh will always choose me over you, I'm willing to gamble. I'm always up for a game, so let us each take a stake here. If you decide to stay silent, I will not kill Pharaoh for one year. At the end of the year, if he still trusts me over you, I win and you will be my wife once the boy passes in a horrible accident and you will do as I say when I say it until the day you journey west. If he believes you over me, however, we will call it even. You get to live as Queen to the crippled child the rest of your days."

He let her digest what he said and then continued.

"But if you speak of the horrors"—he raised his fingers to the air as if to mock her pain and began to circle her—"that have gone on here, and he believes *me*, I will make him execute you and your lovers, and then the same nasty fall will kill him . . . and who shall take the throne? Me." Pawah came to face her again and then shrugged. "But if he believes you over me and my many witnesses, then I will leave Aketaten."

"No, you will leave *Egypt*. I am no fool." Her hot breath sizzled in the morning heat. "You would leave Aketaten to only go back to Waset and live in Malkata as King."

"My dear," he said as he reached out to touch her face, but then pulled away at the last second, his eyes flitting to the royal guards standing in sight. "You are no fool."

"You will address me with my title: chief royal wife." Ankhesenpaaten's nostrils flared as she spoke.

"No. I won't." The words tailed the end of a chuckle. "Not while we are alone. Those are my terms. Do you agree to a wager?"

"You will leave Egypt if Pharaoh trusts me over you."

"No, I will leave *Aketaten*." Pawah shook his head with a *tsk-tsk*. "What leverage do you have over me? What would you do to make me change my own terms?"

"I know you killed my mother." Ankhesenpaaten's voice cracked but grew more bold with each passing statement. "And I will let the people know. I will scream it until my throat is—what did you say, ripped out? I will plant the seed of doubt in the people's minds. No one kills Pharaoh."

"Ah, I admire your strategy. Sounds a little like mine."

Ankhesenpaaten swallowed. "I am not like you." She paused to make sure he knew it, then she lifted her chin and rolled her shoulders back. "You will leave Egypt if Pharaoh trusts me over you," Ankhesenpaaten repeated. Her knees shook as she stared this man down, but her feet stayed firmly planted. She held her breath for fear he might hear her racing heart.

"I have waited sixteen years for this crown," Pawah grumbled. "A woman will be the last thing that keeps me from it."

"What's the matter?" Ankhesenpaaten smirked, satisfied to have finally upset him. "Are you afraid? Do you think there is a small chance I can win?"

Pawah narrowed his eyes. "No. There is no chance, girl."

"Then make the deal. You have nothing to worry about."

She had him. She'd found his ego and squeezed.

After a moment, Pawah nodded. "You're right. If you win, I'll leave Egypt."

"Good." Her senses told her it had been too easy to get him to agree to her terms, but she accepted her small victory nonetheless and felt free to take a relieved breath.

"Good," Pawah repeated in a low hiss as Ankhesenpaaten turned and walked away.

When she reached Hori and Ineni, she peered over her shoulder to Pawah, who still watched her.

"Are you all right, my Queen?" Hori asked her.

"Yes, I am," Ankhesenpaaten said, rolling her shoulders backward and standing straight. "I'm ready to go to the training yard."

Sennedjem will teach me to defend myself. I will teach Tut—no, General Horemheb is teaching him now and telling him the truth about Pawah. I will learn to defend myself. I will kill him if he touches me again. I will kill him. I will kill him.

She would take poison before she ever allowed him to take her by force, she reasoned, and wished her grandfather Ay were in Aketaten to help keep her safe. She didn't like feeling all alone. But maybe in Waset he would be rallying the people for her and Tut and leading them to disown their precious Pawah.

"Yes, my Queen." Hori bowed his head and took up the tail as they went onward toward the training yard.

Pawah watched her leave as he muttered to himself with a nasty sneer, "I have no intention of keeping my end of the bargain if you win, girl . . . but I will delight in seeing your own husband sentence you to death for your betrayal of his bed." He remembered changing the sweet little Nebetah into his conniving late wife, Beketaten, with the same tactics. He remembered plunging Jabari's spear into her heart, and chuckled at the utter confusion on her face as the light in her eyes dimmed dull. He watched Ankhesenpaaten round the corner. "And in the off-chance he does not, you'll meet the same fate as she when I have no more use of you." He rocked back on his heels and sneered, his eyes hidden in the shadow of his brow. "Bide my time," he whispered. "Bide my time."

Read the rest of *Scarab in the Storm* today.

GRAB THE COMPLETE SERIES AND COLLECTIONS

THE LOST PHARAOH CHRONICLES

The Complete Quadrilogy

Be sure to check out the *The Lost Pharaoh Chronicles Prequel and Complement Collections.*

Sign-up at www.laurenleemerewether.com to stay updated on new releases!

Go further into the past with the Prequel Collection and find out how Tey came to Ay's house in ***The Valley Iris***, why Ay loved Temehu so much in ***Wife of Ay***, General Paaten's secret and struggle in the land of Hatti in ***Paaten's War***, how Pawah rose from an impoverished state to priest in ***The Fifth Prophet***, and the brotherhood between Thutmose and Amenhotep IV in ***Egypt's Second Born***.

The Prequel Collection

Dive deeper into the story with the Complement Collection and find out where General Paaten and Nefe end up in ***King's Daughter***.

The Complement Collection

Nefe, the innocent daughter of Nefertiti, flees her perfect palatial home to save her life from a madman obsessed with usurping the throne.

Her mother, Pharaoh of Egypt, is betrayed and murdered; her last living sister abandons her for a fool's errand, sure to end in death. Nefe is left alone under the protection of General Paaten, her mother's steward, and a mysterious man named Atinuk. After narrowly escaping the corruption in Egypt, they head toward an unknown future in a foreign land.

Will Nefe learn to trust her seemingly faithful companions, despite the secrets they carry? Can she pick up the shattered pieces of a life she once believed was perfect and embrace her future as a refugee in the vast lands of Canaan?

Find out in this gripping coming-of-age drama set in the New Kingdom of Egypt.

King's Daughter will contain spoilers for Salvation in the Sun, Secrets in the Sand, and the series prequels, The Mitanni Princess and Paaten's War.

THE LOST PHARAOH CHRONICLES COMPLEMENT COLLECTION

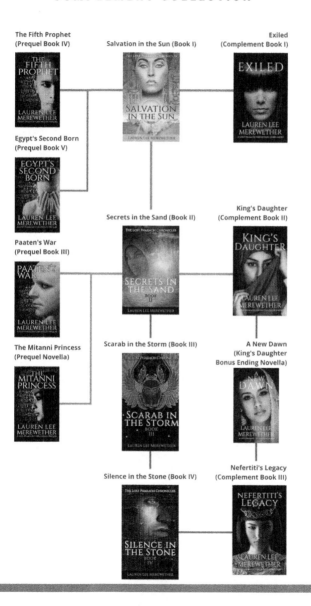

The Fifth Prophet
(Prequel Book IV)

Salvation in the Sun (Book I)

Exiled
(Complement Book I)

Egypt's Second Born
(Prequel Book V)

Secrets in the Sand (Book II)

King's Daughter
(Complement Book II)

Paaten's War
(Prequel Book III)

The Mitanni Princess
(Prequel Novella)

Scarab in the Storm (Book III)

A New Dawn
(King's Daughter
Bonus Ending Novella)

Silence in the Stone (Book IV)

Nefertiti's Legacy
(Complement Book III)

A LOOK INTO THE PAST

As readers may have gleaned from this novel's prologue and epilogue, the account of Pharaohs Akhenaten, Smenkare, and Neferneferuaten were removed from history by a later Pharaoh. Only recently, archeologists have uncovered and continue to uncover bits and pieces of what happened during the Amarna period, the period of time this series covers. The author has taken liberties in *Secrets in the Sand,* book two of The Lost Pharaoh Chronicles, where there were uncertainties and unknowns in the facts, or to better craft the story.

Secrets in the Sand covers the most unknown section of time during this lost period. Many sources discount Pharaohs Smenkare and Neferneferuaten in their entirety and skip over them, saying the next Pharaoh after Akhenaten was Tutankhamun; but, after researching more, it has become clear that there were two additional Pharaohs between those two reigns.

After dealing more with religious reforms and neglecting or dealing poorly with foreign relations, Pharaoh Akhenaten did not keep the nation at the height his father and mother had achieved for Egypt. There was an extremely high presence of military in Aketaten for Akhenaten and Nefertiti versus other Kings. It was assumed there were more threats and fears of Pharaoh's life during this time especially since the country would have been near poverty and starvation, yet Pharaoh Akhenaten ordered over 800 offering tables of the best cuts of meat and crop laid to spoil in the sun as offerings to the Aten disc on an assumedly regular basis. It has been assumed he suffered from Temporal Lobe Epilepsy, Marfan's syndrome, Loeys-Dietz syndrome, or some other disorder, which looks to explain why he believed the sun made him feel better—perhaps due to a severe vitamin D deficiency. Visions were common in his family line and only intensified in each generation, most likely due to inbreeding, which the author carried through to Smenkare.

There are two main theories on why Akhenaten led Egypt to monotheism: Akhenaten was trying to take power from the cult priesthood of Amun, or he just simply held different beliefs for Egypt. It is accepted that he died in Year 17 of his reign. Despite the economic poverty and decline in foreign relations, Akhenaten and the cult of the Aten still had its followers. Akhenaten would have been mourned by some. However, the majority of Egypt was hungry and suffering from starvation and poverty both physically and spiritually.

Smenkare could have been another brother, half-brother, son, or lover of Akhenaten. There are a few who attribute Smenkare and Nefertiti as one and the same, only dressed like a man. Some DNA tests have shown that Smenkare could also be the father of Tutankhaten. Additionally, some believe Tut's nurse, Maia, is actually a reference to his true mother, Meritaten. Tutankhaten's children's mother presumably was his chief royal wife, as well as a daughter of Akhenaten; however, the DNA of their mother shows no father-daughter relation to the mummy identified as Akhenaten. If the children's mother was not Akhenaten's daughter, then their mother is an unknown lesser wife of Tutankhaten; if the children's mother *is* Akhenaten's daughter, then Akhenaten's mummy is actually someone else (presumably Smenkare) and Smenkare's sister bore Tutankhaten, not Akhenaten and his sister.

There is little known about Smenkare as Pharaoh, as no facts have been presented and only theories have been produced about who he was and the length and type of his reign. Some say he was Pharaoh for no more than a year, some two years; others say the length of his reign is indeterminable, but they suggest he was more strict and more Aten-istic than Akhenaten. It appears Smenkare stayed in Aketaten, as no evidence has been presented to the contrary. A few believe Akhenaten was still alive at this time and Smenkare could have been his lover or Nefertiti portrayed as a man, as mentioned above. They believe Smenkare reigned as Coregent with Akhenaten for a while before Akhenaten's death. Again, no one is sure about anything regarding Smenkare. We only know he was a Pharaoh between the reigns of Akhenaten and Neferneferuaten, and some attribute Smenkare as the successor to Neferneferuaten.

It is believed that Nefertiti died sometime between Year 16 and Year 17 of Akhenaten's reign; some say she was Smenkare or Coregent Neferneferuaten during the time of Akhenaten's reign. Although some experts attribute Pharaoh Neferneferuaten as a female and the Coregent Neferneferuaten as more likely a male, she is both Pharaoh and Coregent in *Secrets in the Sand*. Others say she lived past Akhenaten's death and was the Pharaoh Neferneferuaten who reigned after Smenkare, but some associate two separate individuals under the same name and attribute the later Pharaoh to one of her daughters: Meritaten, Ankhesenpaaten, or Neferneferuaten Tasherit. A new theory suggests Pharaoh Neferneferuaten was the name under which two Queen Pharaohs, Meritaten and Neferneferuaten Tasherit, ruled. Regardless, the reign of Pharaoh Neferneferuaten was brief, lasting no more than one or two years before Pharaoh Tutankhaten took the throne, where, presumably sometime before or in the third year of his reign, he moved the capital back to Waset and changed his name to Tutankhamun to give glory back to Amun. There is also a theory that Neferneferuaten reigned during Tutankhamun's first three years, since he was only nine and a Coregency existed. In *Secrets in the Sand*, Neferneferuaten reigned for a little more than two of the three years prior to the move back to Waset.

In addition, the letters to the Hittites and the slaying of Prince Zannanza is majorly contributed to Ankhesenamun after her husband dies; however, there are minor theories and arguments that attribute those letters to Nefertiti, Meritaten or Neferneferuaten Tasherit. The Hittite letters did not name a queen, but rather stated, "the wife of the King [of Egypt]."

Lastly, as Nefertiti's existence past Akhenaten's reign is unknown, book II is largely based in the author's interpretation and imagination of what could have happened.

An example: there is absolutely no evidence of the romance between Horemheb and Nefertiti, their child, and her subsequent murder by Pawah. In fact, Pawah was a lay prophet and scribe of Amun in the 18th Dynasty noted during the reign of Neferneferuaten, and although his quest to take the throne could have been a possibility, there is no evidence to support Pawah as the villain in *The Lost Pharaoh Chronicles* or as a leader in the fictional rebellion group, The People's Restoration of Egypt. The author wrote a prequel collection, and one of the stories is the character Pawah's backstory, ***The Fifth Prophet***.

Additionally, the tomb of General Paatenemheb (Paaten)

was found empty (some believe Paatenemheb and Horemheb were one in the same) and no one really knows what happened to Neferneferuaten Tasherit (Nefe); therefore the author decided to write for them their own story as they journey to Canaan with Aitye and Atinuk (both fictional characters) as part of the series complement collection. Read their story in **King's Daughter**.

The successor to Pharaoh Neferneferuaten, whomever he or she was in history, was Pharaoh Tutankhamun, born Tutankhaten. He is the famed boy King Tut whose coffin was opened in 1925 by Howard Carter, revealing the pristine, golden funerary mask that has come to be associated with Ancient Egypt just as much as the Great Pyramids and Sphinx of Giza. An analysis of his mummy showed he had a cleft palate, a club foot, an overbite, and DNA traces of Kohler disease, which is a painful bone disorder of the foot found in children, and since there were many canes found in his tomb, it is assumed he walked with a cane all of his short life.

A little peek into the author's mindset:

- Horemheb was probably already married to a prophetess of Amun, Amenia, at the time *Secrets in the Sand* took place. She presumably died during the reign of Tutankhaten. They had no children.
- There are only a handful of named fictional characters in the story. The majority of the main characters are based on and named after their real-life counterparts. She wanted to stay as close to the historical account as possible, yet still craft an engaging story.
- The author used "Pharaoh" as a title in the story due to the mainstream portrayal of Pharaoh to mean "King" or "ruler." *Pharaoh* is actually a Greek

word for the Egyptian word(s) *pero* or *per-a-a* in reference to the royal palace in Ancient Egypt, or, literally, "great house." The term was used in the time period this series covers; however, it was never used as an official title for the Ancient Egyptian kings.

- Ancient Egyptians called their country *Kemet*, meaning "Black Land," but because the modern term *Egypt* is more prevalent and known in the world today, the author used Egypt when referencing the ancient empire.

- The term "citizen/citizeness" is similar to the modern "Mr." and "Ms."; Whereas, "Mistress of the House" is what they called a married woman over her household.

- The phrase, "in peace" was the standard greeting and farewell.

- Regnal years were not used during the ancient times, but rather used by historians to help chronicle the different reigns. The author decided to insert these references throughout the novel to help the reader keep track of how much time has passed and to have a better idea of the historical timeline.

- Additionally, the people of Egypt seemed not to celebrate or acknowledge years of life; these were included in the story for the reader's reference. The only "birthday" celebration was every month of Kaherka, which is somewhat equal to December in the Julian calendar. It was a symbolic celebration of the king's coronation, for the gods to renew his life-force. To read a free short story the author created as a winter gift for her readers surrounding this time for Amenhotep III, visit her website and download "King's Jubilee."

- *Amun* can be spelled many ways—Amen, Amon, Amun—but it refers to the same god. Likewise, the *Aten* has also been spelled Aton, Atom, or Atun. The author chose consistent spellings for her series for pronunciation purposes.
- Ancient Egyptians did not use the words "death" or "died," but for ease of reading this series, the author did use "death" and "died" in some instances. The Egyptians instead used euphemistic phrases such as "went to the Field of Reeds," "became an Osiris," and "journeyed west" to lighten the burden of the word "death."

The author hopes you have enjoyed this fictional story crafted from the little-known facts surrounding this period. Find out what becomes of Paaten and Nefe in **King's Daughter** and find out what happens next with Ankhesenpaaten, Pawah, Ay, Horemheb, Mut, Tut, and the rise (or fall) of Egypt in book three, **Scarab in the Storm**!

Go to www.LostPharaohChronicles.com to receive the Free Reader's Guide for *Salvation in the Sun*. Visit www.laurenleemerewether.com also to receive a free starter library and alerts when new stories are on their way.

GLOSSARY

CONCEPTS / ITEMS

1. Chief royal wife – premier wife of Pharaoh, Queen
2. Commander – second-in-command of Pharaoh's Armies; third-highest ranking beneath Master of Pharaoh's Horses and the general
3. Coregent – ruler, second to Pharaoh
4. Deben – weight of measure equal to about 91 grams
5. Decan – week in Egypt (ten-day period); one month consists of three decans
6. Dynasties – Lines of familial rulers in the Old Kingdom, then Middle Kingdom, then New Kingdom (where this story takes place, specifically the 18th Dynasty)
7. General – highest ranking position of Pharaoh's Armies
8. "Gone to Re" – a form of the traditional phrase used to speak about someone's death; another variant is "journeyed west"

9. Great royal wife – chief royal wife of the Pharaoh before

10. Hedjet – white crown worn by Egyptian regents of the 18th dynasty

11. Ka – spirit

12. Kap – nursery and school for royal children in the royal harem

13. Khopesh – a sickle-shaped sword made of bronze

14. Master of Pharaoh's Horses – highest ranking position of Pharaoh's Chariotry; second-in-command to the general

15. Modius – the crown for a queen

16. Pharaoh – the modern title for an ancient Egyptian king

17. Pshent – the great double-crown of Pharaoh

18. Royal harem – palace for the royal women, usually headed by the chief or great royal wife

19. Royal wife – wife of Pharaoh

20. Season – three seasons made up the 360-day calendar; each season had 120 days

21. Sed festival – traditionally, the celebration of the Pharaoh's thirty-year reign, and then every 3–4 years; Akhenaten celebrated several Sed festivals although his reign was not that long

22. Shendyt – apron / skirt; a royal shendyt was pleated and lined with gold worn by Pharaoh

23. Sidelock – long lock of hair above the ear, kept despite a shaved head, to signify childhood; usually braided

24. Sistrum – a musical instrument of the percussion family, chiefly associated with ancient Iraq and Egypt

25. Steward – main person in charge of the estate(s); position held by a man or a literate woman

26. Vizier – chief royal advisor to Pharaoh

GODS

1. Ammit – goddess and demoness; "Devourer of Hearts"
2. Amun – premier god of Egypt in the Middle Kingdom
3. Amun-Re – name given to show the duality of Amun and Re (the hidden god and the sun, respectively) to appease both priesthoods during the early part of the New Kingdom
4. Aten – sun-disc god of Egypt (referred to as "the Aten"); a minor aspect of the sun god Re
5. Bes – god of childbirth
6. Ptah – god of creation, art, and fertility
7. Re – premier god of Egypt in the Old Kingdom; the sun god
8. Tawaret – goddess of childbirth

PLACES

1. Aketaten – city of modern-day area of El'Amarna
2. Akhe-Aten – necropolis for the city of Aketaten
3. Ipet-isut – modern-day Karnak of Luxor; "The Most Selected of Places"
4. Malkata – palace of Pharaoh Amenhotep III
5. Men-nefer – city of Memphis; south of modern-day Cairo
6. Saqqara – necropolis for the city of Men-nefer
7. Waset – city of modern-day Luxor
8. Valley of the Kings – royal necropolis across the Nile from Waset

PEOPLE

1. Aitye – steward of Nefertiti
2. Amenhotep III – Pharaoh; father of Amenhotep IV and Thutmose; journeyed west in Book I, *Salvation in the Sun*
3. Amenhotep IV / Akhenaten – second son of Amenhotep III and Tiye
4. Amenket – royal guard
5. Anen – Second Prophet of Amun; brother of Tiye and Ay; journeyed west in Book I, *Salvation in the Sun*
6. Ankhesenpaaten – daughter of Amenhotep IV / Akhenaten and Nefertiti; royal wife of Akhenaten
7. Ay – father of Nefertiti and Mut; brother of Tiye and Anen; Master of Pharaoh's Horses (second-highest military rank)
8. Beketaten – daughter of Pharaoh Amenhotep III; born with the name Nebetah; wife of Pawah
9. Beset – priest who performs burial preparations for the deceased
10. Henuttaneb – daughter of Pharaoh Amenhotep III; royal wife of Pharaoh Amenhotep IV / Akhenaten; mother of Tutankhaten; journeyed west in Book I, *Salvation in the Sun*
11. Horemheb – Commander (third-highest military rank); future Pharaoh
12. Hori – royal guard
13. Ineni – royal guard
14. Iset – daughter and royal wife of Pharaoh Amenhotep III; journeyed west in Book I, *Salvation in the Sun*
15. Jabari – chief royal guard
16. Kasmut – daughter of Anen

17. Khabek – royal guard
18. Kiya – Mitanni Princess sent to seal foreign relations through marriage to Pharaoh; friend to Nefertiti; journeyed west in Book I, *Salvation in the Sun*
19. Maia – nurse of Tut
20. Maya – First Prophet of Amun during the initial reign of Amenhotep IV; succeeded Meryptah
21. Meketaten – deceased daughter of Pharaoh Amenhotep IV / Akhenaten and Nefertiti; journeyed west in Book I, *Salvation in the Sun*
22. Meritaten – daughter of Pharaoh Amenhotep IV / Akhenaten and Nefertiti; chief royal wife of Pharaoh Smenkare
23. Meryptah – First Prophet of Amun (highest-ranked prophet of the Amun priesthood / cult of Amun); journeyed west in Book I, *Salvation in the Sun*
24. Merytre – steward of Nefertiti
25. Mut ("Mutnedjmet") – half-sister of Nefertiti; daughter of Tey and Ay
26. Nakht ("Nakhtpaaten") – Vizier of the Lower to Pharaoh Smenkare
27. Neferneferuaten Tasherit – daughter of Pharaoh Amenhotep IV / Akhenaten; also called Nefe
28. Neferneferure – deceased daughter of Pharaoh Amenhotep IV / Akhenaten and Nefertiti; journeyed west in Book I, *Salvation in the Sun*
29. Nefertiti / Neferneferuaten – daughter of Ay; chief royal wife of Pharaoh Akhenaten; Coregent of Pharaoh Akhenaten and Pharaoh Smenkare
30. Paaten ("Paatenemheb") – General (highest military rank)
31. Paramesse – high-ranking comrade of Horemheb

32. Pawah – former Fifth Prophet of Amun; husband of Beketaten; Vizier of the Upper to Pharaoh Smenkare

33. Sennedjem – tutor of Tut; Overseer of the Tutors in the royal harem

34. Setepenre – deceased daughter of Pharaoh Amenhotep IV / Akhenaten and Nefertiti; journeyed west in Book I, *Salvation in the Sun*

35. Simut – First Prophet of Amun during Pharaoh Neferneferuaten's reign

36. Sitamun – daughter and royal wife of Pharaoh Amenhotep III; mother of Smenkare

37. Smenkare / Smenkhkare – son of Pharaoh Amenhotep III and Sitamun; half-brother and nephew to Pharaoh Akhenaten

38. Suppuluiuma – King of the Hittites

39. Temehu – deceased mother of Nefertiti; journeyed west in Book I, *Salvation in the Sun*

40. Tey – wet nurse and step-mother of Nefertiti; mother of Mut

41. Thutmose – firstborn son of Pharaoh Amenhotep III and Tiye; journeyed west in Book I, *Salvation in the Sun*

42. Tiye – chief royal wife of Pharaoh Amenhotep III; sister of Ay and Anen; journeyed west in Book I, *Salvation in the Sun*

43. Tut ("Tutankhaten") – only son of Pharaoh Amenhotep IV / Akhenaten; son of Henuttaneb

44. Wennefer – First Prophet of Amun during the reign of Pharaoh Horemheb

45. Zannanza – Hittite prince

ACKNOWLEDGEMENTS

First and foremost, I want to thank God for blessing me with the people who support me and the opportunities he gave me to do what I love: telling stories.

Many thanks to my dear husband Mark, who supported my early mornings and late nights of writing this book.

Thank you to my family, beta readers, and launch team members, without whom I would not have been able to make the story the best it could be and successfully publish.

Thank you to Spencer Hamilton of Nerdy Wordsmith, who put this story through the refiner's fire, making this piece of historical fiction really shine.

Thank you to RE Vance, bestselling author of the GoneGod World series, who offered guidance in the series' framework and structure.

Thank you to the Self-Publishing School Fundamentals of Fiction course, which taught me invaluable lessons on the writing process and how to effectively self-publish.

Thank you to Slobodan Cedic for the wonderful book cover concept design.

<u>Finally, but certainly not least, thank you to my readers.</u> Without your support, I would not be able to write. I truly hope this story engages you, inspires you, and gives you a peek into the past. I've created a Reader's Guide to help you delve into the history and into book one a little bit more—just go to www.llmbooks.com to receive it.

My hope is that when you finish reading this story, your love of history will have deepened a little more—and, of course, that you can't wait to find out what happens in the next book of the series!

ABOUT THE AUTHOR

Lauren Lee Merewether, a historical fiction author, loves bringing the world stories forgotten by time, filled with characters who love and lose, fight wrong with right, and feel hope in times of despair.

A lover of ancient history where mysteries still abound, Lauren loves to dive into history and research overlooked, under-appreciated, and relatively unknown tidbits of the past and craft for her readers engaging stories.

During the day, Lauren studies the nuances of technology and audits at her job and cares for her family. She saves her nights and early mornings for writing stories.

Visit www.llmbooks.com to get her first novel, *Blood of Toma,* for **FREE**, say hello, and stay current with Lauren's latest releases.

facebook.com/llmbooks

twitter.com/llmbooks

bookbub.com/authors/lauren-lee-merewether

goodreads.com/laurenleemerewether

amazon.com/author/laurenleemerewether

instagram.com/llmbooks

tiktok.com/@llmbooks

ALSO BY LAUREN LEE MEREWETHER

Salvation in the Sun

(The Lost Pharaoh Chronicles, Book I)

This future she knows for certain—the great sun city will be her undoing.

Amidst a power struggle between Pharaoh and the priesthood of Amun, Queen Nefertiti helps the ill-prepared new Pharaoh, Amenhotep, enact his father's plan to regain power for the throne. But what seemed a difficult task only becomes more grueling when Amenhotep loses himself in his radical obsessions.

Standing alone to bear the burden of a failing country and stem the tide of a growing rebellion, Nefertiti must choose between her love for Pharaoh and her duty to Egypt in this dramatic retelling of a story forgotten by time.

Scarab in the Storm

(The Lost Pharaoh Chronicles, Book III)

Egypt is divided and conspiracy runs deep—the boy King Tut inherits a nation of chaos, and his wife, Queen Ankhesenamun, is desperate to earn his trust.

Pharaoh Tutankhamun must decide Egypt's path amid political turmoil and corruption while Queen Ankhesenamun struggles to convince Pharaoh that their lives are at stake.

With truth shrouded in mystery, doubt attacks the royalty as a power mercilessly pursues the crown. Egypt's fate is determined by Pharaoh's and Queen Ankhesenamun's success or failure in the coming storm.

DON'T MISS THE LOST PHARAOH CHRONICLES COMPLEMENT COLLECTION.

King's Daughter

(A Lost Pharaoh Chronicles Complement)

Nefe, the innocent daughter of Nefertiti, flees her perfect palatial home to save her life from a madman obsessed with usurping the throne.

Her mother, Pharaoh of Egypt, is betrayed and murdered; her last living sister abandons her for a fool's errand, sure to end in death. Nefe is left alone under the protection of General Paaten, her mother's steward, and a mysterious man named Atinuk. After narrowly escaping the corruption in Egypt, they head toward an unknown future in a foreign land.

Will Nefe learn to trust her seemingly faithful companions, despite the secrets they carry? Can she pick up the shattered pieces of a life she once believed was perfect and embrace her future as a refugee in the vast lands of Canaan?

Find out in this gripping coming-of-age drama set in the New Kingdom of Egypt.

King's Daughter is the complement story to this book, *Secrets in the Sand*, and follows General Paaten and Nefe into the land of Canaan. To avoid spoilers, please read the prequels, **_The Mitanni Princess_** and **_Paaten's War_**, first.

The Complement Collection

The Mitanni Princess

(A Lost Pharaoh Chronicles Prequel Novella)

Her future is pending.

The Mitanni Princess Tadukhipa weighs her options: happiness in exile and poverty, death in prison, or a luxurious life of loneliness. Cursed to love a servant and practice a servant's trade, Tadukhipa rebels against her father, the King, for a chance to change her destiny.

Grab your copy for free at www.laurenleemerewether.com.

The Mitanni Princess sits alongside four talented authors' stories in an anthology, *Daughters of the Past*.

If you have read both *The Mitanni Princess* and *Salvation in the Sun*, find the bonus ending of *The Mitanni Princess* at www.laurenleemerewether.com.

King's Jubilee

(A Lost Pharaoh Chronicles Prequel Short Story)

A secret. A brotherhood. A father's sin.

Crown Prince Thutmose's auspicious future keeps his chin high. Striving to be like his father, Pharaoh Amenhotep III, in every way . . . until his eyes open to one of his father's biggest failures.

What will Thutmose decide to do when he takes the crown one day?

Grab your copy for free at www.laurenleemerewether.com.

The King's Jubilee, a short story, also sits alongside sixteen other authors' stories in a young adult multi-genre anthology, *Winds of Winter*.

Note: King's Jubilee is the short story version of Egypt's Second Born.

The Valley Iris

(The Lost Pharaoh Chronicles Prequel Collection, Book I)

A forbidden love within a sacred village haunts her mind and troubles her future.

Even the vision granted to her by the goddess Hathor keeps Tey from the man she loves. Tey does not understand why her mother will not fight for her. She cannot see why his family does not accept her, until it is too late.

Is Tey doomed to live a life with someone else or with no one at all? Can she pick herself up in the darkness of the starlit night and seek her own happiness?

Find out in this coming-of-age drama set in the New Kingdom of Egypt.

The Wife of Ay

(The Lost Pharaoh Chronicles Prequel Collection, Book II)

Temehu, the daughter of Nomarch Paser, is expected to live a certain life, marry at a certain age to a man of certain status, and have children.

But in her attempts to pursue what she wants for her life, she finds herself questioning the fate of her heart on the journey to the afterlife. Enduring the wrath of a new jealous stepmother and the nobility's harmful gossip and ostracism does not soothe her reservations either.

Is she reaping divine punishment for her deeds? Will she find peace for her eternal soul?

Find out in this coming-of-age drama set in the New Kingdom of Egypt.

Paaten's War

(The Lost Pharaoh Chronicles Prequel Collection, Book III)

Injured in war. Captured by the enemy. Sold as a slave.

Despite his situation, Paaten believes his future is not in the enemy land of Hatti. As Paaten struggles to find his way back to his homeland of Egypt, he encounters a Hittite woman and finds himself in an unforeseen battle waging the biggest war yet:

that of his heart . . .

Will Paaten's perceived enemy ensnare his love and loyalty, or will he return to Egypt to fulfill his destiny and his oath to Pharaoh?

The Fifth Prophet

(The Lost Pharaoh Chronicles Prequel Collection, Book IV)

Power. Gold. Prestige. That is all he wants.

Young Pawah's life changes when he travels to Waset on his parent's hard-earned savings to become a scribe at the temple of Amun. Facing discrimination in Waset for being the son of a farmer among the wealthy elite, Pawah discovers the ease with which he garners sympathy and subsequent "pity gifts" of gold with lies and deceit.

Growing into his own on the streets of Waset, how far will Pawah take his ever-expanding greed for gold and power that hides behind his charm and wit?

Dive into this dark coming-of-age thriller that chronicles the villain of *The Lost Pharaoh Chronicles*.

Egypt's Second Born

(The Lost Pharaoh Chronicles Prequel Collection, Book V)

Bullied by his brother and disregarded by his father, young prince Amenhotep seeks to belong.

Not expected to live as a babe, Amenhotep beats the odds only to find a life always in his brother's shadow and cast out from his father's glory.

Does Amenhotep succumb to the shadows of his father's great palace or does he rise above the ridicule to forge his own path?

Find out in this heartwarming tale of two royal brothers and their journey to love one another despite past wrongs and shortcomings.

Blood of Toma

Running from death seemed unnatural to the High Priestess Tomantzin, but run she does.

She escapes to the jungle after witnessing her father's murder amidst a power struggle within the Mexica Empire and fears for her life. Instead of finding refuge in the jaguar's land, she falls into the hands of glimmering gods in search for glory and gold. With her nation on the brink of civil war and its pending capture by these gods who call themselves Conquistadors, a bloody war is inevitable.

Tomantzin must choose to avenge her father, save her people, or run away with the man she is forbidden to love.

Lauren's debut work of historical fiction, *Blood of Toma,* won a Montaigne Medal nomination and a finalist award for the Next Generation Indie Book Awards in Historical Fiction and Readers' Favorite Award in Young Adult-Thriller.

Get this ebook for free at www.laurenleemerewether.com.

WHAT DID YOU THINK?
AN AUTHOR'S REQUEST

Did You Enjoy *Secrets in the Sand?*

Thank you for reading the second book in **The Lost Pharaoh Chronicles**. I hope you enjoyed jumping into another culture and reading about the author's interpretation of the events that took place in the New Kingdom of Ancient Egypt.

If you enjoyed *Secrets in the Sand*, I would like to ask a big favor: Please share with your friends and family on social media sites like **Facebook** and leave a review on **book retailer sites**, **BookBub**, and on **Goodreads** if you have accounts there.

I am an independent author; as such, reviews and word of mouth are the best ways readers, like you can help books like *Secrets in the Sand*, reach other readers.

Your feedback and support are of the utmost importance to me. If you want to reach out to me and give feedback on this book, share ideas to improve my future writings, get updates about future books, or just say howdy, please visit me on the web.

www.LaurenLeeMerewether.com
Or email me at

mail@LaurenLeeMerewether.com
Happy Reading!

Printed in Great Britain
by Amazon

39775726R00229